The Pangaean Effect

By

James L. Copa

This novel is a work of fiction. Names, characters, places, plots, and incidents are either the product of the author's imagination or are used fictitiously. Any resemblance to actual persons, living or dead, events, or locales is entirely coincidental.

ISBN: 0-7596-5509-X (e-book)
ISBN: 0-7596-5510-3 (Paperback)

This book is printed on acid free paper.

1stBooks - rev. 12/16/03

This book is dedicated to the Gypsy Witch,
who is a proud Cubana by birth,
And an American by choice.
This book is yours.
You are my inspiration.
2 + 2 = 6
T.C.

Micante,
No words either in voice or written
Can express how I feel about you.
What we can share has not yet been realized.
You are the lady of my life and eternity.
You are my soul mate and so much more.
Like each poem, screenplay, and book,
This is a song of my soul to you.

Acknowledgements:

The Great Spirit and Jesus Christ.

Mom and Dad, for everything. I miss you both.

To Jay DeMarco, my best friend. Thanks for your Complete and total friendship over the years.

Thanks to my family: My son, Cheryl, Malcolm, Julien, Ralph, Lorraine, Charity, Claude and Rose Vann, Bub Vann, Margaret, Chappie and Leah, Gus Lilavois, the Vann family, and all of my relatives.

Thanks to: William Osborne, Paul J. Travers, and Robert Frezza, B.J. Chandler, Lynn Swanner, Joyce Mahoney, Barbara Oakley, Alexandra Vigo, Nieves Gonzalez, Gloria Kelly, Yvonne Binum, Ana Galvez, Cynthia Collazo, Cesia Larrandote, Mari Ojeda, Diana Herrera, Sandi Sylvester, Lily LeMasters, Angie Dowda, Elizabeth Cole, Isabel Bautista, Juan Arango, Kathy Hernandez, C. Smallwood, Eylem Gulchere, Dania Peralta, E. Morales, Alba Grieco, Ana Mesa, Chip Becker, and everyone who has helped me.

Live in Brotherhood, Peace, and Love

True Love Lasts Forever

For more information, to order books or screenplays,
or to contact James L. Copa,
Go to gypsywitchproductions.com

Chapter One

"The Devil's Smile"

The woodland camouflaged Blackhawk helicopter flew over the colorful landscape of the Devil's Tower National Park in Wyoming well above tree top level. The aircraft's thumping main rotors frightened the wildlife that populated the public lands passing below them. The middle-aged pilot, whose puffy sun tanned face was barely visible beneath the tinted visor that protected his narrow eyes from the bright sun, was a career member of the Wyoming Army National Guard. He had a young co-pilot sitting next to him who was fresh out of flight school. The angry looking sergeant seated behind them facing the passengers was the highly experienced crew chief who controlled everything that happened inside the helicopter except flying it.

There were three passengers present in the aircraft who were taking up the space that was normally reserved for the aggressive light infantrymen that usually rode in the helicopter during weekend training exercises. The experienced pilot and his crew didn't mind the fact that they were transporting government civilians. For the extra flight pay and flight hours they would receive for conducting this mission, it was well worth the effort and taking a day off from their own boring desk jobs to fly government scientists out to the middle of nowhere.

For most of the morning, the bright sunlight had been baking the rowdy pilots, who had been trapped in the cockpit during the entire flight. Now that the crew was soaked in sweat and uncomfortable, the pilot decided that they needed a distraction. After directing the crew chief to open one of the side cargo doors for ventilation, the pilot began searching the ground below. The co-pilot looked at his boss, curious about what he was looking for on the surface. The pilot suddenly smiled and looked at his curious partner.

"Hey, Stemm, wanna' have some fun with these pencil necks?" asked the pilot into his in-flight microphone as he pointed out a rough stretch of tree lined mountains and hills off to his left.

"Sure, Chief," agreed his co-pilot, whose smooth face and innocent countenance made him look more like a high school nerd than a highly trained Army aviator.

"Sergeant Sierra, we're going tree top huggin'!" warned the pilot to his crew chief.

Without giving away the pilot's intentions, the crew chief scanned everyone's safety equipment and gripped the seat frame.

"Here we go!" exclaimed the Chief Warrant Officer over the crew radio.

Without any further warning, the pilot pulled slightly to the left on the sensitive, wobbling, joystick. The helicopter instantly responded by rapidly veering to the left as the pilot guided the aircraft into the narrow break between two tall stands of trees. The three passengers, who had not been warned about the sudden change in course and altitude, held on for their lives and watched in horror as the rotary wing aircraft successfully cleared the passage. To the terrified civilians on board, the success was less important than the element of mortal danger that they had endured and the realization that they could easily have joined the wildlife that abounded on the ground below them.

"Son of a bitch!" swore the tall thin male passenger who was wearing the navy blue suit and regimental tie. The tie was now sloped over the man's left shoulder and the can of soda that he had been holding in his hands had splashed over his finely tailored trousers.

The co-pilot looked over his shoulder to see how the civilians were doing. He observed that the black woman was holding an airsickness bag up to her mouth, which she was putting to frequent use while the pilot brought the aircraft back on course. Both of the male passengers were holding onto their seats, obviously terrified by the rapidly executed tactical air maneuvers. The tall male passenger reached for his airsickness bag, too. He was trying not to regurgitate, but the smell of the woman's vomit was getting the best of him.

"Hey, Chief, that babe puked all over her pretty HAZMAT suit and the dude in the blue suit looks like he's ready to upchuck too!" remarked the excited co-pilot with a grin. "God, I love this job!"

"Roger that!" laughed the pilot as he continued on course. "That was more fun than dropping night rappelling grunts five feet higher than their ropes can reach the ground!"

After returning to his original flight route, the satisfied pilot took a long look over his shoulder to assess the damage he had caused. "Hey!" yelled the cocky veteran pilot into his microphone at his civilian charges. The shocked passengers didn't appear to hear him.

"Chief, they're too fucked up to hear anything!" advised Warrant Officer Stemm over the radio.

"I think you're right," agreed the pilot. "I'll give 'em a few minutes to gather their thoughts."

"And pick up their guts, too!" laughed Stemm.

The pilot figured the male and female in the shiny fire fighting suits were too civilian looking and equipped too well to be with the Department of Defense. The pilot noticed that the man wearing the metallic suit appeared to be irritated with him, but the older tall guy wearing the conservative suit and tie appeared ready to lose his lunch again at any moment. None of the passengers were talking much now. They seemed preoccupied with staring at Devil's Tower. The huge mountain had been visible through the helicopter's windows for some time.

"Hey! You people all right back there?" yelled the pilot again, as he raised the tinted visor attached to his olive green Kevlar flight helmet. He glanced over his shoulders a second time to make sure his charges had heard him speaking to them.

The older passenger, who the pilot recalled was a military intelligence civilian from Fort Leavenworth, Kansas, looked at his two companions and feebly waved at the pilot. Outside of the opened side door of the helicopter, the colorful landscape was increasing in altitude as they approached the famous mountain.

"You must be hot in them space suits, huh?" asked the crew chief, who wondered what two government executives in HAZMAT suits were going to do at a remote national park. It made no sense to him since it had been too wet a spring for the wildfires that sometimes burned out of control in the area.

"Not at all," answered the brown haired man into his microphone with an unexpected air of authority to his voice. "We're not the ones baking in the cockpit. Besides, with your cargo door open in an unauthorized manner, and from the way you just flew this helo like you're at a hot landing zone in Baghdad, I'm glad to be wearing something that protects me from the elements and two soon to be unemployed rotary wing jockeys."

The stunned pilot and co-pilot had been listening to the conversation and nervously looked at each other as the big mountain came into full view. They were both keenly aware that real civilians never called helicopters by that name or used military terminology so easily. The pilot glanced over his shoulder, deciding to pay more attention to the brown haired man. After he observed the close haircut, well-trimmed regulation moustache, and the eyes of a man who knew how to bear the burden of authority, the pilot realized that he had made a terrible mistake about this plain looking passenger.

"You ain't no civilian. I can see that all right. You Air Force or Navy?" asked the pilot as he concentrated on banking the helicopter around the peaks and hills that were in his normal flight plan.

"Air National Guard!" yelled the man into his microphone without smiling. "I'm the commander of a C-130 support unit in Maryland!"

"A logistics officer, huh?" asked the co-pilot, who was suddenly nervous about having a commissioned officer on board their flight.

"No, a commander," corrected the officer as he stared at the pilot. "I lead men, and those men fly, service, and supply the aircraft for which I am responsible. Any other questions?"

"They didn't tell us we were flying any brass on this mission, Chief," remarked the co-pilot to his boss.

The pilot ignored him.

"How about that shit?" remarked the pilot, whose eyes showed their concern for pissing off a real officer. "You field grade, sir?"

"Yeah, I'm a major, Chief. I graduated from Officer Candidate School after doing my time as an enlisted man," explained the officer with the dark brown hair and Mediterranean facial features. He showed the pilot and crew his military identification card.

"Major Michael J. Valenti, U.S. Air Force Reserve," read the pilot over the radio.

"Now, do I have to prove that I'm a leader, or are you going to make the intelligent decision and take my word for it?"

"Welcome aboard, Major Valenti," offered the crew chief, whose slight Spanish accent failed to hide the nervousness in his voice. He was glad he wasn't a pilot at that particular moment. "It's always good to meet a commissioned officer who did enlisted time before earning his bars."

"Thank you, Sergeant," acknowledged Major Valenti, who still wasn't smiling.

When the Air National Guard commander turned to pay attention to the sick woman seated next to him, the sergeant didn't need to bet his stripes or paycheck to realize that the officer cared for her in more than a casual way. He reached into his flight bag and pulled out an olive drab water bladder.

"Sir, I've got a full three quart canteen here if the lady needs it," offered the crew chief as he handed the canteen to the officer. The sergeant's forearms were covered with air cavalry tattoos.

"Thanks," said the major as he accepted the water and assisted his friend as she drank from the canteen. "I know the water will make her feel better and I can use it to clean up her HAZMAT suit."

The Chief Warrant Officer listened to the conversation between the crew chief and officer.

"About that last maneuver, Major," remarked the pilot with a compromising look on his face. "We were just having a little fun with you."

"I understand, Chief," replied Major Valenti, who pointed at the pilot's battle dress uniform. "By that Third Infantry Division patch on your right shoulder, you flew combat missions in the Iraq War."

"That's right, sir," acknowledged the pilot. "I was there on one year orders and flew enough missions to have fun with you today without getting us all killed in the process."

"I was there, too, Chief, on short orders to support the effort," advised the Major. "So, I'll overlook your deviation from the flight plan on the condition you apologize to my colleagues. If you do, I'll forget about using my authority to make you a sergeant again."

"Works for me, Major," quickly agreed the Chief Warrant Officer.

"I thought it would," remarked the Air Force National Guard commander.

The nervous Chief Warrant Officer quickly turned in his uncomfortable seat and looked at the queasy African American woman.

"I'm truly sorry sir, ma'am," apologized the pilot, who couldn't help but feel guilty when he saw the fear in the woman's exotic blue eyes. The other male passenger just nodded. "I'll make sure we land near the Chief Ranger's facility so you can get cleaned up."

"Thank you," said the attractive woman through the paper bag that covered her mouth. After answering, she threw up again. The attentive major was helping her keep the bag in place.

"Sir, as one vet to another," began the pilot with a worried look on his face that the major had already figured out.

"Chief, why don't you just fly this aircraft and we'll get along just fine from here on out?"

"I appreciate that, sir," said the pilot. "By the way, the rest of us never did get properly introduced."

"Well, Chief, this beautiful woman next to me is Glenda Moses. This gentleman is Tom Ward. He's the other passenger you made sick with your flying."

"Nice to meet you all," greeted the pilot. "I'm C.W.O. Gray. My right seater is Warrant Officer Stemm, and my back seater's Sergeant Sierra. We were ordered to take you to Devil's Tower, but we weren't told why. Any info you want to give me?"

Mike handed the canteen back to the crew chief. Glenda Moses appeared to be feeling better and had stopped throwing up.

The gray haired man that Mike Valenti had identified as Tom Ward spoke up now that the tension had been reduced.

"This mission is classified under the authority of the President. You know what that means, right?" asked Tom Ward in an official but weak tone of voice.

All of the aviators were aware of military security classifications.

"Yes, Mr. Ward. That means we don't hear nothing, know nothing, or see nothing but this here helicopter and our charted course, roger?" responded the pilot on behalf of his crew.

"That's correct," agreed Tom Ward. "I may not be a hotshot aviator, but if I learn of any leak of this information, I'll see to it that you all spend the rest of your lives making model helicopters at Leavenworth."

The pilot and crew just nodded their heads and paid attention to their flying. After one sharp maneuver around a few tall trees, the pilot leveled the helicopter and they could all see buildings scattered at various places close by. The co-pilot took control of the aircraft and slowed it down as Chief Gray consulted his flight plan. The crew chief began preparing for the landing.

"That's our destination," Chief Gray said, as he checked his flight controls. "What a shit hole this place is, huh, Stemm?"

"You got that right, Chief!"

"Hey, put her down next to that landing zone near that main building so our guests can get cleaned up," ordered the pilot as a few people approached the landing zone from the direction of the mountain. "Looks like there's a welcome group waiting for our guests, too."

Warrant Officer Stemm landed the helicopter while Chief Gray directed Stemm to keep the large rotors turning. The crew chief unharnessed his passengers.

"You know something, Major, it was a pure pleasure!" shouted Chief Gray after he turned in his seat and shook hands with Valenti and Moses. "You know how to handle your shit and keep things tight. I like that in an officer! Are we picking you up on the return trip?"

Tom Ward nodded his head.

"Looks like we are!" shouted the pilot now that he was aware of the new information. "Major, we usually have a happy hour after a mission. How'd you like to get together with us for some beers later? Your lady friend's invited, too."

Mike Valenti motioned for Glenda Moses to walk to the ranger's building without him. He turned and leaned close to the pilot to share a private word with him.

"That would've been fine before that stunt you pulled, Chief. But, it had no purpose," remarked Mike Valenti. "I only drink for a purpose. Understand me?"

"Roger that, Major Valenti," acknowledged Chief Gray, whose smile had disappeared.

Mike Valenti hopped out of the helicopter and followed Glenda Moses. Tom Ward prepared to hop out, too, but the crew chief grabbed his arm.

"Where you going, Mr. Ward?" asked the crew chief, who didn't like people leaving his helicopter when it wasn't listed on the flight plan.

"I'll be right back, Sergeant," replied Tom Ward, who had a hand over his crotch. "I've got to go to the rest facilities."

Sergeant Sierra looked at Chief Gray, hoping for the pilot to order the intelligence officer back on board. "Let the man go to the john, Sarge," shouted Chief Gray. "I guess he has a right to go take a piss after that shit we pulled."

As the three civilians walked away from the aircraft, the crew chief grabbed Chief Gray by the shoulder and shook his head. He pointed at Tom Ward.

"Rest facilities," Sergeant Sierra remarked as he tucked a flight clipboard into one of the many pockets in his flight suit. "Chief, that dude's so straight that he walks like he's got a two by four shoved up his ass!"

"Yeah, Sarge, he's a real rear echelon mother fucker," remarked Chief Gray. "Those M.I. types are so far back in the rear that they couldn't find their nuts in the dark with both hands wearing night vision goggles!"

"You got that right, Chief!" laughed the co-pilot, who wanted to appear more experienced that he actually was. The pilot wasn't going to let that happen.

"Stemm, you can't talk," admonished Chief Gray with a frown. "You ain't done shit yet, either! Fresh out of flight school after basic training and A.I.T., you're greener than a second lieutenant wearing camo paint!"

The pilot and crew chief laughed at the young Warrant Officer's expense.

"Roger that!" agreed the co-pilot, who realized it was time to change the subject. "What's taking that Ward guy so long, Chief?"

"Damned civilians can't hold their water!" interjected Sergeant Sierra, laughing.

"Yeah, I know, but I have yet to get any suit to piss into one of our portable waste bags during a flight," said Chief Gray, who held up a new waste bag and opened it. He leaned forward in his seat and began to urinate into the bag. "I figure the guys are scared they'll fall out of the chopper while they're holding their peckers, and the split tails ain't going to piss in a bag on board and show us their pussies!"

The three soldiers continued laughing and joking. The aviators had to speak loudly because the helicopter's engines were making a lot of noise as the rotors churned through the air and whipped the loose dirt on the ground. "Damn, it's hot out today!" remarked the crew chief as he continued looking for Tom Ward. "It's no wonder prairie dogs stay in them holes all day long."

"Yeah, I pity those folks wearing those HAZMAT suits," added Chief Gray. "God only knows what they're doing up here in the high lonesome."

"I heard on the tube that some geology school's testing out here for commercial development," explained Warrant Officer Stemm as he handled the helicopter.

Chief Gray took over the flight controls and settled into his seat again. He began checking his gauges and flight systems.

"You know what, guys? That don't make sense when you think about it," remarked Sergeant Sierra as he observed Tom Ward walking toward the aircraft. "Everyone knows commercial development is banned on park property, and feds don't do commercial research."

"That's true," agreed Chief Gray. "This major reminds me of some of those Agency types we used to fly around Iraq during the war."

"What were they like, Chief?" asked the co-pilot.

"Some were special ops guys with no name tags or I.D. that did the nastiest, most violent shit I've ever seen done in combat, and the others were so high up you just knew better that to fuck with them. I think this officer is the second sort. But it ain't none of our concern and nothing we can talk about, so I'm all for breaking some wind! What's the word, Sarge?"

"Crank the rotors, Chief!" shouted Sergeant Sierra. "Our passenger's back on board!"

When the military intelligence civilian was seated and his seat belt had been secured, the crew became quiet again and prepared to concentrate on flying. As the pilot and co-pilot observed Mike Valenti and Glenda Moses shaking hands with members of the welcoming committee, the Blackhawk lifted into the air and her engines roared as she rapidly disappeared from view.

***

At the rocky base of the mysterious funneled mountain located at the Devil's Tower National Park in Wyoming, a discreet government research site being funded and conducted by the U.S. Department of the Interior was crowded with busy scientists. There was a late model helicopter parked on a helipad farther down the mountain's base that was painted with the emblem and lettering of the U.S. Geological Survey. Most of the busy government technicians were located near several weathered unmarked canvas tents that provided only moderate protection against the terrible heat.

In a public camping area not far from the small government research site, a large noisy group of First Nations protestors was demonstrating against commercial development of the park. Bored National Park Service Rangers dressed in gray and green olive drab uniforms were providing security at the site. The deep booming voice of the excited protest leader being projected over the loudspeakers was almost drowned out by the war drums being beaten by his enthusiastic supporters. There were curious tourists scattered around the area at guide points who appeared to be uninterested in the government scientists, the park rangers, or the protesters.

At various places around the thick base of the vertically etched mountain, there were more scientists working within areas marked with evidence tape. The scientists were dressed in the metallic silver protective colored suits worn by hazardous materials specialists or firefighters. They were using long steel probes to extract molten rock samples from small pools of magma that were scattered around the base of Devil's Tower.

Brumes of acrid smoke were rising from the various liquid rock wells, which were hissing and crackling as the liquid rock on the outer edges of the pools was beginning to cool. Mike Valenti and Glenda Moses were among the scientists and were assisting them in the investigation of the geological hazards. Both Mike and Glenda were dressed in gold colored metallic protective suits that were much more sophisticated than the silver ones being worn by the site workers. Unlike the workers from the Geological Survey, the two visiting scientists were wearing oxygen tanks to protect their lungs from the potentially toxic magma fumes.

"Well, Church, this isn't good," remarked Mike Valenti, as he inspected the black lava that was cooling into shiny black rock in his collection tray. The sweat on Mike's tanned face was visible through his glass visor, as was his affectionate gaze at the woman in the matching protective suit standing next to him. "What the hell are magma channels and toxic gases doing near a mountain that isn't even supposed to be an old or new volcano?"

Glenda Moses nodded as she continued her work. She was a very attractive black woman in her thirties with stunning natural blue eyes. Her male companion noticed how much she was sweating under her visor.

Glenda appeared to be ready to be overcome by the heat, but he knew better than to say anything to her about it.

"You know something, Church," observed Mike as he pointed at the series of magma pools that were scattered around the scientific site. "You see the way the magma pools circle part of the base of the Tower?"

Glenda looked toward the area where Mike was pointing, "Yeah, I noticed it when we flew in. The pools make it look like Devil's Tower is smiling at us."

"Well, if the devil's smiling at us, I hope he's going to help us figure all of this out!"

Glenda wasn't pleased with Mike's humor.

"Okay, sinner, so do I have enough samples for this test batch?" asked Glenda playfully as she bumped a hip against Mike's.

Glenda called Mike "Dim" because his agnosticism made his acceptance into heaven a little dim in her eyes. He called her "Church" because Glenda was a devout Baptist who had a real interest in making it to the upper floors of the Almighty's house.

"There's enough there, Church," said Mike. "It's rare to have so much basalt in magma this far from the coast. Look how the lava's shining as it's cooling off."

"You're right, Dim. This is rare! I'm going to send these samples out for priority analysis!"

"Alright, I'm going to get with the site supervisor and see what else I can find out, but let's keep the reasons for our interest a secret. We don't know what we're dealing with yet!"

"Neither do these guys! It's amazing to me that we weren't notified of this find sooner. The sulphur levels in the fumes alone should've gotten Washington's attention," remarked Glenda. "This is ARK level intelligence for sure!"

"I agree, but I'm not convinced it's pangaean intelligence. The timing's all wrong and the stats don't support my hypothesis. At least Geology was smart enough to publicize this site work as a preliminary step in commercial development. Everyone's focusing on protesting against that rather than figuring out why the government's really here," observed Mike.

"True," agreed Glenda. "I'll be back, Dim."

As Glenda cautiously made her way down the slope with the samples in her hands, Mike admired the way her hazardous materials suit conformed to her body as she was walking. He was wondering if this use of their vacation time would allow them more time to develop their relationship. With an appreciative sigh, Mike turned his attention back to the research site and walked over to speak with the site supervisor. Both men walked a safe distance away from the steamy hot temperatures around the magma pools and removed their head covers. They were drenched in sweat. A site attendant brought both scientists some cold bottled water to drink as they talked. The scorching sun was already beginning to burn their faces.

"Sam, we're going to stay on another week if you'll let us. I know Vernie and I are just guests, but we need to get more data about the origins of this magma!"

Mike usually called Glenda by her nickname.

"Look, it's no big deal if you stay. Hell, if it was, this whole program would be classified or something by the C.I.A. and we wouldn't be here, right? Besides, we've been collecting lava samples on the west coast for the past six years and it seems to be a normal release valve for upper mantle magma that's surfacing from what we think is a subterranean oceanic magma relief channel somewhere out in the Pacific around the area of the Hawaiian Islands."

Mike ignored the comment about the Central Intelligence Agency. The geological scientist was fishing for information about whether or not Mike and Glenda worked for the "Agency."

"It seems like the basaltic lava that's similar in type to what we've been seeing in Hawaii, California, and at Yellowstone. Why hasn't this been completely investigated?" asked Mike.

"Because there's really nothing we can do about it, Mike. Our agency's philosophy is fucked up. If our research doesn't support commerce, it's put on the back burner under President Fairchild's policy of facilitating commerce rather than investigative research. Our Chief Geologist could care less about national or world magma problems. If California dropped into the sea or the Devil's Tower sprouts a volcano, this administration wouldn't care as long as the oil wells kept pumping and the public rangeland remained fertile for cattle. Until these magma finds result in a danger to citizen lives or our commercial natural resources, this will remain an insignificant matter with our agency."

Mike was amazed, "You don't think these magma pools are symptoms of a serious problem?"

"I didn't when they were first detected at Yellowstone National Park," replied Sam. "But now that we have this Devil's Tower puzzler to deal with, who knows? You're welcome to stay, though."

"Thanks, Sam. Vernie and I are actually here on our vacation time, so I appreciate that," remarked Michael

Valenti with a grin. His tanned skin, thin dark moustache, and wind blown brown hair made Mike look like a man more suited to the great outdoors than working behind an optical telescope.

"Well you picked a good time to visit us, Doctor. Those Indian demonstrators give this project a carnival atmosphere. You couldn't have planned this any better!"

"Yeah, there's always been a lot of interest in this place. Some think aliens navigate here by using Devil's Tower as a landmark," said Mike as he gulped down the last of his water. "I personally think it was chiseled to its present state by a flood."

"A flood? Whatever, man. To me it's just a chunk of rock I'm real tired of seeing right about now," complained Sam as he prepared to don his head cover again.

Mike shook hands with Sam and walked down the rocky slope to find Vernie.

Formerly assigned to the defunct National Aeronautics and Space Administration (N.A.S.A.), Michael Valenti was a promising scholar who was hired as a Space Department galactic topographer in 2003. He was one of the few respected scientists who had never accepted conventional arguments that global warming and the effects of the deteriorating ozone layer on Earth's fragile environment were the causes of the Earth's maladies. Mike Valenti also firmly believed that the continent of Antarctica held the most important scientific keys to the Earth's sketchy evolutionary history. As a result of the doctor's progressive opinions, he came under increased scrutiny and pressure from the Space Department to conform to their more conservative policy that the Earth's geology was incapable of being harmed by orbital influences in the near future.

Following the brutally competitive election and successful campaign in 2004 of the Republican Party candidate, President Alexander Montgomery Fairchild, Dr. Valenti was appointed by the new Director of Central Intelligence to head a highly classified planetary project that was on the verge of being discontinued. While the Director believed that Dr. Valenti could salvage the operation, most of the subordinate agency executives were pleased that it had been comfortably banished to the cellar vault. The majority of highly conservative Central Intelligence Agency (C.I.A.) officials were confident that the struggling intelligence science project, like so many other risky classified ventures before it, would be cut from the increasingly tight C.I.A. investigative budget before the end of the fiscal year. With just less than 120 days to go before the beginning of the new fiscal year on October 1, 2006, even the members of the secret task force were aware that they might be seeking employment elsewhere within the next ninety days.

Chapter Two

"Vision Control"

The countryside around the small port city of Qiqihar was mountainous, with small farms interspersed between the rugged terrains. Qiqihar was a city in Heilongjiang province with over one million residents that is located on the Nen River near the Hinggan Mountains in northeastern China. The main occupations of most of the town's inhabitants were mining, brewing, and farming, but the increasing influx of computer technology and a successful semi-conductor industry was beginning to create a small, educated middle class in the area. Most of the occupants of Qiqihar still rode bicycles as the primary method of transportation. Occasional cars could be observed traveling along the poorly paved roads, but most of the traffic consisted of damaged mining trucks, poorly maintained farm vehicles, and rusty bicycles. On the extreme northern outskirts of the town, the land of the struggling family farm collectives yielded to the mountains that provided iron ore and other mineral resources.

There was an abandoned old farmhouse on a once cultivated small knoll that could only be reached by using the rocky dirt road that meandered up to it. The secondary road below the farmhouse led north to the nearby Russian frontier. It was raining, and the higher elevations were shrouded in fog. Scattered among the overgrown furrows that were still visible in the uncultivated field, one could see remnants of the cabbage, carrot, and bean plants that used to grow in abundance there.

A Chinese man wearing a white laboratory coat was sitting on the wet ground near the farmhouse. Chiang Ma Loo cautiously crawled into the musty building where he activated the laptop computer that had been stored in the cache. While waiting for the connection, Chiang thought about his current situation and decided that he could never return to China again.

In 1985, Chiang Ma had been the only Chinese nuclear physicist that the Soviets were able to convert to their espionage payrolls. After several years spent earning the respect and trust of the scientific apparatus of the People's Republic of China, Chiang Ma was eventually assigned to China's elite nuclear weapons program. He had been an inactive espionage agent who had not made contact with Russia since he was transferred to Qiqihar a year ago. Chiang Ma Loo was fat, well educated, and used to enjoying the financial and social benefits of the technical elite of the People's Republic of China. He was not accustomed to living at a remote secret Chinese scientific site where there was no place to socialize and no cultural places to enjoy. Confident of Russian promises to transfer him to a prestigious technical post in Moscow, Chiang Ma could not wait to leave Qiqihar.

There was a Burmese made bicycle lying on its side near Chiang that he had used to reach the secret communications site. There was also a well that provided bitter fresh water and a cache of rice rations that could last Chiang Ma a week. The rain was having a terrible effect on the satellite transmission, so Chiang placed another call. This time his attempt was successful.

"This is Vision Control," answered the rough voice on the other end of the connection that Chiang Ma was relieved to recognize. "Identify yourself."

As he verified his code number in the authentication book, Chiang Ma wondered why everything in the cache was Soviet issued. He expected at the very least that the Russians would've issued him modern technical equipment. The identification and travel documents that Chiang Ma was supposed to use to enter Russia were issued by the former Soviet Union.

"This is Operative 1032," answered Chiang Ma excitedly into the handset.

"I don't know you. Authenticate," directed the voice from Russia. This was the order to give the code word indicating that Chiang Ma was alone and not under duress. If Chiang Ma was being detained, or if he was unable to speak freely, he was to give a different response.

"Stalin," replied the Chinese man with a little more control in his voice.

"Speak, 1032," directed the Russian with a sense of calm in his voice.

"Sergei, I'm exfiltrating immediately!" exclaimed Chiang Ma, who began to lose his composure.

"No names, Operative 1032!" directed Sergei angrily. "What's wrong?"

Chiang Ma fumbled to open the disk drive on the ancient Soviet computer.

"I have important information," advised Chiang Ma as he inserted a compact disk into the computer and began to transmit the information. "All the project data from my research section is here! It's transmitting now!"

"Fine, 1032, and I can tell by your voice that there's a problem," remarked Sergei. "Why must you exfiltrate now when you haven't been compromised?"

"Something went wrong with the project, Vision Control! I think it was the earthquake!"

"How do you mean?"

"I don't know what's going on, but I've been removed from the test program!" exclaimed Chiang Ma nervously. "You'll have to check the data on the disk!"

"Have you been detected? Are they watching you? Answer me, 1032."

"Everyone in the test department is being transferred! An hour ago, our staff was instructed to report to the political commissar for reassignment! We're going to be liquidated!"

There was silence at the end of the line.

"1032, what device was tested?" asked Sergei.

"We weren't allowed to see it!" explained Chiang Ma. "And when I heard they were looking for me, I left the facility using my security pass, got on my bicycle, and went for a ride in the countryside. I don't have much time, but I have everything I could take on disk for you."

Sergei waited for the data to be received.

"The transmission is complete," advised Chiang.

"Standby, 1032," instructed Sergei, as he checked to confirm that the transmission had been received. "You were right to consider the importance of your information the way that you did. Exfiltrate if you can to the safe zone, then call me again. Insure you reach the safe zone for pickup no later than three in the morning five days from now. There will be only one rescue attempt. If you miss it, use your Russian credentials to cross the border. Destroy all of your technical materials, bury your diskette, and throw the computer into the first water source you see. And remember to liquidate yourself if you're captured."

"Of course," muttered Chiang Ma, who had not considered committing suicide as he had been trained to do so many years ago. "I'll make all necessary preparations now."

There was a distinct sound on the telephone that indicated that Sergei had terminated their conversation. When Chiang Ma observed a Chinese troop transport truck approaching on the road, he realized that it was time for him to leave.

"Buddha help me!" shrieked the Chinese spy, who cautiously backed away from his observation spot and returned to his cache.

It took less than fifteen minutes for the searching soldiers to find evidence of Chiang Ma Loo's presence at the farm. After the political officer checked the Chinese issued computer and laboratory coat that had been left in a Soviet military waterproof bag, the security apparatus of the People's Republic of China committed the unlimited resources of the People's Army into action to locate the fugitive scientist.

***

Nestled in a classified old vault area in the chilly bowels of the C.I.A. at Langley, Virginia, a classified technical investigative group functioned under the name of Operation "NOAH'S ARK." Chartered by the C.I.A. in 1990, the TOP SECRET project served as the primary intelligence developer of abnormal planetary phenomena. The original purpose of NOAH'S ARK was to categorize and research potential disturbances and determine their long-term threat to the United States. This mandate included the use of interstellar intelligence.

The operational name was derived from early task force assumptions that geological and climatic changes were the result of complex planetary environmental factors. The planned response to these potential climatic catastrophes was to prepare the United States for long-term survival by creating "ARK" or survival locations where artificial human habitats would sustain carefully selected populations of humans, animals, and plants. While data developed since the program's inception indicated that the ARK concept was antiquated in many ways, the task force had retained its operational name.

By 1994, global warming and other climatic factors had erroneously led top government officials and international agencies to believe that the repair of the ozone layer would stop or slow the Earth's erratic changes. In complete opposition to the ozone argument, a few controversial scientists were advancing dramatic new theories that predictable galactic astronomical patterns were causing Earth's planetary changes.

The investigation of those new theories was limited to a few rogue scientists within the United States. The rest of the world's foremost researchers were guarding their conservative theories through the U.S. Space Department and the politically influenced and highly corrupt United Nations Framework Convention on Climate Change in Bonn, Germany. Although the United States was a primary investor in the U.N. program, the C.I.A. had determined long ago that any sharing of new space and geological intelligence with the U.N. could pose a serious threat to national security.

There were many startling examples to fuel the various arguments. Immense sections of time hardened glacial ice from our polar regions were dropping into the ocean in numbers that were causing the oceans to rise. Long dormant fault lines of deep subterranean rock were shifting at alarming rates. Intense earthquakes and violent volcanic activity were occurring in greater and stronger numbers. With the increase in the frequency and severity of tornadoes, hurricanes, and other natural disasters occurring in the United States, the C.I.A. was attempting to secretly decipher the Earth's violent signals and provide precise intelligence about its future. Operation NOAH'S ARK was then tasked in 1995 to find the answers and be prepared to react to the threats.

As a result of major advances in American geological research and technology, new methods had been developed to more accurately analyze magma and link geological data around the world. Since magma was the common denominator of earthquakes, volcanoes, and other geological disturbances, it provided scientists with an efficient means of locating and diagnosing the Earth's geological problems.

***

Dr. Seth Tayman, the Assistant Director of Operation NOAH'S ARK, strolled into the executive office area of his supervisor with coffee cup in hand hoping for some good morning news. Although Seth was late for work, it didn't bother him. Dr. Valenti's voluptuous Venezuelan secretary, Alexandra Charles, was seated behind her desk. Alexandra always wore clothing that accentuated her stunning figure. A woman in her late twenties, Alexandra was an exotic, shapely lady who was also half African American.

"Good morning, Alex," greeted Seth with an appreciative smile as he strained his neck to stare at her exquisitely long cinnamon brown legs. The slow talking man from Idaho was a bit too obvious. "You look nice today. Do you mind if I ask if you a personal question?"

"Thank you, Dr. Tayman, and yes, I do mind," she answered with a sexy Spanish accent. "I only associate with gentlemen and that you are not."

Seth winced at her answer.

"Sorry about that. I didn't mean anything by it. Hey, is Mike back yet?"

"Not yet, Dr. Tayman," replied Alexandra as she turned in her swivel chair to adjust the volume on her compact disk player. In an effort to get rid of Seth, she increased the volume of the salsa music playing on the radio. Alexandra could always tell when Seth was leering at her because his bird like eyes would get bigger.

"Damn, I guess that means I'm still filling in for Mike then!"

"Yes, sir. Here's the morning mail, Doctor. You missed the classified documents courier, but he said he'd return after the rest of his rounds."

"Okay, Alex. There's nothing much going on here anyway," commented Seth.

Seth walked into Mike's office just as the telephone on Alexandra's desk rang. As he took a seat in his supervisor's chair hoping the call wouldn't interrupt his coffee time, the intercom sounded. The office was cooler than usual, so Seth pulled up the zipper of the plaid flannel jacket he always wore to keep him warm while at work.

"Sir, Mr. Champion's on line two. Bad mood...."

"Thanks, Alex," he yelled without bothering to use the intercom to respond to her. He picked up the telephone and pushed the button for line two.

"Good morning, Mr. Champion."

"That you, Tayman? You still acting? I'm on my way down there to see you! Champ out!"

"Oh, shit!" swore Seth as he looked at the mess on Mike's normally pristine desk.

Knowing the Chief of Advanced Projects was on his way down to Mike's office, Seth clamored to get the mass of paper that had accumulated on his supervisor's desk into a neat pile. His eyes became even bigger when he realized that he hadn't reviewed the morning world information briefs or the memorandums from the classified documents courier. That meant Seth had no idea why Mark Champion was on his way to see him!

The Office of Advanced Projects was under the C.I.A.'s Directorate of Science and Technology. It was one of eight offices within the directorate assigned the tasks of collecting, analyzing, and reporting scientific information for the Director of Central Intelligence.

After Mark Champion stopped to greet Alexandra Charles, the tall man entered the office with his usual cynical attitude. Out of breath from his short walk, Mark tossed a large brown envelope at Seth with a little too much force. A Standard Form 703 cover sheet was on top of the document in the envelope. The cover sheet was marked "TOP SECRET" in bold orange lettering. Mark sat down and put his own C.I.A. logo coffee cup on the desk. Champ tucked one leg under the other and rested his big hands on a knee.

"Hey, got anymore of that coffee," asked Champ with a smile. "All I'm looking at in the bottom of my cup are the grounds."

Seth personally went to get his obnoxious boss some coffee. After handing Champ a fresh cup of coffee, Seth settled into Mike's worn chair to receive the bad news. Mark Champion usually didn't visit NOAH'S ARK unless there was something wrong. The Advanced Projects chief slowly relaxed in his chair and sipped his fresh cup of coffee.

"Good joe," breathed Champion, savoring the gourmet blend. He pointed at the parcel. "That was shuffled my way by the Director for your boss."

Few people cared much for Mark Champion, who was a fifty seven year old former University of Connecticut basketball player who never forgot to remind everyone that he had once been a National Basketball Association draft candidate. During service as a logistics officer in the U.S. Army in the Republic of Vietnam in 1970, a knee wound received during an ambushed truck convoy ruined all of Champ's professional athletic hopes.

Since Seth had been a Marine during the same time period, Champ liked to deal with him more than with Mike. Seth opened the bulky envelope and withdrew the series of messages and photographs contained there. He scanned the pages until something caught his attention.

"This is amazing, Champ! There's a terrain rip in the American Highlands area of Antarctica that's got to be at least 20 miles long!" exclaimed Seth as he examined one of the photographs more closely.

"So what?" moaned Mark, who was irritated by Seth's enthusiasm over the information. He decided to occupy his mind by looking at a picture of an F-16 fighter jet on Mike's office wall.

"The terrain rip's cracked open a glacier and exposed a huge oil field. This quake was big!"

"What's that intercept got to do with NOAH'S ARK's mandate?" asked Champ as he attempted to calmly drink more of his coffee.

"Actually, this information's from the National Security Agency," explained Seth, who casually slid the photograph in front of Mark to review. "N.S.A. provided this information to us from their own Taiwan desk. This data was intercepted during an encrypted transmission from a Russian satellite terrain surveyor to Moscow. According to this, the Chinese contracted the Russians to conduct a classified subterranean survey of the American Highlands area of Antarctica. If you look at this photograph, you'll see that significant petroleum and natural gas reserves are now vulnerable to exploration."

Champ shrugged, and then ran a wide hand through his brittle brown and gray hair.

"Big fuckin' deal, Seth! So who cares outside the U.S. Geological Survey if there's oil, gas, or a gash on Antarctica? It's a big piece of continental rock covered with ice!" exclaimed Mark, who was now playing with the laces of one of his expensive wing-tipped shoes. "Everyone, including the idiots on my noon basketball team, knows that Antarctica has rich mineral resources!"

"C'mon, Champ, you know Mike's been saying for years that Antarctica's the key to the world's geological problems and a prime location to signal the beginning of the Pangaean Effect," explained Seth. "This gash, as you call it, could be a result of early pangaean activity!"

"Yeah, or just a crack in the ice that the Chinese want to take advantage of! Gimme a break! They probably just see this as an opportunity to tap the oil fields down there!"

Seth flipped through some of the papers until he found one of the statistical lists.

"I disagree, Champ. There's no rational reason for the Chinese to have an interest in exploiting Antarctica. They have no international right to any mineral resources there, and even if they did, international treaties and their poor technological ability to exploit the resources all but exclude China from the continent. They don't even have the ability to do their own subterranean surveying from space!"

"Christ!" moaned Mark in a bored tone as he shot an imaginary basketball in the direction of Mike's empty trashcan. "Get to the winning shot, Seth! I've got to shoot some hoops at lunchtime! You know something, it sounds to me like this whole thing needs to be passed on to the U.S. Geological Survey."

"That would be a waste of time, too, Champ. You know as well as I do that under current administration policy, the U.S.G.S. doesn't do anything with technical intelligence from the People's Republic of China. The last president didn't like China, and President Fairchild's even worse," explained Seth.

"Whatever," muttered Mark Champion with a shrug of his shoulders. He uncrossed his legs, appearing to be ready to leave. "I'm just an old C.I.A. logistics project manager, not some weird science dork like Valenti. So why don't you tell me what you think Mike's going to do with this information?"

"If I know my boss," speculated Seth, as he began to put the Antarctic data away. "He's going to send an ARK Team to the survey area to obtain accurate scientific intelligence."

Champ didn't like the fact that any international information that fell within Dr. Valenti's ARK objectives was automatically assigned to the operation. Mr. Champion knew that any scientific findings made by NOAH'S ARK would be a big boost to an operation that Champ wanted shut down as soon as possible. A foreign mission could ruin his plans to close the operation.

"I'm not convinced, and you're not helping. Now, where's that maverick boss of yours anyway?"

Seth shrugged, "Still on annual leave, sir. We haven't heard from him since last week. Why?"

"Dammit! I've been worldwide paging that little bastard for two days now and he hasn't answered me yet! The Director's calling for a National Security Council meeting and Valenti's got to be there! Now, activate their G.P.S. body locator chips so I can schedule a videoconference with the Director!"

Mark Champion stormed out of the office, leaving Seth to examine the Chinese information more closely. After he notified the ARK Communications Chief to locate Mike Valenti, Seth returned to his analysis of the Chinese data as he hummed to the salsa music that was playing on Alexandra's radio.

***

After an exhilarating morning subway ride on the improved Beijing transit system from the city of Ping Guo Yuan, Vice Premier Sang Jiyun was escorted by state security officers into his armored black Mercedes limousine at the downtown Beijing subway stop at Xi Dan. As the head of state special projects for the People's Republic of China, Sang Jiyun was responsible for coordinating and managing the secret mission to survey the earthquake site in Antarctica.

The Premier and Head of Government, the ruthless Hu Quichen, had assigned Sang Jiyun this expedition in hopes that it would prepare him for more important activities at the highest levels of the government and party. The Chinese Communist Party General Secretary, Jiang Zhaoping, had disapproved of Sang's assignment. Fortunately, Premier Hu had more power than the party leader when it came to bureaucratic decisions. As a result of his superior handling of the assignment thus far, Sang Jiyun was hoping that President Zhu Le Ho would reward him for his service by placing him in charge of one of the many profitable government owned businesses in Hong Kong.

After getting comfortable in his chauffeur driven car, the seventy-year-old fat man placed an encrypted cellular telephone call to his Russian counterpart in Moscow. Because there were only a few cellular sites around Beijing, the connection was not very good.

"Sergei! Good to talk you!" greeted Sang Jiyun with a genuine touch of friendship in his voice for the veteran Russian project leader. "Sergei, we know that Chiang Ma Loo contacted Russia after his escape from one of our laboratories. Need I tell you more?"

Sergei was too experienced an intelligence officer to provide unnecessary information to an adversary.

"I don't know anyone by that name," replied Sergei. "We have many operatives, but we keep them nameless. It's much more professional, no?"

Sang Jiyun took a deep breath that Sergei could clearly hear over the telephone.

"We knew him by that name here in China," advised Sang Jiyun with a knowing laugh. "But the expired papers in his possession identify him as your Boris Chiang. His documents listed him as an agricultural attaché with your embassy in Peking."

"Ah, I know that name," acknowledged Sergei, who feigned remembering the spy. "He was developed years ago under the old regime. When he called us, he used old equipment that was placed at a safe zone located at a farmhouse a long time ago. The idiot's identification number was so old that my communications staff wouldn't authenticate the transmission!"

Sang Jiyun was surprised that Sergei was admitting to the contact with the scientist. He took a moment to gather his thoughts. The Chinese intelligence officers that had inspected the safe site and Chiang Ma's possessions confirmed that the scientist had not had the opportunity to transmit the stolen intelligence. Sang

Jiyun also knew that the telephone call had been too short to permit Chiang Ma Loo the time to tell the Russians about the important information he had obtained at the nuclear facility.

"He was indeed an imbecile, Sergei," advised Sang Jiyun. "This scientist single-handedly bungled a radioactive container of plutonium that was being removed for arms destruction and it resulted in the deaths of his entire team. Chiang Ma was contaminated and dying when we found him. He was attempting to reach your border before he died like his comrades."

"Then you've done Russia a valuable service, my friend," chuckled Sergei. "I'll wager a month's Rubles that the traitor didn't discard our secure telephone?"

That made Sang Jiyun laugh. His agents had indeed found the classified telephone in Chiang Ma's possession when he was captured, but the spy liquidated himself before he could be interrogated.

"Yes, my friend, we seized the telephone. It will not be returned. A matter of procedure, you know," advised Sang Jiyun. "He was caught spying for Russia, and that isn't appreciated by the Politburo. They don't understand the art of our profession, Sergei."

"I understand, old friend," responded Sergei. "Our profession never changes, only the rhetoric of it."

"Of course, and when the politicians recognize the significance of our respective contributions, you might finally get that large office in the Kremlin you've always wanted!" teased Sang Jiyun.

Sergei laughed so loud that Sang Jiyun had to hold the receiver away from his ear.

"That day will never come, old comrade! The Kremlin is now a place for politicians and the Russian

Orthodox Church! Soon it will be more like the Vatican than the life blood of the Russian state!"

Both men laughed at the thought.

"So, are you prepared to send your two scientific officers here to meet with my project commander?" asked Sang Jiyun, who was still laughing.

"The Kremlin has agreed to accept your request for assistance," answered Sergei, who was also still laughing. "We'll be sending you Vitaly Chin and Natasha Svetkov, two of our best polar scientists."

"Very good, Sergei," noted Sang Jiyun. "Their experience will be most appreciated."

"I'll advise my superiors of this good news, Sang, and inform them that it is reliable information."

"Thank you, Sergei. I'll contact General Fu immediately. Coordinate directly with him from now on. Farewell, Sergei."

Vice Premier Sang Jiyun contacted General Fu Wen Han next. As the People's Liberation Army Joint Military Commander of Beijing, General Fu was entrusted with the mission of obtaining much needed research from Antarctica. The Vice Premier informed the general that two Russian scientific advisors would be accompanying the daring expeditionary force.

***

As the afternoon shift changed at C.I.A. headquarters and the halls filled with personnel, a nervous Seth Tayman was in the Office of the Director of the C.I.A. with Mark Champion. Champ was standing behind the Director with his arms crossed. A state of the art classified video conferencing screen had been extended from its concealed compartment in the office ceiling. It was raining heavily, so the video link was being affected by the storm. The interference was sporadic.

"Initiate contact," ordered the Director into her intercom. She was dressed in a flattering suit and the room smelled like her expensive perfume. Rosy's disability and confinement to a wheelchair did not deter from the fact that she was a beautiful woman.

The screen illuminated showing Mike Valenti standing at the base of a foreboding mountain. The Department of the Interior's helicopter was in the background with the setting sun in the distance.

"Doctor," began the Director in a concerned tone of voice. "I've been waiting all morning to speak with you, and Mr. Champion tells me that he's been paging you for two days. Are you aware of that?"

"Yes, ma'am. I apologize, but I've been tied up here on a project I think is related to NOAH'S ARK."

"Where you hiding this time, Mike?" interjected Mark Champion, who wanted to cause as much trouble for Valenti as he could. He nudged the Director's shoulder to get her attention.

Mike smiled like a kid caught hooking school.

"I'm vacationing at the Devil's Tower National Park, about 1,267 feet above the Bell Fourch River in the wonderfully remote state of Wyoming!" answered Mike.

The Director smiled, appreciating that Mike used his own time to bend the rules. Mark noticed the Director's change in attitude and realized that she liked the young scientist.

"You're supposed to be relaxing after that series of ARK field operations in Europe, Doctor, not using personal time to expand on your theories," remarked

Myrna Ramirez. She was paralyzed in both legs after being shot during an unsuccessful assassination attempt against the former Chinese premier in Peking in 1999.

"I am relaxing, ma'am," replied Mike nervously. "I just figured I'd see what the Interior folks are so worked up about. Did you know they found new magma pools here? They've been conducting studies for awhile and NOAH'S ARK didn't know about it!"

"Never mind that right now," cut off Myrna as she shifted in her wheelchair and caused the worn frame to squeak. "I need you to do an info brief to the N.S.C., and I need you here A.S.A.P. I've got it scheduled for June 6 at nine in the morning. When can you be here?"

"Well, it's the fifth, so I can finish here today and catch a flight out of Cheyenne tomorrow," offered Mike.

"No, get to Cheyenne tonight. I need you to prepare for the meeting. A company jet will be there for you in your Space Department cover name. We also need a creative location for the meet."

"I know just the right place!" replied Mike. "The National Observatory at Kitt's Peak, Arizona. That's the site where I first confirmed the Pangaean Effect!"

"The politicos will hate that location, but I like it! I'll let the pilot and everyone know. You'll be flown directly to Kitt Peak where you can prepare for the tour and briefing. Fax me the info on the magma find as soon as we disconnect. Get moving, Mike! Later."

As the screen turned black and the monitor retreated back into it's hidden compartment, the Director returned to her work. Mark Champion and Seth Tayman departed to continue their duties.

***

It was a cloudy day in Moscow as the Russian human espionage coordinator waddled down the hall of the Kremlin into the offices of Yuliy Matviyenko, the Deputy Premier of the Russian Republic. As he walked down the ancient corridor, Sergei passed more Russian clerics than civil servants. The dimly lit office was lavishly furnished in the traditional Russian style. The secretary was as ancient as the furniture.

"I'm Sergei Stankovich from the Foreign Intelligence Bureau here to see the Deputy Premier," stated Sergei in a heavy Russian accent.

"Please be seated, sir," smiled the secretary.

Mr. Stankovich watched her as she walked to the heavy, polished wooden door and entered it without looking back at him.

"Mr. Stankovich?" asked the secretary in the soft voice of a librarian.

"Yes, madam?"

"The Deputy Premier will see you now."

"Thank you," said Sergei, who sounded more nervous than he had intended.

As the intelligence agent entered the deputy's office, he quietly approached the portly, balding man who was responsible for Russia's International Relations.

"Be seated," directed Deputy Premier Matviyenko, who did not look up from his work at Sergei. "I'll be with you in a moment."

Stankovich read the certificates from the defunct Soviet Union and new Russian Republic that spanned the Deputy Premier's long career of public service.

"You are Stankovich?" asked the Deputy Premier as he looked up from some papers he was reading.

"Yes, Premier Matviyenko!" nearly shouted Sergei as he rose to his feet. "Of the Foreign Bureau!"

"I know, Stankovich. Be seated," directed the Deputy Premier again. "I've read this information you obtained from our operative in Qiqihar. Is it accurate?"

Sergei turned red when he heard the question. He was confused about the reason for it.

"I don't know," Sergei muttered, suddenly worried that he had not properly prepared the information for dissemination. "I was not made aware of the exact technical data 1032 sent to our bureau."

"You do not know what 1032 sent?" asked the Deputy Premier with concern in his voice.

"No, Deputy Premier. The data was sent directly to the compartmented department, which consolidated the information according to intelligence directives. I've always followed procedure. The information you received is for your eyes only."

The Deputy Premier leaned back in his chair and played with the ink pen he was holding.

"You spoke with the Chinese intelligence chief. What did that conversation reveal?" he asked.

"Sang Jiyun is extremely intelligent, ruthless, and an expert liar," advised Sergei. "That fat man could pass a lie detector test without an error."

"You've actually met him?"

"Yes, Premier, I met him in 1968 at a truck buying exhibition in the Ukraine when I was new to the K.G.B.," answered Sergei. "He was part of a large Chinese agricultural entourage, but I recognized him as an intelligence operative as soon as I saw him."

"How did you know he was an intelligence agent?"

"His eyes," advised Sergei. "He not only had very observant eyes, but they also betrayed his military or paramilitary training. I've had encounters with him, some of them involving gunfire."

"He's killed before?"

"Yes, Premier. He's trained in the old Communist ways, and his dossier indicates he served as a human intelligence officer during the Cold War and the Vietnamese War of Independence."

"What else did he tell you during your conversation with him?" asked the Deputy Premier.

"That operative 1032 died of radiation poisoning as a result of a leak at the Qiqihar facility that was caused by an earthquake," responded Sergei.

"Our operative took his own life," opined Premier Matviyenko, who popped a chocolate into his mouth. "Otherwise the Chinese would never have called us."

"Do you think we should investigate this more?" asked Sergei, who was suddenly worried that the Chinese agent could still be alive.

"No," snapped Premier Matviyenko with an air of authority that emphasized that his answer was final. "I would like to hear the details of the conversation you had with 1032."

After Sergei spent over three hours in discussions with Premier Matviyenko, the debriefing was finally over. Both men were tired.

"Your work has been exemplary, Stankovich," complimented Premier Matviyenko. "You have the wisdom to go with your white hair. There will be a bonus in your monthly check, and a much needed holiday to Denmark."

"Thank you!" beamed Sergei Stankovich.

Sergei stood and shook the Deputy Premier's hand. He was glad to have been recognized by such a powerful man. After the intelligence agent closed the thick, wooden door, Yuliy Matviyenko picked up the telephone and made some very important telephone calls.

***

The unmarked Lear 25D jet took off from Cheyenne's small international airport before midnight carrying two passengers. After flying above the usual turbulence associated with western jet streams, Mike Valenti used the secure in-flight telephone to contact Seth Tayman at home. As Mike spoke with Seth, Glenda Vernell Moses turned to stare adoringly at her boyfriend. Although the aircraft could seat eight passengers, Mike and Glenda were the only guests on board. Prior to making his telephone call, Glenda had made both of them mixed drinks from the well stocked hot and cold refreshment center.

Even though Doctor Michael Joseph Valenti was a brilliant thirty six year old theoretical astronomer, Vernie had known from the first moment she met Mike that they were meant to be together. They became friends after Mike's assignment to head the operation in 2004, and their relationship progressed from there. Neither one of them publicized their relationship, which was suspected by many within NOAH'S ARK.

"That was Seth, Church," explained Mike as he ran a hand through his dark brown hair. He smoothed down his narrow moustache next. "This exposed Antarctic fault's big. I mean big! I'm going to send an ARK Team down there to check it out!"

"Great, Dim," she breathed in a relaxed voice that suddenly showed signs of tension. "That means Bubba's going to choose ARK One, and that means I'm going to freeze my butt off in bitter cold Antarctica."

Mike removed his glasses and rubbed his tired eyes.

"Maybe, Church, but you don't have to go if you don't want to. I can fix that."

"C'mon, Dim, if Ranger's team is selected, then I'm going with them. Besides, we've never done an Antarctic mission before," Glenda noted. She remembered something important. "Hey, it's June 5th, did you remember that it's your son's birthday?

"Really? Why should I? I never remember birthdays, and you know I haven't seen Steven in years!" replied Mike in an irritated voice. "Dad says Steven's doing fine working as a Navy S.E.A.L. at Little Creek, Virginia, and for me that's too much information."

"I can't believe you, Mike. Your dad told me Steven wants to meet you, and I think it's a great idea."

"Oh yeah, meet a child by a girl I screwed when I was fifteen? She's married and her squeaky clean husband adopted him. He's had the best of Maryland educations at Gilman, Church, and he's been raised like his mother to be a deck shoe wearing, squash playing preppie! I haven't seen him since he was two, and it's better that way!"

"It's still not right, Dim," pressed Vernie as she sipped on her bottled water. "Steven's still your son!"

Mike stood, looking for the lavatory. He was so upset that his face was red.

"Look, Church, no more talk about Steven! End of subject, okay? It's his birthday, he's not my son, and he's got a family that loves him very much!"

Mike headed for the bathroom, where he disappeared with a science magazine and an attitude. Glenda crossed her arms and stared out of the aircraft's window again at the night sky with tear filled eyes. The rest of the flight to Arizona was uneventful.

***

A large crowd of scouters was gathered under the June sun around the base of the Abraham Lincoln statue at the Lincoln Memorial in Washington, D.C. Secret Service agents were keeping well-wishers and fans of President Alexander Montgomery Fairchild at a safe distance as he cheerfully presented honorees of various ages with plaques for their faithful service with the Boy Scouts of America. When the final handshakes began, Myrna Ramirez moved her manual wheelchair forward to intercept the President as he prepared to depart. Mr. Fairchild was dressed in tan chinos and a tan scouting shirt that was filled with all the regalia of an Eagle Scout. As a former scouter himself, President Fairchild was also wearing the white sash and red arrow of the Order of the Arrow scouting fraternity. Cameras flashed everywhere as the President waved at his cheering supporters. The C.I.A. Director relinquished control of her wheelchair as one of the agents in her own protective detail began to push her along next to the President.

"We need to talk, Mr. President."

"Okay, Rosy, go ahead. Let me put on a little sunscreen so we can walk a bit," said President Fairchild as they turned away from the armored car and headed down the promenade from the Lincoln Memorial. People began to flock around him. "That way the press can get some good shots of us, and I won't look like a pop up roaster chicken while they do it."

The President's decision to change his itinerary by walking along the Lincoln Memorial promenade and his comments about letting the press take shots at him put the Secret Service agents into a panic. The agents scattered and rushed around the area as they coordinated to make sure the vehicles and protective details provided security for the President and C.I.A. Director at all times.

"Sir, we've now got a serious magma field growing under Devil's Tower National Park."

"I know, Rosy! I read your brief!" advised President Fairchild. "But is there a link between Hawaii, Yellowstone, California, and this new problem?"

"I don't know that yet, sir. Geology is dragging their feet on this again. They're supposed to be testing and comparing magma samples from the four locations, and my crew hasn't been receiving the information from Geology. The bottom line is something's causing all the problems and it has to do with a disturbance of the molten rock at the Earth's core."

"Maybe, or this is all some normal way for our planet to blow it's nose," said the Chief Executive. "I mean, really, Rosy, there's not much we can do but monitor the situation and advise our citizens if some kind of volcanic disaster appears to be imminent."

Myrna stopped her wheelchair and waited until she had the President's complete attention.

"Mr. President, that's the weird thing about all the magma fields except our problem in Hawaii. They're not going to erupt because there's nothing stopping the magma from rising to the surface. This isn't normal! It's like the Earth's letting the magma rise like water through a sponge," explained Myrna. "And the Geological Survey can't explain why it's happening either."

"Okay, Rosy, so if it's natural and can't be explained, why can't we just leave this to God and nature? If the planet's got a fever, it's got to sweat it out just like a human being does, right?"

The Director of the C.I.A. began moving forward in her wheelchair again. She was quiet for a moment. The agent that had been pushing Myrna's wheelchair walked behind her at a discreet distance.

"Mr. President, I think Dr. Valenti's right about his astronomical theory. If our magma problems aren't based on Mike's theories, they're just as bad."

"Rosy, you said yourself that he was a whack job a few months ago! I still don't see what these regional problems have to do with his galactic theories anyway!" exclaimed the President as he stopped to shake some hands. "What do you have this time?"

"It's very new, sir, but we've now got fresh data that a major earthquake's occurred in Antarctica," began Myrna as she wiped the perspiration off her brow with a colorful silk handkerchief.

"More classified information?"

"Yes, Mr. President, courtesy of Russia and China this time."

The President stopped in his tracks. As he did, the Secret Service agents fanned out to deter citizens from killing the leader of the world's most powerful nation in the world.

"Interesting," remarked a concerned President. "But why didn't we find out about this first?"

"The Geological Survey obviously hasn't been including geological research from the Park Service or Antarctic sub-stations in its intelligence reports," replied Myrna, who was irritated by the errors.

"Look, Rosy, do large earthquakes or geological mysteries have to apply to the C.I.A., too? What's NOAH'S ARK's mandate?"

"Everything applies, Mr. President. You see, NOAH'S ARK investigates these geological disturbances and considers the unconventional factors that the Geological Survey wouldn't think to consider."

"The Pangaean Effect again, right?"

"Yes, Mr. President. I can give you an information briefing on that again if you like," offered the first Mexican American C.I.A. Director with a smile.

"No, I've got a better idea," declined Alexander Fairchild as he scratched his sunburned chin. "Frank told me we're scheduled for an N.S.C. meeting, so if I know you, you'll want us to address our geological problems then. Am I right, Rosy?"

"Yes, sir."

"Good, I'll be there. Let the National Security Advisor know when and where, and make sure your star counter's there, too. I want to know more before this blows up in my face and hits the press."

As more crowds gathered to observe the President of the United States taking a rare unscheduled walk in public with one of his key cabinet members, the two political celebrities ended their discussion and entered the vehicles that had been following a safe distance behind them. As the President entered his limousine, the crowd cheered. When Myrna Ramirez settled into her armored vehicle, she rubbed her eyes and began thinking more about the relevance of Operation NOAH'S ARK and whether her previous decision to cancel the classified program had been too premature.

Chapter Three

"The Pangaean Effect"

Carrying a popular national full color newspaper dated June 6, 2006, Dr. Valenti walked briskly out of the lavish elevator that had gently stopped at the lobby floor of the Mayall 4-Meter Telescope building complex located at the remote National Observatory at Kitt's Peak, Arizona. He walked through several reinforced steel doors before arriving at the soundproof conference room that was guarded by stoic Secret Service agents and the protective details of the various department heads in attendance. After the agents checked his C.I.A. badge and credentials, Mike entered the conference room and discreetly took a staff seat behind the Director.

The prestigious National Security Council was present for the meeting. All of the major N.S.C. members had just completed a V.I.P. tour of the observatory and the Mayall telescope. None of them appeared to be happy to be so far from Washington, even though the National Observatory executives were completely delighted to have the President and the N.S.C. take a tour of their facility.

"Rosy, this place is in the middle of nowhere!" complained Levan Salazar-Balart, whom Mike quickly recognized as the Vice President of the United States. The Cuban American had a Romeo y Julieta cigar in his mouth that he smoked in spite of the embargo on Cuban made cigars. "Who's idea was it to meet on an Indian reservation of all places?"

Rosy spoke up without letting Mike answer. He was new to National Security Council politics and she didn't want him to get on the bad side of its influential members too soon.

"That was C.I.A.'s decision, Mr. Vice President," replied Rosy, irritated by Mr. Salazar's attitude.

"Well, the C.I.A.'s got a lot of nerve pulling all of us out of the District to come way out here for a damned science project!" growled Mr. Salazar as his lips turned brown from the wet cigar in his mouth. He looked very distinguished with his graying dark brown hair and thick lavish moustache. "We're 50 miles south of Tucson near the Mexican border, in the middle of the Sonora Desert, and it's already 100 degrees outside!"

"This location will help us all understand what's going on, sir," explained Rosy.

"Yeah, yeah. So, where's Monty?" asked Mr. Salazar, changing the subject and using the President's nickname to remind everyone that he was the one person in the room who could. "Do I need to get him?"

"No, sir. Frank went to get the President. He was on a call with the Prime Minister of England when I last saw him," replied Rosy.

Except for his monthly weekend military duty and two weeks of Air Force service each year, Mike had little contact with intimidating government executives, powerful godlike flag officers, and presidential advisors. Aside from familiar political figures from the Senate and House of Representatives, Mike recognized few of the people in the room. The designated agency heads had nameplates at specific places on the conference table while staffers sat along the wall. While they waited for the President, Myrna Ramirez briefed him on the National Security Council.

"Working in the vault, you don't get to interact with these power players," she began. "But this is where national security policy is formed, analyzed, and executed. You already know the President's the head of the National Security Council, but it also consists of statutory members, advisors, and invited guests. The Council's responsible for advising the President on national security and foreign policy matters. The decisions he makes here ultimately affect the world, the government, and the citizens of our country. The statutory members, in addition to the President, are the Vice President, Secretary of Defense, and Secretary of State. The Chairman of the Joint Chiefs of Staff and I are the military and intelligence advisors. The usual invitees are the National Security Advisor, Homeland Security, and the U.S. Representative to the United Nations, the Secretary of the Treasury, the Assistant to the President for Economic Policy, and the President's Chief of Staff. As you can also see, a member of the Senate and the House Intelligence Committees is here, too."

Mike was confused, "What's the difference between the N.S.C. and…?"

"Shh!" exclaimed Rosy quickly. She moved some hair away from her face. "We're on!"

Mike nodded, even though he was lost somewhere after hearing about the economic advisor. It was a lot to digest. As Mike wished for a cigarette, a Hispanic man dressed in a trendy double breasted suit entered the room while two observant Secret Service agents in bulky conservative suits held the conference room doors open. Just as Mike recognized the man as the president's National Security Advisor, the political appointee made the formal announcement.

"The President of the United States."

Everyone stood as the tall balding man with the slim build and small paunch entered the room and sat down at the head of the long conference table. President Fairchild wasted no time beginning the meeting as he reached for some coffee and donuts that were on the table. Mike noted that the President resembled the late comedian Bob Hope.

"Good morning," began the President with a charismatic smile that everyone returned. "I see that everyone's here. You mind if we get right into the guts of the meeting, Rosy? I've got to get back to the White House for a meeting with the President of Panama on the Chinese military expansion there."

"Not at all, Mr. President. You have a copy of the agenda," noted Rosy. "Shall I open the meeting?"

The President acknowledged the presence of Senator Talia Georgoulis and Congressman David Unger, who were both very powerful and influential political figures. He looked around the room with his predatory eyes as the C.I.A. Director started the meeting.

"The objective of this N.S.C. meeting is to address current issues that pertain to our long term geological problems," began Rosy. "This meeting is TOP SECRET.

No notes, please. N.S.A. will prepare a transcript for each attendee, which will be delivered to you after it's processed. There's to be no discussion of this meeting outside of this group. The President's been briefed, and he's very concerned about our national and international geological problems as they may relate to environmental national security. Mr. President."

"Thank you, madam," took over President Fairchild as everyone looked at him. He was dressed in a bright green polo shirt and tan canvas shorts. "We haven't made decisions on our long term geological problems in quite a while, but I want information about this geological dilemma of ours. I also want to know more about NOAH'S ARK and related theories from the subject matter expert. When I consider our problems in Hawaii, along the Pacific coast, and now in the Midwest, it seems this all comes down to two opposing geological theories. That's why I invited the C.I.A.'s expert and the head of the Geological Survey to be here. So, let's get started with Doctor George Donaldson, the Chief Geologist of the U.S. Geological Survey. George."

As the head of the nation's primary geological intelligence organization, Dr. George Donaldson was appointed by the President to support programs that expanded opportunities for commercial exploitation of national and offshore mineral resources that had traditionally been restricted by the more environmentally friendly Democratic Party. The powerful oil and energy lobbies that had supported President Fairchild's campaign with their generous cash contributions had pushed for the appointment of the independently wealthy oil tycoon and Texas wildcatter to head the Geological Survey. Dr. Donaldson turned out to be more interested in conducting surveys for mineral exploitation of national land areas than the investigation of other international geological problems that also fell under the jurisdiction of his agency.

The gray haired, fifty eight year old geophysicist had been exposed to many years of severe climates that made him appear to be seventy. His lean face and arms were extremely wrinkled and weathered, but he had the bright blue eyes and cocky nature of a vibrant field researcher. George was also not your typical beltway insider, which he demonstrated by coming to the meeting wearing a cowboy hat, boots, and western clothes.

"Talk about your boring jobs," remarked the high voiced, heavily accented Texan to the conservatives in the room. "Hell, I've had more fun with a shelf full of rocks than y'all! I can't believe I'm here wasting your time and my tax dollars talking about problems the Earth's been having since the creation! Next thing you know, we'll be making weather policy, too!"

Some in the room laughed, but the President grunted his disapproval of Donaldon's remarks.

"Get on with it, George," directed the President to his old friend. "You know I don't like Texas bullshit unless it's served with lone star beef and beer."

"Sorry, Mr. President," apologized Dr. Donaldson. "The United States Geological Survey, or U.S.G.S. to you suits, has the responsibility for monitoring a wide range of geological programs and abnormalities. I'll address the situation in Hawaii first. According to space based research and a lot of hard work by my geo-scientists, three of the five existing volcanoes on the big island of Hawaii are showing signs of imminent eruption. The most exigent situation is Mauna Loa, which has widened its caldera five to six centimeters in the past three months. Mauna Loa is located in the center of the island. Kilauea and Hualalai, which are on the eastern and western sides of the island, will probably erupt before the end of the year. The three I mentioned are the most active volcanoes in Hawaii."

"Do they all have these magma pools like we've been seeing on the mainland?" asked President Fairchild.

"No, sir. As a matter of fact, what we're seeing more than magma pools are subterranean indicators like volcanic earthquakes and steam geysers. If Hawaii had the magma pools, there wouldn't be much of a concern about an eruption. Anyway, we've also got current indications that Haleakala, which is a volcano on East Maui, is experiencing a tremendous buildup of magma in its crater. If the trend of magma growth continues, Haleakala will erupt within a year. To add to our problems, there's an intense amount of magma pressure under Lo'ihi Seamount, which is a submarine volcano about thirty miles off the coast of Kilauea. Initial magma research shows the lava of all these volcanoes in the past consisted of scraps of recycled rock that covered Earth in its early years. That's been changing, though. Now we're seeing rock from the deepest parts of the Earth's mantle that consist of much purer basalt."

Frank Benavente raised a hand. He always squinted his eyes when he was concerned about something that interested him.

"Doctor, we've been told that three to five major eruptions in the Hawaiian chain would be catastrophic. Is that accurate?" asked Frank, whose trendy closely trimmed goatee and wet looking thick hair made the

National Security Advisor look more like a hit man than a top government official.

"Mr. Benavente, volcanic hazards are extreme," explained George Donaldson. "Not only do you have the slow to moderately rapid lava flows that destroy developed areas and cause deaths, but you've got to consider explosive eruptions, airborne lava fragments, sulfur dioxide gas and other volcanic gases, and ground cracks that could swallow entire buildings. When three or more erupt, life becomes difficult and can become fatal within hours of a volcanic event."

"Can we stop it from happening?" asked the Vice President.

"No."

Everyone became quiet after Dr. Donaldson gave such an abrupt answer. George nervously chewed on the snuff that was in his mouth.

"Which leads me into the situation in California," continued George. "The magma channels appear to be deteriorating the San Andreas Fault. The San Andreas is actually a continuous narrow break in the Earth's crust that extends from northern California well into southern California. It's a place where the Pacific fault meets the North American fault. It's a complex area of broken and crushed rock that can extend a mile wide in places. The concern right now is that the magma is weakening the junction of the San Andreas and could cause a major earthquake anywhere from San Francisco to Los Angeles within the next six months."

"Okay, so what's being done to prevent a major catastrophe there?" asked the President.

"Well, Mr. President," began George Donaldson. "We've got sensors over the entire fault area that should give us early warning. Unfortunately, predicting earthquakes is less accurate than predicting eruptions."

"It seems that way to me, too," muttered the President, whose sunburned cheeks became redder.

"Of course, we've taken magma samples from the pools in the area of the San Andreas and they're also basaltic like those in the Hawaiian Islands. As for the magma pools popping up at Yellowstone National Park and Devil's Tower National Park, they're basaltic, too. What we've got, Mr. President, is a deep magma buildup under the Earth's crust that should subside after the pressure's released. This should pass after a year or two with a possible major earthquake in California and the eruption of three to five volcanoes in Hawaii."

"You say it like we won't have any problems," remarked the President. "Are you also saying this is a short term issue?"

"Yes, Mr. President. Magma buildups always subside after the pressure is reduced, whether it's through magma pools or a major eruption," opined George Donaldson with confidence in his voice.

"I appreciate your decisiveness, George," said the President. "I want your results to be accurate."

"They are, sir," said George Donaldson.

"So tell me about the Chinese and Antarctica," directed the Chief Executive.

"In the course of the last year or so, we've received a couple of formal requests from the Russians to assist them in the research of some mysterious geological problem that's been affecting their oil production. 'Cause of budget limitations and our own reduced resources, we didn't respond with any assistance. Since the requests were too vague, we also didn't investigate the situation.

We're also not aware of any significant geological problems concerning China, except for the intelligence brief I received prior to this meeting."

"Okay, so what about Antarctica?" asked Myrna of the Chief Geologist.

"Well, ma'am, the South Pole's always been a hotbed of geological activity," advised George with a smile again. "The worst earthquakes in the world occur there due to the magnetic and orbital conflicts associated with Antarctic geology and polar mathematics. The earthquake that occurred in the area of the Chinese sponsored survey was a 12.5 on the Richter scale. It was a beauty that would've been bad had it hit a large city in the United States. There's always the potential for others there, but Antarctic quakes have always been limited to affecting that polar region only."

"Have we had any other interaction with Russia or China regarding geological problems?"

"Yes, Mr. President," spoke up Andrea Mangone, the Secretary of Defense. She was a tough 1975 graduate of the U.S. Military Academy and a retired Major General. "In 2002, the Russians submitted a request to the U.S. Army Corps of Engineers for assistance in researching rare Siberian seismic fluctuations. We referred that request to the Geological Survey, which Dr. Donaldson denied because our political relationship with Russia has been poor. In the summer of 2004, Dr. Donaldson received more specific requests from the Russians, who began detecting serious seismic fluctuations near the Russian-Chinese border. He didn't do anything with that information either."

"George?" asked the President for clarification. He was not happy with the information he was receiving from the Chief Geologist.

The Secretary of Defense raised an inquisitive brow and turned her blonde head in Donaldson's direction. The head of the Geological Survey kept his confident eyes on the President.

"That's a fact, sir. Since your policy's not to provide unnecessary technical assistance to Russia, we didn't," remarked George with casual confidence. "We haven't heard from them since."

"Okay, so what do you think they wanted to find in Antarctica?" asked President Fairchild.

Donaldson clicked the remote control and a topographical display of the border area between eastern China and Russia appeared on the screen. Mike examined the map from his seat. It contained current Asian geological information he had never seen.

"I've reached some preliminary conclusions about Asia's role in this," continued Dr. Donaldson. "There are still a lot of unanswered questions, but it appears as though a small earthquake occurred in northern China in early June."

"Dammit, George, do we know the date or size of the quake?" asked the President.

"Not really," stammered George. "I mean, no."

"So what do you know?" the President pressed.

"I figure the cause was a minor fault that became unstable," answered Dr. Donaldson. "Approximately 800 square miles incorporate the areas of the reported seismic activity between Russia and China. More importantly, information and data obtained from U.S.G.S. and Space Department satellites show that a magma leak near the

Sino-Russian border has tainted the oil fields as a result of the earthquake. There's a major fault that runs roughly southwest for 600 miles from the Nen River valley through Beijing, Xi'an, Chengdo, and into Burma. It also runs well into the northeastern heartland of Russia. The damaged fault has restricted the ability of the Chinese to continue extracting petroleum deposits in the affected areas. I believe China is interested in Antarctica for future mineral exploitation and they're asking the Russians to do the job for them."

"Antarctica does have some vast mineral resources," noted Frank Benavente, whose narrow eyes squinted hard to read the fine lines on the topographical map on the screen. "It could fuel the world for years!"

"Forget about the world, Frank. What about the U.S.? Why haven't we thought about that, too?" asked the President of his advisors.

"Because the international agreements banning exploitation of Antarctica are as precious as the public opinion behind them, Mr. President," answered Aramentha Washington, the U.S. Ambassador to the United Nations. Her educated Jamaican accent was unique. "Breaking those agreements would severely damage our credibility in the rest of the world."

"Okay, so why would China want to risk that, too?" asked General James Beckwourth Vann, the Chairman of the Joint Chiefs of Staff. He was an Army R.O.T.C. graduate of Hampton University who grew up in the historic black community of Aberdeen in Hampton, Virginia. "Wait a minute! I do know that within the last couple of weeks, the Navy located Chinese diesel subs lurking around Antarctica twice. They were running silent at the time, so we figured they were tracking merchant vessels passing through the cape. Now I'm thinking differently. They were probably protecting their interest in the oil reserves, but even the Chinese can't afford that kind of international fallout by deploying forces in Antarctica or drilling for oil there!"

"Exactly," agreed Myrna Ramirez, as she changed the course of the discussion. "It makes no sense for Russia or China to attempt to exploit Antarctica. Are there still Chinese subs in Antarctic waters, Andrea?"

Andrea Mangone checked her military intelligence reports, and then conferred with General Vann.

"According to our latest satellite imagery and underwater monitors, there are no Chinese submarines in that area, Rosy," answered Andrea Mangone.

"Do we have any naval assets patrolling that area?" asked President Fairchild.

"No, Mr. President," responded Secretary Mangone. "There hasn't been a mission requirement to patrol those waters in the past."

"Until we figure out what's going on down there, you have one now," directed the President.

"Yes, sir," acknowledged Andrea Mangone. "Is a thirty day patrol window satisfactory?"

The President nodded.

"All right, George, any other ideas as to why the Chinese are interested in the area?" asked the President in an increasingly irritated voice.

"Mr. President, there's no covert reason for it," opined Dr. Donaldson. "I'm pretty much done with my briefing. Any comments or questions?"

Mike raised his hand, which quickly drew the scrutiny of everyone in the room.

"China didn't sign those agreements, so it's quite possible the subs were protecting their increased interest in the oil fields," advised Mike, who turned his attention to the Chief Geologist. "But there's another factor to consider that you haven't addressed."

"And that is?" asked Dr. Donaldson suspiciously.

"Aren't you failing to consider how tectonics affects Earth's physical behavior?" asked Mike, who pointed to a spot on the map. "You keep mentioning faults, but you haven't said one word about the fact that they're plates. Isn't the San Andreas in fact a junction of two tectonic plates that traverse into the ocean and along the South American coast into Antarctica?"

Willard Farrell, the head of the National Security Agency, looked up from his fact sheets, clearly impressed with Myrna Ramirez's staffer.

The Chief Geologist ran one of his sun-splotched wrinkled hands through his thinning gray hair. He didn't appear to be wealthy to Mike, just old and weathered.

"Possibly, if you like to play connect the dots with the many faults scattered around the world. Doctor Michael Valenti, isn't it?" inquired George Donaldson, who appeared to be recalling some knowledge about the brilliant young astronomer.

Mike nodded, but he continued concentrating on the map. According to the topographical information provided by Dr. Donaldson, the Asian fault was limited to the local area of the Sino-Russian border. Mike took a moment to remember the disposition of the planet's tectonic plates as George continued speaking.

"I remember you, too, sir. I read your works on Antarctic glaciology. Interesting work. As I recall, though, you're not a certified geologist like I am."

"Thank you. I'm not a certified geologist, just a well read student of the science," acknowledged Mike with a sincere smile. "But, I am an Antarctic expert, Dr. Donaldson, and that includes having a wide range of experience in geology and other related areas. I've read your works, too. Now, I'm sorry to interrupt you, but what are the specifics on the fault associated with the unstable area in Asia?"

"Well, the affected area is a very small division of the Eurasian fault," began George, only to be interrupted by Mike Valenti again.

"Eurasian plate," corrected Mike with a slight smile. "The faults are the seams between the plates."

"The Eurasian plate," continued George. "It's composed primarily of igneous stone deposits. It runs through China, Burma, and the Bay of Bengal. Of course, the fault that's giving the Russians and Chinese their difficulties is only a sub-fault. It's not going to be a problem, and we don't forecast any significant geological activity for that area of Asia."

There was silence in the room while George Donaldson consulted his notes and papers. Myrna knew there was a battle brewing that was necessary for the progression of the meeting.

"Thank you, Dr. Donaldson," said Rosy with a smile. "While you check your notes, I'd like Dr. Michael Valenti to present his progressive views on our problems and the Pangaean Effect. Most of you haven't heard about this theory, and I think you'll all find it interesting. Doctor Valenti, could you explain your pangaean theory to the members of this group, please?"

"The Pangaean Effect?" asked Donaldson, who was now clearly defensive about the discussion of a different point of view. "Now what the hell's that?"

Myrna Ramirez motioned for Dr. Donaldson to be seated. The council members began conversing. President Fairchild raised a hand for silence. He made Dr. Valenti wait for the group's complete attention.

"Doctor, tell the Council a little bit about yourself before you get into the technical aspects of your presentation."

"Yes, Mr. President," agreed Mike with a humble smile. "I graduated from Loyola College in 1993 with a Bachelor of Science degree in Physics."

"Loyola Chicago?" asked the President.

"No, sir, Maryland."

"I know the one. It's that little liberal arts college with the nationally ranked soccer team," responded the President. "They've got one hell of a basketball team!"

"I agree, Mr. President. In 1996, I received my Masters in Astronomy from the Massachusetts Institute of Technology," continued Mike, who was once again interrupted by the President.

"Is that a fact? I'm from Massachusetts myself!" boasted President Fairchild. "M.I.T.'s a tough school!"

"I liked living there, sir," continued Mike with a more comfortable smile. "In 1999, I received my Doctorate in Theoretical Astronomy from Johns Hopkins. Between '99 and 2004, I was a galactic astronomer at Space before being hired by the Agency."

"So you're a Marylander?" asked the President.

"Yes, Mr. President," replied Mike with as much pride as he could muster. He could tell the rest of the attendees were getting bored with the conversation.

"I do like those Chesapeake Bay crabs!" remarked Alexander Fairchild. "Well, if you went to all those institutions of higher learning, you come from good stock. Where did you prep?"

"At Loyola at Blakefield, Mr. President," replied Mike with more pride.

"You went to Blakefield? No wonder you're moving up the intelligence chain so fast! There's nothing better than a Jesuit education! I went to The Fessenden School up in West Newton, Massachusetts. Then to Harvard, of course!" grinned the President with pride, as his Chief of Staff reminded him of his busy schedule. Alex Fairchild waved him off. "I know! I know! Carry on, Dr. Valenti, you have my ear!"

"Thank you, Mr. President. The Pangaean Effect," spoke up Mike with greater confidence. "Is a term I coined to explain the planetary phenomena that occurs when the Earth changes its entire axis from one forty five degree angle to another in response to solar systemic stimuli. If you give me a chance, I can make this easy to understand."

"Please do, Doctor," urged Myrna Ramirez as she looked around the conference table at several confused but interested faces. "We need to know more."

"According to new theories that I believe to have been substantiated, our continents are still evolving at a rate that may appear to be very slow to us, but which is very important to our existence. Approximately 60 million years ago, one huge super continent called Pangaea separated to form two: Gondwanaland and Laurasia. Several severe astronomical effects from our galaxy and solar system that span millions of years caused continental drift to our current configuration. The results of course are that Earth now has seven continents. Council members, it's an astronomical fact that the Earth completes one precessional cycle every 25,920 years."

Dr. Valenti held up a colorful crystal baseball sized globe of the Earth to demonstrate the concept of precession. The use of the training aid caught the attention of even the most bored attendees.

"Even though precession causes the Earth to rapidly change its axis from one 45 Degree angle to an opposite alignment, there's still a lot of disagreement about how quickly the change occurs. But approximately 13,000 years ago, the Earth's axis did change. A mid-cycle planetary precessional adjustment also occurs approximately 12,960 years."

"Okay, Doctor, so what is the effect of precession that should concern the N.S.C.?" asked Myrna Ramirez.

"The last precessional event was so catastrophic that it caused a secondary Ice Age that made many active glaciers in equatorial and northern hemispheric areas rapidly recede. There was such a great deluge of flooding, earthquakes, and volcanic activity that stories from our greatest civilizations still speak of the event. The immense earthquakes that accompanied these natural disasters were major tectonic shifts of the terrestrial plates deep under the ground that float on the Earth's molten rock mantle. The Pangaean Effect was also a very human event that was so catastrophic that mankind did not emerge to form new civilizations until approximately 8,000 B.C. There is documented proof that bears witness to this."

"Maybe, but give me some examples to make me feel better," directed the Vice President.

"Scientists have documented that the Sphinx and Egyptian pyramids were once entirely covered by salt water. The remains of well-preserved prehistoric mammals were discovered on Antarctica in 1982. Classified carbon dating places the animals on Earth approximately 13,000 years ago. There are many other examples, least of which should be mentioned that the Russians found thirteen thousand year old tropical animals and plants in Siberia in the 1980s. Those animals were found in the same general area in which Russia and China are currently experiencing problems. All of these documented events support my hypothesis. Based on the information provided in this meeting today, I personally believe the Chinese surveyed Antarctica to examine the earthquake there for evidence that would explain their unstable fault fluctuations. That would provide them with a lot of information about the potential consequences if a corresponding tectonic event occurs in Asia."

"The Chinese don't have the technological ability to examine tectonics, Doctor," interjected Donaldson with a frown. "Given the speculative nature of the science of tectonics, there hasn't been much concrete evidence to even support your thoughts or confirm your exaggerated theories."

"But the Russians do have the technology," replied Mike as he removed his reading glasses to clear up the fog that formed there when he became nervous. "And because they're being affected by the Chinese earthquake, there's a motive for the Russians to support them. Quite frankly, no government really wants to make doomsday predictions or contemplate preparing to survive them. Governments want to guarantee stability and prosperity, not chaos. The Pangaean Effect would toss the planet into 5,000 years of near total darkness with a toxic atmosphere, famine, disease, and possible human extinction. It could knock mankind back into the Stone Age again, if we survive it at all."

Mike paused, allowing the attendees to excitedly chat amongst themselves. It only took a moment for several hands to be raised. The Secretary of State appeared to be very interested in making a comment.

"But why would the Chinese be concerned about Antarctic links to their unstable fault?" asked David Tokuhisa. "I know from experience that the Chinese don't even believe in western science!"

"That's true," agreed Mike.

"When do you think the Pangaean Effect will occur again, Doctor?" asked Willard Farrell, the head of the National Security Agency.

"The most significant date to consider in that calculation is May 5, 2000, when the planets of our solar system were in a rare alignment with the sun. I believe that date to be the beginning of the countdown to a mid-precessional event, which should occur in 2025."

"This is bullshit!" exclaimed George as he stood up to challenge Mike. "How the hell did we get from analyzing our fault problems to a discussion about the Earth flipping on her axis?"

"This is a little much on theory, Monty," admitted Levan Salazar with a concerned frown. "The United States can't make policy based on astrology!"

"What do you say, Rosy?" inquired the President.

Myrna looked at Mike, seeming to silently give him permission to make any comments that he deemed to be important. She wanted the issues between U.S.G.S.

theories and Mike's put on the table. Myrna motioned for him to come closer.

"Mike, you don't get many chances to tangle with political appointees like Donaldson. You have to risk ridicule sometimes to make an impact. If you have opinions about this, you'd better speak up now while you've got the opportunity!"

George was preparing to speak again when Mike decided to offer more information.

"Doctor, I know theoretical tectonics like you know geophysics," advised Mike with a bit of irritation in his usually calm voice. "You're way off on that Eurasian fault you've been showing us. During my own brief examination of the radio glacial and satellite topography relief areas on your map, I clearly see that your sub-fault's much deeper and more extensive than you're revealing."

"Sir, even though this discussion of the science of crustal plate dynamics is fun, it isn't pertinent to our meeting here today. We're not talking about the plate shifts of huge tectonic sections of Earth in this meeting. I'm merely discussing a sub-fault associated with China and Russia," explained George Donaldson.

Mike wasn't that easily dismissed.

"So you say, Doctor, but in fact, galactic and solar systemic influences affect the Earth's mantle. Changes in the mantle put pressure on the plates. Pressure on the plates causes faults to shift. And those shifts are called earthquakes."

"That's theory!" argued George, who was now getting very upset. "There are so many unanswered questions about tectonics that we have to form conclusions based on current scientific procedures."

"Very good, then, Doctor," continued Mike. "But pangaean theory holds that even though the Earth's plates are still moving within normal patterns, galactic and solar orbital influences will affect plate movements over the long term in much stronger ways."

"You're talking about that pangaean thing again?" asked George with a sneer. "Give me a break! Maybe I could believe the solar part because the Earth is orbiting around the sun, but galactic influences? At a National Security Council meeting! Maybe you should try a U.F.O. convention or something!"

There was some laughter, and a few supportive smiles for George Donaldson's comments. Everyone looked at the President for a remark, and the President looked at his Director of the C.I.A.

"Go on, Doctor Valenti," urged Myrna Ramirez.

"Thank you, ma'am. The continental-to-continental plates that we've been discussing, which involve the boundary between the Eurasian plate and the Indian plate, are examples of continental convergence. Tectonic junctions are like hinges on a door, and the faults are like the seams that keep in the heat. However, tectonic plates don't know the difference between land and sea, and a plate boundary can traverse all of Earth's areas. The continental to oceanic, and oceanic to oceanic plates that exist under the sea south of Asia are called the 90th East Ridge, Southwest Indian Ridge, and the Southeast Indian Ridge. These plates run down from Asia separating the Southwest Indian Ridge from the other two ridges. The plates then run south to East Antarctica where they turn west and traverse back into the Weddell Sea.

"The areas around the Hawaiian Islands, the Pacific and Asian coastlines are known as the "Ring of Fire."

That's because it's such an active location for volcanoes and earthquakes. Since Dr. Donaldson's noted that Antarctica is the site of the most active geology in the world, I believe it's the center point of all major geological events on Earth. And I believe that our national magma problems, and I might add the continuing problem with the potential Hawaiian volcanoes, are going to be associated with this Antarctic quake whether you believe in the Pangaean Effect or not."

"Interesting," noted Congressman Unger, as he placed his donut on a napkin. He was still chewing. He was very impressed with Mike's last comments. "You're saying that if something major in geology happens anywhere, it can be traced back to Antarctica?"

"Exactly, Congressman," smiled Mike with a nod. "I even suspect that there's a magma presence under Antarctica, too."

"And what about China?" asked President Fairchild.

"Well, just analyzing Geology's map here, I agree that a magma leak penetrated their oil fields," explained Mike, as he examined the map on the screen. "But it doesn't explain the reason for the contamination. Magma is the heating element that turns biological matter into oil or coal over the course of time. It doesn't contaminate oil with its heat."

"What do you think is causing these leaks?" asked the Vice President. "I mean, can liquid rock just permeate solid rock and rise to the surface?"

Dr. Donaldson stood up and interjected, "It could, sir. Magma can literally permeate any rock between the mantle and the surface."

The President grunted. One of the congressmen had a question.

"So does that mean that galactic or solar orbital effects could've caused the earthquake in Antarctica, and that Antarctic geological instability could've caused the problem in China?" asked Senator Georgoulis, as she played with her pen by twirling it around in her fingers.

"I have to say again that this is all highly speculative, Senator," spoke up George in anger.

"But you're possibly right," added Mike as he approached the projector screen. He pointed to various geographical areas that Donaldson had on display. "I'm an astronomer, and I learned long ago that each part of our great universe affects all the others. Remember that the core of liquid rock influences our geology and is influenced by our orbit. The sun controls the orbit of the Earth, and our galaxy controls the movement of our solar system. If a small geological event occurs separate from Antarctic precursors, then something, usually man-made or extra-terrestrial, caused it. So the working theory now is that the small earthquake in China was a factor in the tectonic earthquake in Antarctica. In our national case, I think the Pangaean Effect is slowly arriving. In the case of the Chinese, an unstable fault can be indicative of a rupture of an entire plate that could result in a tectonic quake in China. This is something that needs to be investigated very quickly."

"C'mon, Doctor, are we supposed to investigate every earthquake that occurs in the world?" complained George Donaldson.

"Yes, if it helps solve our national problems and saves lives!" commented Mike.

The room became even quieter as the occupants looked at Myrna Ramirez to see how she would respond to Valenti's challenge of Donaldson's presentation. In order to be fair, Frank Benavente asked George Donaldson to elaborate on Mike's comments.

"You're full of shit, Doctor!" observed the U.S.G.S. Director critically, as he crossed his thin scaly arms and rested his chin on a raised hand. "A minor earthquake would explain the unstable fault, but there's no evidence that the major fault's been affected."

"If there's been no effect on the major fault, Doctor, then what caused the deep core magma to become tainted in the first place?" asked Mike. "China could have a first class plate disruption that could cause one hell of an earthquake!"

"I believe one thing, Doctor Valenti," reassured George Donaldson. "Oil is a strategic requirement for a superpower, and China needs oil now. I think that's why they wanted a survey of the exposed Antarctic area."

President Fairchild had finally heard enough. The meeting had turned into a near argument between the C.I.A. and the U.S.G.S. It was clear to the President that Mike Valenti believed that the magma dilemma was long term and global, while George Donaldson believed it to be short term and regional.

"Well, I can see from your different viewpoints that we've got a real policy problem," noted the President as he leaned forward in his chair. "Whether the Chinese want to exploit Antarctica or merely investigate their own geological problems, it doesn't sit well with me that we found out about the problem this way. I don't know much about geology or tectonics, but I do know Geology's been sitting on Russian requests that should've been investigated, including this Park Service information. Intelligence is intelligence, and it should at least have been brought to Rosy's attention, or Frank's, for future development! You got that, George?"

"Yes, Mr. President," acknowledged George Donaldson, who was angrier over being reprimanded.

"And I don't like the prospect of Hawaii being threatened by volcanoes or California facing a serious earthquake. I'm not going to sit back and watch Mother Nature kill people or destroy property without this country or government doing everything we can to prevent it or reduce the damage!" lectured the President to everyone in the room. "Kurt, contact the governors of Hawaii and California and arrange for them to meet with me as soon as possible."

Kurt Farley, the President's overworked Chief of Staff, made a note of the directive.

Myrna Ramirez knew the discussion had proceeded to the point of making a policy determination, so she tapped the side of her water glass to get everyone's attention.

"It's time for a decision, which means that all non-statutory members must leave the room. We'll open the doors when we're ready. Thank you."

The affected people left the conference room. When the doors were opened again, Mike followed the remainder of the group into the conference room where the President was waiting to address the Council.

"George, I think you've made your point, as has Dr. Valenti," Alexander Fairchild summarized. "Since Operation NOAH'S ARK's inception as a classified operation, the C.I.A. has been investigating cutting edge theories that might explain Earth's problems. Since I have to assume that most of the Russian and Chinese geologists are familiar with progressive theories regarding tectonics, I think it's in the best interest of this council to consider the probability that our Asian neighbors have detected a major geological problem. Unfortunately, Dr. Donaldson is also correct in his position that this may only be a minor issue. Therefore, I'm tasking the U.S.G.S. with the responsibility of monitoring the American and Russian-Chinese fault areas and making accurate determinations about the dangers there."

"Excuse me, Mr. President, but if you attach a F.E.M.A. element to one of our rapid deployment units, we could discreetly respond to any affected area in record time," suggested Andrea Mangone. "All it would take is your approval and General Vann will make it so."

General Vann nodded in agreement.

"Approved," decided President Fairchild. "Next, I'm tasking C.I.A. to investigate the Antarctic problem and any other international issues as they may relate to the Pangaean Effect. Comments?"

"With one dissenting vote," added Levan Salazar, who sat back in his chair and looked at Mike Valenti. "I don't buy your line of crap for a minute!"

George Donaldson added, "Got that right!"

"I didn't ask for a vote or dissent! This isn't the Supreme Court, but one of my damn meetings!" reprimanded the President. "All I asked for were comments. Now are there any comments?"

Everyone in the room remained quiet as the President conferred briefly with Myrna Ramirez.

"Thank you, everyone," concluded the President. "Frank will be in touch with all of you. In the interim, I want a priority assessment conducted by everyone in one week on this Chinese problem. Now, with the exception of the National Security Advisor, the C.I.A. Director, and the Vice President, have a nice day, everyone."

Chapter Four

"Operation NOAH'S ARK"

On June 9, 2006, Michael Valenti was in the chilly NOAH'S ARK conference room in a planning meeting with his primary managers and staff. In the event that more complex missions and planetary developments required the authorized expansion of the operation, the unit's Table of Distribution and Allowances (T.D.A.) could be rapidly adjusted. Dr. Valenti already had at his disposal a huge array of classified highly technical logistical assets that were suitable or designed for extreme weather missions.

Prior to the scheduled briefing, Mike and the staff leaders had submitted several logistical support requests in preparation for the upcoming Antarctic mission. The scientific staff had prepared most of the initial technical requirements and had sent them forward for action. There was an obvious feeling of excitement in the air as the work activity of the NOAH'S ARK group increased. Even Mike was excited to be involved in an Antarctic expedition that was sanctioned by the President.

"This briefing is TOP SECRET and ARK sensitive," stated Mike, as he put on his glasses. Information that was ARK SENSITIVE was not to be disclosed to C.I.A. members outside of the operation or C.I.A. chain of authority without Dr. Valenti's approval. "Everyone knows why we're here. A tectonic earthquake registering about 12.5 on the Richter scale has caused significant damage in Antarctica, and we're going there to find out how why."

Everyone in NOAH'S ARK knew about the Pangaean Effect and its arrival in 2025. A tectonic event anywhere in the world was always of interest to the task force members, who spoke amongst themselves.

"Simmer down, guys," said Mike, who was proud of his group's enthusiasm. "You all know we're mandated to investigate planetary phenomena, but our Antarctic mission has the full blessing of the President. Our mission is much more vital because our research will assist the government in determining what's causing our magma problems. If we don't find the source of the problem, Hawaii and California could suffer fatal earthquakes and volcanoes within six months."

There was even more excitement and concern among the management, who had all been worried about the rumors of the operation being cancelled. A few of the managers asked Mike that very question.

"NOAH'S ARK isn't being terminated, people. We're being regenerated with a greater purpose of finding out why our nation has these magma problems and investigating how to nullify them. While I believe the Pangaean Effect is alive and kicking, I've got a hunch there's more to our geological problems. Either way, NOAH'S ARK is in business!" exclaimed Mike, whose comments caused a spontaneous applause by his managers. "Now, Geology's responsible for domestic research and investigation of our problems, while we're responsible for international areas. If we're lucky, I'm betting we'll find magma vents around the area of the quake that we can compare to our own. Those samples of liquid rock could allow us to diagnose the geological problems and find effective solutions that could delay or prevent prolonged damage to the Earth!"

"How 'bout that?" remarked one of the managers. "You know how cold it is on that rock?"

"Now we're going to be rock doctors, too!" laughed another.

"Yeah, first the higher ups wanted to fire us, and now they want us to solve the problem," complained another manager. "C'mon, Doc, don't they know the Pangaean Effect's going to do the whole planet? Even if we prevent the geological forecast this time, Earth's going to flip out on 2025 no matter what!"

Mike was about to speak when his right hand man intervened.

"Simmer down," cautioned John Klinesmidt, the ARK Operations Officer, who glared at anyone else who dared to speak up during Valenti's briefing.

"You're all correct," advised Mike, who understood their frustration. "But you've all been aware that when the effects of precession were going to be felt, we'd be the ones called on to solve the problem. Unfortunately, our job security is guaranteed on future human misery and our planet's near destruction."

After waiting for any questions or comments, Mike continued, "I think you're all aware that seismic readings and samples of oil, glacier, and rock obtained from Antarctica will provide documented physical evidence that cannot be refuted. That evidence can be used as the baseline for other similar evidence collected in other parts of the world. We'll be able to map more accurately the region's history and its relationship with the rest of our planet. Our investigation will be used by the President to form national security policy that must incorporate the Pangaean Effect! This mission will legitimize our operation and our existence!"

Several attendees applauded, while some others complained about the terrible location. One woman whistled, impressed by the mission's overall intent. Most of them knew that any new government expedition to Antarctica would be a rare professional achievement that might never become available again.

"Look, I can't disclose the details of any National Security Council information, but our mission is literally a matter of life and death. We need to get on the ground there and investigate this A.S.A.P. I want a complete ARK force in Antarctica in four weeks," directed Mike to John Klinesmidt. "Our summer is Antarctica's wintertime, so it's going to be as cold as Pluto down there in July and August. The missions are to confirm and test the presence of fossil fuels, accurately document geological evidence, conduct glacial analysis, and conduct preliminary seismic evaluations of the affected area. I want this op to be completely secure and clandestine, using the U.S.G.S. as our cover. Give the team one month to get results. Confirm vessel departures from the U.S. on June 28th, onsite with the entire ARK force deployed on July 9th. I want all specified objectives completed by August 9th. Plan for mission end by the 25th. John, place ARK Two on stand by as the secondary or alternate mission team, just in case there's a problem or something else develops."

"No problem, boss," responded John, who took notes of Mike's directives.

"Seth, I need you to get N.S.A. to run detailed technical and voice signal interceptions between Russia and China from now until 30 days after mission end. Request that Navy conduct a priority marine geological survey of the Southwest and Mid-Indian ocean ridges, and confirm the task force I've requested to support us. It should at least consist of an Amphibious Assault Ship that can billet ARK One, an attack sub, and an escort vessel. Also, I need the survey information A.S.A.P.! Send Heather McKay out there to be our liaison with the naval researchers, and send Montellero over to N.S.A. to represent us on this one. He did a bang up job on our last mission to Italy."

Seth Tayman always utilized a computerized palm device to record his notes, so he used his little plastic pen to load the information.

"Okay, John, you can go into the operations portion now," directed Mike.

John Klinesmidt nodded, his piercing brown eyes unable to hide the excitement of launching another expedition. While John presented his briefing, Mike pondered over his choices for a deputy. He had to admit that John was currently the only one for the position.

As the Operations Officer, John Robert Klinesmidt was responsible for ARK level plans, operations, and training of the task force. Since the Vice Director's position was vacant, John was also the acting number two man of Operation NOAH'S ARK. Half Mexican and half German American, John was often a loose cannon whose piercing dark brown Aztec eyes could be intimidating. During the last two leader and staff exercises, John had shown a tendency to be too mission oriented at the expense of the welfare of ARK personnel. Mike was no longer certain that he wanted John to be promoted into the powerful position.

"Thanks, boss," acknowledged John, with a nod that threw his light brown hair out of place. "Thanks to the Royal Air Force on the Falklands Islands, we'll get direct support from the base there, which includes a hospital and emergency billets if we need them. And they've already approved the storage of any back up M.U.L.E.S. units we want in the area. My question is if you want to base any of our organic Special Operations units there just in case we need increased security?"

"Only the Green Beret team, John. Since each ARK Team has armed badge carrying agency security officers assigned to it, we need to make this look as normal as possible by keeping the military out unless it's absolutely necessary," determined Mike. "Since the Falklands are available to us, can you make arrangements to billet ARK Two there?"

"Gotcha, boss," responded John. "Good idea!"

Mike looked at Colonel Richard Beahm, who was the Special Operations department head. A twenty-year career Army veteran and Green Beret, Colonel Beahm was short, clean-shaven, and mean.

"Colonel Beahm, I'll need one of your tactical teams on standby and stationed in the Falklands ready to support us on order."

"Airborne, sir, I'll have an "A," Team positioned there with a "B" Team for command, control, and communications. My men are already cold weather qualified," advised the tough field commander. "The "A" Team I've got in mind just came back two weeks ago from the Italian Alpini School. They're my best tactical experts in the ice, snow, and glaciers. I'll attach the proper support units to round them out, sir. My only concern is the transport of the Special Operations M.U.L.E.S. containers. My team leader will load out the M.U.L.E.S. units with most of the equipment they'll need that isn't man portable prior to the carrier's departure. That means our load out and M.U.L.E.S. will have to be coordinated by your staff since my troops won't be traveling with the equipment."

"John," directed Mike as he pointed the Colonel in the direction of the Operations Officer.

"Consider it done, Mike. Okay, everyone, this is your initial warning order! I want the ARK staff to plan to support this deployment as Dr. Valenti's directed. The operations plan will be given in the situation room on 6/27 at 0900 hours. Our mission is to document fossil fuels and geological evidence. Bubba Washington, you're the mission coordinator, so submit all your higher headquarters support requests through me and I'll take care of them. Since the boss has designated the deployment and alternate teams, what are your other two teams going to be doing during this time?"

"ARK Three's standing down from three weeks helping the Brits investigate a mummy find in a bog," explained Bubba. "And ARK Four's leaving tomorrow to assist the South African geographical department in rock layer analysis of a deep diamond mine."

"So everyone's tied up," commented John. "That's good. With ARK Three and Four downrange being supported by the British and South Africans, we won't be tied up doing in-house activities that will distract us from the Antarctic mission."

"True that," agreed Bubba as he twirled a toothpick in his mouth. "I just want my people to have as much trainin' as time allows. That'll make me feel better 'bout this mission."

"Of course, Bubba," continued John nervously. "As we've been planning, both ARK One and Two, along with your deploying staff, will be trained up on cold weather certifications A.S.A.P. I'm scheduling a full mock deployment for the ARK Teams from 6/12 to 6/19 at Fort Wainwright, Alaska."

"Solid," responded the big muscular man who was seated in the front row as he nodded his thanks to Mike. Bubba didn't like or trust anything John did when it came to managing the people in the field. "Doc, you know I always want complete support for my peeps."

"You'll have it, Bubba," reaffirmed Mike. "This mission's too dangerous and important to limit training and readiness. Even though John's the staff coordinator, I'm the man in charge."

"Thas' somethin' I already know, Doc," acknowledged Bubba. "I just wanted John to hear that from you. Sometimes he forgets his self."

Mike knew exactly what Bubba meant.

"John, Bubba's got to have a clear chain of command on this mission that flows freely. Your staff requirements and decisions can't interfere with the decisions that he and I must make."

"Understood, boss," said John, who was disappointed with Mike's statement.

"Continue," directed Mike.

"Thanks, boss. Since the ARK units will be operating under continual night conditions, let's have the primary and back up teams compete limited visibility training at our Frederick, Maryland facility, and they'll be evaluated during the mock deployment in Alaska. Bubba, you and Ranger can brief the boss on your operations order on 6/26. ARK One must be ready to depart from Norfolk on 6/28. Modification one, I want an ARK advance party on the ground in Antarctica by dawn on July 8th, and operational on the 10th, if that's acceptable to you, Doctor Valenti?"

Mike stretched as he nodded. He often found himself walking a constant tightrope when he had to deal with John's overbearing nature. While John was talking, Theodore Bolte, the Deputy Director of the C.I.A. quietly entered the conference room to listen to the briefing. He discreetly stood at the back of the conference room.

As the head of NOAH'S ARK, Dr. Valenti controlled over 600 employees. He managed a Mission Staff that handled support activities, a Special Staff that was responsible for scientific and technical support, and four operational departments that contained their own field operations teams. Each of the four departments was named for their specific areas of responsibility: Domestic, International, Field Operations, and Special Operations. The Special Operations section was comprised of active and reserve military units that were attached to the operation as ARK missions required.

"Neil, enhance these photos for the boss and improve the detail. Seth, get hopping on the N.S.A. task and assign one of your people to be there during the mission. I'll coordinate with Navy today, so tell me what you need from them before the close of business. Randy, get the equipment and logistics set. Any questions?"

Deputy Director Bolte raised his hand.

"Yes, I have one," spoke up the career C.I.A. executive. "Doctor Valenti, I've read your initial staff estimates. The operations estimate appears sound, and your logistics estimate was particularly detailed given the short time that has passed since you took on this mission. However, the intelligence estimate was a little vague about the transition plan. What's the extraction plan specify about sanitizing the objective area and making it overt when the primary mission has been completed?"

Mike stood. He was prepared for any questions the Deputy Director might have. Mike knew the executive was there to report back the progress of the mission planning to Myrna Ramirez.

"Thank you, sir. We've planned for a steady transition from covert ops to routine activities as soon as mission objectives have been met," began Mike with a confident smile on his face. "The seismic analysis will be continuously conducted during all phases of our mission so that any foreign satellite or aviation reconnaissance will detect our seismic activities and lead their intelligence analysts to believe we're conducting routine geological studies. As our mission ends, NOAH'S ARK will import Geological Survey personnel and equipment to Antarctica on our re-supply aircraft. We'll gradually replace our group with members of the Geological Survey, who will keep the base as a semi-permanent research station."

"Excellent, Doctor," said Ted Bolte, who made a note of the information. He took a moment to address the group. "The Director and I have approved this mission because the United States needs to know more about our geological situation. Thanks to NOAH'S ARK, the

President has a mobile scientific team that can secretly investigate this problem in Antarctica."

Without any more fanfare, Mr. Bolte walked to the front of the room, shook hands with Mike, and departed. The Deputy Director's presence had helped to reduce the stress levels of the NOAH'S ARK planners.

"Boss, can I get going on this?" asked John as he rose to leave the room.

Mike nodded, and Klinesmidt quickly departed the meeting to complete numerous operational actions. Bubba Washington glared at John as he left the room.

As the supervisors and staffers in the room completed their notes on Klinesmidt's orders, Seth Tayman, the Assistant Director in charge of the Special Staff and the third man in the chain of authority of Operation NOAH'S ARK, issued instructions to his managers. Seth wasn't a big fan of John Klinesmidt, but he had no desire to be the Deputy Director of NOAH'S ARK. When Seth was finished with his portion of the briefing, Mike took over again.

"People, a lot rests on this mission. There's no room for error where ARK One is going," advised Mike, who was interested in capitalizing on the Deputy Director's comments. "I'll be reporting our activities to the Director herself. That means we need to function first and foremost as a team. Seth, I want members of your staff in our Situation Room during the entire mission. Bubba, I need you to manage this one personally and be where you can help Ranger the most. I want you to coordinate field activities from the mission vessel until full deployment, then be at the hotspots to insure everything's running smoothly."

Seth Tayman and Bubba Washington both nodded. Bubba liked Seth and got along well with him. The big man knew that Seth always considered Bubba's field teams and their needs during all phases of mission planning and execution.

As the Chief of Field Operations for NOAH'S ARK, Bubba supervised a total of four numbered ARK deployment teams. Washington also managed his own Mission Staff, which consisted of Air Operations, Marine Operations, Communications, and Services. The Chief of Field Operations and each of the ARK Team leaders were also experienced C.I.A. Special Agents.

As the conference concluded, the task force worked out the objectives and details of the mission for their particular divisions. It was shaping up to be a long day for the normally quiet basement organization.

***

ARK One was assembled in the hot lecture room. The entire ARK element had traveled by air to Fort Wainwright, Alaska, where they had just completed a full mock exercise of the Antarctic mission using the specialized equipment they would take with them. It was June 19, 2006. The training exercise had gone well.

In order to simulate realistic weather conditions, the mock deployment included an air insertion using the actual helicopters and flight crews from the U.S. Marine carrier that was assigned to conduct the mission. ARK One was flown to an area where arctic conditions were present, even though it was the warmest time of year for the State of Alaska. While there were technical problems and mild cold weather injuries, the mock mission gave ARK One members a little more confidence.

After only three days into the mock deployment, the arctic weather began to affect the morale of ARK One. Some personnel were beginning to complain about the mission requirement to travel to the coldest continent on the planet, so Mike Valenti traveled to Alaska to assess the situation. He could clearly see that everyone was apprehensive about conducting the mission on the most intimidating continent in the world.

"Afternoon, gentlemen, ladies," greeted Mike in a motivated tone of voice. "Take a seat, please."

Bubba Washington eased into a seat with the nervous ARK One team, which was a conglomeration of technical, field, service, and scientific experts. He sat next to his best buddy and subordinate, Elton Rance. Rance was the leader of ARK One and the most experienced field supervisor that Bubba had. After Mike finished arranging his papers, he turned on the audio-visual screen. When a slide of the mock encampment was illuminated on the screen, the room quieted down. There was a video screen against one of the side walls that was filled with the camera images of the Science Staff and Mission Staff, who were participating in the critique of the mock deployment from the NOAH'S ARK offices at Langley, Virginia.

"This meeting is TOP SECRET and ARK sensitive," began Mike, who turned on a red light pointer and highlighted a photograph on the audiovisual screen. "This will be brief. I'll address general issues here. I'll discuss specific points with each of my staff leaders and management later. I'll leave the mock deployment after action review of Field Operations and ARK One in the capable hands of Bubba Washington and Elton Rance."

Dr. Valenti walked over to the screen showing the NOAH'S ARK staff.

"First of all, I'd like to thank John Klinesmidt and the staff at Langley," began Mike, who led the applause for the staff leaders on the screen. "Their constant attention to detail and coordinated communications with Bubba Washington's field staff was one hell of an example of how the command and staff process should function. I've already received critiques from the Defense Department liaisons, and they had nothing but praise for our operation. Thanks, John, Seth, everyone."

"No problem, boss," responded John. He had an overly confident and arrogant look on his face.

"Thanks, Mike," chimed in Seth Tayman, who was applauding the staff, too. "My Science Staff did well, but we need to streamline the transport of field samples from the objective area. With the weather ARK One will be facing, timing is everything."

"I agree, Seth. We'll discuss the fine tuning as soon as I return to Langley," said Mike. "As for the operations portion of the mock deployment, the field exercise went well. We simulated flight from the helicopter carrier using the carrier's assigned helos and crews. According to the Marine flight commander, the helos had no problem with the weather or carrying the M.U.L.E.S. units and ARK One personnel. The sling loading went well, as did the deployment of the Advance Team to the objective area. Vernie's leadership proved itself when the weather delayed the connection of the M.U.L.E.S. units. In spite of the freezing temps, the Advance Team was hooked up and operational on schedule. Great job, Advance Party."

Glenda and the members of the Advance Team clapped. The mock deployment had done a lot to convince everyone that the mission could be accomplished in spite of the Antarctic weather.

"Vernie's unit allowed for the rapid transition to Main Body mode," continued Mike. "As the helos dropped the follow on M.U.L.E.S. containers, Vernie's people attached the umbilicals and assisted arriving Main Body members in getting oriented on the ground. By the time the O.A.S.I.S. and M.A.I.D.S. hardware arrived on site, the operation was ready to go green for research and drilling. I know there was a problem with some moisture seeping into the extended umbilical couplers for the M.A.I.D.S. hardware, but the Logistics Staff has already solved the problem by inventing rubberized insulator bands that will be wrapped around each umbilical extender coupling. Great job, Randy."

Randall Cummings, Mike's Logistics Staff Officer, nodded and smiled.

"Bubba, I've never seen Field Operations function so well," continued Mike. "You were constantly coordinating with Ranger from the air base, where you were simulating being on the carrier. When there were problems or slow downs, you went to the objective area and worked with Ranger to resolve them. I like how you put Irene and Warren with the Advance Party. Your decision to do that placed Field Operations staffers right there on the ground with Vernie to make for a smoother transition during the most difficult phase of the mission. Outstanding job, Bubba and crew."

"The credit goes to my people, Doc," spoke up Bubba from his place in the crowd.

"I noted some confusion during the Main Body phase," explained Mike. "That was because the O.A.S.I.S. facilities were located too closely to one another. We'll make a change on the Antarctic layout to make sure they're at opposite ends of the base camp. That way each ARK One team assigned to each project will be able to function separately from the others. Bubba's Chief of Staff will have to insure that as samples arrive from each O.A.S.I.S. facility, they're received in such a way that the flow of work won't be delayed or interrupted. Even though we didn't do any deep drilling with the M.A.I.D.S. hardware, they functioned well in the Arctic ice. The generators were impressive during this entire exercise and provided more than enough power for our mission requirements.

"So, based on the results of this mock deployment, the mission is a go," determined Mike with a smile. "Having said this to you, I need ARK One to find the facts. We need to deploy to Antarctica, and we need to do it fast. Bubba," said Mike Valenti as he passed the briefing over to the tall, muscular black man.

Washington took control of the briefing after giving Mike a concerned look. Mike listened as Bubba presented a professional warning order to the 120-man ARK One expedition team. Washington's funky voice and easygoing style awakened even the most bored team members. As a former competitive body builder, Bubba's size was also very intimidating.

"Awright, people, listen up!" demanded Bubba John Washington. When he lifted his arms to get everyone's attention, Bubba's wide back always caused the female members of the group to admire his physique. “Y’all heard the Doc on his concerns, but I know there ain’t gonna be no problems from the field ops side of this house when we hit the ground down south, right?”

Everyone on Bubba’s staff responded with enthusiastic grunts and several thumbs up.

“It’s jus’ a mission, like every other one,” continued the big man, who had a green toothpick in his mouth. “But it will be dangerous if we don’t do it right. So ah figger that’s why me an’ my staff will stay down range with ARK One, sittin’ right on that naval boat or on site making sure things go my way. The Doc’s staff, at least most of ‘em, will be back at Langley or the Falklands keepin’ the brass off our asses and protectin’ our lives as best they can. Now, the only problems I seen were with Ranger’s Mission Staff. The communication between my staff and Ranger’s Special Staff was smooth. Brian Olson’s science boys coordinated directly with the Doc’s Science Staff as planned, but Roger Conyers didn’t do like I instructed. As Ranger’s Mission Staff chief, you were supposed to make things easier for Ranger’s teams while they were in the field.”

“I did, Bubba, but Oto Yee and Warren Wells kept trying to direct the way my staff was supposed to operate. That’s not their job,” defended Roger Conyers in his whiny voice.

“Roger,” warned Elton Rance, who had been listening to Conyers talk back to Bubba Washington.

“It’s okay, Ranger,” calmed Bubba. “You know, Roger, staffs have to interact on any mission, but especially this one. Ranger and I make the decisions, and your staff coordinates with upper headquarters. True, you work for Ranger, but if my staff leaders need something done, you'd best believe you're answerable to them, too, because they work for me."

"He copies, Bubba John," interjected Elton Rance, who was irritated with Conyers for taking up their valuable time. "Go on ahead with your critique."

"Solid, now, I liked the way each team of yours worked, Ranger," continued Bubba. "Glenda, Webster, Karyn, and Terry, y'all got my respect during this mock exercise. In spite of the cold and snow, y'all accomplished each mock mission on time and as a team. Just remember when y'all step foot on that cold rock that God ain't got no say in a plan that's man made!"

Everyone in the room grunted and yelled when Bubba made that last comment. The big man's employees were always inspired by his leadership.

"Ranger, since my staff's up on the mission, I'll leave the rest to you to explain."

Elton Rance hopped to his feet, grinning as he approached his friend. Elton was just as motivated as Bubba, but he was shorter, lighter, and more energetic.

"Charlie Mike, Ranger!" directed Bubba, with a hip nod of his head at his much shorter and smaller friend. "Charlie Mike" was military jargon that means to "Continue the Mission." "It's all yours."

"Roger that, Bubba John!" took over Elton Rance, as he turned his iron jaw line towards his attentive employees. Washington left the conference room to find Mike Valenti. "Look heah, people! Y'all heard the Doc and Bubba John, an' ah hope y'all understood them! Mission first is my rule! Ah don't want any whinin' or complainin' now that the decision's been made, and bitchin' ain't no longer authorized on ARK One! Y'all did good! Now let's get back ta' Langley and get this show on the road for real! Brian, Roger, and my team leaders, pack up and let's go home!"

Brian Olson, Elton's second in command and the Special Staff leader, took over for Rance as he quickly left the conference room to catch up with Mike Valenti and Bubba Washington. The former paratrooper hurried down the cold hallway, not pleased with the way the operation was shaping up. Elton was a direct opposite of his friend, Bubba. A born and bred Tennessee mountain redneck and former racist, Elton had the rebel battle flag tattooed on his right forearm. It had been placed there during a drunken evening with high school buddies in Nashville back in '86, but Elton was no longer that kind of a redneck. After serving in the Army in an elite Ranger unit, Elton had no problems with anyone. Bubba was his best friend, and the flag tattoo now bore the motto, "Stars and Bars for All Southern Colors."

Elton caught up with the two men, mostly because Mike was short and tended to walk slowly. Valenti stopped long enough to ask Rance for his opinion about the mission. Elton was more abrupt than most, once you got him over his conditioned military courtesy.

"Doctor, if you want us to deploy to the fuckin' moon, I'll get us there an' back," answered Elton in his thick Tennessee drawl.

"That will be necessary one day, Ranger," advised Dr. Valenti, with genuine concern. "But it will also include a trip to Mars, too."

"That don't matter none to me, Doc, cause ah ain't concerned with politics. No sir! Mission first, ah always say. Roger that, Bubba John?"

"Roger that!" yelled Bubba.

Bubba and Elton slapped hands with each other, pleased with their practiced expressions of male bonding. They always fed off of each other's attitudes. Both of the country boys shared a common military background, a love for largemouth bass fishing, and a natural lust for adventure. Washington had been an intelligence sergeant during Operation Desert Storm. Neither man knew the meaning of mission failure or a bad attitude.

"Very good," noted Mike Valenti, who knew the two men were still concealing some mission issues. They continued walking in silence toward the office Valenti was using while in Alaska. After they passed Alexandra Charles and her seductive smile, Bubba Washington graciously opened the door for Mike. He was as black as ebony, and every bit as capable of being mean as his two hundred and twenty pounds of gym enhanced muscle were of being powerful.

"Gyat damn, Doc, she sure is fine! I didn't know you brought her along for the critique! I need me a secretary like that!" whispered Bubba with a long look back at the sexy woman. "That sista's got all tha' flava ah need in this lifetime, Ranger!"

Mike grinned, understanding but not sharing the big man's reaction.

"Keep your voices down, guys!" cautioned Mike. "Alex's not the type you can joke around with like that!"

Elton glanced around the edge of the door for a peek before closing it.

"Oh, son, that's one bee-yoo-tiful woman! Tha' marryin' kind, I've always said a' her," Elton remarked to Bubba. "Ah'd take her home an' watch proudly as all my dead racist rebel ancestors would rise up outta their graves an' disown my young ass for marryin' her!"

Bubba laughed as he slid into a seat. Washington was a hard worker and very intelligent. In spite of his smooth demeanor and hip street language, Bubba had a Masters degree in European history from Georgetown University. Coupled with his street-smart common sense and military discipline, Washington had the unique ability to lead people of different skill and occupational levels in ways that achieved superior results.

"Don't let my future wife hear yo ass, Ranger," warned Bubba. "Cause then I'll have ta' kill ya!"

Mike just listened and enjoyed the earthy banter.

"Shit, B.J., your big ass would hurt somethin' fragile like that! Did you see that cinnamon skin on her?" asked Elton. "Son, they don't make 'em like that north of Miami, and you don't speak any Spanish!"

Mike knew the two agents still wanted to talk about the Antarctic mission. Bubba had his big hands jammed into his baggy blue jeans, and Elton was stuffing his mouth with a leafy moist chaw of Beechnut chewing tobacco. The three men sat in silence while Mike withdrew a cigarette from his shirt pocket and lit it. He took a long drag, savoring the flavor of the tobacco. Bubba and Elton waited patiently for Mike to speak.

"Okay, so what's bugging you guys?" asked Mike, who was now able to speak privately. "And don't give me any more of that military "can do" bullshit! You've both been too quiet and irritable since we conducted this mock exercise."

Elton was first. He had a tendency to cover for Bubba's brash manner whenever possible. Bubba fumbled around in his pockets for something, then pulled a toothpick out and inspected it. Satisfied, he began to clean his front teeth with it as his buddy spoke.

"Well, sir," began Elton with sincere country manners. "Me and Bubba John ain't science dicks like the rest a' the team, but we know a tough mission when we see one. I reckon the military's tough enough for this, but puttin' these civilian college boys in Antarctica for sixty days is like puttin' me an' B.J. here in a girl's college dormitory for the same amount of time. It's gonna be fucked up fer sure with long term results!"

Mike laughed at the thought, which drew scornful looks from the Tennessee native. Bubba grunted, concerned that Mike was laughing at his friend.

"Shit, Doc," spoke up Bubba. "Ranger's not bullshittin' ya on this one! We can deploy a bunch of cherries to a war if we have ta', but that don't mean they're gonna' fight like men when they git there! Up till now, our ARKs have only been to easy digs in the country or to well supported disasters in third world areas where the comforts of home haven't been far from camp. We're both winter warfare and deployment certified, baby, but damn, even Elton's ARK Team ain't up for this one! This mock deployment was staged, so we need to practice it a few more times to get me feelin' cozy about doing the real deal."

Mike attempted not to laugh at Bubba's colorful language. He did take their points seriously, though.

"I understand, and you're right - both of you," agreed Mike, who removed his glasses. "Unfortunately, you agents get paid to achieve the impossible. You're the big dogs this agency pays for the impossible mission! Whatever you need, you can have. You make changes as required, but you've got to accomplish this mission."

"What about more time, Doc?" asked Bubba. "Can't you give us a few more weeks of training?"

"Copy that, Bubba John," supported Elton. "What about it, Doc? Can we have another month?"

Mike shook his head, "No, sorry, guys. The mission goes as planned. We used the time we had to get as ready as we could. That's the way it is."

"No problem, baby, but bein' a GS-14 at N.S.A. or Defense is becomin' a sweeter thought ta' me every day!" remarked Bubba, as he crudely grabbed his crotch and shifted in his seat. "This ain't right, Doc!"

"Copy that, B.J.," agreed Elton, with that natural drawl that made the two letters sound obscene. "Ah'm just a thirteen, but ah know some fellas the same pay grade as me who don't do half this much shit here at C.I.A., much less anywheres else. We'll get it done, Doc, you know that, but it ain't goin' to be no tiptoe through the goddamned tulips!"

"That's right, brutha. Me and Ranger will accomplish any mission you give us," reassured Bubba. "I jus' don't want any shit if soma these science boys don't make it back, Doc. And watch Klineshit. I've got nuff problems without him micro-managin' our asses or pretendin' he's runnin' the show! If he fucks up any of my people with his bullshit decisions, I'm going to break off a pair of my size thirteen shoes in his little ass!"

"Done," Mike agreed as the two men stood up.

Bubba tugged on Elton's arm, stopping his exit.

"Doc, have you wondered yet how the Russians and Chinese got onto this Antarctic gig? They're 'bout as conservative as they come, so why are they so interested all of a sudden in the South Pole?"

Mike leaned back in his chair, thinking about that one question as the two men departed.

"Yeah, Doc, what do they know that we don't know?" asked Elton.

Mike remained silent as the two men left. Mike picked up the phone and made some calls, confident that the task force was finally getting into the mortal fight to save the Earth from her scheduled date with disruption.

***

Mike's standard government desk calendar showed the date as June 21, 2006. After exchanging morning pleasantries and getting their morning cups of coffee, the NOAH'S ARK Mission Staff gathered in the Director's office for a final mission conference. By noon, the meeting was still going strong. Even Mike Valenti was weary from all of the planning.

"We're almost done, ladies and gentlemen," commented Mike as he nursed a fresh steaming cup of coffee in his hands. "ARK One boards the U.S.S. Wasp tomorrow morning, so our planning nightmares are almost over. We'll be faced with a different set of headaches when we enter the movement phase tomorrow. Now we're done with personnel, so let's hear from intel, ops, and logistics. Neil."

Neil Fowler, the NOAH'S ARK Intelligence Officer, addressed Mike and the rest of the staff.

"I have several topics, but I'll address foreign intelligence first," Neil began. He was a ruggedly handsome man with a scar on his left cheek from a wound received during Operation Desert Storm. "The Navy has reported that there are subs and other ships of war along our task force route from Russia, India, France, China, Japan, Brazil, Venezuela, Argentina, and

Great Britain. This is mainly due to a huge international sea show that's being held in Montevideo, Uruguay."

"I didn't know so many countries had submarines," remarked Randall Cummings. "Amazing!"

"Oh, yeah! Most developing countries are still using diesel boats," explained Neil. "But the major powers and the Chinese will have nuclear missile submarines there, too."

Mike didn't like the idea of Chinese naval forces being anywhere in the region, but there wasn't any proof that the People's Republic of China was interested in NOAH'S ARK activities. Neil read his thoughts.

"Doc, the Navy will report any deviations from the normal routes for these vessels. All of them will be monitored," reassured Neil.

"I guess that will have to do, then," breathed Mike. "Just stay on top of this, Neil."

"The Naval Submarine Force, United States Atlantic Fleet, which is known as SUBLANT, will be patrolling all waters between Norfolk and Antarctica during our mission," stated Neil. "Of course, the Jimmy Carter will be with the carrier at all times. We'll also have satellite and space reconnaissance, too."

"That's great, Neil! Now that's what I call intel support!" exclaimed Mike. "Okay, John, you're next."

"Yes, sir. The Wasp, with the destroyer escort John S. McCain, and the submarine escort Jimmy Carter, are supporting us in this mission," began Klinesmidt as he flipped some papers on his clear plastic clipboard. "The Wasp and McCain will depart Norfolk at dawn on the 24th, while the Jimmy Carter will rendezvous with them on the 30th off the coast of the Bahamas."

Mike was concerned about air readiness, "What about the helicopters, John?"

"The Navy has reported that the Marine CH-46 helicopters have been equipped for extended cold weather operations, but our experience in Alaska proved that their rotary wings limit their use under severe conditions," replied John. "To preclude any problems with wind shear, the Navy's modified the carrier's helicopters by installing stabilizers so they can function under stronger wind conditions. They've also come up with a way to keep the rotors from icing during flight."

"That's good, considering where we'll be going," remarked Randall Cummings, the ARK logistics officer.

"Information will be critical at all times, but especially during deployment. That means you have to be on top of the weather, John," advised Mike, who was concerned about the safety of ARK One. "You've already started, Randy, so tell me about log ops."

"Our equipment's been loaded, Mike. The M.U.L.E.S. containers, M.A.I.D.S. drills, and O.A.S.I.S. field sites are certified ready. Our pilots and our organic Blackhawk helicopter departed for Andrews Air Force Base this morning. As far as I know, we've made no such modifications to our own chopper."

"Get that done during the voyage, Randy," ordered Mike.

"Count on it, Doc," acknowledged Randall Cummings.

"Since ARK Two will be based on the Falklands, the Navy assigned a Marine Expeditionary Force to act as the rescue force. They'll be billeted on the Wasp with ARK One," advised John. "And the ship's Harriers will also be dedicated to patrolling our immediate operations area during the mission."

"That's excellent, John. Randy, are we set for immediate replacement of M.U.L.E.S., M.A.I.D.S., or O.A.S.I.S. units and their components?" asked Mike.

"Sure, Mike, that's all taken care of. All supplemental equipment will be flown down to our logistics support base in the Falklands. If any parts, components, or units are needed, the LC-130 transport aircraft will fly them directly to the Antarctic site," answered Randy Cummings, who handed Mike a piece of paper that detailed the re-supply plan.

"Well, it looks like our planning is over," decided Mike, who was deep in thought. "Okay, ARK One disembarks as scheduled. If you have any changes or concerns, call me. I don't care what time it is."

With little fanfare, the NOAH'S ARK staff departed Mike's office. Now the work would really begin for the members of the operational support staff. As they departed, Mike sat back in his chair and looked at the various staff support plans on the table in front of him. It was going to be the most complex and dangerous mission they had ever conducted.

Chapter Five

"The Way of the Rock"

The blowing ice and bitter temperatures of the Antarctic continent slowed the progress of the Chinese workers who were attempting to rapidly set up camp. They had unloaded their expeditionary equipment from a distant cargo ship and transported it overland to the scientific site. It had taken hours working in extremely long shifts for the soldiers to make the site habitable.

After taking shelter in a portable building that was heated by insulated diesel generators, two Chinese soldiers with ice on their faces and goggles quickly removed their white parkas and gathered around the nearest heater for warmth. The taller of the two men was a colonel is the People's Liberation Army.

"Our landing was unsatisfactory! From the time the freighter unloaded our equipment, we've been delayed by the weather! Do you still think we deployed without detection, Commander Jia?" asked Colonel Doctor Quien Lo Chen. His cheeks were frosted from the severe cold weather.

"I doubt it, sir," answered the security officer, Commander Jia Yonguan. "The only thing that may actually keep western sources from detecting our deployment is this weather you're complaining about!"

"I served in Upper Mongolia, and never experienced anything like this!" remarked Colonel Doctor Quien through shivering teeth. "I tried to explain to the general that this life support equipment was substandard, but the General Staff wouldn't fund the purchase of better goods. Now I'll have to accomplish this mission without my men being comfortable enough to perform their duties at 100 percent!"

As he spoke the door opened and the two Russian advisors entered. Their uniforms and clothing were different, and they appeared to be much more comfortable with the elements.

"This isn't bad weather, Colonel!" exclaimed the male Russian in perfect Chinese as he stamped snow from his thick boots onto the shelter's floor. "Zemlya's got bad weather!"

"Zemlya?" asked Commander Jia. "Where's Zemlya?"

"In the arctic, Commander," answered the woman, Natasha Svetkov. Her Chinese was also flawless. "It's a scientific site for Russia, and it's very nasty there. The conditions are very similar to Antarctica's. We've worked there, and we learned to function efficiently in extreme temperatures."

"We Chinese aren't accustomed to such deployments, so for us it's difficult to be effective under these harsh conditions," admitted Colonel Quien. "We learned much just making camp, but we survived and will complete our mission."

"So you will," agreed Vitaly Chin with a friendly smile. "We Russians are used to polar expeditions to search for mineral resources."

"Mr. Chen, you know very well this mission has to do with China's problems!" growled Commander Jia, who cared little for Russians. "Don't insult me by assuming that I'm stupid!"

"Calm down, please," insisted Vitaly Chin, who looked to Natasha to ease the situation more.

"We're merely here to assist you," offered Natasha in genuine friendliness. "You're a Chinese security officer, so this must be difficult for you. But as scientists, we're all seeking knowledge."

Colonel Quien agreed, "Come now, Commander, we're here to work together. Remember that we'll be conducting twenty-four hour operations, so we have to get along. Your special troops are providing security, but there are no enemies here."

"I obey orders, Colonel Quien, but I don't have to like Russians!" hissed Commander Jia. "I'll stay out of your way until I'm needed."

As Commander Jia found a seat at another heater, the three scientists sat down and planned the continuation of their mission in Antarctica. While they spoke, the rest of the members of the Chinese expedition were busy working in the blowing wind and freezing temperatures.

***

Moving in a protective patrol pattern in the murky waters off the Antarctic coast between the Weddell Sea and Enderry Land, the U.S.S. Jimmy Carter (SSN-23) was at the western end of it's patrol route as a screening element of the NOAH'S ARK mission. Running silent at three hundred feet below the surface of the rough South Atlantic waters, the Seawolf class fast attack submarine had deployed it's towed passive sonar array as a routine part of it's mission to detect any hostile surface or submerged vessels that might pose a threat to the deploying task force.

Captain Elroy Logan, the commander of the Jimmy Carter, had just returned from inspecting the nuclear missile tubes when his sonar operator broke the peaceful silence.

"Conn, sonar, tonal contact, center bearing 2-4-5," reported the young petty officer as his control panel and screen reflected the new activity being detected by the towed array's sensitive hydrophones. Even though the vessel was quiet, the command area of the submarine was alive with computer screens and lighted dials.

"Can you identify it?" asked Captain Logan from his seat. He was six feet tall and lean, and just happened to be one of the first black submarine commanders in the United States Navy.

"Captain, the tonals show it's a Chinese Xia class submarine!" exclaimed the normally reserved sonar man. "The computer reports it's a boomer called the Revolution. She's bearing course 0-6-0, speed 18 knots, range 60,000 yards. She's at periscope depth."

Elroy Logan looked back at his Executive Officer with a surprised look on his face. It took a lot to surprise a sub commander who was three months away from being approved for promotion to the admiral ranks. As the 353 foot long attack submarine continued to stalk it's new prey, Captain Logan made some split second calculations and decisions before issuing his orders.

"All engines stop, passive array," ordered the Captain as he rose from his chair. "Retrieve the TB-23 sonar array. Fire control, make tubes one and two ready."

The sailors on station repeated his orders as they performed their duties. As they executed the captain's commands, the submarine came to a stop as quietly as it had been moving through the water.

The more technologically advanced Seawolf class boats were slowly replacing the Virginia class submarines. Compared to submarines of other nations, the U.S.S. Jimmy Carter and other submarines in the Seawolf class were the most lethal ships of war in the world. With four torpedo tubes, vertical launch missile tubes, and an armament of MK-48 torpedoes and tomahawk missiles, the Jimmy Carter was capable of complete anti-ship and anti-submarine warfare.

"Mr. Willis, do our data files show the last time a Chinese sub was reported in the South Atlantic this far away from the cape and normal shipping lanes?" asked the Captain as he sat back down.

"Negative, Captain," responded Commander Cain Willis, the Executive Officer. He was a Naval Academy graduate, just like his boss. "According to our intel files, the Chinese don't venture into these waters except to navigate around the cape. When they do, they don't steer far from normal shipping routes out of fear they might run aground or get in trouble. And a Chinese boomer never strays far into the Atlantic as far as I know!"

"That's what I've come to learn myself," remarked Elroy Logan, rubbing his chin.

"What do you think, Captain?" asked Commander Willis. Captain Logan had recommended Willis for his own command following their return to port in Groton,

Connecticut. As a leader and sailor, Captain Logan knew that as much as he enjoyed working with Willis, it was time to pass on command of the Jimmy Carter to his right hand man.

"Wait a minute!" exclaimed Captain Logan, who rose from his seat to walk over to the intelligence station. "I just read an intel message that there's a Xia at that international naval show in Uruguay, but she's way off course and was supposed to be heading back home through Panama. That means we've got a strategic sub where she isn't supposed to be, and we don't know how the hell she got into these waters without us knowing about it! Mr. Willis, deploy the floating wire antenna. We're going to send this through channels now!"

As the U.S.S. Jimmy Carter silently stalked the Chinese submarine, Captain Logan notified his headquarters. Within minutes, every submarine in the South Atlantic was advised of the presence of a Chinese strategic nuclear submarine lurking in the treacherous waters near Antarctica.

***

The slippery snow covered gray deck of the U.S.S. Wasp was crowded with naval technicians and Marine aviators who were preparing their CH-46 Sea Knight helicopters for flight operations. As the flight crews prepared to depart, other technicians were attempting to keep the deck from being covered with ice.

The flight deck personnel were being whipped by biting forty mile per hour gusts of wind that blew icy moisture from the Antarctic coast into the sea. As the constant darkness continued to shroud the U.S.S. Wasp, the Officer of the Deck and those other lookouts unfortunate enough to be on deck caught a brief glimpse of the savage continent in the distance. Even in the middle of June, Antarctica was a foreboding land covered by ice and snow.

As Elton Rance read a flash message that was dated July 16, 2006, the ARK One Advance Party began to assemble near their assigned aircraft. Bubba Washington's Field Operations group was already exhausted, having been tasked with completing support activities before ARK One boarded the rotary wing aircraft. As the Field Operations personnel exchanged greetings with ARK One, Bubba Washington and Elton Rance paused for a moment to assess the weather situation. They were dressed in extreme cold weather gear that was not keeping them very warm.

"Gyat damn!" swore Bubba as he pulled his hood tighter around his insulated facemask. "You sure the cap'n said these were fine weather conditions? Shit, I haven't seen weather this bad since the winter of '94 on the DMZ! Even on the Korean border, we didn't do shit when the weather got like this! You ready, bruh?"

Elton rubbed his mittens together, attempting to warm his throbbing fingers. The former Ranger knew the mission began once the Advance Party left the vessel.

"Yeah, Bubba John, piece a' cake," replied Elton through his chattering teeth.

A carrier flight officer appeared and handed Elton another plastic sealed message. Bubba waited, running in place to keep himself warm.

"John and them ARK weather folks back at Langley confirmed we're good ta' go, Bubba John," advised Elton with a frown. "If this wasn't transmitted through the sensitive compartmented information facility, ah wouldn't believe it!"

"Uh huh, and I'll bet my virgin ass at a downtown sissy disco that the Doc don't know all of what's going on down here," speculated Bubba. "And I'll bet Klineshit's got his dick skinners all over this weather situation! I say we don't do it. Not now."

Elton was unsure of his friend's decision.

"I don't know if that's tha' right thing at this point, B.J. Them Navy boys are sayin' we're a go right now, but the weather's gonna get worse. So if we don't kick it into gear, we could be stuck on this tub for weeks!" cautioned Elton. "The choppers are loaded and our people are on deck and ready. It'll take us more time to gear down and get everyone back below decks than it will take us to go!"

"I know, Ranger. But I'm goin' to make sure Vernie's got as much field support as we can give her! As soon as the Advance Team's on the ground, she'll need the essential M.U.L.E.S. hooked up A.S.A.P. Them cherries cain't last more'n a couple of hours in this weather! Make sure she knows deployin' the O.A.S.I.S. and M.A.I.D.S. equipment can wait 'til the base camp's up. We have to frag our original Advance Party plan and do this in one lift. Roger that?"

"Ah copy," acknowledged Elton with a frown, as the last of the Advance Party and ARK support personnel trickled on deck. "Just for shits and giggles, I'm flyin' in with Vernie, but I'll return with the choppers. I just want to get a good look see of what she'll be dealin' with."

"That'll work, bruh!" agreed Bubba as he coughed a few times. He was worried about Elton, too.

"Well, B.J., I'm gonna go get this show started! It's time to cross the line of departure!"

"Do it, Ranger," said Bubba. "I'm gonna make contact with the Doc. Get em' off safe, Ranger!"

"Hoo-ah!" exclaimed Elton with the motivated grunt that was common to the armed forces. "Alright people, let's board these choppers and go wheels up! This is where the rubber meets the road!"

***

As the American expedition deployed by helicopter to the American Highlands region of Antarctica, the scientists from the People's Republic of China had already established their encampment to the northwest of the American site. Their poorly constructed and badly insulated research structures were arranged in a tight rectangle. The Chinese had stored their few trucks and other light vehicles in the middle of the rectangular community. Two officers, who were wearing the white winter parkas and trousers of the People's Liberation Army, stood near the orderly collection of parked vehicles.

"Our buildings and equipment are functioning well, considering the terrible weather we had at the beginning," noted Colonel Doctor Quien Lo Chen, the expedition commander. "How are our casualties?"

"Twenty have died so far, Colonel," cautiously answered Commander Jia Yonguan, the commander of the special military detachment. "The frostbite was too severe for them. Ten more have had amputations, but they're expected to survive until the mission ends."

"If it had not been for your security concerns, I could have the supply plane arrive here regularly rather than at the time we leave Antarctica," complained Colonel Quien. "It bothers me to have the wounded suffer for so long."

"That's far too risky, Colonel, especially now that our deployment was delayed," defended Commander Jia. "If your units had been detected too soon, your mission would have come to an end before any of your precious testing could have been completed."

"Perhaps, Commander, but I have much more to worry me than being detected by the Americans or any other claimants to this terrible land," noted the scientific leader as both men watched the two Russian liaison officers approaching their location.

"Your men need to turn on their vehicles more frequently, Doctor," advised Vitaly Chin through his white polar fleece face covering. His attractive associate inspected the vehicles as he spoke. "I'm sorry, did we interrupt something?"

"Not at all," replied Colonel Quien with a smile. He summoned one of his men and ordered them to turn on the vehicle engines of the unused vehicles.

The four leaders huddled together for warmth.

"This expedition has been hard on the vehicles, madam," agreed Colonel Doctor Quien Lo Chen in Russian as he lit another cigarette. Natasha rudely ignored Commander Jia Yonguan, whom she had already decided was not a good source of information. "And our testing is being accomplished at great human cost."

"Yes, I was informed by one of your doctors that you've had fatalities and amputations. Unfortunately, cold weather injuries are to be expected in such extreme climates as this," explained Vitaly Chin, who was a minerals geologist. "If you shorten work shifts, and lengthen their rest, they'll work more efficiently."

The Colonel considered Chin's advice. He would make the changes when the next work shift began.

"Thank you, Dr. Chin," said Colonel Quien, who was grateful for Chin's experienced advice. "The constant darkness is more debilitating than the weather, I think. Our bodies aren't made to work without sunlight."

"How is the seismic testing going, Doctor?" asked Natasha Svetkov, who was slowly attempting to get a little more intimate with Colonel Quien. "Are the results positive?"

Colonel Quien was silent for a moment, unsure of how much information to provide. He removed his clipboard from under his arm to consult his notes. If Commander Jia had not been present, he would have shared more data with his counterparts. Colonel Quien was about to speak when Natasha noticed something on the data sheet Colonel Quien had on his clipboard.

"Something is wrong here," advised Natasha to her colleagues. "See?"

"What do you mean?" asked Colonel Quien as he looked at the data sheet. "The earthquake?"

"No, the oil," remarked Natasha.

"I don't understand, Doctor," said Vitaly Chin. "The oil's been tested and re-tested."

Colonel Quien suddenly realized what Natasha had detected and he attempted to distract them.

"Dr. Svetkov, I was just about to take both of you to the oil site to discuss this," said Colonel Quien, who tucked the clipboard out of sight under his arm.

"That's exactly it, Doctor," remarked Natasha. "The Antarctic oil is hotter and has been heated by direct contact with magma, but it hasn't been contaminated."

"I see what you mean, Natasha!" exclaimed Vitaly Chin. "But how do we explain how China's oil field was contaminated when the Antarctic oil was not?"

"I'm afraid to speculate about it, but I believe the differences in climate and magma pressure tainted our oil," stated Colonel Quien, who realized that he was revealing China's true problem.

Colonel Quien knew the experienced Russian scientists would quickly determine that another heat source had tainted China's oil.

"Magma under an oil field keeps the oil fluid," remarked Chin. "Magma over an oil field would taint it, possibly, but how is magma going to form over an oil field as a result of an earthquake?"

"Exactly, Vitaly," agreed Natasha. "Only volcanoes could generate the heat and possess the contaminants that could taint an oil field from above it."

Doctor Chin realized that the Chinese officer was watching him. He made eye contact with Natasha, who was deep in thought.

"Natasha, it's time to eat and leave Dr. Quien to his tasks. Are you ready?" asked Vitaly Chin, as he reached out to guide her by the elbow.

"I was hoping to remain here with Quien Lo and discuss scientific matters," answered Natasha, who alluringly blinked at the expedition commander.

"That's fine. I'm going to dry out my garments," stated Chin. "Excuse me."

Vitaly Chin departed, slowly making his way through the deep snow to his shelter. Natasha stood next to Colonel Quien and remained quiet.

"Natasha, please give me a moment to speak with Commander Jia. He needs a lot of guidance when he becomes frustrated," explained Quien Lo Chen.

"Of course, Quien Lo. I'll wait in your quarters, if that's agreeable with you."

"Make yourself comfortable there, Natasha. I'll be there in a moment," said Colonel Quien, who looked forward to coupling with the Russian beauty."

Doctor Svetkov departed, walking as seductively as possible toward the portable building where Colonel Quien was living.

"Commander?" asked the Colonel into his communications headset.

It took a moment for him to receive a response.

"Yes, Colonel," came a response over the radio. "I apologize, but I've never been able to stomach Russian bullshit."

"That's irrelevant. I need your services," advised the expedition commander, who was not enjoying having to ask the arrogant Special Operations officer for assistance.

"I am at your service, sir," he responded.

"I believe Doctor Chin just became aware of our country's blunder and may be attempting to contact his superiors in Moscow," explained Quien Lo Chen. "He needs to meet with an unfortunate natural accident now."

There was a moment of silence over the radio.

"My pleasure, comrade," acknowledged Commander Jia. "What about the woman?"

"She will be my pleasure for a short while, and then you can dispose of her as well," advised Colonel Quien. "See to your duty."

"Yes, Colonel," acknowledged Commander Jia. "Their fate will be very natural and easily explained."

Colonel Doctor Quien Lo Chen turned and followed Natasha's footprints in the snow to his commander's billets, where he entered and found her naked and huddled under his woolen blankets. When Colonel Quien pulled back the covers and leered at the buxom enticing body of the Russian scientist, he smiled.

As Colonel Quien Lo Chen and Doctor Natasha Svetkov added themselves to the small list of people who have had steamy sex on Antarctica, Commander Jia Yonguan and some of his trusted men knocked on the door of Vitaly Chin's small room. When the Russian scientist answered the door, Commander Jia found him dressed in a pair of wool underwear. There was a satellite telephone unit on the bed that had not been opened.

Commander Jia stuck a Type 89 5.8 mm Assault Rifle in Chin's face and guided the confused man off into the frozen Antarctic tundra. As the Chinese Special Operations officer sat in the snow and relaxed, Doctor Vitaly Chin quickly succumbed to the horrific Antarctic elements and died of exposure.

When Natasha Svetkov finally stirred and decided to return to her quarters, Commander Jia Yonguan was waiting for her there. He would kill Natasha in the snow, and then make it appear as though the two scientists had taken a snowmobile ride to the petroleum site. Commander Jia had already procured a snowmobile that was malfunctioning. The stage was set to show the Russians that their two scientists had died while serving on the mission. To guarantee the authenticity of the ruse, Commander Jia had also selected two inept Chinese scientists to ride two snowmobiles to the liquidation site. Those two Chinese scientists would unknowingly be sacrificing their own lives in the name of the People's Republic of China.

***

The President of the Russian Federation was caressing a goblet of German Auslese wine during his scheduled afternoon meeting with the Head of Government and the two Deputy Premiers. Premier Grigoriy Gaydar, who was appointed to his position as part of a coalition Pro-American government, was drinking vodka from a heavy crystal glass. The two Deputy Premiers were also drinking vodka. It was their third bottle of the evening.

"We made several million Rubles on the Chinese contract, gentlemen," noted Vasil'yevich Tomskaya. As President of Russia since 2004, he was just becoming comfortable being the leader of the former Soviet Union. "Even though it took some effort to convince the Chinese to pay us in Hong Kong dollars rather than Rubles."

"You know it was necessary, Vasily," provided Grigoriy Gaydar with a belch. "Our Swiss accounts are better served converting the strong Hong Kong currency rather than our weak national toilet paper. Had we been paid in Rubles, our profit would have been reduced."

"I know, but our profit is worth so much more than money," remarked the President of Russia.

The Russian Head of Government poured himself another helping of vodka as he added, "This is true,

Vasil'yevich, but without their strange request we would not have known the problems we too will be facing along our southeastern border with China."

"I agree, Grigoriy," replied the Russian President. He examined the fine long legs of the rich Auslese wine as they slowly ran down the sides of the goblet. "Our mountain town of Chita appears to have the most seismic activity, which extends into China, too. There's no predicting what this might mean to the stability of that area, but our scientists are quietly monitoring the situation. You're responsible for domestic matters, Alek. Even though we're keeping the details of the situation secret, I'll need to advise select members of the Duma in order to obtain the Rubles needed to restore the damage to our own oil fields. Did you investigate the Chinese?"

Aleksandr Yefimovich was the seventy-year-old Deputy Premier of Russia. He was responsible for investigating the Chinese reasons for the covert contract to conduct satellite surveys of portions of Antarctica.

"Of course, Vasil'yevich," replied Aleksandr Yefimovich confidently. He had extensive service in the former Union of Soviet Socialist Republics. "These disturbances are the result of subsurface Chinese nuclear testing they conducted approximately two months ago. That disturbed a small geological fault."

President Tomskaya laughed out loud, pleased to hear that the Chinese had botched yet another technological advancement that the Russians had perfected long ago.

"That's fantastic information, Alek! Who says our intelligence network has become too weak?" asked Vasil'yevich.

The four men toasted their good fortune.

"This is to the days of fortune, not the days of honor!" offered the President as they drank together.

After their glasses were refilled, the four government executives sat down again.

"Alek served in the days of honor like I did, President Tomskaya. Now that was a time when our nation could keep state secrets!" remarked Yuliy Matviyenko, who was five years younger than his counterpart. "Let me tell you, sir, that the Americans aren't aware of the Chinese problems because our Chinese neighbors have an iron grip on the proletariat and the press. We haven't heard a word about this in the liberal American newspapers."

"That's fine, Yuliy, but tell us more of this great secret you've obtained from our Chinese spy at the nuclear facility," directed President Tomskaya. "Let's adjorn to the secure room where we can talk!"

After an hour of discussions and a few more drinks, the four men ended their meeting about the sensitive Chinese information.

"If this is true, China has more trouble than a geological problem," remarked President Tomskaya, who loosened his belt and undid his silk Italian tie.

Yuliy Matviyenko provided President Tomskaya with classified color photographs of the area where the fault was damaged.

"The Chinese are masters of deception," Matviyenko explained as he pointed at the different photographs. "At the exact date and time of the nuclear test, ten Chinese Xian Hong 7 supersonic nuclear strike bombers conducted a test run over the bomb site and dropped fuel air explosives. The Chinese have been conducting those tests regularly for the past six weeks."

"Fine, but could fuel air bombs mask a nuclear detonation?" asked Premier Gaydar."

"Yes, President Tomskaya, if it was a small yield for training purposes that was detonated underground," replied Yuliy Matviyenko. "The multiple fireballs of the bombing run could mask such a test."

"Brilliant," remarked President Tomskaya as he leaned forward to untie his designer shoes. "I compliment the Chinese on their planning, even if their execution was poor. If it had not been for our own espionage agents and the satellite contract, we would be wondering what had happened in China ourselves."

"We still don't really know," advised Premier Gaydar. "Even with the information we have obtained, there's much we need to learn."

"But we do know a great deal, Premier," agreed President Tomskaya, who now sank more into the plush chair that he was occupying. "If the information that Yuliy obtained from the Foreign Intelligence Bureau is correct, it will be both profitable and beneficial to us and the Russian people. The problem with the operative's information is that we haven't corroborated it."

"They haven't tested anymore nuclear devices since then," advised Alexandr Yefimovich. "Whether the spy's information is accurate or not, the Chinese have been much too quiet and cooperative."

"What about our Antarctic efforts, Yuliy?" asked Premier Gaydar.

"Our two operatives are there, Premier, but they haven't made contact as scheduled," explained Yuliy Matviyenko. "I'll advise as soon as they provide any information to corroborate our intelligence."

"That's the only reason why we sent our own researchers along to assist our Chinese neighbors," added Premier Gaydar, who at fifty-six was the youngest man in the room. Unlike the others, he didn't smoke anymore. He had already lost a lung due to cancer.

The men in the room waited for the Russian President to issue instructions. He took his time thinking as he drank the contents of his goblet. He refilled his glass again before speaking.

"We can't ask the Americans for information on a matter such as this," remarked President Tomskaya. "Our own secrecy and national security is paramount. I believe the Chinese will provide us with the information we need through our people in Antarctica. In the meantime, Aleksandr, continue researching the Chinese geological problems internally. I need you to formulate a complete plan on how we can exploit this information. We can't trust the Secretary General of the United Nations since he began receiving compensation from President Quien, so, Yuliy, I want you to use all your international resources to find out if any other nations are concerned or aware about this Chinese blunder."

Aleksandr Yefimovich and Yuliy Matviyenko both agreed to comply with their leader's directives.

"Premier Gaydar, I task you with handling the Duma. We don't need legislative problems concerning these issues. And I want you to handle any foreign inquiries," ordered President Tomskaya.

The four men continued drinking as they moved onto other issues. Until more intelligence could be gathered regarding the matter, issues such as the devaluation of the ruble were much more important to the intoxicated men.

***

Elton Ronald Rance was verbally motivating his ARK One personnel when Bubba Washington gave him the final mission thumbs up. The twelve CH-46 Sea Knight medium lift helicopters that had been covered with waterproof tarps and lashed down on the pitching deck of the Wasp cranked up their loud engines in succession. Their mission had originally been to transport the ARK One Advance Team and their equipment to the objective area in consecutive waves. The helos were each 45 feet in length and powered by two cold weather modified General Electric T58-16 turbine engines that gave the rotary wing aircraft a cruising range of 132 nautical miles. Each helicopter was capable of lifting 22 troops and 5,000 pounds of cargo under all weather conditions.

Warren Wells, Washington's ARK Services Officer, approached Rance with Oto Yee, the ARK Chief of Air Operations, following close behind him. Both men were having trouble walking on the slippery deck. There were naval personnel all around them. A loudspeaker was continually blaring flight instructions. The huge amount of noise and extreme weather conditions made any conversation difficult.

"Ranger, all the helos are ready and everyone's loaded. I put a full complement of M.U.L.E.S. conduits on bird two and the extra set on bird three. Bird one's got Vernie on board with her key people dispersed on birds one through four. I made space on bird one for you to ride in with Vernie and recon the drop zone!" advised

Wells, yelling against the strong wind. "Any changes I need to know about?"

Elton nodded his head, realizing that some changes had to made right away if the mission was going to be a success. "Get as many choppers as you need to get our people and the most essential equipment to the objective area in one lift!"

"No way, Ranger!" exclaimed Wells. "It's too late for that!"

"One lift?" asked Oto Yee. "That's impossible, Ranger! That requires using almost every bird on the carrier! We've got twelve loaded and ready to go now, but the rest aren't ready!"

"Yeah, Ranger, I've sling loaded our most essential M.U.L.E.S. to the twelve we've got! The follow on M.U.L.E.S. will have to wait until the weather clears!" added Warren Wells. "That's why I'm flying with the Advance Party! I'll be right there with Vernie to make sure our support is as good as it can be!"

"I don't like it, gents!" shouted Elton. "Glenda's crew will be short some critical items and we don't know how long she'll have to last out there!"

The Flight Operations Officer joined the three men, wondering why there was a delay.

"What's the hold up?" asked the naval officer. "We've got to go now!"

"I want all the essential equipment taken to the objective in one lift!" explained Elton.

"Sir, what you want and what you get are two different things!" shouted the naval officer. "Either you go now as is or I'll terminate this launch myself!"

Elton hopped onto the helicopter with Glenda and told the pilot to take off. Wells boarded his assigned helicopter after falling twice on the icy deck.

As Oto Yee waved at Elton Rance and the departing Advance Party, the weather seemed to dissipate for a moment. It seemed to last long enough to permit the helicopters to launch from the deck of the carrier without difficulty. Bubba Washington was on the bridge of the carrier coordinating with the Captain Burke to insure that the landing went as smoothly as possible. Everyone on board was concerned when the helicopters could no longer be heard in the distance.

Chapter Six

"Trouble in the Darkness"

The flight time from the vessel to the terrain safe landing zone was approximately thirty minutes. The first helicopter was carrying an extra sling load of emergency survival gear that made the flight more difficult. The second Sea Knight, which transported members of the Communications Section and the Geographical Section, was carrying extra umbilical cables for the M.U.L.E.S. modules. The third helicopter transported the Services Staff Section and the Meteorological Section. The remaining Sea Knights were loaded with the rest of the Advance Party.

"Look there, Vernie!" shouted Elton Rance as he pointed past the pilot's head into the darkness."

When the lead helicopter's lights illuminated the terrain during its bumpy descent, the nervous passengers caught a glimpse of their new temporary home for the first time. It was a desolate flat landscape, sporadically peppered with snow covered hills or mounds.

Glenda Moses was already shivering during the flight while the helicopter doors were closed. After the pilot released the sling load that was attached and hanging from the belly of the aircraft, the crew chief shouted for his passengers to unfasten their canvas seat belts. The pilot lowered his aircraft and held it steady until the wheels touched the top of the drifts.

"Go!" bellowed the crew chief as he motioned for the passengers to exit the aircraft. They remembered to keep their heads down to avoid being beheaded by the wide rotor blades. Glenda and her four team members jumped onto the ground.

"Vernie!" yelled Elton from the helicopter as he grabbed her by the parka and took a moment to scream into her ear. "The shit's going to hit the fan, darlin'! Ah know you're cold, but suck it up an' take care of your people! Ah'll be back soon as ah can!"

Glenda attempted to wave, but the rising helicopter's rotor wash caused her to turn away to protect her face from the snow that was whipping around in the air. Just as quickly as it had landed, the Navy helicopter lifted off to return to the ship. The follow on helicopters were also conducting their respective landings, well away from the location of Team One.

"L.T., take the G.P.S. and confirm our current position. Then find the exact location of our base camp," directed Glenda Moses in the complete darkness. They were all wearing headlamps. "Let's get this gear and move it to our preplanned emergency area!"

Lewis T. Griffith, the assigned archaeologist from Eugene, Oregon, was a solid outdoorsman. At twenty-six, he was one of the few scientists in the NOAH'S ARK program who was at home in the wilderness.

While Glenda Moses worked, other team members that had just landed made their way to her location. The wind blown ice made the approaching researchers difficult to see.

"Team One, ARK One Elton, over," sounded the radio. Ranger's voice was unmistakable.

"ARK One Ranger, Team One Moses," responded Glenda into the transmitter. "Over."

The others had almost reached her location. Even with their powerful flashlights, it was difficult for them to see Moses in the darkness.

"Vernie, we're only going to have time for one more lift! The weather's goin' to force us to shut the choppers down in about one hour! You copy, over?"

Glenda replied affirmatively. Warren Wells looked worried, as did the rest of them.

"Copy, Ranger, what's the plan? Over," asked Glenda, who had ice forming on her parka.

There was an uneasy silence on the other end of the tactical radio. Glenda used the radio silence to get her people motivated. L.T. Griffith shouted that he had found the benchmark coordinates for the base camp.

"Wells, get your people to set up the emergency services station where L.T. marks the spot," ordered Glenda. "Get the secondary cables covered and secured there. Irene, L.T. will show you where communications will be set up. Stretch out the primary M.U.L.E.S. cables in your area, and mark each cable with a signal flag in case the storm arrives before the helicopters do."

"You got it, Vernie!" agreed Warren Wells, who appreciated her leadership."

Everyone was busy setting up camp when the radio crackled again.

"Vernie?" announced Elton Rance as he broke the radio silence. "Them choppers are arriving back heah now. Me an' Bubba John are goin' to sling load them bad boys up with the M.U.L.E.S. power unit, one dormitory, and a fuel unit. That'll at least keep y'all safe and warm til the weather breaks, over."

Glenda knew the arrival of the other essential M.U.L.E.S. modules was critical to their survival.

"Roger, Ranger," responded the Advance Party leader. "We'll be just fine, over."

"Vernie, we've been retransmittin' using the aircraft. Once the airlift's done, the boat's goin' to back a safe distance away from the coast. When your communications station is up, contact us per S.O.P. Don't use the satellite phone unless you have an emergency. If the weather's goin' to be as bad as it sounds, any communications will be disrupted anyway. If we lose radio contact, we'll attempt contacts at the beginnin' of every hour. You've got your emergency kits, so use 'em, over," said Elton in a serious tone. "Make sure all your people eat and drink, too."

Glenda tried to hide her emotions. When L.T. approached her, he knew there was something wrong.

"Roger, Ranger, out," finished Glenda.

"Out heah," ended Elton.

Glenda put the portable radio back on her hip.

"Get everyone over here, L.T. We've got to get some of the M.U.L.E.S. equipment set up as soon as it arrives. This is going to be one hell of a storm," related Glenda Moses.

M.U.L.E.S. was a government acronym for Mobile Umbilical Laboratory Excavation System. It was a modularized, air and sea transportable, temporary base system that contained it's own power and sustainment systems. The complete M.U.L.E.S. package consisted of forty insulated structures, all of which could be delivered by rotary wing, fixed wing, or vessel transportation systems. M.U.L.E.S. allowed people to conduct government activities in a secure human habitat.

When the members of the ARK One Advance Party were gathered around Glenda, their faces betrayed a mixture of apprehension and fear. The increase in winds and decrease in surface temperature were hints of what Glenda was about to tell them. Their C.I.A. training kicked in, and the group handled the news well.

"That's it in a nutshell," finished Glenda. "Irene's team will hook up the communications station. Warren's guys will hook up the dormitory unit. Geography will attach the power station umbilical. Ted, I want your meteorological team up A.S.A.P. As soon as we're generating power, we secure loose equipment and get the hell out of this weather! Clear?"

Everyone agreed. By the time the helicopters could be heard in the distance, Ted Harding and his meteorological team had activated their portable unit and connected the umbilical attachment. Weather data was being input into the sensitive machines as the last helicopter released its load. After it hovered away to a safe staging area, the crew chief walked in the deep snow toward Glenda. He had a brown envelope in his hands.

"Are you Moses?" asked the aviator.

Glenda nodded, unsure of the problem.

"Here, ma'am," said the crew chief as he handed Glenda the brown envelope. "I was told by that crazy mountaineer to give you this with orders not to open it until you're safe and warm in your M.U.L.E.S."

Glenda thanked the man and tucked the envelope in her parka. It would take an hour to attach the unit umbilical, and it would take another to warm the modular units. Warren Wells flipped on the power switch on the big M.U.L.E.S. generator and yelled when he was rewarded with the buzzing of a working machine. Ted Harding, the head of Meteorology, approached.

"Vernie, we've got about a half hour before we get buried in snow," warned Ted Harding, the meteorologist. "It's coming from the west! I figure four feet of snow today, ending tomorrow night."

Glenda figured the time schedule out in her head, fully aware that it would take more time than that to get the M.U.L.E.S. equipment functioning.

"What about the temps, Ted?"

"Well, it's ten degrees above zero now, and dropping. We've got another hour, then it'll drop down fast, maybe even to thirty below."

Glenda thanked Ted and went back to work. They hooked up the small communications module first, and quartered that team safely inside it. In another fifteen minutes, the dormitory unit was connected. Everyone worked hard to get the emergency equipment inside the residence. As they completed their work, Glenda pulled Warren Wells aside.

"Warren, how's it look from your point of view?"

"Well, Vernie, my concern's the dormitory unit. It's built to hold ten people. Minus the communications guys, who can cram their group into the commo unit, we're still forced to house twenty three people in a ten man unit."

Glenda shrugged, causing the ice on her parka to crack and crunch.

"What's the difference, Warren? Ten or thirty, as long as we fit, we should be fine," said Glenda. "Right?"

"We'll arrange for hourly watches all night. For now, we need to finish and get out of this weather!"

The Advance Party finished securing their essential equipment just as the worst of the storm hit the encampment. It quickly caused all the members of the party remaining outside invisible. The snow struck so rapidly that Glenda didn't have a chance to get all of her people inside the dormitory. L.T. and Quentin Smith were still out in the storm placing bright orange magnetic banners on the sides of the M.U.L.E.S. units.

"Irene," spoke Glenda into the hand held radio.

"I was just getting ready to contact you, Vernie. Have you seen any of my people wandering around the dorm? I'm missing two!"

Glenda swore.

"After the snow hit, the meteorological unit came here. They're all present, but they're jam packed in this module. What do you want to do?" asked the communications chief.

Glenda looked at the others gathered around her. None of them could go out in the cold again, and she was still wearing her cold weather gear.

"Stay put, Irene. I'll go find them," Glenda said into the wet radio.

Nobody protested. No matter her gender, Glenda Vernell Moses was the person in charge.

"Here, Vernie," offered Warren Wells, holding out a length of nylon parachute cord. "Let's go outside. We'll tie one end to you, and the other to the door. That way, you won't get lost, and we won't have to answer to Ranger if we lose you."

Glenda smiled gratefully, but told Warren to stay inside. She would tie off the rope herself and find her people. When she was all zipped up, Glenda opened the door against the biting winds and stepped outside.

The Advance Party leader huddled against the door as a blast of wind almost knocked her down. She diligently tied the rope to the dormitory unit doorknob, wondering if being a government employee was worth the sacrifices she made for her job.

"I can't see shit!" she said to herself.

With the hum of the generator unit to guide her, Glenda blindly walked toward it. She figured the men would be at the generator or near the communications unit. She hoped they hadn't wandered off.

As she stumbled against the blowing wind, Glenda got close enough to the power unit to be shielded from the gales. L.T. and Cowboy Smith were leaning against the sheltered side, enjoying the warmth and protection from the wind that the generator created.

"Hey, Vernie! We're sure glad to see you!" shouted Cowboy Smith with a grin even Glenda could see. The force of the terrible winds was muffling cowboy's words. "Let's get out of here!"

Glenda took shelter next to her subordinates and asked about the two men who were still missing. Both men had seen them walking toward the commo unit when the worst of the winds had hit them.

"It was some terrible shit, Vernie," described L.T. "The winds blew me and Cowboy all the way over here. Hell, I hit the generator headfirst! That's how we found it! If those guys were heading back to the commo unit and didn't make it, they could be in the ocean by now."

Glenda instructed the two men to follow her rope back to the dormitory, but Quentin Leon Smith wouldn't hear of it. A bi-racial man born in Stockton, California,

Quentin was the child of a rugged white rancher and a black Agriculture Inspector. Quentin's light brown skin, straight brown hair, and green eyes made him an exotically handsome man who had no trouble attracting the opposite sex. He was also as tough as nails, and every bit a cowboy like his tough father.

"Vernie, you're the boss, and you're too valuable to lose," Cowboy said as he untied the rope from around Glenda's waist. "You guide L.T. back to the dorm. I'll find the two missing men!"

Glenda was already too cold to argue, and Cowboy seemed less affected by the terrible temperatures than either one of them. As Glenda slowly led L.T. back to the dormitory unit through the blinding wind, Quentin headed in the direction of the invisible communications unit. Halfway there, Cowboy found the two lost men lying on the ground desperately holding onto each other for warmth. They were almost completely covered with snow. Both men were motionless, but alive. One team member attempted to speak and began crying instead. His tears froze as they ran out of his eyes. They were both a sad sight to see.

Cowboy tied his rope around the most stricken man. It took almost a half hour for Quentin to drag both men back to the dormitory unit. By the time Cowboy arrived at the dormitory, one of the cold weather victims was slipping into a coma. The other was suffering from deep frostbite. L.T. Smith assisted Cowboy.

"They're both bad off, Vernie," observed Cowboy. "This one's got hypothermia, and this one's got deep frostbite on his hands, feet, and face."

Warren Wells retrieved the first aid kit while others used emergency blankets to warm the men. Vernie notified Irene over the radio.

"Vernie, our commo system's down while this storm affects us. As soon as I can get through to Ranger on the emergency channel, I'll let him know we've got two casualties," advised Irene. "Thanks for finding my crew for me."

Glenda didn't pay attention to Irene's last comment, but her people did. Most of the team had been critical when Glenda was selected to lead the Advance Party. Her performance that day had gone a long way in changing their views.

***

Mike Valenti was sitting at his desk with the door closed. Alexandra had brought him a cup of coffee, but the project director was too worried about the Antarctic mission to drink anything.

"Mike, Seth Tayman's here to see you," announced Alexandra. "Shall I send him in?"

With a huge sigh, Mike gathered himself and told Alexandra to let Seth enter. The wire-haired action officer's big nose was red with stress.

"I've got Bubba Washington on the secure line, Mike. He's really pissed," advised Seth.

"Do you blame him?" remarked Mike.

Bubba Washington was calling from the naval vessel. It was a pristine connection, so the big man's deep voice had its full effect.

"Doc, what the hell's goin' on up there? My Advance Party's gyat damn stranded, and tha' weather's gone ta' complete shit!" shouted Washington. "Somebody up there fucked over my people wit' a bad weather briefin' that's caused injuries!"

Before Mike could do it, Seth asked about the specifics. John Klinesmidt entered the office, too.

"Fuckin' surface temps are at thirty below!" bellowed Bubba without regard for anyone's hearing on the other end of the transmission. "Gyat damn wind chill is anywhere from fifty to a hundred below! Ranger had some broken up emergency communications with Glenda's crew. She's got two injured - exposure and deep frostbite, all cause a' some bullshit staff fuck up!"

"Damn!" swore Mike, who punched his intercom button and summoned Heather McKay, his Chief of Meteorology. "Go ahead, Bubba."

"Doc, Vernie's good people. She'll keep her crew together and continue the mission, but whoever gave the "go" for the weather fucked this up bad! ARK One didn't know shit 'bout this weather system 'till it was playin' gyat damn Rocky Mount'n High and shit on their poor asses!" remarked Bubba. "You gotta get some ass on this one, Doc!"

Mike agreed, took responsibility for the situation, hung up the phone with a promise to call back with an answer. Seth sat down, while John unprofessionally shouted into the paging system for Heather McKay.

"Look, John, Heather's under my control," warned Seth, whose eyes got wider when he was angry.

Mike thought Seth looked like an albatross when he started to get upset.

"No way, Seth!" countered John. "I run this staff. If anyone fucked up, I'll get my pound of flesh first!"

"Kiss my ass!" swore Seth maliciously. "I'll get to the bottom of this without your fucking help!"

Alexandra ushered Dr. Heather McKay into Mike's crowded office. She was an attractive thirty nine year old brunette with the dry weathered skin of a professional scuba diver. An oceanographer and marine meteorologist, Heather always had the pale look of a woman who wasn't regularly exposed to the sun. She had a proven reputation for being tough, and she didn't take much verbal abuse from anyone.

Heather was holding a thick tan folder in her right hand that was filled with Antarctic meteorological data. She casually leaned against Mike's wall, focusing her eyes on Mike. Mike could see by the sharp look in Heather's eyes that she was eager to defend herself.

"What's the problem, Mike?" asked the blue eyed marine expert.

"Doctor McKay, the problem with ARK One is weather related. What was your mission forecast?" interjected John.

Heather ignored Klinesmidt and directed her answer to Mike.

"Three hours before mission start, that storm wasn't even on radar or satellite, Mike. It developed extremely quickly, and changed directions more times than John's temper."

"Now hold on a minute…." started John.

"Calm down, J.R.," cautioned Mike, who knew the operations officer didn't like to be criticized. "I'm responsible for this fuck up, okay everyone? Now, Heather, do you have the data on that."

Heather produced a file and gave it to Mike.

"Doctor, I notified John about the change in weather as soon as it was detected. I constantly kept him informed of changes in the front's direction, and made him aware of it's dangerous potential for compromising the mission and being life threatening," advised the oceanographer with a vengeful look at John. "When I wanted to bring my concerns to you, John instructed me to return to my duties."

"Thanks, Heather, that will be all," said Seth to his employee.

After Heather left and the door closed again, Seth confronted John.

"You cowardly son of a bitch! You knew about this before the mission and didn't tell Mike? How could you?" Seth screamed as he tried to grapple with John.

John stared hard at Seth, but he backed away from any confrontation with him.

"The storm wasn't a threat at the time, Seth!" growled Klinesmidt, who raised his hands in a gesture of hopelessness. "Mike made the right decision!"

Mike stood, suddenly aware of the anger that had welled up inside of him.

"Out, Seth!" order Mike, who looked hard at John.

"Look Mike," began John in that nervously high voice of his. "I've made calls like this before. That storm wasn't a threat when I made the big decision."

"John, you failed to inform me about the severity of the storm," reprimanded Mike Valenti in his even, confident tone. "People's lives, our mission, rest on my ability to make sound decisions based on accurate data. As my operations officer, you don't have command authority, sir. I do. Clear?"

Klinesmidt turned red. A C.I.A. case officer for two years before being assigned to NOAH's ARK in '99, the forty three year old government employee was unused to being reprimanded.

"Very clear, sir," acknowledged Klinesmidt with a nasty attitude. "Anything else, sir?"

Mike shook his head. John Klinesmidt departed, visibly enraged by Mike's counseling session. Minutes passed before the secure telephone's unique ringing interrupted the silence. It was a much calmer Bubba Washington on the line this time.

"Hey, boss, Bubba here," announced the operations chief. "We just received word from ARK One! Both of my people are going to recover. Chenovsky's in fair shape. The deep frostbite's mostly in his feet, and the medical technician's sure he'll lose a couple of toes on each foot. His face and hands will need a lot of therapy, too. Milne's out of his coma and is respondin' well, but he's gonna lose most of his fingers."

Mike directed that his injured employees be evacuated at once to the Bethesda Naval Hospital, one of the best government hospitals in the United States.

"How's Vernie doing, Bubba?"

"She's a soldier, Doc!" praised the big Louisianan. "Irene Johnson told me Vernie was tha' one that went out an' looked for them missing snow victims! Quent'n Smith's tha' one helped her, Doc. He wouldn't let Vernie risk her life a second time. This mission's bringin' tha' team together tight, baby - tight!"

"That's good news, Bubba," agreed Mike, who was relieved to learn that Glenda was safe. "We'll have to give her an award when this is over."

"That'll work, boss. "I'll type it up when we get back. Hey, wanna' here somethin' funny, Doc?"

"Sure, Bubba, what is it?"

"Ranger sent ole' Vernie a note jus' before the weather shut us down sayin' that stayin' warm will win this war! Don't that sound like Ranger, Doc?"

Mike thanked Bubba, hung up, and continued to coordinate the mission. He began planning for more operational changes and future task force requirements. Dr. Valenti had to be prepared to implement and follow the classified Single Integrated Operations Plan (S.I.O.P.) that specified the expanded mission role of Operation NOAH'S ARK.

***

It took two snowbound days for the immense weather system to dissipate. Alone in the vast frozen wasteland, the ARK One Advance Team was finally reinforced on June 21st by Elton Rance and the Main Body. The main elements rapidly arrived by helicopter to find all of the M.U.L.E.S. structures covered in a thick lumpy blanket of freshly settled snow. The ailing nuclear generator, which had remained functional during the treacherous storm, was covered with several dense layers of ice that had conformed to the shape of the unit. Elton Rance was the first member of the Main Body to attempt to locate the snow-covered door of the frozen dormitory unit where Glenda's party had taken refuge.

"Son of a bitch!" swore the Tennessee country boy as he kicked and shoveled the crunchy snow away from the M.U.L.E.S. unit. "Glenda! Y'all in there?"

As muffled shouts of joy erupted from inside the containerized unit, Rance and the Main Body members attempted to force the housing unit door open.

"Git your hand held working!" directed Elton to one of his people as he labored. "And git a hold of the squids. We're gonna need some help with this!"

As they attempted to establish radio contact with the snowbound team members, Rance determined that the occupied M.U.L.E.S. units had survived the blizzard too well. The heat from inside the units and the snow that had pummeled the unit exterior had resulted in the weather tight seams of the insulated doors becoming completely sealed with two-inch thick ice.

"Vernie, y'all doin' awright?" shouted Elton as the crews worked to open the sealed units.

"My injured people are in bad shape!" came back the muffled voice from inside the dormitory unit. "We need to get them back to the ship A.S.A.P!"

"Roger that, Vernie!" shouted Elton again.

It took a vessel emergency maintenance team using specialized extraction equipment and heat blasters two hours to open the icy M.U.L.E.S. units. During that time period, the helicopters took advantage of the improved weather conditions to transport the rest of the M.U.L.E.S. modules to the encampment. By dusk, the forty units were onsite and the camp was fully manned.

Rance held his first staff meeting in the M.U.L.E.S. main office unit, named O-1, while the rest of the team members continued to set up camp. The office unit was centrally located within the confines of the research base. O-1 was warm and equipped with standard government furnishings and no windows. Every item of equipment was secured inside the portable structures for immediate use.

"It looks like we're ready to be operational," declared Elton Rance to the gathered staff and team leaders. "Bubba John's sent Otto Yee and Warren Wells to represent 'im cause he's puttin' out some fires on tha' boat before he joins us here. They're gonna give us an overview, and then ah'll say my piece. After me, ah' want Brian an' Roger to give their staff briefings. We need to keep this meetin' short. Awright, Otto."

The Chinese American engineer with the high forehead, heavy shadow on his jaw, and thick dimples stood up and assumed control of the session. Yee's wire framed glasses were still fogged over as he flipped through his notes.

"I have only a few comments and a little guidance from Mr. Washington," remarked Oto in his naturally laid back California accent. "Air Operations first. The New York Air Guard LC-130 transport will arrive with service on Mondays, Wednesdays, and Fridays. Arrival times will be at 0800 hrs. Departures are at 1700 hrs. Any questions?"

Arn Bruhard, the head of Anthropology and Archaeology, raised an arm. With curly bright red hair and a freckled face, Bruhard was hard to miss in a crowd.

"Oto, is this aircraft going to be properly outfitted to transport our delicate scientific samples?"

Yee shook his head. His glasses had finally cleared up.

"Yes, Doctor Bruhard," answered Oto Yee. "Anyone else?"

With no more questions, Yee moved on to the intelligence portion of the briefing.

"Mr. Rance, everyone, I just received notice over the secure link with Mr. Washington that an unknown expedition team has landed on Antarctica twenty five miles northwest of our position."

"Come again?" exclaimed Elton with a frown. "We're just now findin' that shit out?"

Yee adjusted his wire rimmed glasses, "Yeah, Ranger, the unknown units apparently arrived in an old Iranian registered freighter that was tracked passing through the Drake Passage of Cape Horn two days ago. Mr. Wells will provide the vessel intel after the meeting. According to the latest estimates, they're fully deployed. Langley estimates that two hundred personnel landed in that expeditionary force. The probable identity of this group is Russian."

Lemuel Stokes, Rance's Operations Officer, raised a hand. A balding black man from Summit, New Jersey, Stokes was a retired Air Force officer.

"Russian? I'm going to need more than that, Oto! Who knows what these guys could be doing down here? Are you going to leave me with a detailed S-2 intel report so I can get working on our own intelligence estimates and plans?"

Yee acknowledged that he would.

"Marine operations," Oto continued. "Once Mr. Washington and the rest of ARK One deploys, the McCain will withdraw to a patrol route in the South Indian Ocean. There will be no further vessel support until the planned extraction date."

"That's just great," remarked Roger Conyers, Rance's opinionated Mission Staff Specialist. "The Russians are knocking on our door, and the Navy's pulling out on us! Who's going to guarantee our safety and kick their asses?"

Yee looked up from his notebook and raised his eyebrows.

"Dr. Conyers, we're not at war with Russia," Yee advised.

"Thanks, Otto," acknowledged Elton. "Warren."

The career C.I.A. logistician stood and took over. The bald area on top of his pale head was shiny under the bright office lighting.

"That vessel's definitely Iranian, Mr. Rance," began the slow talking man from Toma, Wisconsin. "Satellite photos indicate she was loaded, but we currently don't know the origin of her cargo or passengers. We do know the vessel departed Hong Kong and over three weeks ago enroute to Port Everglades, Florida. I have a full report for you, Ranger."

Rance nodded. The part about Hong Kong and Bangkok bothered him. The Russians usually used other locations for clandestine maritime missions.

"Ranger, 100% of the M.U.L.E.S. units have been deployed - 75% are cabled to the power unit. Priority of service to M.U.L.E.S. is dormitory units, main office, laboratory unit, and other units. The heat should be kicking into full gear in three hours, tops. We'll place the two O.A.S.I.S. and the M.A.I.D.S. modules on our pre-planned excavation and drilling sites as soon as they arrive. As soon as the transport vehicles and heavy equipment arrive, we'll prepare the runway for the resupply missions. Resupply will coincide with the aircraft schedule. Food replenishment will be on Mondays, spare parts on Wednesdays, and fuels, batteries, and energy needs on Fridays. Medical, scientific, biohazard, and human waste removal go with all departing flights. Oh, and satellite telephone use is restricted to Saturdays and Sundays. Any questions?"

There were no questions, so Rance thanked the two Field Operations staffers and waited for them to leave before speaking with his ARK group. He paced a few times before addressing his group.

"Well, people, y'all heard it. The Russians have prob'ly deployed here, too," began Elton. "That means we've got ta' get results! Roger, git your staff hoppin' on gettin' intel on that other expedition. Firm up Warren's logistics schedule, and formulate our personnel needs. Now, Roger, let's hear from you."

Conyers redirected the briefing to Frasier Owens, his Movement and Deployment Officer.

"Equipment transport's at 50%, Ranger," advised Owens, who was holding a personalized clipboard filled with logistics schedules. "The current base priority is the hydration modules, fuels and subsistence, transport vehicles, and mission equipment. Upon completion of the lifts, our organic aircraft will remain with us, stored and lashed down in the aircraft and vehicle storage unit. The two naval Seasprites will return to the vessel for sea containment."

Elton Rance shook his head, "Change your priority to mission equipment in place of them hydration modules an' we'll be cookin' with grease! We've got 'nuff of the planet's cleanest snow here to drank for the resta' our lives. Now that we're onsite, I need them O.A.S.I.S. units and M.A.I.D.S. up A.S.A.P., Frasier."

Owens sat down and occupied himself by updating his clipboard. O.A.S.I.S. was another acronym for Outdoor Arctic Site, Igloo System. It was a mobile, state of the art, triangular insulated tent system that contained a field laboratory. The O.A.S.I.S. could be coupled by varying lengths of umbilical cable to the M.U.L.E.S. system and placed on top of a dig or light-drilling site. Only the length of umbilical cables limited the distance that an O.A.S.I.S. unit could function away from the M.U.L.E.S. encampment.

M.A.I.D.S. is another government acronym that stood for Multi-purpose, All terrain, Independent Drilling System. The M.A.I.D.S. were capable of conducting deep site drilling and debris excavation in remote locations. The equipment could function with minimal human supervision, and it was powered by state of the art nuclear energy. M.A.I.D.S. were air, sea, and land transportable units that could penetrate glacial ice and various types of stone at depths of up to 1,000 feet.

"Here's the deal for now," advised Elton to his personnel. "Teams One and Two will function under Vernie Moses and work at Site One. Teams Three and Four will be under Terry Friarson and work Site Two. They'll each be using two O.A.S.I.S. units and the M.A.I.D.S. units. Each team'll have two M.A.I.D.S. units to do the drillin' at their locations. Site One's responsible for researching the glacier. Two's got the job of findin' the petroleum."

Elton covered a few more items then proceeded on to the Science Officer, whose staff directly supports the actual field researchers. Brian Kevin Olson, looked more like an innocent teenager than a shrewd biochemist. At fifty-one, Brian was still youthful. He was a slow talking farm boy from a rural area on the outskirts of Minneapolis, Minnesota.

"Glenda's team's on site, Ranger," said Brian. "My staff's getting the M.U.L.E.S. laboratory facility hooked up right now. Once the O.A.S.I.S. and M.A.I.D.S. units land on our planned research sites, we'll work in shifts until results force us to adjust our hours as necessary. If you ask me, Ranger, digging straight through the glacier is a lot quicker than analyzing every layer of ice and sediment as we drill down. I'm not sure the slow way is worth the effort."

"Quit yer griping, Brian," directed Elton, who knew Olson to be a whiner. "We ain't politicians out here. Bubba John's the head mutha' in charge a' this overall mission, and we're gonna do this right by the numbers. Now, what else ya' got?"

"I've task organized my staff. The Anthropology, Botany, and Zoology Sections will be in direct support of Glenda's site. The Geology and Geography Sections will in direct support of Terry's drilling operation, and can reinforce Glenda's site operations, too. The Meteorology Section will be in general support of both sites. The Eugenics and Ecology Sections will be general support of the entire operation," finished Brian, with an attitude.

Elton looked at his special polar safe watch and did some mental calculations, then dismissed his group. In the distance, Rance could hear the sounds of the arriving Blackhawk helicopter. Anticipating the arrival of Bubba Washington, Rance donned his cold weather clothing and went to welcome his friend.

Chapter Seven

"The Revolution"

The Chinese submarine was on the second leg of its patrol route when the chief scientist assigned to the vessel called for the ship's captain over the intercom system. When Captain Than Jai arrived at the operations room, Commander Park Hong was already there. Both men appeared to be excited.

"I notified Colonel Doctor Quien, Captain," advised the scientist with a look of satisfaction on his face. "We've located increasing seismic fluctuations along the plate ridge that extends from the American Highlands into the ocean. The most interesting part is that the new fluctuations begin in Antarctica and increase as they move away from the continent!"

The Captain frowned, unsure whether the news was good or bad.

"Comrade, what does this mean for the people?" asked Captain Than Jai.

"We don't know, sir," admitted the scientist. "We need more vessels along the path of the potential threat. If we had accurate maps and readings of the plates, we would know without a doubt the actual threat to our homeland."

"Aren't plates terms for western theoretical plate boundaries, Doctor?" asked Captain Than Jai critically.

"Yes, Captain, they are," advised the scientist as he continued reviewing the data. "Unlike our government's denial of tectonics, I study western research when it makes sense. Tectonics makes sense, and it seems to apply here. I'm just not sure how."

"I will request the deployment at once, but I question the ability of mere seismic readings to adequately provide the data we need to protect our homeland. Can this fault instability in Antarctica really affect the stability of our fault back in China?" asked the commander of the Revolution.

"Theoretically, yes," replied the scientist as he flipped through some reference pages."

"Doctor, I need more if we're going to convince the Premier that Antarctica may affect our geological problems at home," presented the Captain.

The scientist nodded and returned to his work. Captain Than Jai, deep in thought concerning the seismic discovery, returned to his quarters for a glass of Napoleon brandy. While the vessel moved to research the tectonic plates between Antarctica and Asia, the commander of the Revolution was more concerned about repairs that were required on the vessel's ballast tanks.

***

The Premier of the People's Republic of China was completing a meeting with his Minister of Foreign

Affairs when he was notified that the Secretary General of the United Nations was on the telephone.

"Asi Fanon Mtume! Good to hear from you, my friend," greeted Premier Hu Quichen. He knew that the Secretary General was fluent in the Chinese language. "I'm with Lee Jiang Ping and he greets you as well."

The Secretary General was in a good mood.

"Greetings, Premier Hu, and Minister Lee," returned Asi Mtume, whose accent bore just a hint of English influence. "I'm always pleased to serve the People's Republic of China."

"Can you assist us in conducting the underwater surveys we require?" asked Minister Lee Jiang Ping.

"Yes," answered Asi Mtume. "The specialized vessels you need are limited to Russia, India, Pakistan, and the major western powers. I can discreetly provide you with Pakistani support. Their survey vessels are already near the area you have indicated. I must caution you, though, that this assistance will be expensive."

"Most assuredly," acknowledged Minister Lee. "Please provide me with a point of contact, Secretary General, and I will see to the payment. China would also like to provide you with a small token of our appreciation for your expeditious handling of this matter."

"Thank you!" remarked Asi Fanon Mtume. "Any contribution would be appreciated."

"Would one hundred thousand British pounds suffice?" asked Premier Hu, who preferred to be the one to make the illegal bribe to the Secretary General.

"That is most generous, Premier Hu! You have my account number, sir," provided the Secretary General, who ended the telephone call with the usual pleasantries while his distant Chinese benefactors smiled.

***

By the fifth day of full operations, the ARK One encampment was an efficient military base. White painted electric transport vehicles and snowmobiles could be observed traveling between the scientific sites and the main camp. Military type trucks and all terrain vehicles were parked in the vehicle storage unit, along with the Blackhawk helicopter.

The petroleum site was ahead of schedule. With no requirement to conduct glacial analysis, the Site Two team was using industrial diamond and titanium alloy drills that quickly penetrated the five hundred foot deep glacier. The team had quickly penetrated the ice to drill into the crust in search of the exposed oil field.

The glacial site was behind schedule. M.A.I.D.S. units had penetrated the dense permafrost, but they had more than 200 feet to go before reaching the glacial base. At specified intervals, ice layer samples were obtained for analysis. The major problem with Site One was operational. Roger Conyers was pressuring researchers and assuming control of the field site, which was organized to function independently of the main base.

***

Bubba Washington and Elton Rance knew about the problems with Site One and they made it a point to make an unannounced visit to the glacial dig site. Roger was present at the site. There was a light snowfall, but the wind chill was lighter than usual. The two supervisors entered the O.A.S.I.S.

"Gyat dammit, Ranger," swore Bubba Washington as he removed a worn toothpick from his mouth. "What's Conyers doin' here? Don't he know Vernie likes to work independently?"

Elton shook his head, recalling how much Conyers had been absent from his assigned staff area.

"B.J., Conyers always boasts about being a damned site expert, so ah' reckon he's out here to earn some recognition back home. Look lively, Bubba John, cause here he comes."

"I see 'im, bruh. I'll try an' let you handle this problem, seein' as he's yo' chief of staff an' all."

Roger Conyers joined his supervisors. Bubba had tossed his toothpick away and was fumbling for another one in a container he had stashed away in his cargo pants. He had a taste for one of the mint ones.

"I'm directly monitoring this site," stated Roger, irritably. "Moses is operating this place like an amateur, gentlemen. She's behind schedule, and has failed to provide daily status reports, as I require. I've been attempting to streamline her operation and bring it back online, but her people are absolutely hopeless."

Bubba glanced at the white and black camouflaged O.A.S.I.S. tent as Conyers briefed them, observing its pyramid shape and weather tight construction. Each corner contained a cylindrical stabilizer. Each stabilizer contained a power unit, heater, and lavatory, respectively. On each of the three sides, there was a covered entrance where the field laboratory tables were located.

"Plus," continued Conyers. "Nobody else has been here to make sure they're meeting our planned objectives. According to Brian, neither one of you regularly supervises this site or crew! Did you know that Moses has used so many cutting blades that we're going to have a shortage of them soon? Her team's wearing out our inventory of blades on that glacier because she's moving too slowly," criticized Roger, with his hands on his hips. "She's drilled one hundred feet into the ice in two different places, and all we've detected is old ice, in a damned old place."

Roger was a critic of anything but his own ideas. Since Bubba didn't like him, Elton didn't like him much either. The comment about their lack of site supervision did not pass by either leader unnoticed.

"Look, Conyers, you need to leave the work here to Vernie," warned Bubba, who pointed his big index finger about an inch from Roger's shallow chest. He couldn't wait for Elton to give Roger a formal reprimand. "I suggest you git yo' tired ass back to the operations hootch and run Ranga's Mission Staff. Thas' your gyat damned job, not dickin' around Vernie's site disruptin' her work! Vernie's doin' a great job. If she has ta' dig up this whole fuckin' cont'nent, a mile under this here ice, she'll do it! And if some evidence is here, we're gonna' find it, even if I have to order a thousand more drilling blades! Gyat damn!"

Bubba walked away from Conyers, his quick temper getting the best of him. Elton quietly guided Roger away from the workers and Washington's considerable wrath. In the background, the repetitive pumping and lubricated grinding noises of the M.A.I.D.S. units seemed to be getting louder.

"That fellow's a real true believer," remarked Roger about Washington, shaking his head. "I don't know how you tolerate that cretin's earthy behavior."

Elton didn't know what a cretin was, but he knew it wasn't a compliment.

"R.W., Bubba John's a pisser when thangs don't go right," confided Elton, who put an arm around Conyers' bony shoulders. "But that's besides the point, son. The real problem at this heah site is you!"

Roger looked in Bubba's direction, unsure of his bargaining position with Elton Rance. He detested common men, and he believed that both Washington and Rance represented the epitome of the wretched class. He also hated being called "R.W." by Elton Rance.

"Mr. Rance, my Mission Staff's quite capable of working independently. They're like that because I run a tight ship that gets you positive results. Your problem is that Site One is a shambles. I don't think we're going to find the evidence Doctor Valenti is seeking because there's no evidence here," advised Roger, whose exposed pale long neck made him look sickly. "I've said all along that this was going to be a fruitless mission."

Rance nodded, listening intently to Roger's opinion. When the scientist was finished, Elton removed his arm from around the man's shoulders and spit a foul stream of dark tobacco juice into the trampled snow. In spite of the heating system, it was still cold enough in the O.A.S.I.S. unit that a little spittle froze at one of the corners of Rance's mouth.

"R.W., you're a nice fella," commented Elton. "But ah don't cotton to quitters and slackers, and you're both. You're one backstabbin' son of a bitch."

Conyers blanched, and then squinted hard at Rance. Roger was paler than the Antarctic snow.

"I beg your pardon?"

"Beggin' won't help, young blood. You've insulted B.J. an' me, and you've disrupted Site One's op. You're an asshole, son, and you're fired," decided Elton, followed by another spit. "Git yer shit packed, and be on the first bird outta here back to Langley. Copy?"

"No, I don't, you damned redneck bastard!" bellowed Roger, loud enough to get the attention of everyone at the site. "You can't fire me! Who the hell do you think you are?"

Elton Rance was boiling inside, willing himself not to get violent with the snotty scientist or lose his cool. Bubba quickly placed himself between them before the situation could escalate.

"Ease up, baby," advised Bubba to his angry friend. "Look, Conyers. If Ranger said somethin' to offend you, he didn't mean it. He's jus' rough 'round the edges is all."

Conyers took a step back, spreading his arms in feigned acceptance of Bubba's advice.

"Well, well, Mister Bubba John Washington! The big boss man!" sniped Roger with a sneer that made him look even more elitist. "You're both just back country trash I've avoided my entire life - until now!"

Bubba raised his hands and removed the mint toothpick from his thick lips, then cautiously moved from between the two men.

"Ranger," said Bubba with raised eyebrows. "Ah apologize for buttin' into yo' personal bizniss."

Roger took a cautious step backwards, with his hands raised in mock surrender.

By now, everyone in the O.A.S.I.S. unit was watching Rance and Conyers. Most of the team members could hear what was being said, and they knew the men were not having a friendly conversation. Bubba was the only one who suspected what would happen next. When Conyers attempted to walk away from a full confrontation, Rance boldly stepped in front of him.

"Son, you cain't walk away from them words you said," explained Elton as he removed his parka. "And ah won't let you insult me an' Bubba John an' git away with it. Ah don't care how god damned cold it is. You're asshole deep in some warm nasty shit right now! I figger that if you apologize ta' me an' Bubba John, I'll forgit what's happened since I fired you. But if'n you don't, ah'm gonna whoop yer ass like a natural born man."

Conyers was an inch taller than Rance, and about five pounds lighter. A former gentleman boxer at the St. Thomas Academy in the U.S. Virgin Islands, Roger believed he could protect himself. Without any warning, Conyers swung quickly at Elton Rance and hit him solidly on the jaw with a crisp right hook! The punch made Elton's head snap back, but he stayed on his feet. Elton swung back with lightning speed. The first punch was a jab that Conyers barely blocked, but it was the smooth loaded right that followed that landed flush on Roger's cheek and dropped him like a rock!

"One, two, it's through! Well, now, Ranger," chuckled Bubba as he rubbed his jaw. "Ah think you knocked tha' dude clean out."

Glenda and some of the others instinctively rushed to Roger's assistance. Conyers was not responding to Glenda's efforts to revive him.

"Damn fine punch fer a rich kid," remarked Elton as he worked his jaw around. "That prick musta' been aimin' to knock my teeth out, huh? Ah was hit once at the Aztec Club at Fort Benning back in seventy-nine by some drunk S.E.A.L. that felt about as bad as this. Ah lost a tooth that time and a half hour outta my life ah still ain't found yet. Roger cain't take a punch, though."

Bubba laughed and slapped Rance on the back.

"Ranger, ah about shit my pants when he punched yo' ass!" chuckled Bubba. "That took some balls of rusted iron I didn't think the chump had!"

"Copy that, Bubba John, that sure woke my ass up quickly," agreed Elton. "Ah didn't feel so bad when I had ta' hit 'im. Man's got a fine glass jaw to go with his big assed head, though. I went easy on 'im and went fer his cheek instead of that fine dental work. You know, ah' almost like 'im now that he's stood his ground."

Bubba and Elton watched as the workers helped Conyers to his feet and loaded him onto a snowmobile. Rance would recommend that Willian Penellas, the Site Processing Officer, be promoted to the position Conyers had held as the Science Officer.

***

The two ARK leaders met with Glenda Moses as soon as Roger Conyers was out of the area. Washington and Rance joined Glenda Moses at her dig site.

"Vernie, darlin'," began Elton Rance. "Roger's been fired. I want you to supervise this heah site and git the job done as you see fit."

Glenda thought about the offer, and about the way Rance had handled Conyers.

"Sure, Ranger, as long as you promise not to hit me when I argue with you!" responded Glenda. "Roger had a big problem with the slow sampling process, but the M.A.I.D.S. are working just fine. He didn't believe that glaciers are like big freezers full of well-preserved leftovers. If we continue to take samples at planned intervals in the layers and core, our chances of achieving good results improve. I know. I'm boring you, right?"

Bubba had retrieved his toothpick and occupied himself with cleaning his large teeth. Elton was also getting bored, and had begun fishing around inside his snowsuit for his chew.

"A little, Vernie, but that's okay cause it means you know what you're talkin' about," advised Bubba. "Now what's the real deal with the samples?"

"Well, the dense layers of glacial ice can provide us with material that can be used to track the path and plane of the glacier over time. If we get really lucky, we'll be able to match glacial samples and pinpoint the origins of more evidence like this," said Glenda as she tossed Elton a rectangular section of opaque ice containing the faint shape of a dragonfly imbedded in it.

"Now that's one big assed bug," observed Bubba as Elton took the ice block from Bubba's gloved hand.

"No shit, Bubba John! Can you imagine bass fishin' with a dragonfly like that?" said Elton. "I'd catch a lunker fer sure with bait like this!"

"Only if you were around a few hundred thousand years ago," advised Glenda.

"What do you mean, Vernie?" asked Bubba with a questioning look.

"If we go with accepted theories, this is a very old dragonfly, Bubba. When this guy was flying around the tropics, Antarctica was probably situated somewhere else. The thing is that I studied a similar species of dragonfly which was discovered imbedded in sedimentary rock near alleged four thousand year old ruins in Peru," wondered Glenda. "Radio carbon dating and potassium argon analysis of this will give me an idea of the time period we're dealing with at this layer level."

Both men were confused listening to Glenda.

"Look, why don't you guys let me get back to work," Glenda suggested as she placed the fossil into the evidence bag.

"Damn," swore Elton in astonishment. "Ah didn't know a damned chunk a' ice with a dead ol' bug in it could be so all fired important!"

"So, look heah, Vernie," offered Bubba. "You're sayin' the bug in tha' limestone's the same type as this bug in tha' ice?"

Glenda smiled, and put a hand on the shoulders of both men.

"Not yet, guys, but I've seen enough old bugs in both places to know that they're quite similar. Now, I need to get back to work if I'm going to complete this mission on schedule, if that's okay with you guys?"

"Hell, yes!" exclaimed Rance with a grin. "Right Bubba John?"

"You go, Vernie girl! We got yo' back!" reassured Bubba.

Elton pulled Vernie aside and leaned closer to whisper something in her ear. She could barely hear him above the sounds of the M.A.I.D.S. machines.

"Since I know how bad your temper is, Ranger, I'll answer that question later!" replied Glenda Moses, who left the two men to return to her duties.

"What was that all about, Ranger?" asked Bubba Washington.

"Nothin' much, B.J.," replied Elton. "I was askin' her what a cretin is. Do you know?"

Bubba shook his head and led his confused friend back to the all terrain vehicle, which the two men drove back encampment. By the end of the day, the glacial team had resumed their original research methods that allowed them to once again take advantage of the opportunity to examine each layer of the ancient glacier as they had been tasked to accomplish.

***

Mike Valenti attacked his work with newfound energy, amazed at how much a simple telephone call could motivate a man. With the ARK mission progressing well and Glenda in good health, Mike wondered what else could make his day any better.

"Dr. Valenti?" Alexandra's cinnamon brown smiling face peeked into his office. "Mr. Champion's here to see you."

Mike groaned. That would kill anyone's day!

"Mike, I've got a slam dunk for you!" announced Marcus Champion as he hastily entered the office. "Have you heard anything about your hard case Rance knocking out Roger Conyers down south?"

Mike had heard, but he kept that to himself.

"Well, it appears that Washington and his henchman Rance physically removed Roger from the glacial site. Can you believe that crap? And to top it off, they had a brawl in the middle of Antarctica! That's a big foul, Mike, and I want this rectified now!"

"First of all, Champ, it wasn't a brawl. Conyers hit Rance first after a few angry words, then Rance simply hit Conyers in self defense," clarified Mike. "And second, Roger insulted both Bubba and Ranger in front of witnesses. Since the dumb ass was stupid enough to hit the wrong fucking guy, I won't even discuss how he ended his career by hitting his own boss!"

"Enough!" bellowed Mark Champion in a higher voice. "You get Roger back onsite and working, or I'll take this upstairs!"

Valenti looked up from his papers, thinking about Mark's demand and threat.

"Champ, what happens in the field stays in the field," reminded Mike.

"Bullshit, Mike! I outrank everyone in this op, and I say Roger stays in the game!" demanded Mark.

"Don't come into my office and threaten me, Champ!" warned Mike Valenti as he rose from his chair. "If you want to take the issue upstairs to the Director, got for it! Until then, you back off, Marcus!"

The Chief of Special Actions stormed out of Mike's office. Since Mike had already informed Myrna Ramirez about the scuffle in Antarctica, he wasn't worried about Washington, Rance, or the ARK One mission. Mike Valenti would transfer Conyers to a more suitable research department within the Agency.

***

As the United States Navy reacted to the presence of a fully armed Chinese strategic nuclear submarine in the South American shipping lanes, an aging athletically built Asian man in a deep olive military uniform was reading a detailed message from the "Revolution." This senior officer was dressed in the uniform of the People's Liberation Navy. On top of his narrow shoulders were the gold shoulder boards of a Rear Admiral. He was the commander of the Directorate of Foreign Military Operations for the Guangzhou Military Region.

As the next higher commander of the Chinese expeditionary force in Antarctica, Admiral Long Fu Min was in constant communication with the Revolution and the expedition commander. The Premier of the People's Republic of China was concerned that the presence of the submarine could jeopardize international relations with China's valuable capitalist trading partners.

"Have you heard from the vessel commander, comrade Long Fu?" asked General Xuesen Chang, the portly regional commander. He had a Burmese cigarette in his hand that he was attempting to light.

"Yes, comrade General, Captain Than sent a routine message that the deployment of the Russian seismic pods is proceeding on schedule. Sir, I believe our use of the Iranian freighter helped us to achieve the important element of surprise. Our good fortune is a credit to your strong leadership."

General Chang exhaled a long stream of smoke from his brittle lips and slowly took a seat behind his finely tooled enamel desk. Due to an injury sustained while battling opium smugglers some years ago, the commander's back still bothered him. His tailored uniform was immaculate and contained many ribbons and medals from his distinguished campaigns.

"That will not last long, Long Fu," breathed the General. "The Iranian freighter indeed permitted us to deploy without incident or notice. I am surprised that the Americans didn't intercept our sub when she passed into Atlantic waters en route to Uruguay."

"It's ironic, comrade Long Fu, that Antarctic faults and isolated oil fields may be the keys to our country's ability to survive our mistake. That area has rarely been anything more than a passing interest to us."

"Yes, General, but I just hope Quien Lo Chen's expedition fails to find the evidence we seek. It would be better for China and the world. This geological problem cannot be our fate."

The Guangzhou Commanding Officer took a long drag on his bitter Asian cigarette. Xuesen Chang preferred American cigarettes, especially Camels.

"Fate is for Buddhist priests, Long Fu. Keep me informed. I'm going to prepare for the inevitable meeting with General Fu Wen Han. When the Americans or British contact President Zhu Le Ho, or send their warships to the area to investigate us, General Fu Wen will be worried about our precious western trade relationships and pull us out of Antarctica before our mission is complete. With all due respect to his honorable service, our commander has been in Beijing far too long lining his pockets with private corporate profits. He's a politician now."

Rear Admiral Long Fu Min saluted and left his commander to his planning. After he returned to his own tastefully furnished office, he drafted a message to be sent to the commander of the submarine. Admiral Min had to prepare for the probability that westerners would soon be interested in the Chinese presence in Antarctica.

***

Doctor Mike Valenti arrived at the highly secret National Security Agency located at Fort George G. Meade, Maryland well ahead of the scheduled two o'clock meeting. The imposing concrete super complex was clearly visible from Maryland State Road 295, which linked Baltimore to Washington, D.C. The guard checked Mike's credentials, and then instructed him to check in at the visitor center.

When he pulled into a visitor parking spot, Mike was grateful to see the C.I.A. Director's Agency car parked in the VIP section. Mike approached and waited while her armed driver assisted Ms. Ramirez in getting out of the armored car. Myrna was in good spirits and motioned for Mike to assist her.

"Mike, this Chinese expedition has definitely boosted visibility for your operation," explained Rosy Ramirez. "For the last four days, I've had to personally brief most of the Intelligence Community members about NOAH'S ARK. I briefed the President again early this morning over breakfast, and I've invited the Intelligence Community members to this meeting."

Mike was nervous about the sudden increase in exposure for the black budget operation.

"Ma'am, what's the situation? Have we determined why the Russians are in Antarctica?"

Myrna shook her head as the two of them passed through the main lobby area and into the quiet pristine hallways that led to the N.S.A. executive offices. Electronically controlled identification devices protected every steel door at each entrance. Two N.S.A. special agents in suits escorted the pair of C.I.A. officers through the glossy tile hallways to the large secure conference room and lobby area on the first floor.

"You've had blinders on, honey, but the people looking at the big picture didn't care about your operation until now," said Ramirez in a subdued tone. "And that's only because there's a lethal Chinese sub working near an unauthorized expedition on Antarctica. That means that your operation is suddenly very big news. You're moving up the intelligence food chain, but I'm not sure you're going to enjoy it. And to answer your question, I think we've dug up some good theories that I'll tell you about in a minute."

Mike thanked his boss and drifted into a safe position behind Myrna's wheelchair. She greeted the military and civilian officials that slowly crowded around her. Mike nervously nodded and shook hands as his boss introduced him to the distinguished attendees.

"You know I'm the head of the Intelligence Community, but do you know how it's organized?"

"No, ma'am," answered Mike.

"Don't worry, most intel types don't know all the ins and outs either," reassured Myrna with a supportive smile. "But you need to know for obvious reasons. The Intelligence Community consists of two staff elements and twelve intelligence agencies. But I also have other responsibilities. I have a Community Management Staff that coordinates the activities of all the community members. My other staff is the National Intelligence Council, a group of appointed officials that deal with specific intelligence priorities. After that comes the members, which are the National Security Agency, Defense Intelligence Agency, and the four military departmental intelligence agencies. There's also the National Reconnaissance Office, the Space Department's National Imagery and Mapping Agency, the Departments of State, Energy, Treasury, and Justice. Everyone here fits into one of those categories, with the exception of the National Security Advisor, who works independently for the President."

Mike nodded. The meeting had come to order.

"Good afternoon, for those of you that don't know me, I'm Frank Benavente," introduced the retired Navy admiral in his firm bass voice. "The objective of this meeting is to advise you about this Chinese boomer. This meeting is TOP SECRET."

One of the N.S.A. agents entered the conference room and handed the security advisor a note. Admiral Benavente read it, scribbled an answer on it, and handed it back to the agent before he continued.

"Sorry about the interruption," apologized the National Security Advisor. "We've learned a great deal about the identity of the other expeditionary unit. The President has been briefed, to include an update on the C.I.A. Operation, NOAH'S ARK, and he's very concerned about Antarctica. Rosy."

Myrna leaned forward in her wheelchair and comfortably addressed the prestigious group.

"Thank you, Frank. Good afternoon. Over the past few months, intelligence agencies around the world have been monitoring Chinese and Russian activities. Based on information from Britain and our own sources, the expedition team that deployed from the Iranian freighter is Chinese. There are two Russian advisors with the Chinese team. Now I'd like Admiral Ethan Berman, the Chief of Naval Operations, to provide us with a basic knowledge of the Chinese Xia class submarine. Admiral."

The Director of the C.I.A. motioned to Admiral Berman and he stood up. A descendant of one of the original Jewish families to establish roots in Lincoln, Nebraska, Ethan Berman was a foul-mouthed, cigar smoking, career sailor who graduated from the U.S.

Naval Academy in 1981. He had a nasty habit of criticizing the roles of women in the Navy and Marine Corps. He had been unpopular with the public when he adopted the ancient notion that if the Navy wanted a sailor to have a wife, they would have issued him one.

Admiral Berman punched a remote control device that activated two audio-visual screens on the long walls of the conference room. The dark room illuminated with a color photograph of a dark gray submarine with a red star on its conning tower that was moving on the surface on the ocean.

"Thank you, Rosy, and thanks for keeping your intro short there, Frank. Hell, I remember when you could jack your jaws all day long about nothing! Retirement must've calmed your ass down a little bit!"

Most of the people in the room laughed, fully aware of the rivalry between the two general officers.

"On this screen you'll see a Chinese Type 092 Xia Class nuclear ballistic missile submarine. The Xia's a submersible metal dildo with a motor, but they're effective enough. The class was first introduced in 1958, and underwent improvements in 1965, 1967, '78, '81, '83, '95, and in 2003. A Xia has a general displacement of 6,500 tons dived, and is 120 meters long. She's capable of confirmed dived speeds of 22 knots, and maintains a standard complement of 140 officers and enlisted men. This vessel is China's primary strategic naval weapon. She's armed with 12 JL-2 strategic long-range ballistic missiles that have a range 8,000 kilometers. Each missile can be armed with 200 to 300 kiloton yield nuclear warheads, to include neutron warhead devices. The Xia also is equipped with six 533 Millimeter bow tubes, and an inventory of 18 Yu-3 active and passive 205 kilogram homing torpedoes capable of reaching targets at a speed of 40 knots and a range of 15 kilometers. This vessel is extremely quiet at speeds under 10 knots. Over 10 knots, and your senile granny could hear this boomer without her hearing aid. The Xia also has advanced snorkeling capabilities that allowed her to stay submerged long enough to sneak past us in the South Atlantic. Questions?"

The admiral's eyes could bore holes through anyone who dared to look him in the eyes.

"No questions? Good," remarked the husky Chief of Naval Operations in his deep intimidating voice. "The sub on the screen is a boomer named the "Revolution." She was launched in 2004 from the legendary submarine shipyards at Xiamen. Captain Than Jai currently commands her. The exec is Commander Park Hong. Naval Intelligence has observed Captain Than Jai evolve into a first class blue water submariner. Hell, I wish he were one of my officers! He transitioned into Xia vessels after mastering Russian Kilo Class subs that China purchased from the former Soviet Union. Commander Park Hong is also a master seaman and will no doubt have his own command in the near future. He's been driving Xia vessels since his graduation from the Chinese naval academy. My vessel-tracking officer, Captain Phil Dust, will provide you with specific movement details. Captain."

Captain Dust stood and waited as the display screen changed. He took a moment to consult his notes, which he had left on his chair.

"The Revolution returned to Xiamen from her normal Yellow Sea rotation on June 5, where she was serviced and refitted. Contrary to naval show regulations, she's carrying a full complement of nuclear warheads and mines. On June 9, the vessel departed Xiamen and our satellite lost contact with her soon after she cleared Hainan through the South China Sea. On June 20, she arrived in Uruguay, where the vessel remained for four days for a naval exhibition. The Revolution departed Montevideo on the 24th. Our monitors suspected the sub would traverse Cape Horn and head back home. When the Revolution went silent in the Atlantic east of Cape Horn, the chain of command was notified. On that same date, the Revolution came to periscope depth within sight of the Iranian freighter."

Myrna Ramirez presented the N.S.A. director, Willard Ray Farrell, as the next advisor. Will confidently scanned the attendees with his soft blue eyes.

"This is an interesting case," began the N.S.A. Administrator. "At the end of May, the Iranian freighter Mashhad departed Bandar-e-Abbas, Iran, with a cargo of textiles. Her itinerary was standard, moving to Sri Lanka, Singapore, and Ho Chi Minh City before arriving in Hong Kong and unloading her cargo on the ninth of June. On June 10, the Mashhad had an early morning rendezvous with two Chinese junks and received unknown cargo prior to her afternoon departure. The Mashhad then proceeded to Manila, Brisbane, Tahiti, and into the Drake Passage where she made contact with the Revolution and deployed the Chinese expeditionary force on Antarctica."

Myrna deferred the next portion of the briefing to Theodore G. Bolte, the Deputy C.I.A. Director. He was responsible for routine Intelligence Community matters on a day-to-day basis.

"Ted Bolte, good afternoon," began the Deputy Director. His wide smile and happy eyes were charismatic. "According to human intelligence sources, the Joint Military Commander of Beijing, General Fu Wen Han, met with Russian advisors at his headquarters on June 6. They're identified as Nikolas Chin and Natasha Svetkov. Chin is a Siberian researcher with the Special Projects Division of the Ministry of Defense. Svetkov is a space and geological researcher under the Security Communications Division of the Ministry of Space. Both are members of Russian intelligence.

"On June 7, the Russian advisors met with Colonel Quien Lo Chen, the commander of the Chinese expedition, at the office of General Fu Wen Han. On June 8, the Chinese team with its Russian advisors traveled to Guangzhou, where Admiral Long Fu Min and the commander and executive officer of the Revolution briefed them. Thank you."

"Big Mack," said Myrna to the Air Force Chief of Staff.

Francis Xavier McKenna was a Class of 1979 Air Force Academy graduate. He was known in Pentagon circles as "Big Mack," which was his aviator call sign. Frank was athletically built, even though he was beginning to develop the fleshy jowls of a man of forty-seven years old. He was young for a four star general, but McKenna's distinguished service in Desert Storm, Desert Thunder, Somalia, Bosnia, and Serbia had quickly boosted him up the ranks during a time when most Air Force pilots were taking early separations to fill lucrative commercial airline positions.

"My people have developed intel on this sub and the freighter, too," began the deep voiced fighter pilot from

Dover, Delaware. "We observed the Mashhad depart the Strait of Hormuz on May 31. She was heavy in the water, fully loaded, and passed through the Palk Strait south of India on June 3. As for the Chicom sub, one of my C-130 cargo birds that has been resupplying an international research outpost in western Antarctica observed a sub matching the Chinese description snorkeling with her E.S.M. mast raised east of the Falkland Islands on June 24th."

General McKenna nodded at the National Security Advisor and took his seat. Frank Benavente stood up again and cleared his throat.

"Look, people, it's clear the Chinese are in Antarctica for no good reason. And thank God for Rosy's NOAH'S ARK expedition that we've got people on the ground there," praised the National Security Advisor. "The President wants the Chinese monitored, and he wants Rosy's people to find out what the hell they're looking for down there."

Rosy motioned for Frank to be seated. She had a concerned look on her face.

"Thanks, Frank," she began. "One of the reasons I asked Dr. Valenti to provide us with an updated estimate of the situation. I spoke with him this morning about Antarctica and China, and he has an opinion he'd like to share. Mike."

Mike stood and looked at the assembled faces. Most of them were vacant, but some of them seemed genuinely interested in listening to what he had to say.

"As you are all well aware, I sent a field team from NOAH'S ARK to search for evidence of past precessional effects based on the tectonic earthquake that occurred there. I didn't consider at the time that the problems with China's geology and Antarctica's were directly related to each other."

"I don't understand," spoke up Willard Farrell. Other attendees agreed with him.

"I've been researching the Pangaean Effect as the probable cause of the Antarctic earthquake," explained Mike. "But my calculations indicate that earthquake occurred well in advance of pangaean precursors and it did not occur in response to the pangaean time table."

"So what?" asked Frank McKenna with irritation in his voice. "Are you saying you've been wrong about your previous briefings?"

"No, General, I'm not saying I was wrong. The Pangaean Effect will occur as I've explained it," reiterated Mike. "But I've examined the data regarding this Antarctic tectonic quake and believe that something else caused it. It wasn't caused by the Pangaean Effect."

"God dammit! Spit it out!" demanded Admiral Berman in his rough authoritative voice. "I don't have all day to sit here listening to your C.I.A. bullshit presentation! If he was one of mine, Rosy, I'd rip him a fresh new wide open asshole for dancing around the point like this!"

The Admiral's reprimand caught Mike off guard. Myrna Ramirez observed this and stepped in to rescue Mike from the Chief of Naval Operations.

"Relax, Ethan," said Myrna in a soothing voice. "Dr. Valenti's attempting to explain this as simply as possible."

"Well, Rosy, he's wearing thin on my patience!" growled Admiral Berman.

Myrna nodded for Mike to continue.

"Basically, I think China's unstable fault caused the larger Antarctic earthquake," stated Mike as all eyes in the room were on him. "And I think the Antarctic quake's going to cause a tectonic one in China."

"You gotta be shitting me!" exclaimed Admiral Berman with his usual flair for profanity. "What are we playing now, ping pong?"

"Rosy, do you believe him?" asked Frank Benavente. "Is this a hunch, or do you have proof of this prediction, Doctor?"

Rosy nodded as Mike decided to defend himself this time.

"No, Mr. Benavente, I don't have proof that this earthquake will occur. It's only a prediction based on decreasing seismics coming from plates associated with China, and increasing seismic emanating from disturbed plates in Antarctica."

"You're basing this on tectonics?" asked the Director of the Defense Intelligence Agency.

"Yes. At first, I limited my thinking to Antarctica being the mother of all other tectonic regions, rather than consider that Antarctica can be just as affected by the instability in other regions. I also considered the magma problems in Hawaii and the continental United States. They are related to the Chinese instability because the Asian plate junctions interact with our west coast, too. That being the case, our magma problems and the Antarctic quake are signals that the Chinese have a super earthquake coming their way."

"Now that makes more sense, Doctor," admitted Admiral Berman as he twisted his tobacco stained lips. "It still sounds like bullshit, but it makes more sense."

"So what about the Pangaean Effect?" asked Willard Farrell.

"I'm concerned that whatever caused China's problem has accelerated the deterioration of our fragile tectonic plates and increased the progression of the Pangaean Effect. How rapidly, I don't know."

The room was quiet as everyone considered what Valenti had said. Myrna Ramirez broke the silence.

"Thank you, Doctor," she said. "Okay, everyone, let's get cracking on finding out what's causing the Chinese problem," directed Myrna. "Mike, what happens if there's a large earthquake in China?"

"Well, ma'am, if the Chinese have a big quake, more quakes and volcanic activity could be triggered in that region, our country, and Antarctica, of course."

"Of course," responded Myrna. "Since the President wants answers, I need good intelligence to provide them. Antarctica, the Chinese presence, the submarine, our geological problems, they're all pieces of a huge puzzle. Unfortunately, we need to complete enough of the puzzle to satisfy the President and members of Congress that we haven't been caught in a planetary crisis with our pants down."

"Rosy, what about the Chinese quake forecast?" asked Ted Bolte. "You want any of that disseminated to the P.R.C., or not?"

Myrna shook her head.

"Absolutely not. Any release of an earthquake prediction to the Chinese at this point would indicate to them that we might know the extent of their problems when we really don't. This information is still highly classified, and it's still a prediction. China hasn't shared the cause of their geological problems with the rest of the world, so we're not showing any of our cards yet. Now, any other questions?" Myrna asked.

There were none. Mike finally felt it was a good opportunity to take his seat.

"Good. I'd like to thank everyone for coming, and I'll be in touch with all of you within the week to provide you updates. Have a nice day."

Chapter Eight

"Asia's Fault"

The results of the examination and clinical classification of the glacial dragonfly arrived in Antarctica via secure C.I.A. communications systems one week after the sample had been received in Washington. During that time period, Site One continued working at the glacier to identify and document evidence of ancient ice, soil, flora, fauna, and insect life on Antarctica. This was the first expedition to the southern continent that attempted to use DNA technology and scientific dating techniques to link Antarctica to other regions of the world.

The Site Two team penetrated the oil field a few days after the discovery of the insect sample. Analysis of the petroleum was conducted within one week of submission to the C.I.A. During the daily morning supervisory meeting at the O-1 main building, Elton Rance was advising team leaders of the schedule changes. There was a snowstorm blowing outside that had disrupted operations for the day.

"Look heah, everybody," continued Elton Rance, who held a steaming cup of coffee in his gloved left hand. "The Doc's happy with our progress so far. Vernie and her people have a good glacial dig goin' on, and the oil drillin' team's been successful. In spite of the weather, we've accomplished our primary mission objectives already. We're goin' to continue tha' mission and await further orders from higher headquarters."

Bubba Washington interrupted the meeting and motioned for Elton to meet with him. After a few whispered words, Elton called for Glenda Moses to leave the meeting and go with Bubba, too. Glenda followed Bubba into his designated office and took a chair. The office was drafty due to a strong wind that could be heard whistling through tiny gaps in the M.U.L.E.S.

"Is there a problem, Bubba?" inquired Glenda, who chose not to remove her parka. She hadn't been warm since she arrived at Antarctica.

Washington pulled a small folder out of the iron safe that was chained to his floor and handed it to Glenda. Elton had a curious look on his face. He raised his wide brows as Glenda read the classified paperwork.

"Get this, Vernie," began Bubba as he showed her the message. "Jus' the ice alone is somethin' else! It says here that dirt we found mixed with the ice is damn near fourteen thousand years old! Gyat damn!"

Glenda frowned as she read the paperwork.

"Vernie, you listenin' to me?" asked Bubba. "I 'member in high school how they said nothing's been happening on Antarctica for millions of years, so how's the dirt in this ice only fourteen thousand years old?"

"Odonata Anisoptera Anax Junius?" whispered Glenda Moses with a look of clear surprise.

"Huh? Odanaka what?"

"Anax Junius," whispered Glenda a little louder, without correcting her boss. She lifted the photograph and examined it. "No shit! It looks like Dim's theories were right all along."

Bubba looked intently at Glenda, drawing a complete blank when he heard the scientific terms again. This time the big man waited, agitated as the seconds passed into minutes. Glenda finally took a break from her reading. She had a satisfied smile on her face.

"Bubba, at first I suspected that the new addition to your tackle box was a previously undocumented specimen dating back approximately one million years ago. Thanks to the Smithsonian's collection of insects, our dragonfly has been adequately classified as Anax Junius. That particular insect still exists today, and the one in our sample shouldn't have been in this glacier if Antarctica has been located at the South Pole for millions of years. Our Green Darner dragonfly is a mystery."

Bubba shook his head, and then pointed an open hand at Glenda as he formed his words.

"So the bug we found ain't new, and it's called the Green Darner? Whas' up, Vernie? Is this bug hot shit on a silver platter or cold shit on a paper plate?"

Glenda laughed in spite of herself. She placed the information back in the classified envelope.

"Bubba, you make work so enjoyable that I almost wish you would've been my professor back at the Tuskegee Institute!"

Bubba blushed and nodded his head in acceptance of her compliment.

"Awright, Vernie, so what's the deal? Is this here green bug the reason why you're smilin' at me, or are you finally learnin' to appreciate my good looks?"

"Sorry, Bubba, but it's the Green Darner that has me smiling. The soil and that dragonfly have been carbon dated to be approximately fourteen thousand years old. That makes this insect very hot shit on a sterling silver platter. It also makes a hell of a lot of thick science books worthless paper!"

Bubba shrugged as he shifted his toothpick from one corner of his mouth to the other.

"How's that?"

"The Green Darner is native to tropical and temperate climates around the world, Bubba. You know, places roughly between Argentina and Canada," explained Glenda. "That means that we've found evidence supporting Dr. Valenti's theory that Antarctica was in a temperate location around fourteen thousand years ago. Current theory argues that Antarctica drifted to the South Pole over a 100 million year time frame that ended at least a million years ago. Our dragonfly sample has verified for us that Antarctica was not at the southern pole when the Pangaean Effect occurred."

"Gyat damn, Vernie. This must be big!"

"It is, Agent Washington, and we may just get a big bonus for this one," remarked Glenda.

After Glenda departed, Bubba Washington eagerly got on the satellite telephone and contacted Elton Rance. In spite of the incredible distance between Antarctica and the C.I.A. headquarters, the digital satellite monitors and cameras made the meeting seem like participants were only a block away from each other.

"Whas' up, boss?" asked Bubba with a grin.

Mike grinned back, "The temperatures, Bubba. It's hotter than the Persian Gulf up here! All this urban concrete's making Langley feel like an oven today."

"Thanks, Doc, that really makes us feel a lot better, seein' as it's fuckin' dark every day and gyat damn cold all the time down heah!" exclaimed Bubba.

"Yeah, me an' Bubba John's been workin' in fuckin' temps that make me wish fer a three week ranger exercise in the Georgia swamps!" added Elton Rance.

"Well, thank God you're not up here with me sitting in on all of these meetings. Things are developing fast up here while you guys are on your cool continental vacation!" teased Mike.

Bubba Washington had already popped a new toothpick in his mouth and sat way back in his chair to relax. Elton was leaning forward in his chair gathering a chew from a new bag of Red Man brand chewing tobacco. Both men laughed at Mike's description of their duty tour as a continental vacation.

"You coulda' picked us a better continent, Doc!" said Elton with a stuffed mouth.

"Awright, Doc, so fill us in on the happenins," urged Bubba as he chuckled.

Mike explained the general situation involving the Chinese and the Russians, to include the expedition, the submarine, and the importance of keeping their outpost area secure. He continued into the report about the Antarctic field samples.

"I'm excited about your findings, gentlemen! The petroleum samples were analyzed with fascinating results. The magma under that oil field is heating the petroleum without tainting it, which indicates that magma probably isn't the cause of the tainted Chinese oil. And seismic analysis indicates that China may be in Antarctica to determine if they'll experience another earthquake. The dragonfly was a bonus for substantiating the Pangaean Effect."

"You don't say," remarked Elton. "So our mission was worth the effort?"

"Definitely! The information about the dragonfly alone would've marked the trip as a success for our operation," continued Mike, who had lit a cigarette. "You've proven that the Pangaean Effect occurred fourteen thousand years ago! Bubba, I need you here to get your ARK teams humping. We've got some new leads to investigate. Return to Langley on the next lift."

"Roger that, boss," acknowledged Bubba with a snap of his chin.

"Mr. Rance," continued Mike. "Prepare ARK One to extract from your station on July 25 as planned. If China experiences a tectonic quake, chances are another one will occur in Antarctica. You'll transfer control of the base to the US Geological Survey. They'll continue the seismic research while ARK One serves as the op's reserve and gets some much needed rest."

Elton Rance was grinning from ear to ear.

"You say rest? Copy that, Doc! How 'bout that, Bubba John? With a big un possibly coming, it's time for ARK One to go wheels up!"

"You got that right, dog!" agreed Bubba.

The two men slapped each other's hands and rejoiced over their good fortune to leave Antarctica.

"Ah need ta' be back home!" responded Elton Rance. "Ah don't like not bein' on solid ground!"

Bubba belched loud enough for Mike to hear it over the satellite link. "No shit, Doc. Heah we are sitting on the ass end of the world, and Oriale Washington's fav'rit chile's on the puckering part of tha' crack!"

"Airborne, brother Bubba!" agreed Ranger Rance while Mike laughed at the comment.

After a brief discussion about base logistics and resupply problems, Mike Valenti ended the video teleconference. When Elton Rance told his group about their confirmed extraction, they cheered and celebrated the good news in the warm day room.

***

On the morning of July 22, the President of the United States was enjoying a light breakfast with his wife, Rebecca Charlene O'Callaghan Fairchild, when his secretary's formal voice summoned him over the intercom. The bright sunlight invading the historic windows highlighted the majestic furnishings and style of the Oval Office.

"Mr. President, Frank Benavente is on line one for you, sir," said Edith Madison, the secretary. "Shall I take a message?"

"Thank you, Edith, I'll take the call," replied Alexander Montgomery Fairchild with a slight touch of irritation in his voice. He had just completed a long morning telephone call with Myrna Ramirez.

Rebecca Fairchild gathered the morning newspapers and left to get the children ready for the rigors of the day. A native of Reading, Pennsylvania, Becky Fairchild always had a variety of newspapers from her home state delivered to the White House every day. She was wrapped in a white linen robe that revealed a bit of her pale legs as she walked. The President watched as his slim beautiful wife glided out of the Oval Office.

"Good morning, Frank," greeted the President. "Sure, come right over and brief me. I've got a light agenda today - a few visitors and awards to distribute. Fine, I'll see you in half an hour."

Rebecca Fairchild had crossed her shapely freckled legs and was now kicking against the beak of the wooden eagle on the front of the desk. She was not pleased. Alex tried in vain to ignore her icy stare.

"Monty," began Rebecca. "You promised Kathleen that you'd spend time with her in the pool, and both boys have invited friends over for a pool party."

Alex looked into his wife's proud green eyes and lied, "This will be quick, Charly. Frank's coming over to brief me, then I'll be right down."

Rebecca knew he was lying when he called her by her pet name, but it had always melted her heart.

"Fine, Monty, but forget getting close to me for a month if you let the kids down. Do you understand?" said Rebecca with a stare that made the President forget he was the most powerful leader in the world.

Alex Fairchild watched his wife leave the Oval Office. At forty, Becky was six years younger than he was and she had become more alluring every year. After his meeting with the National Security Advisor, Alex Fairchild joined his wife and children at the White House outdoor swimming pool.

***

That evening, in the town of Hailar, China, a major earthquake occurred that caused structural damage and significant casualties to the isolated mining area of 250,000 residents. The effects of the earthquake were also felt in Russia, North Korea, South Korea, and Japan. The geological event began with deep subsurface tremors that caused panic in Chinese and Russian residents living within 500 miles of the devastated city.

In a matter of hours, China's slow communications system made notifications to government leaders and departments. By morning, Chinese military and civil units were onsite to assist local authorities in damage assessment and rescue operations. As Chinese authorities determined the extent of the devastation, governments around the world were beginning to receive the news of the huge earthquake.

***

On the night of the earthquake, Captain Than Jai, the commander of the Revolution, was fighting boredom by playing a challenging game of chess with his executive officer. The seismic monitoring was proceeding on schedule and had become routine. When the first major underwater tremors occurred, the slow moving vessel didn't show any physical signs of knowing it. The submarine's keenly tuned internal and external sensors did detect the tremors as they rolled out of Antarctica. One of the technical officers knocked on the commander's door.

"Lieutenant Kwai, sir!" announced the junior officer in response to his commander's loud voice.

The captain swore under his breath, irritated by the interruption when he was contemplating a brilliant entrapment of Hong's knight. When he opened his watertight door, the lieutenant was visibly excited.

"Sir, we just detected an unusual tremor in the fault area, magnitude 2 on the Richter Scale," reported the nervous submariner as he handed his commander a computer report. "The tremor originated in Asia."

The captain read the report while the Executive Officer made his next move. Another officer appeared.

"Captain, one of Colonel Quien Lo Chen's liaison officers would like us to contact the colonel and report the tremors at once," reported the ensign.

The captain nodded and continued reading. His subordinates waited patiently. Since it was dark on the surface and there had been no indication that enemy vessels were in the area, Captain Than was compelled by his classified orders to report the tremors at once.

"Cease monitoring activities!" ordered the captain. "Initiate active sonar! Go to periscope depth. Establish contact with Foreign Military Operations, contact Colonel Doctor Quien Lo Chen, and retrieve routine message traffic. Make our ascent by the book, Park, and be prepared to dive on my order. Carry on!"

"Aye, sir," acknowledged Commander Park Hong as he slid past his commander. The two junior officers saluted and followed the X.O.

Captain Than Jai left his quarters and decided to monitor activities in communications and the main control room.

"Captain, sonar, new contact bearing 2-2-0, range fourteen thousand meters, American S.S.N., Seawolf Class," announced the sonar officer.

"I expected that," remarked the captain to his crew. "X.O.?"

"Mast deployed, sir," stated Commander Park. "Ready for communications, sir."

"Initiate communications," ordered the captain. "Send messages one and two. Advise receipt of all transmissions."

"Transmissions complete, sir," advised Mr. Park. "Messages received."

Commander Than Jai waited for the communications officer to provide him with the messages.

"X.O., return us to our patrol route," directed the captain.

"Aye, sir," acknowledged Park Hong. "What about the American attack submarine, sir?"

The captain casually waved at the air.

"I have no concern with the Americans right now, Commander Park. Neither should you. We are in international waters on scientific business."

As the Revolution returned to her patrol route and research depth, Captain Than Jai reached for the ship's intercom and addressed the crew. He reported the tragic news from Peking in which thousands were believed to be dead or missing as a result of the massive earthquake. A man of extreme patience and calm, Commander Than completed his announcements, turned his vessel over to the X.O., and returned to his cabin to grieve in private.

***

On board the USS Jimmy Carter, a Seawolf class attack submarine based out of Groton, Connecticut, Captain Elroy Logan was filled with pride in knowing that his advanced attack submarine had crept into killing distance of the Xia class boat without being detected. They had arrived in the Xia's patrol area a day earlier and had easily located her.

"Your orders, sir?" requested Commander Willis, the Executive Officer.

"Half ahead, Cain," ordered Elroy Logan. "Four zero revolutions, five down, thirty meters."

The X.O. echoed the commander's orders as the submarine dove deeper into the South Atlantic. The dim greenish black environment of radar, sonar, and computer screens made the interior of the vessel appear more like a space ship than a naval one.

"Down all masts, steer 2-1-0," announced the captain. "Sonar, maintain distance from target at three thousand yards. She's not hiding her activities, so switch to passive array. She didn't blink an eye when we pinged her with our sonar, but she shit her pants when her sensors hit on the tremors."

The captain departed for the wardroom with messages in hand while the Jimmy Carter maintained vigil on the Revolution. By the time the tremors were subsiding, Washington was already receiving the news from his vessel that increasing earthquakes had occurred in the South Atlantic.

***

By the time the C.I.A. Director's telephone rang at her bedside, every news and information agency in the world had been notified about the earthquake. Empowered with the ability to detect large earthquakes from satellites in space, the U.S. government received notification more rapidly than any other country. The call Myrna Ramirez received on her classified line less than an hour after the event was more informative. By the time she hung up the telephone, Dr. Ramirez knew that the Chinese earthquake was the worst in history since the development of the Richter scale in 1935. Myrna decided to travel to her office, where she cleared her schedule and arranged several new meetings for the day. A meeting with Dr. Valenti was first on her crowded agenda.

***

When Mike Valenti entered Myrna's lavish office, he could tell by the lack of makeup and her tired eyes that she'd had as long a night as he had. Mike had received the earthquake notification from several public and classified sources. He went to his office immediately to obtain more data about the Chinese disaster. He was barely functioning on three hours sleep. As he sat down, Myrna rubbed her tired eyes and sighed.

"Mike, I want you to know that I've really been hoping that your opinions and predictions would be completely incorrect," she admitted. "Now, I'm a very reluctant believer in this Pangaean thing. Since I was last notified, U.S.G.S. has been reporting that this quake was the worst on record. We received reports from the sub monitoring the Revolution that they detected tremors moving away from Antarctica in the same time frame."

"A magnitude 8.9 on the Richter scale, said Mike. "This quake actually equals the largest on record that occurred in Chile in 1960. Any other reports?"

Myrna groaned and reached for the coffee pot on the credenza behind her desk. She offered Mike a cup, which he eagerly accepted. Both of them were exhausted.

"Oh yeah, Mike. Every agency with any seismic or surface scanning capability has notified us of the Chinese earthquake," admitted Myrna with a partial smile. "My people are conducting global terrestrial intelligence analysis as we speak. N.S.A. is doing its part, too. The National Imagery and Mapping Agency is going to have something for me by nine."

Myrna savored the taste of the coffee. Some of the sharpness had returned to her tired eyes.

"At least we're busy now," said Mike.

"Honey, we're going to have a long day," Myrna provided. "We can't wait for American or U.N. agencies to respond to China. I'm going to get U.S.G.S. to send an emergency assistance team to Hailar and I want you to send an ARK team with them using your U.S.G.S. cover. We also received notification through NATO that the French have verified the loss of a destroyer and a commercial fishing vessel in the waters off Iles Kerguelen to an unforecasted tsunami at approximately the same time as the Chinese earthquake. Think this is also related to China?"

"An oceanic earthquake would cause a tidal wave like that. If the plate shifted in Antarctica and caused the tectonic quake in China, then every plate in the world is unstable right now," thought Mike out loud."

"Plus," continued Myrna with a sigh. "The Brits have reported that a villager in the Solomon Islands was killed after he fell into a fresh pool of lava."

"I read that one when it arrived over the news service," advised Mike. "The Solomons are within the same unstable tectonic network as the Hawaiian Islands. Hawaii's volcanoes are close to erupting, so this is bad."

Myrna was obviously alert and focused on the events of the day.

"Find out what you can, Mike," she ordered. "I know you've been busy. You need a number two in that vacant spot in NOAH'S ARK. Any thoughts?"

Mike knew the person he wanted as his scientific partner on NOAH'S ARK. He needed someone with vision and experience. He needed someone he could trust and with whom he could share his controversial ideas without being viewed as a maverick.

"Evan Leeper, Myrna," replied Mike. "He's currently working with the Space Department."

Myrna smiled, knowing something Mike obviously didn't know.

"I know him, Mike," Myrna said as she nodded her head. "He's a top notch space analyst and aerospace manager with a lot of astronomical experience, but will he be of service to NOAH'S ARK?"

"Yes, ma'am," replied Mike after a swallow of his coffee. "Evan's a big fan of the Pangaean Effect! I trust him with my life, and he knows more than I do about the long-term methods of dealing with this situation. He and I used to discuss all my crazy theories when we were in college together!"

Myrna was puzzled, "Hey, what long term methods? I hope they don't conflict with any of my other programs."

"Ma'am, I'll advise you about those when you have more time and we're prepared for the fallout."

Myrna thanked Mike for his early morning appearance and sent him on his way. Located on a shelf in Mike's office, there was a thick dusty NOAH'S ARK binder that contained the guidelines for expansion into the C.I.A. level operation. After removing the notebook from the shelf, Mike Valenti opened it and began to read about agency level intelligence operations.

***

At the White House, President Alexander Fairchild was silently enduring the prospect of lifelong celibacy after a series of phone calls from other national leaders had pulled him away from time with his children. Four hours had passed and Edith Madison was still transferring calls to him.

"God dammit! Who's on the phone now?" demanded the President.

"I apologize again, sir," soothed Edith in her unwavering tone. She was happy to be on overtime. "And please watch your language, Mr. President. There are mothers, children, and the press out there who expect you to be a role model."

The President rolled his eyes as she reminded him of his public persona.

"The Prime Minister of Australia is on line three," she continued. "I placed him on hold, sir."

"Thank you, Edith. Hey, can you order me something from the restaurant? I'm starving. Hello?" the President asked as he hung up on Edith and resumed his conversation with the President of Panama. "President Diaz? Sorry about that, sir. You were saying?"

Alex Fairchild listened to the Panamanian president's concerns about the increasing tremors his country had experienced since the Asian earthquake. Edith brought him a cheese steak sub and French fries for dinner. After a lengthy lecture, the Central American chief executive finally ended his conversation.

"Thank you, sir. I'll keep you informed," offered the President as he took a bite of his sandwich and chewed. "My Secretary of State, Dan Tokuhisa, will be contacting you."

After the call with the Panamanian president, Alex Fairchild punched the intercom button.

"Edith, I want the entire NSC here A.S.A.P.," directed the President with a mouth full of food. "Invite the head of the U.S.G.S., too! Hey, and make sure Rosy brings Dr. Valenti along, too!"

The President's intercom buzzed again. This time Edith notified him that the President of France was on hold to speak with him. Monty Fairchild picked up a stress doll that looked like George Washington and tossed it across the room in frustration.

"What the hell else can go wrong today?" asked the President to himself as he picked up the telephone. "President LeSerge?"

President Fairchild listened as the French leader explained in detail how his scientists were worried about the cause of the tidal wave that occurred down near Antarctica at Iles Kerguelen. Alex Fairchild jotted down some notes while President LeSerge was speaking. The President promised American assistance and ended the conversation. He realized that his entire day had revolved around planetary tragedies.

"Edith!" yelled Alex Fairchild in the direction of his secretary's closed office door. "Edith!"

The matronly woman casually entered the Oval Office door to see what her irate boss wanted.

"Yes, Mr. President?"

Alex hated it when she said his title in such a calm way. That irritated him more!

"Edith, no more calls from anyone unless there's a nuclear attack!" he ordered through big rude bites of his sandwich. "I'm going to the pool, dammit! When the NSC arrives, seat them in the Roosevelt Room until I'm finished at the pool!"

"Yes, sir," Edith acknowledged as the President stormed out of his private doorway.

Like any fine executive secretary, Mrs. Madison promptly summoned a staffer and directed him to make all the necessary coordinating telephone calls to the members of the National Security Council. By five o'clock that afternoon, the entire National Security Council was present in the Roosevelt Room.

Chapter Nine

“Recognition”

By the time most of the National Security Council was present in the Roosevelt Room for the meeting with the President, Mike Valenti had been waiting there long enough to overcome the awe of being in the same room with national treasures he had only seen in text books or on television. When retired Rear Admiral Frank Benavente entered the famous room, everyone knew the meeting was about to take place. It was eight o’clock at night.

“The President will be here shortly, ladies and gentlemen,” announced Francisco Benavente as he walked into the room from the direction of the Oval Office. The National Security Advisor was very formal when he was conducting his official duties. “Mr. Vice President, is everyone present?”

The Vice President, Levan Antonio Salazar-Balart, was a Cuban American from Miami, Florida. His brown skin, handsome features, and elegant Latin style had a powerful influence on the outcome of the last national election. His ability to identify with the black community and their concerns helped build a cultural bridge between the nation's two major minority groups.

"Yes, Mr. Benavente," replied the Vice President formally. "I'll get the President."

President Fairchild made his usual entrance after the Vice President announced him. Everyone took a seat after the President was seated and the meeting came to order. The President's Weimaraner dog loped into the room behind him and found a place to lie down under the President's chair.

"I've called you all together because I'm worried about the Chinese earthquake. Since this terrible tragedy occurred, I've had several telephone calls from the Secretary General of the United Nations, and the leaders of Russia, China, Great Britain, Japan, North Korea, South Korea, Laos, Burma, India, Australia, France, and Panama," detailed the President at length. "In essence, every country I mentioned except the Brits experienced some effects of that huge earthquake. I spent half the afternoon denying that a large Asian earthquake could be related to all of the nations involved. By the time I finished on the fucking telephone, I realized that my C.I.A. chief's information briefings about this pangaean thing aren't total bullshit after all! So, I've asked you all here to sort this thing out and find some answers!"

Everyone sitting at the long table remained silent.

"You know, George," began the President as he held up a stack of paper and tossed it across the table at the wrinkled Chief Geologist. "You reported in your last quarterly intelligence report that the unstable sub-fault in the area of Hailar was not a threat to the region. This earthquake traversed half the whole damned world and caused significant damage!"

"Mr. President, I provided what I considered to be an accurate analysis," defended George in his high Texan voice. "That sub-fault was not unstable when I wrote that intelligence summary. Something must have happened to it!"

"Your agency was responsible for accurate geological intelligence analysis," explained Alex Fairchild, who was clearly irritated. His voice showed more of a Massachusetts accent when he was mad, and everyone present knew the President was mad. "What's that in your mouth, George?"

"Copenhagen, sir," replied the man with the weathered face and brittle hands. "Sorry."

"Dammit, George, that report you gave me was wrong! Now take that snuff out of your mouth!"

George removed his dip from his mouth and nervously spit it into his full coffee cup.

"Mr. President," continued Dr. Donaldson. "I stand by my recommendation. This was just a bad earthquake."

"Bad earthquake? The Northridge earthquake was a bad quake! This was catastrophic! Look, George, I appointed you as Chief Geologist as a favor to your old man," explained Alex Fairchild, who face was purple with rage. "But if this happens again, I'll fire you before you can dial your daddy's phone number and scream for help! Is that clear?"

"Yes sir, Mr. President," acknowledged George. He was visibly shaken by the reprimand.

"And in the future, don't come into any Executive Branch meeting again in cowboy boots with a chew in your mouth. You're a political appointee, not some goat roper without an education!"

"Yes, Mr. President."

The President averted his hostile eyes from the shocked Chief Geologist and picked up the detailed seating list. Mike was hoping President Fairchild would not be so confrontational with him.

"Rosy, Dr. Valenti provided the information about the earthquake," reasoned Alex Fairchild as he attempted to calm down. "So let him begin first."

Dr. Michael Valenti partially raised his hand and began to stand until the President motioned for him to remain seated. Mike still felt a need to identify himself.

"Doctor Michael J. Valenti, Mr. President," introduced Mike with unintentional nervousness in his voice. He noticed that he smelled like cigarettes. Smoking was a career killing habit in Washington.

"I remember, son," remarked the President as he placed the list of attendees on the perfectly polished mahogany table. "Your prediction of the Chinese earthquake caught a lot of people, including me, off guard. Unless you're a psychic or something, your theories are holding up when everyone else is dropping the ball on this."

Mike didn't nod his head. He just listened.

"But this whole pangaean thing's going to take time to settle into everyone's heads. It's not natural to think the end of the world's coming, especially when you've already said that something else has caused this Chinese geological problem. I need you to answer some concerns we have."

"That's no problem, sir," remarked Mike Valenti with a confident smile.

"There are always problems, Michael. There are ethical, political, even religious issues associated with considering our current problems and the end time you've called the Pangaean Effect. That's why we're going to discuss our national security from the viewpoint of the Pangaean Effect."

"Monty, this whole notion of an end of the world as we know it occurring by 2025 is inconceivable to me," noted the Vice President critically. "What if young Valenti's wrong and nothing happens?"

"I'm not wrong, Mr. Vice President," replied Mike, who was irritated by the Vice President's reference to his age. "If the Pangaean Effect wasn't going to happen, I'd be sitting in front of a telescope."

"You realize nobody's been right yet about the Apocalypse in over two thousand years?" muttered Levan Salazar as his fingers played with the copper colored band on the cigar.

Mike burned a hole into the Vice President's eyes as Myrna Ramirez came to his political rescue. She was the picture of tranquility in a sea of criticism. Levan Salazar stared right back at him, causing Mike to avert his eyes and remember that he was the peon in the room.

"Mr. President, Mr. Vice President, ladies and gentlemen," soothed the C.I.A. Director. "Dr. Valenti is fully qualified as an international expert on astronomy, geology, physics, and the Pangaean Effect. He coined that term to represent the extensive natural phenomena that encompass our planet's wide-ranging geo-physical problems. You see, Dr. Valenti is a reputable published scientist who has almost single-handedly argued against accepted scientific theories in the ruthless pursuit of world survival and our national security."

"Impressive" remarked the President as he stared at Dr. Valenti.

The Vice President raised a brow, surprised that the man seated next to the C.I.A. Director was so smart.

"Yes, Mr. President," continued Myrna. "The C.I.A. always hires the best and the brightest. When Mike first came into our family, I thought the Pangaean Effect was a millennium hoax. I've learned since then that Dr. Valenti's challenging theories are based on sound hypotheses and accurate calculations. His most recent calculations also include the accurate identification of the main Asian fault as a super-fault that is linked to our national problems. Doctor."

Every eye in the room was on Dr. Valenti as he stood and began to make his presentation.

"Mr. President, I'm not predicting the end of the world, or the apocalypse," replied Mike with a confident smile. "And I don't know exactly why the Asian fault became unstable so rapidly. I do believe that the first pangaean signal occurred back in 1975 when the star in our solar system moved slightly within our galaxy as a result of normal galactic rotation. On May 17th of 2000, the planets in our solar system were aligned in a rare 19.5 Degree span of ecliptic longitude. That event started the countdown to the Pangaean Effect.

"The Pangaean Effect will not mark the end of mankind. In fact, modern man survived the last two precessional events well enough to arrive to our current human status where we as a species are contemplating expanding mankind to the stars utilizing space travel, exploration, and colonization.

"Unlike so called prophets and oracles who claim to see the future, I don't. I have investigated the past, which includes our astronomical and geological history, natural galactic cycles, and the cycles of our solar system. Any fool can dream of a disastrous future, but only a madman will turn a blind eye to the facts of our past. Since we're all educated beings of thought and action, each of us has an important responsibility to prepare the people of our nation and the members of the international community for the Pangaean Effect. By 2025, the event will occur whether you believe it or not. I know it, and the ancient humans of our world knew it."

"You know, Doctor, I find this whole Pangaean thing unsettling," spoke up the Vice President. "For the record, I am a religious man - a Roman Catholic in fact. You're telling me that in twenty-four years, the shit hits the fan whether we like it or not? And you're saying we can't do anything about it? We have emergency agencies in place, fantastic technology, and one hell of a developing space program, so why do we need to prepare anymore for a POTENTIAL catastrophe? There will always be earthquakes and floods, even if they don't last for forty days or forty nights."

More NSC members laughed at the Vice President's attempt to demean Dr. Valenti and his presentation of the Pangaean Effect. Mike stood and began to walk around the group of attendees. As his anger mounted, he forgot he was in a room with the President of the United States.

"History tells us that after the last Pangaean Effect in approximately 13,000 B.C., it took mankind approximately 5,000 years to build new civilizations. Modern man, H. Sapiens Sapiens, appeared on Earth approximately 90,000 years ago. There were two pangaean events that occurred since that time frame at a span or approximately 25,920 years each. And in the past 90,000 years, mankind has been bounced back to the Stone Age each time and survived. Like she has always done in the past, our Earth will provide nature and mankind with the means to survive the Pangaean Effect."

"Now what the hell does that mean?" asked Derrick Jones, the skeptical Secretary of the Treasury. His bald head and goatee made him look more like a rhythm and blues singer than a presidential cabinet member. "Are we dealing with science fiction now?"

"On the contrary, sir," replied Mike quickly. "Darwin proved well over a century ago that evolution is a scientific fact, but since the last Pangaean Effect there has been no active evolution in nature. In spite of skeptics and hard line religious critics, the gentle dance our planet performs in our solar system and galaxy is not a dance she does alone. Our galaxy has preordained Earth's choreographed routine for hundreds of thousands of years into the future. When astronomical cycles dictate, our Earth will signal a time for evolution that will prepare all life forms well in advance of the Pangaean Effect. It is up to us to unselfishly prepare mankind for that time in order to better insure humanity's recovery, prosperity, and readjustment."

"Damn," swore the Secretary of Defense, Andrea Mangone. The retired Army general had a smile on her face. "It's going to be difficult preparing to survive five thousand years of global catastrophe. Its hard enough to pay my bills every two weeks!"

There was nervous laughter in the room.

"Doctor, how do you propose we begin planning for such a catastrophe? This could cost our country millions," noted Nicholas Wasniewski, the Assistant for Economic Policy.

"The cost would be more in the trillions of dollars, Mr. Wasniewski, but our survival is priceless. Money will be a moot point after 2025," explained Mike. "Funding will be necessary from a practical point of view, but gold reserves will be worthless when the world shifts it's axis. Difficult decisions have to be made regarding the colonization of Mars, the creation of nationally stocked and protected population centers, and the formation of a unified world alliance to accomplish simple human survival needs. Also, the children of evolution will need to be identified and secured. We must all realize that trivial things such as currency and national identity will mean little unless the United States propels itself to the stars and establishes itself out there."

Mike pointed his hands over his head towards the heavens as he finished speaking. None of the N.S.C. members was smiling now. The C.I.A. Director rapidly scribbled some notes as she listened.

The room was quiet as everyone silently digested the grim world forecast presented by Dr. Valenti. Mike remained standing, prepared to handle any other challenges to his theory.

General James Beckwourth Vann, who was named after the famous frontier mountain man, James Beckwourth, was the Chairman of the Joint Chiefs of Staff. General Vann was known throughout political circles as a tough authoritarian.

"What kind of changes in human habitat are you talking about after the Pangaean Effect strikes, Doctor?" asked the General.

"The most extreme changes you can imagine, General Vann," answered Mike Valenti in a calm gentle tone. "After regional floods, tsunamis, volcanoes, years of severe earthquakes, and fatal fluctuations in temperature and climate, mankind will be subjected to a toxic atmosphere, polluted or no fresh water, famine, disease, and limited resources. The modern conveniences of civilization, such as electricity, plumbing, government services and security would disappear. Until the tectonic plates stabilize again after several years, the entire planet's landmasses could shift, break, or collide in many different ways."

General Vann nodded, understanding the magnitude of the changes in habitat that would occur. He looked around the room at the other NSC members.

"Thank you, Doctor. I know you've been under the gun since you opened your mouth, but I know from your background that you're a very competent commissioned officer in the Air National Guard," noted General Vann. "Tell me something. If you were advising me, what would you recommend that I do?"

"General, I'd advise you to initiate a long term plan that would disperse domestic military and air forces to temporary bases around the country in preparation for spontaneous pangaean events. I'd advise you to keep naval forces on alert and at sea in greater numbers in order to respond to catastrophes," suggested Mike Valenti. "I'd advise you to prepare the Armed Forces for emergency domestic actions to supplement state and local law enforcement agencies which will have terrible problems maintaining order in the wake of the chaos and devastation that the Pangaean Effect will cause. Finally, I'll advise you to expand the military beyond World War II levels and be prepared to seize any and all natural necessary natural resources from weaker nations that we'll need to stock our survival centers."

"I appreciate that, Captain Valenti," remarked General Vann with a satisfied smile. "I may not be a scientist, Mr. President, but I know how to look a man in his eyes and measure him. This gentleman's put his ass on the line to brief us on some bizarre subjects, and I for one believe him. Doctor, I'm going to consider your recommendations, and I will support you in any way that I am authorized to do."

"Thank you, sir," acknowledged Mike Valenti.

The Attorney General shook his head as he considered what he had heard during the entire briefing.

"I'm trying to imagine the multitude of legal and civil rights issues we're going to face, Doctor," commented Tell Summers. He was a genuine Wyoming cowboy. "This sounds like some kinda' sci-fi action movie, except I'm not hearing about any heroes that will save humanity."

"There will be many heroes in the years to come, sir," answered Dr. Valenti. "I hope that the first ones are the members of government seated in this room."

After the members of the National Security Council were challenged by President Fairchild to discuss the information Dr. Valenti had presented, the invited guests were asked to leave the Roosevelt Room. While he waited in the hall, Mike Valenti could hear shouts and heated disagreements coming from the historic meeting area.

***

After supervising the expulsion of an old political enemy from the Kremlin, the President of the Russian Federation joined his Premier and his two deputies in the royal conference chambers once frequented by Russian tsars. When President Vasil'yevich Tomskaya entered the ornate conference center, an aide immediately handed him a large glass of Auslese.

"Another long day, Vasil'yevich, yes?" greeted the Head of Government, Grigoriy Gaydar. He was already intoxicated drinking only the best Russian vodka.

"That's true, Grigoriy. As Premier, you know how long our days can be. What's the problem?" asked the president after taking a gulp of his wine.

The Premier of Russia motioned for one of the Vice Premiers to close the doors to the chamber.

"We have an opportunity to make a great deal of money and bolster our reputation with the Americans," provided the Premier with heavy vodka breath.

"Nuclear weapons again?" asked Vasil'yevich in a bored voice. "We've disposed of them all."

"No, Vasil'yevich, not nuclear weapons or fuel," responded Grigoriy enthusiastically. "We need to sell the information about the Chinese nuclear test."

"That's rubbish! The Americans must know about that! They're not stupid!" rebuked the Russian leader. "How do you know this?"

"The Americans are interested in knowing why the Chinese are in Antarctica," explained Yuliy Matviyenko, the Vice Premier in charge of International Relations. He was just beginning to drink his first glass of vodka. "And we have that information. The Chinese weapon was not of a yield large enough to be detected by the Americans, and the American intelligence network in China is very limited. According to my sources from the U.N., India and Thailand, the American State Department has been quietly attempting to learn more."

"It's true, President Tomskaya," added Aleksandr Yefimovich, the Vice Premier in Charge of Domestic Relations. "This information is worth millions!"

President Tomskaya looked at each man, and then considered the opportunities.

"Would we need the authorization of the Duma?" he asked his advisors.

"No, unless you want to share in the profits, Vasil'yevich!" answered Premier Gaydar with a laugh. "What do you say? Do I have your approval?"

"Yes, but approach the Americans personally," agreed the Russian leader slowly. "Contact their Secretary of State directly. He's an honorable man, and he would treat this delicate subject confidentially."

"Very well, President Tomskaya," acknowledged Premier Gaydar.

The four men continued speaking, working out the details of their proposal to the Americans. After they were finished sorting out the details, the conference room doors were opened and servants entered with the evening meal. The Russian leaders were in a very good mood.

***

Following the National Security Council meeting, C.I.A. Director Myrna Ramirez made an appointment to meet with the President. She wanted to discuss Doctor Valenti's remarks about evolution. The President was at Camp David for a morning ride on his favorite horse. Since it was early in the morning, the temperatures were perfect for a brisk ride through the Maryland mountains.

"Mr. President, the C.I.A. began monitoring unusual human genetic phenomena back in the eighties under operations like "LIFE CELL" and "BUILDING BLOCK" when D.N.A. testing improved to allow our government to more accurately identify criminal and domestic intelligence suspects. The Federal Bureau of Investigation was originally responsible for domestic classification of criminals and domestic intelligence violators, while the C.I.A. was tasked with foreign intelligence classification. Since D.N.A. classification became cheaper and more practical, C.I.A. ran several new operations to investigate genetic intelligence."

"Go on," directed President Fairchild.

"Since that time, we've classified the D.N.A. of everything from alleged alien life forms to terrorists and enemy agents operating under American identities."

Dr. Ramirez withdrew a TOP SECRET folder from her briefcase and handed it to the President.

"What's this, Rosy?" he asked. "Don't tell me this is Roswell crap?"

"No, Mr. President, that file contains a comprehensive list of Americans who have been identified as possibly possessing a genetic mutation. Mike Valenti coined another term, "The Darwin Strand," sometime back. Our people adopted its use because it appears to be the genetic element that Dr. Valenti has theoretically predicted through his own independent methods. It does exist and has been occurring in our national population at a rate of approximately one out of every 2000 births since 1975."

"Well I'll be damned," swore the President. "This is too much for me to digest in one morning."

"What do you say we get together again at the beginning of next week, sir?"

The President nodded.

"Does Valenti know about this yet?"

"No, Mr. President."

"Tell him, and keep me informed," said the President.

"Do you have any problem with my decision to make some in house upgrades to NOAH'S ARK?"

"No, Rosy. I believe his operation needs more support now," noted the President. "It's your show, so expand as you deem necessary. Use black funds to do it, but get Valenti in on this genetic thing."

"Yes, sir, I'll arrange for him to get together with our Darwin Strand director immediately."

The President issued more operating instructions before departing on his morning ride. By the time President Fairchild had his horse warmed up, the C.I.A. Director had arranged for the meeting she had discussed with the President.

***

Premier Hu Quichen was exhausted. The Head of Government was continuing to coordinate rescue efforts in Hailar. He didn't have time to sleep or worry about Antarctica. Several ministers were meeting with him, which gave the Premier a chance to discuss international and domestic issues.

"Lee Jiang," continued Premier Quichen. "President Zhu Le Ho will be pleased to know that the Americans will be assisting us. Comrade Lee Chao, how are our rescue efforts proceeding?"

The head of the Chinese Red Cross Society equivalent bowed to the Head of Government. Lee Chao

Chong, at 63, was one of the younger departmental heads.

"Premier Hu, our rescue force is having difficulty reaching the disaster area. The air force isn't supporting us, and the roads and airfields into Hailar have been severely damaged by the earthquake. Only 60% of my comrades have been deployed to Hailar," reported Lee Chao Chong. "We require continuous air support."

Premier Hu picked up his writing instrument and scribbled something on his official letterhead.

"Give this to Minister Lin Hyo," directed the Premier. "As the Minister of National Defense, he will support you as I dictate. The people must be rescued and know their government is providing for them."

Lee Chao Chong bowed and departed. The Premier rose from his finely crafted chair and walked slowly around it to join his subordinates. Just as he was preparing to sit down, President Zhu Le Ho struggled even more slowly into the Premier's office. Zhu Le Ho was seventy and in poor health.

"President Zhu," greeted the Premier as he and the other men in the room rose and bowed. Hu Quichen was only six years younger than the President."

"Premier Hu, I have just been notified that the American Vice President, will be arriving to inspect the disaster area at Hailar," provided the President. "I see Lee Jiang Ping is present here as well."

The Minister of Foreign Affairs bowed again, pleased to be recognized by their leader.

"Mr. President?"

"Arrange for this visit, and contact our friends at the United Nations," ordered President Zhu Le Ho in his gentle voice. "Provide normal courtesies to Mr. Salazar, no more. He has always been a critic of our form of government. How is the provincial government supporting Hailar, Comrade Ho Chu Chen?"

The Minister of Civilian Administration slowly bowed. He was seventy-two and looked his age.

"The provincial government suffers, President Zhu. Electricity and basic services have not been restored," explained Ho Chu Chen, with sweat on his brow. "The after shocks have not helped the situation. Food and water are not being supplied in the quantities that are needed. Medical and engineering equipment, which would expedite rescue efforts, are not arriving in a timely manner. Thousands have died."

The President nodded as the Premier whispered in his ear.

"And you, Dung Yeung Song," continued the President. "What of Antarctica?"

Dung Yeung Song was the Minister of Science and the administrator of the Antarctic expedition.

"Our assumptions were correct, President Zhu Le Ho. Our nuclear weapons test altered the stability of the sub-fault and affected our major fault. Seismic readings indicate that our major fault caused Antarctica's earthquake and resulted in our suffering this one. Our after shocks indicate that more earthquakes may occur that may be similar or greater in strength. It is becoming apparent that Western theories involving plate tectonics are an accurate science. I anticipate that our fault will stabilize over time, but we may suffer severe damage in the meantime. It may take five years for this fault area to stabilize, and we still have to keep down the Tibetans, Mongolians, and insurgents."

"We can't appear weak, comrades," cautioned the Chinese President in a weary voice. "Premier Hu, you must insure that the people are rescued and their needs are met as soon as possible. Recall the expedition and supporting ships, and have the Minister of Public Security isolate devastated areas where our people have died in the greatest numbers. It will not bode well for the Americans to learn and publicize we failed to rescue our citizens in the worst areas. The Party already has difficulties with protest movements. We need no more."

The Premier nodded and bowed respectfully as the President lightly shuffled out of the office. The ministers remained with the Premier throughout the evening as the government officials attempted to direct rescue efforts of the disaster at Hailar, China. As they labored, the Chinese officials began to coordinate directly with the United States to arrange for American aid and the visit by Vice President Levan Salazar-Balart.

Chapter Ten

"Glorious Man"

The break between ARK deployments in Field Operations didn't last long for Bubba Washington and the ARK Teams. As C.I.A. laborers and commercial movers were relocating the operation into their newly designated office building in Greenbelt, Maryland, Bubba was directing ARK activities around the world. By the time the ARK One task force arrived from Antarctica, the three remaining ARK elements were already deployed to other trouble spots around the planet.

"How are we looking?" inquired Mike Valenti after he stuck his head into Bubba's partially furnished new office. "Any surprises?"

Bubba frowned, obviously upset at some malfunction on his computer screen and keyboard.

"Naw, Doc, no surprises so far. You know ARK One's standing down right now. They've got equipment to secure and they need to be debriefed before I release them to git some rest. I've got ARK Two investigating the quake in Hailar. Thas' some nasty shit out there! Oh, an' ARK Three's in Iles Kerguelen checking out their seismic fluctuations and whatever it was that caused that tsunami. Four's jus' landin' in Colon, Panama, where they'll deploy by SOUTHCOM choppers to Santiago to check out tremors in that area."

"Very good, Bubba," praised Mike as he placed a new box of mint flavored toothpicks on Washington's desk.

"Thanks, boss, you know how to keep a brutha happy at his work!"

Mike left Bubba Washington and returned to his office for a meeting with an unknown C.I.A. representative. Myrna Ramirez wanted to attend the meeting, but she was attempting to obtain more French support for ARK Four in Iles Kerguelen.

"Dr. Cable Craig," introduced the C.I.A. scientist as Mike arrived at his office door. "I like your setup down here, but it looks like it's moving day."

Mike shook hands with the man in the white laboratory coat who had surprised him near Alexandra's desk. The two men entered Mike's office. Dr. Craig had an assortment of classified files in his possession.

"We have a mutual friend," offered Craig as a way of breaking into informal conversation.

"Who's that?" asked Mike as he took a seat after his guest did. "The Director?"

"Shit, I wish! She's too high up on the totem pole for a little C.I.A. science dude like me. Evan Leeper. I've known him since my soccer days with Greenwood School. Evan played for Gilman in Baltimore, so we became buds from way back. He told me you were good friends and said you'd remember hearing about the Turk from Loyola Chicago."

"You're the Turk? I always figured you'd be an animal by the way Evan talked about you!" recalled Mike. "He said you were one crazy son of a bitch!"

"Yeah, well I still am," informed Cable with a sly smile. "There aren't many guys in I Phelta Thi left to run the streets with me anymore. Hell, most of the older guys are married off by now."

The I Phelta Thi Society was a social fraternal group founded by Loyola College students in 1977. Since actual fraternities were not permitted on Jesuit college campuses, it was a way of having a social organization. Mike was known in the fraternity as the "Dwarf."

"Ah yes, the good old days," reminisced Mike with a nasty laugh he had perfected at Loyola. He looked at Cable's files. "So tell me about your op, Turk."

Turk handed a set of neatly labeled folders and classified briefs to Mike. The Loyola University graduate didn't need a reference sheet to brief Mike.

"As a classified baseline genetic operation that was part of the Human Genome Project, blood samples were obtained from the Red Cross, hospitals, and police departments. The C.I.A. also created a D.N.A. database for the extensive collection of genetic material for research and examination purposes," began Cable Craig. "During the course of the D.N.A. collection and classification, approximately 10% of the samples of persons born since 1975 were found to contain a undocumented abnormal mutation. The genetic strand hasn't been found in any samples of individuals born prior to '75. I figure your theory about the sun's shift in position within our solar system being the evolutionary trigger for the Darwin Strand was right."

"Did you examine all the genome research data to rule out other potential biological causes for the Darwin Strand, Turk?" interrupted Mike.

"We did, Mike, which is why we're so intrigued. You see, a child has a greater chance of being born with hemophilia than the Darwin Strand, but there had been no indication since '75 that the strand caused or did anything - good or bad. Well, that's been changing."

"How so?"

"Little things, really, and not all related to humans," began Cable Craig. "One example that comes to mind is the way that Colobinae are changing."

"Old World monkeys of the leaf eating family? What about them, Turk?"

"Well, it seems nature has kicked in their evolutionary clock. They possess highly specialized stomachs that help them digest leafy plant cellulose, but they're changing their diets now. A scientist in Ogbomosho, Nigeria recently observed a troop of Hanuman Langurs eating a variety of foods. He obtained one of the younger specimens for dissection and found that it had a more versatile stomach that could digest cellulose and other food sources than its normal parents."

"That's amazing!" exclaimed Mike Valenti. "If Old World monkeys have been evolving to adjust to changes in habitat, then all living things will be evolving as the Pangaean Effect approaches."

"That leads me into the human aspects of the Darwin Strand, Dwarf," continued Turk Craig as he slid a videodisk into the disk player.

When the wall mounted television began to show footage of a tropical jungle environment, the Darwin Strand researcher continued.

"We've been researching scientific history to find any influences of the Darwin Strand since the baseline year of 1975. Back in '81, the newsstand tabloids began reporting a story about a five-year-old boy who was born in the remote Brazilian town of Alta Floresta along a tributary of the Amazon River called San Manuel. At the age of two, the boy disappeared in the jungle. He was called "Spirit Boy." The name was given to him after the he was found at the age of twelve prospering in the rain forest. During his medical examination, the boy was found to have adapted to nature too well. He was able to eat raw green plants that were toxic or indigestible to other humans and he could digest raw or partially decomposed meat. His skin had also adjusted to the extreme heat and sunlight by changing naturally to the dark brown hue of an Amazonian native."

"Fascinating," noted Mike as he adjusted his eyeglasses. "Was this an active strand Darwin child?"

Turk nodded, then handed Mike a photograph of the child with his two parents.

"The real clincher is that the boy was born to Swedish immigrants who's own D.N.A. showed no immediate ancestors of color. And neither parent was a carrier of the Darwin Strand. A DNA analysis of both parents also confirmed that there were no mutations in their backgrounds."

Mike leaned forward and slowly traced his finger over his narrow moustache.

"So this child was born with the gene while his parents didn't possess it, and he was born with the ability to adapt to his habitat. Interesting. What was his I.Q?"

"Very high. The I.Q. sporadically increased during those times when biological changes were necessary," replied Cable as he flipped through his dossier and removed a group of pages for Mike to review. "The boy's feet were also unusual. He only had four toes on each foot."

"That's an advanced evolutionary indication."

"I'll leave you with dossiers of all the identified Darwin Strand individuals, Dwarf, but it's interesting to note that the biological ability of strand individuals to rapidly adapt to their environment ends between the ages of eighteen and twenty one. Our research also shows that the I.Q. level needed by Darwins remains at the necessary level at the end of adolescence."

"What's the pattern of inheritance in the offspring of the Darwin carriers?" asked Mike.

"Well, first generation mutational carriers will pass on the Darwin Strand to their offspring, but research suggests that normal genetic probabilities apply to their procreation. One child may have the strain, while another may not. The rate is greater, though, than the rate of probability in the general population as a whole. It changes to about one in four births by then. I have all that calculated for you."

"What about Darwin offspring? Can they procreate with non-Darwin humans? inquired Mike, who was thinking about evolution's effects on human beings.

"Good question, Dwarf. The data is limited, but no," replied Cable. "A Darwin human cannot reproduce with a non-Darwin human. Darwin Strand carriers are the only common genetic bridge between non-Darwin and Darwin humans and they can procreate with either group. In essence, Darwin humans are an entirely new human species. It's disheartening to realize it, but we Homo

Sapiens Sapiens are a dying species. The Darwins are designed to be more capable of surviving."

Mike thought for a moment, considering how the Darwin Strand would fit into his long-range objectives. Cable handed him another file.

"What's this, Turk? I feel bad enough about our species being replaced like the Neanderthals so quickly."

"I figured you might as well receive this from me. It's a classified list of government employees who possess the Darwin Strand," explained Cable. "You don't have the gene, but our friend Evan Leeper does. He's a carrier of the Darwin Strand, so he can pass it on to his lucky offspring one day."

That surprised Mike, who had never considered Evan as being a carrier of anything other than a sexually transmitted disease.

"It sounds like wasted DNA to me! I don't want anymore Evan Leepers on the planet!" laughed Mike. "I won't tell him until he's had that vasectomy he's been talking about getting!"

Cable Craig laughed.

"Anything else you're concerned about, Dwarf?"

"Yeah, any indication of how long the Darwin Strand will last along generational lines?"

"Your guess is as good as mine, Dwarf. Whatever caused this phenomenon no doubt has it's own time schedule. I don't have a clue."

"Best guess?" asked Mike.

"Eight to ten generations, maybe fifteen," guessed Cable. "That's just to dilute the strand and make it ineffective. Of course, this is highly speculative. The Bible might be a good reference for a better guess."

"I understand. Turk, I've submitted a change of organization to the Director for approval. Until you hear otherwise, your entire operation's assigned to NOAH'S ARK," directed Mike with a friendly smile. "In the meantime, plan on being able to locate and make contact with every Darwin subject within one year."

"Why?"

"There's a reason the Darwin Strand has come to town, and we're responsible for taking full advantage of the abilities of these rare individuals before the public finds out and Darwins start dying," informed Mike.

Cable shrugged, "The Turk's all for team efforts, and I'd prefer to work for you anyway. What's the plan?"

Mike Valenti informed the Darwin Strand scientist of his preliminary plans. Committed to insuring that America was prepared for the planetary changes, the NOAH'S ARK leader was forming the basis for a task force to combat the Pangaean Effect.

***

In an effort to consolidate space resources and programs into one Executive Branch organization, President Fairchild created the Space Department in 2004. The Secretary of Space was Mary Ann Smith, an upper middle class woman from Red Bluff, California. She received her Bachelor's Degree in Physics in 1967 from the University of San Francisco. She was a strict and ruthless politician.

"You have a call on the direct line, Mrs. Smith," announced her secretary. "It's the President."

Mary Ann ran her fingers through her graying blonde hair and took a deep breath.

"Mr. President, how are you?" asked the Secretary of Space in her most professional voice.

"Mary? Nice to hear your voice," greeted Alex Fairchild on the other end of the line. "How's Dillon doing? Is he still trying to get you to stop flying?"

Mary Ann laughed. The President and her husband had hit it off well during the last White House reception and it seemed to be paying off for her.

"Yes, Mr. President, he's sixty now and worries too much about his health. How's the First Lady?"

"Becky's just fine, Mary. Look, I'm calling to inform you that one of your people's being permanently transferred to C.I.A. His name is Evan Leeper."

Mary Ann blanched. Evan Leeper was one of her best space analysts and the head of her Mars program.

"That can't be, sir," stammered Secretary Smith. "Evan's the head of our Mars program."

"Assign another qualified person to Dr. Leeper's position, then, Mary, but C.I.A. needs this scientist more than you do," reaffirmed Alex Fairchild. "Rosy will contact you directly. His effective date will be at the beginning of the next pay period, but I want him on duty with C.I.A. starting tomorrow."

Mary Ann sat back in her chair and angrily buzzed her secretary as soon as the President had hung up the telephone. She ordered Evan Leeper to her office.

"You sent for me, Doctor Smith?" asked Evan Leeper as he casually strolled into her domain.

"I'm pissed off, Evan!" remarked Mary Ann as she stood to interrogate one of her best employees. "I just received a call from the President ordering me to transfer you to the C.I.A. effective tomorrow."

Mary Ann watched Evan Leeper's reaction.

“C.I.A.? What’s C.I.A. want with an astronomer who aspires to be a Martian?” mused Evan in a vain attempt to charm his distraught supervisor.

“I don’t know, Doctor, but you’re a C.I.A. man starting tomorrow. What’s going on?” inquired Mary Ann. “Nobody gets pulled from Space for C.I.A. like this, and I want to know the reasons for it. And Rosy, that bitch! She thinks she’s in charge of the whole government!”

Evan listened, fully aware that Myrna Ramirez was about to become his new boss. The truth was that Space’s Mars program had been put on the back budget burner after some tragic shuttle setbacks. Since he didn’t know which project would be of the most interest to C.I.A., Evan was very curious about the role he would play as an employee of the Central Intelligence Agency.

***

That evening, Mike Valenti was frantically attempting to complete a steamy sizzling meal of steak fajitas when the security button from the first floor entrance of his apartment building signaled that his special guest had arrived. Swearing out loud, Mike checked to make sure that the tortillas were stacked safely within their steamer before he lowered the heat on his steak. Mike answered the doorbell in a hurry.

“Ready for some religion, Dim?” whispered Glenda Moses as her rare blue eyes softened when she observed his nervous face. She was carrying a dusty bottle of wine in one hand and two crystal wine glasses in the other. She was wearing a sexy blue floral sundress. “I brought along a 1990 Chateau Neuf de Pape to convert you, but I need a corkscrew!"

"Church, I've missed you!" exclaimed Mike as he swept her into his arms.

Glenda let him hold her for a moment, and then she pushed her way past Mike into the apartment and waited for him to close the dark wooden door. She was upset.

"Doctor Michael Joseph Valenti, the next time you send me on a mission, it had better not be without you!" Glenda scolded him as she put the bottle on his dining room table.

Mike couldn't wait any longer. Without thinking, he pulled her into his arms again and passionately kissed her. She vainly struggled to stop him. It only took a moment for Glenda to melt in his firm arms. The sizzling steaks were the only things that caused Mike to pause in his efforts.

"My steaks!" exclaimed Mike, as he raced into the kitchen.

"You're cooking, Dim? That's so sweet," praised Glenda with a giggle. "What are we having for dinner?"

"Steak fajitas and salad," yelled Mike over the noise in the kitchen. He was really making an effort to prepare a nice respectable meal.

Glenda took a slow walk around the apartment, making her way to the smoke filled kitchen where her boyfriend was attempting to impress her.

As Mike finished preparing their meal, Glenda made her way into the bedroom where she quietly changed into a sheer white negligee that magnificently accentuated her busty one hundred and thirty pound figure. She slowly stepped into a pair of stilleto heels.

"Church! Dinner's ready!" announced Mike as he placed the meal on the table and lit some candles for that romantic effect. "Where'd you go?"

Glenda provocatively made her way back into the dining area with her heels announcing her arrival on his pinewood floor. Mike stopped in his tracks with two plates of food in his hands. He was stunned by Glenda's breathtaking beauty.

"Church?"

Glenda smiled and slowly walked past him as she picked up the bottle of wine.

"You bring the glasses," she ordered, as she walked back into the bedroom holding the bottle by the neck and swinging it in cadence with her sultry walk. Mike couldn't help but notice Glenda's awesome butt.

Mike quickly grabbed the wine glasses and rushed into the bedroom. With an entire night to make love, the two lovers kissed and caressed each other, exploring their bodies with the sensual need and profound desire to be joined in love as one. Mike inhaled the fragrance of her hair and tasted the sweat of her body as they made love. He caressed Glenda's skin and experienced the wonders of her body in a way he had never done before that night. In response to his deep love for her and the passion it aroused in her, Glenda explored his body with a newness that consumed her with emotion. They both cried tears of joy that evening because they had found each other again. By dawn, Mike and Glenda had rekindled the fire of love that had always drawn the two soul mates together.

***

Evan Leeper had been to the C.I.A. enough times to know how to find the highly secure office of Dr. Myrna Ramirez. She welcomed Evan on board and gave him a brief orientation. After they were finished, she buzzed Mike Valenti and asked him to join her in her office. It was a pleasant surprise for Mike when he arrived to see his best friend sitting in one of the Director's guest chairs.

"Evan!" exclaimed Mike Valenti in shock. "What brings you to the Agency?"

"You, brother! Doctor Ramirez summoned me here this morning!"

Myrna smiled as Mike hugged Evan and took a seat next to him.

"You bastard! Why didn't you tell me when we talked last night on the telephone?" asked Mike, still amazed that his best friend was standing in front of him.

Myrna Ramirez laughed at the two friends; pleased to see they were so close. The mission would require them to work very closely together.

"As you requested, Evan's your new number one man beginning today, Mike," began Myrna. She opened a folder that was on her desk. "I also approved your expansion requests. You'll have a Darwin Department that will be headed by Cable Craig. Seth Tayman will head the Pangaean Department. I'm putting your Mars Department under Mary Elizabeth Blalack. Evan recommended her highly, and she also works at Space."

"That's fine with me, ma'am. Mary Ann will love that!" interjected Evan. "Hey, Mike, I'll bet you weren't expecting to run into Turk Craig, were you? Small world...."

"I know!" agreed Mike with a grin. "This is going to be one hell of an undertaking!"

"Yes, this is an ambitious operation, gentlemen," cautioned Myrna. "And I'm concerned about how the American people will react when they learn that we control such a powerful operation."

"Ma'am, I don't care how classified the Pangaean Effect is, it won't remain a secret for long," advised Mike. "It's just a matter of time."

"I know, Mike," acknowledged Myrna Ramirez with a sigh. "I'll work on that."

"What about the Darwin program's mandate?" asked Mike.

"The Darwin Department will be free to handle Darwin research and implementation as you determine, Mike," replied Myrna. "As for the Mars Department, you know the mission. It will be responsible for our most critical objective - to colonize Mars," stated Myrna.

"Get outta here!" exclaimed Evan. "So that's what I'm doing here, huh?"

"Yep," grinned Mike. "Our survival also means starting a successful colony in a safer place."

"That's one hell of an objective, brother! We haven't even mastered landing on the moon yet!"

"That's an intermediate objective," advised Myrna. "The Mars Department will, in this order unless otherwise specified by me, establish an Earth orbital space station capable of conducting docking, refueling, and providing transient quarters for space vessels and travelers. Second, establish a permanent lunar colony that will provide water and other lunar resources by means of a lunar orbiting space station. Of course, the lunar colony may be vacated if the precessional shift of the Earth's axis is expected to affect the safety of the people located there. Third, establish a Mid-Space Station between Earth and Mars with capabilities similar to the Earth station, and fourth, establish a Mars orbital space station and planetary colony for the permanent settlement of human beings by January 1, 2025."

"Fuck me running!" swore Evan Leeper in shock. "You C.I.A. guys ain't right! That's not much time to accomplish this huge mission!"

"Twenty four years, brother," reiterated Mike.

"Well, since I've been running the program at Space, I can tell you we weren't even thinking about putting a man in Martian orbit by 2015! Hell, we're still losing robots and tinkering with new ionian engines during computer simulated research launches!"

Myrna and Mike looked at Evan, fully confident in his professional and technical abilities.

"You're talking serious risk here, people," Evan warned. "Americans shit their pants every time an astronaut dies on the job, but if we go for this program we're going to lose a hell of a lot of astronauts. We won't have much time to reduce the flight risks!"

"I know, Evan, which is why Mike wants you to have oversight of the Mars Department. You're a risk taker, and that's what we need if America is going to survive. Can we accomplish the Mars mission?" asked Myrna again. "Or do we give up?"

"We'll do it," Evan replied confidently. "Since the Earth's about to shake us off her like dogs do fleas, I don't see where we have much choice in it. How are we specifically going to use the Darwins?"

"Mike and I have discussed this," answered Myrna. "Right now we're planning on using Darwin humans only in support of the domestic survival plan. They'll survive on Earth if our species can't, and that's the whole purpose of their presence."

Mike Valenti put a file in front of the Director.

"Like Evan and Cable, I agree that the Darwin Strand has created an entirely new human being," opined Mike. "It's inevitable with the presence of the Darwin Strand that mankind's time on Earth is numbered as we know our species to be now. I already have a scientific name for the Darwin offspring: Homo Sapiens Gloria."

"Glorious man? I like that!" admitted Evan. "I can see we have a lot of work to do and things to learn."

"All of us do," agreed Mike, suddenly serious. "We also have several moral issues that will have to be resolved before this whole operation gets cranking and the planet's real fate goes public."

Myrna wrapped up their meeting on a high note, "You know, guys, have fun with this project, no matter how difficult it becomes. Deal with this like I deal with my handicap - with a positive attitude. And remember that you're not in this alone, even though it's may feel like it at times. Anything else, gentlemen?"

Both men shook their heads.

"Good. SethTayman, Mary Blalack and Cable Craig are waiting outside," provided Myrna. "Let's get together with them now and get them on track. Mike, I want daily briefings from you until you hear otherwise."

The NOAH'S ARK executives met with Myrna to expand the operation into a flexible Pangaean Task Force, which would bring many different agencies into the battle against the world's geological problems. While

NOAH'S ARK would continue as a classified operation, the creation of the Pangaean Task Force prepared it for eventual public recognition.

***

Secretary General Asi Fanon Mtume was pleased to meet with Aramentha Washington for lunch in his magnificently decorated office. He had just completed a presentation to a group of Danish businessmen who had been gathered in the Dag Hammarskjold Library of the United Nations. A former marathon champion, Asi Mtume was a proud Kenyan cattle rancher who was born in Mado Gashi, Kenya. He was a former Secretary of the Kenyan State Department whose keen diplomatic skills had resulted in his selection to the prestigious United Nations position.

"Ambassador Washington, so good to see you again," greeted the Secretary General in his soft-spoken voice and cultured English accent."

Aramentha Washington removed her eyeglasses as she greeted the leader of the United Nations.

"Secretary General, thank you for meeting with me on such short notice," said Aramentha with a mild Jamaican accent she had inherited from her immigrant parents. "The President has sent a letter for you, and I'm to discuss the information which it will provide, sir."

Asi Mtume gestured for the ambassador to sit in one of the beautiful Kenyan great chairs that decorated his office. Each chair was hand made of ebony and genuine cheetah hides. As an assistant arrived with a well-stocked food tray for them to enjoy, Aramentha presented the Secretary General with an exquisite linen envelope bearing the presidential seal and Mr. Mtume's name in genuine gold lettering. The Secretary General took a few moments to read the correspondence.

"President Fairchild is requesting U.N. support for the victims of the earthquake disaster in China," advised Asi Mtume as he continued to read the letter. "He's concerned about the after shocks that may occur there. Even though I'm tired of American failings in Iraq and your leader's manipulation of the General Assembly by withholding international aid to non-supporters, I've already coordinated for immediate aid and assistance."

Aramentha selected some finger food and placed it on the plate of Kenyan china on her lap. She knew better than to eat while the formal phase of the meeting was taking place. Aramentha also knew that Secretary Mtume was a first class intelligence gatherer. They were first acquainted back in the late nineties when they were both pursuing advanced degrees at the prestigious United Nations University in Tokyo, Japan. Mr. Mtume was well known at the university as a man who possessed special skills in dealing with different cultures and learning languages.

"Secretary Mtume, President Fairchild has empowered me to reach terms on arranging a summit of interested world leaders as soon as possible to address disaster efforts and planning for the Asian earthquake."

Asi Mtume ate another grape and joined Aramentha in the matching great chair next to her own.

"I see you have blonde highlights in your hair, Aramentha," complimented Asi Mtume with his charming smile. "I wish the women of my country would adopt similar styles."

"Thank you," accepted Aramentha with a diplomatic smile.

"May I be candid, madam?" Mtume asked as he rubbed his manicured hands together.

Aramentha nodded, "Please do."

"I've had several contacts with other U.N. representatives since this tragedy occurred. As a matter of necessity, the U.N. World Meteorological Organization in Geneva received scores of scientific and eyewitness data following China's earthquake. The potential for another seismic event is of great concern. Everyone is apparently under the impression that the other tremors around the world are all unrelated. That may be their ignorant opinion, but you and I both know that they are incorrect assumptions. Like Africa itself, the Earth is a complicated planet that remains a mystery."

Aramentha knew that Asi Mtume was an Animist with a deep reverent relationship with the Earth and the environment. His concerns about conservation were legendary. It was rumored among people in Kenya that Asi ran barefoot during Kenyan marathons as a youth so as not to disturb the Earth's surface.

"Secretary General, I am not at liberty to discuss any details about the earthquake with you."

"You already have," smiled the legendary leader. "This summit will not assist the victims in Hailar, madam. After seventy-two hours, most trapped people will die if they are not rescued. This summit is clearly to discuss the cause of the earthquake. Inform President Fairchild I must also be invited to attend. In the meantime, I'll arrange for the summit and notify you as to the date and time. The Chinese have already demanded that any summit be held in Beijing."

"That's unacceptable to the United States, Secretary General," spoke up Aramentha. "Our current detente with China is severely restricted."

"I understand, Ambassador Washington, but the Chinese have demanded that any international discussions take place in Beijing. Their vote in the Security Council, and their power in the U.N., must be respected in this matter."

"Very well, sir. I know the Vice President is in China now, and I'll relate this problem to the President this afternoon," accepted Aramentha.

The two diplomats continued discussing minor details over their delicious meal. As a Jamaican American, Aramentha appealed to the Secretary General's preference for dealing with diplomats with international backgrounds. Both of them were avid cricket fans, so the rest of their leisure conversation involved the upcoming championships in Great Britain.

***

President Fairchild had just returned from a road trip to the Capitol when Daniel Tokuhisa arrived at the White House. It was a rainy evening that made the downtown streets look like polished glass. After the limousine passed through the southwestern gate of the national residence, the President exited the armored car with his Secret Service agents swarming around him. Frank Benavente was traveling with him.

"Dan, how are we looking for the summit?" asked Alex Fairchild. He quickly shook hands with the head of the State Department as they walked into the historic building.

"Fine, sir," responded Dan with a broad smile that displayed his thick dimples. Frank nodded a greeting, too. "We have a long list of respondents, and I'll be arranging the official invitations in the morning."

"Nix that, Dan. I just talked to Aramentha. Mtume's making this a United Nations show, which is just as suitable for our needs. Get with his people and coordinate it. The Reds want the summit in China. You get it anywhere but in China. That Chinese puppet in New York is supporting Beijing over us. I knew it when he agreed that we meet there!"

"Beijing? Mr. President, we're going to catch hell in the public opinion polls if we hold a humanitarian summit in China!"

The trio entered the Oval Office with a sense on urgency. Alex Fairchild sank into a finely upholstered love seat and slouched back into the comfortable fabric.

"You know, that bastard Unger can be a pain in the ass when you want something from him!" complained the President as he pulled off his damp Brooks Brother's loafers. "I had to kiss his ass during the whole meeting to get him to support the summit!"

"Well, Mr. President, he is the Chairman of the House Intelligence Committee, and he's hated China since their last attempt to block the Taiwan Straits," advised Frank Benavente. "At least Senator Georgoulis stepped up to the plate and persuaded Congressman Unger to support this. She's got a lot of pull as head of the Senate Intelligence Committee."

The President leaned back in the love seat and closed his eyes.

"Dan, try to locate the summit in New York. If that's impossible, I'll only accept London, Tokyo, Geneva, or

Paris," directed the President. "The Vice President's out there now. I've directed him to win the respect of China as much as he can while he's there."

Dan liked that idea. He could always count on the President to turn a public disaster into a political tool.

"Secretary Tokuhisa, you have a telephone call from the Russian Premier on line one," announced the night secretary over the intercom."

"Thank you," replied Dan, who was wondering what could be on the minds of the Russians at this time of night. He forgot that it wasn't late at all in Russia.

"Go on ahead, Dan. We're pretty much done here," stated the President.

Both advisors departed, with Secretary Tokuhisa going to the Roosevelt Room to speak with the Premier of China. Alex Fairchild left the Oval Office for his private residence on the second floor of the White House.

***

The Secretary of State was tired when he picked up the telephone in the brightly lit Roosevelt Room. He wasn't prepared for the Russian premier to ask for ten million American dollars for the sale of information.

"Premier Gaydar, why would the United States want to pay you ten million dollars?" asked Dan Tokuhisa with a laugh.

"I can trust you with such an offer," replied Grigoriy Gaydar. "And the information I have for you will be worth much more than what I'm asking."

"Fine, I'll bite, sir," replied Dan, who was more interested in the information. "If I like it, I'll make sure you're wired the funds as you desire. Talk to me."

"How would you like to know the real cause of the Chinese earthquake?" asked the Premier.

"You're kidding, right?" responded Dan Tokuhisa. "The cause was an unstable fault."

"You may know about the unstable fault, but would you like to know how it became unstable?" asked Premier Gaydar. "Or what activity made the fault become unstable? Or how it affects China now? You'll find that this information is priceless."

"Okay, Mr. Gaydar, you've got a tentative deal," agreed the Secretary of State.

"Good. The power of the Russian government was used to obtain this very important information," explained Premier Gaydar. "Ten million dollars is a small price to pay for national security and the ability to become the only true nuclear superpower."

Daniel Tokuhisa knew the information was essential.

"When will the information be available?"

"Immediately, Secretary Tokuhisa," responded Premier Gaydar. "In a gesture of good faith, I will send Yuliy Matviyenko to Washington to meet with you personally. He will bring all the data I have, and he will bring wire transfer information for my account."

"That's smart, Premier Gaydar," agreed Dan with a sigh. "Advise me of his itinerary and we'll provide him full diplomatic honors, sir."

With the deal arranged, the Secretary of State completed his conversation with Premier Grigoriy Gaydar and wearily departed the White House for his home in Gaithersburg, Maryland. During the ride in his State Department limousine, Secretary Tokuhisa notified the President of the Russian offer. President Fairchild approved the decision praised his Secretary of State for taking the call as expeditiously as he did.

Chapter Eleven

"A New Archipelago"

Vice President Levan Salazar-Balart did little to improve relations between the United States and China. After arriving in Beijing, he failed to listen to his aides and control his arrogance. Instead of lodging at Chinese government V.I.P. quarters, Mr. Salazar decided instead to obtain unauthorized quarters at the Hyatt Beijing. He aggravated the situation even more by ignoring President Fairchild's specific instructions to visit the earthquake zone immediately upon his arrival. By the time Levan Salazar was taken to the disaster site at Hailar, the entire diplomatic corps of the Ministry of Foreign Affairs was alienated by his brash personality.

The Vice President also complained about being transported in a Chinese aircraft to Hailar. With his entourage of Secret Service agents and neurotic White House aides, the Vice President's large contingent easily occupied the majority of the seats on the dilapidated Chinese Air Force transport airplane. The big propellers of the pea green aircraft were scarred and speckled with paint chips. The beige interior of the airplane was old and smelled like damp canvas.

"I've seen Cuban rafts built better than this bird," complained the Vice President in his loud voice.

A few aides attempted to quiet Mr. Salazar, to no avail. The Chinese officers and advisors accompanying him on the trip ignored his remarks, silently hoping that the seven hundred and fifty mile flight to the disaster area would be a quick one.

"What do you think of China, Mr. Vice President?" asked one of the more courageous Chinese aids who was there to assist the Americans.

Mr. Salazar took a long drag on his fine cigar and blew the pungent smoke into the faces of the irritated Chinese escorts.

"It reminds me of Vietnam in your lowland areas," replied Levan Salazar. "And your bullshit communist system reminds me too much of Cuba."

"Mr. Salazar, you fought in the Vietnamese War of Liberation," added another dedicated Chinese attendee to change the subject. "Weren't you an Army officer?"

"An officer? Hell no! I worked for a living! I was an infantry sergeant in the 25th Infantry Division. I did three tours as a tunnel rat at Cu Chi before I took shrapnel in the gut from a Chinese hand grenade," boasted Levan Salazar. "That was back in '71. I hated the communists. Still do."

The Vice President's hatred of communists did not escape the ears of the Chinese diplomats. Not wanting to continue discussing sensitive subjects with the American, the Chinese escorts spoke amongst themselves for the rest of the flight. When the aircraft finally began a slow turn and bumpy descent, one of the Chinese escorts pointed out of the window.

"There is Hailar!"

Everyone scrambled to look out of the blurred cracked windows at the horrific scene below. There was a huge fresh gash in the land that was clearly visible from the air. From their descending altitude of three thousand feet, the devastation was immense. Many buildings that had been caught in the rift had toppled like dominos into the deep gash in the ground. Bodies were lined up at designated locations, and the injured were lying on blankets and cots without the benefit of overhead shelters.

"God," swore one of the Vice President's aids in amazement. "Look at all the buzzards! It looks like a war zone down there. How many people were killed?"

A Chinese delegate interjected, "Twenty thousand, with another ten thousand unaccounted for."

"Damn, how far's that rut part the Earth from the primary earthquake zone?" asked the Vice President. "It looks like it goes on forever."

Another Chinese escort answered, "The rift moves north and south of Hailar for approximately thirty kilometers. Some of the depths along the rift are considerable. There are after shocks every day, but they're subsiding in intensity."

The cargo aircraft bumped and rolled down onto the poorly maintained and earthquake damaged asphalt runway before coming to a noisy halt. It taxied around some huge cracks and came to a stop near the small terminal that was overflowing with refugees.

"They're using the airport to house as many of the wounded and homeless as possible," advised one of Salazar's aides. "Look at that! The buzzards are actually bold enough to peck at the wounded on those cots!"

"Dammit!" exclaimed Mr. Salazar as he watched the vultures trying to feed on the dead and defenseless. "Can't you get someone to get rid of the buzzards? I can't believe your disaster program is so fucked up!"

Lee Chao Chong, the Administrator of the Red Cross Society of China, could no longer remain quiet, "Vice President Salazar, the people of my country will be well served by our rescue programs, but the after shocks have limited the response time of our relief effort. I resent your remarks about our national problems."

A White House aide discreetly identified the cabinet minister to the Vice President.

"Mr. Lee, a pleasure, sir," greeted Mr. Salazar in a vain attempt to smooth over his harsh criticism of the Chinese situation. "I'm sure your country will handle this disaster just fine, and I meant no insult."

There were no flight attendants to direct the passengers to exit the aircraft, so everyone followed the Chinese diplomats. The Vice President was complaining about the change in climate and lack of a welcoming committee just when the revolting odor of rotting bodies invaded his nose. The stench was so bad that several American aides rushed back into the aircraft to find the lavatory. Mr. Salazar retched in spite of himself just as an aftershock moved the ground under his feet.

"Now you see how it is in Hailar, Mr. Salazar," remarked Lee Chao as he noted and then admired how well the Vice President handled the revolting stench. "Our rescue workers must transport the vital supplies from Qiqihar by land and air to Hailar. There have been over one hundred after shocks per day, which makes it difficult to conduct rescue operations. When the ground is shaking, aircraft can't to land and trucks can't be driven safely. Of course, if you have any positive suggestions, I would welcome them."

The Vice President nodded as they walked toward the crowded concourse area where four all terrain vehicles awaited them. There were hordes of flies everywhere, and the Earth violently shook more as they entered the vehicles. During his one-day tour of the disaster area, Levan Salazar experienced twenty after shocks, one of which brought down a roof in the concourse area and killed more people. For the first time since his return from Vietnam, the Vice President was surrounded by death. He was also ready to leave China as soon as possible.

***

The U.S.S. Dolphin was a diesel electric, deep diving research submarine that was assigned the mission of performing special surveys between the Coral Sea and the Hawaiian Islands. This unique 165 foot long vessel was capable of conducting deep-water research and ocean floor surveying to depths of 3,000 feet. On this particular mission, the Dolphin was on a solitary voyage being conducted at the request of the Australian government. The Dolphin was at the southern portion of its patrol route near the Solomon Islands.

"Captain, sensors, sir," sounded one of the 46 enlisted personnel on board. "We've detected a new unstable oceanographic signature."

"What do you have?" inquired Captain Frederick Herman, the vessel commander.

"Sensors indicate a large subsurface fissure at the following coordinates," responded the sensor technician as he read out the coordinates.

"It's going to be marine volcanic activity," predicted Doctor Milton Robelot, the scientist on board.

"Go to 2500 feet, speed five knots, left standard rudder," ordered Captain Herman. He intended to pass along the outer edge of the fissure. "Full sensor array."

"Full sensor array, aye," responded the sensor technician. "Incoming analysis, sir."

The submarine slowly made her way along the fissure as the vessel's special computerized sensors analyzed the data. The scientist reviewed the results.

"Captain Herman, this is a rare geological event!" exclaimed the scientist, showing unusual surprise. "Based on infrared and survey data, there are six volcanoes developing underwater funnels even as we speak."

The captain was educated in marine geology, though not as extensively as the scientist.

"Six? That's impossible, Milt!" commented Captain Herman. "Granted, we're on the outer edge of the Bougainville Trench, but it would take one hell of a fissure to create six volcanoes!"

Dr. Robelot cleared his throat and removed his reading glasses. He mentally calculated some of the data he had just read. The Bougainville Trench was a name for a banana shaped archipelago that extended out from New Guinea to the Solomon Islands. It was an area known for significant and violent volcanic activity.

"Captain, I'm uncomfortable with our current position. A powerful eruption column could cause significant aquatic turbulence and seriously damage this vessel. I'd give these new volcanoes a wider berth of at least two miles."

Captain Herman agreed, "Left standard rudder, all ahead full, steer course 160, speed twenty knots."

"I don't think we have to worry much about any eruption clouds at this point," continued Dr. Robelot. "It will be some time before the growing funnels reach the surface, but tephra and pyroclastic flow from these eruptions can affect the ecological systems in the area. We need to report this to the U.S.G.S., Washington, and Australia, Captain. This fissure is growing fast and will destabilize the entire region."

The captain ordered the vessel's mast be raised as soon as he was a safe distance away from the volcanoes and sent notification messages. Huge rumbling underwater explosions from the distant volcanoes could be felt inside the research submarine. As the eruptions continued, the sensor and sonar displays lit up and alerted technicians.

"Subsurface eruptions, Captain," advised Doctor Robelot as he pointed at one of the computer screens. "Look at the effects they're having on the currents. We need to find the ends of the fissures and survey them. We also need to get some acoustic ships and more surveying vessels to assist us."

As the U.S.S. Dolphin silently continued it's new research pattern, the U.S. Intelligence Community received the information that newly formed and active volcanoes had been detected in the South Pacific.

***

President Zhu Le Ho gingerly strolled along the main hallway of his traditionally decorated residence with his hands behind his back. Hu Quichen, the frail Chinese Premier and Head of Government, walked next to him. They were having a serious discussion about the upcoming Chinese summit.

"Hu, the Vice President's behavior was typical," continued the Chinese Chief of State. "He is an American capitalist and an outspoken critic of Cuba and our successful communist state."

The Premier walked with the President in silence.

"I wanted this summit in China to share our culture, but this could be done in New York without exposing our society to their alien cultures," said the Chinese president.

"I agree, Zhu Le Ho."

"Very well," continued President Zhu. "I will contact our friend Asi Mtume and accept the American counter-offer to host the summit in New York. I will insist that it be held at the United Nations, and that we continue to be the hosts. It will be well accepted by the Kenyan since he understands that our recent earthquake has deeply affected the morale of the Chinese people. This will also permit us to inspect American geological laboratories and learn more about tectonics without appearing to be weak or damaged by our own disaster."

As the two men continued down the dimly lit hallway, they discussed Antarctica. Their Mandarin dialect was cultured and educated.

"What about the American expedition?" asked the Chief of State. "Do you believe they know the extent of the earthquake's effects on our country?"

Hu Quichen abruptly stopped.

"The Americans are there because they don't know our initial earthquake was man made and the cause of the one in Antarctica," Hu cautiously replied."

"And the Russians?" asked President Zhu Le Ho.

"The two liaison officers were expertly liquidated before being able to notify Moscow that our first earthquake was our own fault."

"Good," stated President Zhu. "How many special guards were sent with the expedition?"

"Twenty," replied Hu, suddenly realizing the President's intentions. "They were only sent as a security detachment."

"Of course, but it was necessary to use them to liquidate the Russians. We need to use them again," Zhu Le Ho said as he raised an index finger to silence the Head of Government. "Send them to the American encampment. I want them to obtain one captive, a scientist, for interrogation. One man lost to bad weather will not be missed. Like the Russians, they will presume he fell victim to the climate."

"This is very risky, Zhu. Any error could result in an international incident."

The President laughed, "The Americans won't go to war over a lost American! The Americans only create incidents or wars against inferior enemies!"

The two men completed their discussions and retired to their respective rooms for the evening. The groundwork was set for the Chinese summit and the infiltration of the American research site. High above the residence, an American Boeing 767 was climbing higher into the star filled sky. The Vice President of the United States was on his way back home.

***

Before the Vice President's aircraft landed at Andrews Air Force Base near Camp Springs, Maryland, Mike Valenti was had been informed of the six new submarine volcanoes that threatened the South Pacific. Mike's telephone was already ringing off the hook.

"Mike, the Director's on line three," advised Alexandra Charles. "She sounds upset!"

He got rid of the other two calls.

"Mike, do you have a team available to check out the new volcanoes near the Solomon Islands? I've got New Zealand and the Aussies sending some research and survey ships to the area, but I'd like to have your people there to insure our concerns are addressed and analyzed."

Mike told his boss that all the teams were deployed, and then remembered ARK One.

"Which team is operating in the area closest to our research sub?" she asked.

"ARK Three. They're assisting the French on that tidal wave at Iles Kerguelen," advised Mike. "They'll be done in about a week."

"That won't work, Mike," said Myrna. "I need one of your teams there now. Is every team deployed?"

"No, Rosy. ARK One's resting."

"Activate ARK One, Mike," Myrna directed. "We don't have time to wait for your deployed teams to be re-equipped to operate in the Solomon Islands. I'll give you five days to get them there. Thanks."

Mike hung up the telephone. His teams were already stretched too thin. As Mike picked up the telephone to call his father for their weekly conversation, Mike Valenti was wondering if the world was going to turn upside down too soon.

***

Alexander Fairchild was having a bad day. Amidst State Department complaints about the way the Vice President behaved in China, and headaches associated with convincing the American public and Congress that the summit was necessary, the President was beginning to wish for a quick escape to California to shoot eighteen holes at Pebble Beach! It didn't help that Edith Madison was sending him calls without a break.

"Dammit, Kurt, I can't get in a five minute meeting with you without the phone ringing!" remarked the President to his Chief of Staff, Kurt Farley, as the phone buzzed again. "We've got to clean up this mess with Salazar and the Chinese! He made it worse for us!"

"I agree, Monty. Take your time," replied Kurt.

"This is the President," answered Alex Fairchild over the telephone. "Yes, Aramentha? That's fantastic! You can give him my approval! Goodbye!"

Kurt Farley looked at the President, expecting an explanation following the telephone call.

"That was Washington. The Chinese don't want the summit in Beijing now. They want it at the United Nations, but they still want to be the hosts," explained Alex in a more upbeat tone of voice. "Levan might have actually helped us, even though I don't know how."

"Maybe, sir, but that Balart's a raging asshole," opined Kurt, who was also known for being one himself. "I believe in being direct, but your sidekick abuses the privilege. What do you want me to do about the flak over his China trip?"

"Well, let's turn this around our way. Leak to the press that the Vice President presented the Chinese with an invitation to hold the summit in New York," he explained. "The Chinese accepted, of course. And gloss over the bad political blood Balart caused by emphasizing that we were there to assist in rescue operations."

There was nothing more that needed to be discussed, so the Chief of Staff excused himself. Alex Fairchild continued taking telephone calls and dealing with Edith Morgan.

***

Bubba John Washington was swamped with time sensitive issues that had to be resolved. It didn't sit well with him that Mike Valenti had just ordered the deployment of ARK One again. The big man lumbered up to Mike's office to complain.

"Mike, this is some bullshit!" complained Bubba as he interrupted Mike's telephone call. "You're sendin' ARK One southbound again? They ain't had time to unpack their flight bags or defrost their asses!"

"Bubba, it's necessary," explained Mike. "The Director's orders. ARK One goes in five days!"

Bubba shook his head.

"You need ta' grow some balls, cuz ah' expect more from a boss than this shit here," advised Bubba."

"Sorry, Bubba," apologized Mike.

"This is some bullshit!" growled Bubba as he left his supervisor's office.

Mike knew that Bubba Washington and Elton Rance would deploy on time. He was used to dealing with both men and their protests. Mike admired the way they defended their people when it was necessary. As he continued planning for ARK One's deployment, Mike was already beginning to miss Glenda Moses.

***

When Secretary General Asi Mtume received the sealed communiqué from the President of China, there was also a Swiss cashiers check inside of the envelope made payable to him in the amount of $200,000.00. When Aramentha Washington arrived to meet with him, Mr. Mtume was well prepared for his conversation with the U.S. Ambassador to the United Nations.

"Ah, Mrs. Washington, a pleasure, madam," greeted Asi Mtume as he ran his eyes over her shapely mature body. He rubbed a hand over the one she offered. "How have you been?"

"Fine, Mr. Secretary. I heard the Chinese have rescinded their offer to host the summit in China?" asked Aramentha as she sat in one of the Kenyan great chairs.

"That is quite correct, madam. It took quite a bit of convincing on my part, you know. Your Vice President's visit strained Sino-American relations."

Aramentha was prepared for Asi Mtume's political maneuvers.

"Secretary Mtume, the President is fully aware of the problems Vice President Salazar caused during his trip.

We'll support the summit, with restrictions on Chinese access to controlled areas, of course."

"Of course," smiled Mr. Mtume. "I've already discussed these options with President Zhu. He's a very reasonable man and able diplomat."

Aramentha wasn't satisfied.

"I need the Chinese and U.N. agreements in writing before the President will authorize the necessary travel and other permits. We will not finance the Chinese summit if they will be hosting it."

Mr. Mtume nodded with understanding; secretly pleased with the amount of money he had been paid by the Chinese for his assistance.

"Aramentha, the key to this summit is to gather interested and affected countries under our glorious blue flag with U.N. resources and American technology to assist the world in their efforts to avert future disasters like this one," advised Asi Mtume, deep in thought. "I will speak with President Fairchild about the budgetary aspects of this summit, but I feel it is detrimental to Chinese detente and their disaster efforts to place financial responsibility for this conclave on them. If the Americans won't sponsor the summit, the bill should be absorbed by all the other member nations."

Aramentha didn't expect that response from the Secretary General of the United Nations. Mtume was usually quick to place billing requirements on the nations with veto powers.

"I'll inform the President of your concerns," replied Ambassador Washington.

"My decisions," corrected Secretary Mtume. "The decision to support the summit in New York stands on my authority. I just want to spread the cost of the summit over the broader pockets of the veto and other member nations who will be attending it. China has too many problems to be able to finance the summit, too."

Aramentha Washington concluded her meeting with Secretary Mtume and made telephone calls to the White House. By the end of her communications, the Ambassador to the United Nations learned that the United States would finance fifty percent of the summit.

***

ARK Four leader Derrick R. Blasdale was in the process of changing a compact disk in his portable C.D. player when he received orders from Bubba Washington to evacuate Panama via SOUTHCOM choppers to a small U.S. Air Force airfield in Cali, Colombia.

"I'm getting tired of these satellite messages," complained Derrick to one of his team members. "We just arrived, get good data, then we're told to split."

One of Derrick's employees wearily sat back in the dirt next to him and retied one of his steel shanked boots.

"It's difficult figuring out what the Doc wants these days," added a team member."

"I don't care, personally," responded a scientist as he regained his feet. "These monitors say the ca-ca's about to hit the fan, and I don't want to be here for it."

"Hey, Derrick, what about that cute Chinese chick in the nice car taking photos of us?" inquired a team member. "Did you tell Bubba about her?"

"Hell, no! You know how many Chinese there are in Panama since we handed over the canal? That broad was probably lost or something, and besides, she didn't ask us any questions or do anything suspicious."

As the sun rose higher in the cobalt blue sky, the ARK Four team hastily packed their research equipment and prepared to depart the area. Since sunrise, the town of Santiago had been occupied by Panamanian troops who were directing the evacuation of vulnerable areas to makeshift shelters at higher elevations.

***

The resident intelligence officer at the Chinese embassy in Panama City received the classified report from Santiago with a look of concern on his face. As a result of the keen observations of Intelligence Agent Chang Daihua, the ambassador had already alerted Peking that civilian American spies were operating in Panama. The presence of unidentified American researchers with unmarked geological and research equipment in Santiago was enough to warrant sending an immediate message to Lee Jiang Ping, the Minister of Foreign Affairs.

In his conservative office in the Beijing district, Mr. Lee Jiang Ping prepared orders for his military commander in Panama to defend the canal and Chinese interests there in the event of an American attack.

***

The United States Southern Command is located in Miami near the famous Doral Country Club in the heart of Miami's expanding international cargo district. General Louis R. Frederick, the commander of the joint Armed Forces of U.S. SOUTHCOM, was upset over the report he had received from his J-2, Joint Intelligence Officer.

"Dammit," he swore to himself as he scratched his perfectly sculpted high and tight haircut. "The C.J.C.S. wants me to disperse forces in Panama because of an earthquake threat? Sounds like another Hailar."

General Frederick picked up the telephone and issued some verbal orders for the American unit commanders in Panama. You just couldn't temp fate with precious troops and expensive military equipment.

***

It took three weeks for Santiago to experience the predicted earthquake, which occurred at 02:30 hours on September 23, 2006. The most dramatic shifts in the subterranean fault under Panama lasted less than two minutes, but the effects were devastating. Most Panamanians were sound asleep when the huge earthquake jolted the country and made the Peninsula de Azuero on the Pacific coast disappear from the face of the Earth. The President of the United States was the first American to be awakened and notified of the tragedy.

"Fairchild here," answered the President as he groggily pulled the receiver over to his ear. He looked as bad as he sounded. "My God, you're serious? Are we talking about a large land mass? Damn! How many dead? No shit! What do you mean it's gone? It can't be gone! Fine, summon the NSC immediately."

Alex Fairchild quickly woke up and turned on the antique table lamp.

"Monty? Can't this wait, honey?" she begged him as she hid her head under her goose down pillow.

The President slapped his face a couple of times to get focused, which irritated Rebecca even more.

"The whole damned world's coming apart, Charly," remarked Alex to his slumbering wife as he pulled on his designer slippers. "I hate this! First there's the earthquake in China, then volcanoes in the South Pacific, and now this crap!"

"What's that, honey?" mumbled Rebecca from under the down filled pillow.

Alex Fairchild ignored her and stumbled through the halls of the West Wing into the Oval Office. He ordered the staff to bring the dormant White House to life. In less than an hour, the heads of the National Security Council trickled into the operational heart of the United States of America. As head of NOAH'S ARK, Doctor Michael Valenti was summoned by the Director of Central Intelligence to attend the meeting, too.

***

When the National Security Council was gathered in the Oval Office, there was already a steady stream of staffers and intelligence personnel walking back and forth in the White House. All the members were present in spite of the early morning hour. The President attended the meeting in his pajamas, robe, and shower shoes. Thurgood had already found a place in a corner to lie down and sleep some more.

"Give me a report, people," the President ordered as an aide placed a piping hot cup of coffee in front of him. Alex lifted the steaming cup to his nose and inhaled the aroma. "I need to know more about Panama."

Defense Secretary Andrea Mangone briefed the President on the tremendous damage to the Panama Canal and the extensive efforts of the U.S. Southern Command to recover from the effects of the earthquake. Her thin blonde hair was frumpy and the wrinkles around her green eyes were more severe under the bright lights of the Oval Office. As she spoke, the President made contact with Panamanian President Oswaldo Diaz, whom he convinced needed immediate American assistance to insure the rapid recovery of his country and guarantee the strategic security of the isthmus. Alexander Fairchild decided to send troops, engineering, and emergency aid to Panama before the Chinese government or the United Nations had time to respond.

After her in-depth lecture, Andrea Mangone deferred the rest of the briefing to General James Beckwourth Vann, the Chairman of the Joint Chiefs of Staff. He was in a camouflaged uniform that displayed his subdued jump wings and other professional military qualifications. When he spoke, all eyes were on him. The general's tight jaw line commanded the attention of those who were in the room.

"The SOUTHCOM commander submitted reports from vessels and aircraft in Panama via secure satellite communications. Mr. President, utilities and government services are completely out down there. People are scared, and there's a real probability for civil unrest and panic. After shocks are forecasted to continue for at least a month. 12th Air Force reports that the entire peninsula dropped into the ocean within ten minutes of the earthquake, which caused major marine events. The Atlantic Fleet documented tidal waves that emanated from Panama and also affected the Pacific coasts of adjoining countries. US Army South and Marine Forces Atlantic both report significant damage to the Panama Canal, which includes estimates that it will take a year to repair. We sustained 1,422 dead, and 3,114 injured as of ten minutes ago."

General Vann's face reflected the loss he felt for his dead and wounded troops.

"Thank you, General. I still can't believe it took a split second to make all that real estate disappear," muttered Alex Fairchild as he completed taking notes. "How will all this affect our military and rescue capabilities?"

"15% of our airbases are functional, Mr. President, as are 25% of the ports. I'm ordering the 10th Mountain Division to be airlifted into the area just north of the peninsula to support rescue and security efforts there. I'm sending the 82d Airborne to act as a security force along the border of the Canal Zone. They're both rapid deployable units that are capable of sustained operations over rugged terrain. Of course, engineering and theater support command units will also be deployed to begin repairs where they're needed. We'll work with civilian agencies and the Red Cross to perpetuate relief efforts. The logistics units will be able to supply fresh water, food, shelters, and medical support, but it will take approximately one week to get advance units and equipment on the ground. It'll take another thirty days to really make a difference."

"Thirty days? That's bullshit!" swore the Vice President, as he raised his thick eyebrows in surprise. "That's no better than China's efforts! We need to help these people immediately!"

"What about that?" asked the President.

"Unfortunately, Mr. President, disasters require huge logistical support," explained General Vann as he looked hard at Levan Salazar. "We don't keep disaster materials stockpiled in every American stronghold in the world, sir. Even if we did, there wouldn't be enough to help all the affected people of Panama."

"That'll have to change, General," advised Levan Salazar, who pulled a monogrammed leather cigar case out of a pocket and withdrew one of his cigars.

"You go ahead with your plans, General," directed the President. He was tired, and that made Vice President Salazar's comments irritate him more. "What's going on at State? Things any better?"

Secretary of State Daniel Tokuhisa flipped open his executive notebook and addressed the council. He was visibly sleepy, and his dimpled smile was missing.

"Well, our embassy's on auxiliary power, Mr. President, but we're also in touch with President Diaz. Colombia and Costa Rica were also affected, mostly by the tidal waves associated with the earthquake. President Diaz is reporting that approximately 250,000 people lived on that peninsula," explained Dan in his slow deliberate voice. "Deaths besides those on the peninsula are conservatively estimated at over 250,000."

"That's still hard for me to comprehend!" remarked the President as he ran a hand through the uncombed sides of his otherwise balding head. "Over 250,000 deaths. Unbelievable!"

"This makes the Hailar disaster look like shit," added Levan Salazar. "Was this a bigger quake?"

"Definitely. We're estimating eleven points on the Richter scale, but the quake itself occurred at a deeper, more damaging subterranean level," interrupted George

Donaldson from the U.S.G.S. The change to business wear did little to improve George's unkempt appearance. "Survey satellites also recorded that the mountain range north of where Santiago was located gained about six yards in elevation. This was some fault disturbance."

The President shook his head, upset by the whole catastrophe. "Zip, just like that, and a chunk of Panama drops into the drink! We've got to do something! When the people wake up and hear about this on the television, we're going to be bombarded with questions that I'm not sure we know how to answer!"

Myrna Ramirez was wearing a warm up suit, which was her standard attire when she had to respond to emergencies on such short notice.

"Mr. President, most of the information we have must remain classified," advised Myrna Ramirez in her soft voice. "Any reference to tectonics and planetary damage must be avoided, if only for consideration of world political dynamics. George Donaldson's people can present the routine facts to the media as public information. Very few people know or care about the development in the South Pacific. We're not prepared to go public, sir, and neither is the U.N."

"Good suggestion, Rosy," noted Alex Fairchild with a long yawn. "Excuse me people, I'm still trying to wake up. I just wonder how long we can keep this government conspiracy a secret, especially with all the news and Internet sources out there."

"Doctor Ramirez is correct, sir. With the summit approaching, China and the other involved nations will have a hard time dealing with budget problems, much less panic," noted Aramentha Washington. "The less the world knows at this point, the better I think. Also, Mr.

President, we're in a delicate situation with China now that we're going to send military troops to monitor a canal that the Panamanian government has authorized them to maintain."

Alex Fairchild nodded. Aramentha had made a good point. The whole mess would have to remain classified. The State Department was going to be busy keeping the other countries off balance.

"Thanks, Aramentha. Rosy, let's get moving on NOAH'S ARK," continued the President. "Where do we stand on their expansion to a pro-active posture?"

"The Pangaean Task Force is in its new location, sir. I need your signature to move into phase two," explained Myrna Ramirez.

"Phase two? What's that?" asked the Vice President. "You know, even with all these disasters, I'm still skeptical about this pangaean thing. It's hard to believe the Earth's about to shake and bake mankind."

"Phase two involves switching NOAH'S ARK from an investigative operation to a proactive one, Mr. Salazar," spoke up Mike Valenti. "Since it's inception, NOAH'S ARK has been limited to investigating planetary phenomena that may be associated with pangaean based theories. During phase two, we will begin actual planning to survive the Pangaean Effect and whatever outside factors are causing these planetary problems."

"Which will include?" urged Tell Summers, who as Attorney General was always considering the legal implications of classified operations. A true Wyoming cowboy, Tell Summers was dressed in tasteful western business wear, to include a tan Stetson hat.

"Which will include many missions, the most applicable one right now being finding solutions to our current geological threats," finished Dr. Valenti.

The President moved on, concerned more about future public opinion relating to the disasters.

"Well, George, what do you have to say about all this?" asked Alex of his alienated political appointee. They had spoken little since the reprimand. "Anymore about the volcanoes near Australia?"

"Mr. President," began George formally. He was dressed in chinos, a shirt and tie, and a blue blazer. "I'd like to apologize to Dr. Valenti for my criticism of his tectonic theories. A new archipelago is forming near the Solomons. It's centered near an expanding rupture in the middle of an existing tectonic plate system. It's clear that the Chinese and Antarctic quakes are causes of the volcanic activity in the South Pacific. The good thing is that the new volcanoes have solved our continental magma problem by becoming the relief valve for our magma buildup here. However, the Hawaiian buildup of magma is increasing more as a result of these new volcanoes. We're still waiting for the results of what these new volcanoes mean for Hawaii's instability. They should be available in a few days."

"Thanks, George," said the President, as he looked in Valenti's direction. "Solutions, Doctor?"

Mike Valenti shook his head.

"Not good enough," said the President. "Not for me. We've got six volcanoes that threaten the Solomon Islands and the Hawaiian Islands. I need a solution, I need one fast, and you're the expert who's been right on the money so far. Get me a solution within a week."

"Yes, Mr. President," acknowledged Mike.

"Rosy, you've got the green light now. Organize and supply the NOAH'S ARK task force yesterday, but be careful with the spending. Kurt, I want 100% staff support on this. You're Chief of Staff, so I don't want to hear about any leaks to the public. Frank, I want you to work closely with Rosy to make sure the good doctor's not going to be bogged down with political bullshit from the Congress or us. Valenti's got this emergency and twenty-four years worth of work to do. Aramentha, you and Dan are responsible for the summit. Andrea, I want you to coordinate with the Vice President on the Panamanian relief mission. Tell, I need a legal brief on how we can fund this pangaean operation until the mission is accomplished."

"You got it, boss," acknowledged the Attorney General of the United States.

Everyone else remained quiet, not wanting to prolong the meeting.

"Levan, Panama's your baby, but only as it pertains to supporting that country and our Department of Defense. Be a positive influence and don't fuck this up," warned the President. "You don't have any authority to modify my orders. Don't make any policy decisions with President Diaz. Clear it through me."

The National Security Council, and especially the Vice President, answered affirmatively. Alex Fairchild looked haggard as he stood up and retied his robe. He needed a shave and a lot more sleep, which did not escape the observations of the Chief of Staff and the National Security Advisor. The strain of a world in crisis was taking its toll on the President of the United States.

***

There were too many reports about missing persons and isolated communities for the Panamanian government to handle. President Oswaldo Diaz had been awake for the two days since the earthquake and he had personally immersed himself in every step of the rescue effort. The Americans were assisting his defense forces. Without power, water, food, and communications, the Panamanian government was unable to meet the demands of a shocked populace. In one more day, those who were trapped or isolated would also begin dying.

"Many have taken to the countryside to forage for food and make shelters," reported one Panamanian officer over a Vietnam era field telephone to his president. "The American 10th Mountain Division is arriving in the area with water purification units and packaged meals, but our people in rural areas will be starving and dehydrated before they'll be of any assistance. The airdrops have been effective, but they're only delivering food and medical supplies in limited quantities. Can you ask the Americans to increase their drop shipments?"

"Of course, general," responded President Diaz irritably. He wondered what had happened to his own military stockpiles that they had purchased from the Americans. "I will speak with President Fairchild soon. Was there any outlying damage?"

"The coastal areas were devastated, my president. There are many dead. I don't know how many yet. There are also small guerilla groups forming in the hills that are calling for a rebellion."

"What about the Chinese, General? Are they within their restricted areas?"

"I don't know, sir," stammered the general over the telephone. "Our communications systems are down, and I haven't received any reports."

Oswaldo Diaz had reached the limits of his endurance twelve hours ago and had no patience for military commanders who lacked initiative.

"General, instruct our forces to provide assistance as best we can. As for our own stockpiles of goods and equipment, find the wiring and field equipment you've been issued and establish communications with every town that has been isolated. Order the commanders in each town to make contact with all the villages in their districts. I want radio outposts or wire communications stations established throughout the outage areas by the end of tomorrow! Serve the people, General, and serve them now!"

President Diaz slammed down the telephone and swore at the top of his lungs. The Chinese were no longer requesting authority to send military units from the Canal Zone to assist in the rescue operation. With each passing hour, Oswaldo Diaz resented their presence in his country. He had denied the Chinese request to deploy troops from the Canal Zone. At least the Americans were self sufficient and uninterested in occupying his country again. In this crisis, the Chinese were proving to be as imperialistic as the United States had once been.

Chapter Twelve

"The Doctor Knows Best"

It was approximately five degrees Fahrenheit when the Chinese special operations team arrived within view of the American expeditionary site. Designated men photographed and sketched the details of the encampment while the rest of the twelve-man team provided security. The members of the unit were dressed in white tactical clothes. Their skis and white packs had been left at their last assembly location. They had also left a human drag sled at their temporary base to transport the hostage.

Each soldier was armed with weapons that were suited to his particular task or area of expertise. Commander Jia Yonguan, another officer, and the senior sergeant on the team were armed with Tokarev 7.62 mm pistols and Type 89 Xin 5.8 mm military assault rifles. The team sniper was armed with a silenced Type 89 sniper rifle with an improved scope, night vision device, and a modified barrel. The two four man assault teams were each equipped with one Type 89 squad machine gun and three Type 87 assault rifles. All of the team members were wearing night vision goggles.

As they scouted the encampment, Commander Jia Yonguan quickly learned that there were no American military troops present to protect the research site. A few of the modular buildings also appeared to be empty. There was one location, a research area well away from the main area, where some Americans occupied a triangular tented shelter. The leader observed for an hour, selected their target, and informed his sniper.

With great discipline and stealth, one assault team maneuvered close enough to the O.A.S.I.S. unit to hear the researchers as they worked. The interior of the tent appeared to be empty, while a wide variety of monitoring equipment was being installed in the area around it. Their selected target, a white male in his forties, appeared to be one of the supervisors or experts at the site. It took another hour and a half before the target became isolated. When the target walked to one of the all terrain vehicles with a large package in his hands. The sniper waited until the package was placed in the truck, then fired his silenced Type 89 rifle. A narrow stream of gas escaped the end of the barrel as the dart took flight.

The dart that was fired at the American contained a dose of medication that would instantly disable any human target. It hit the shocked man in the neck. The geologist stumbled, reached for the bumper of the truck, and then fell to the ground without uttering an alarm.

The assault team silently crawled to the stricken man and dragged him away. No American researcher at the site noticed the supervisor's disappearance until it was too late. In the constant late summer Antarctic darkness, only a trained military man or seasoned hunter would have been able to locate the human footprints left behind by the elite Chinese soldiers. While the Chinese departed the area, the Americans at the Antarctic site were becoming aware of the missing scientist.

***

Doctor Michael Valenti was in the middle of a planning meeting and a discussion about ARK Four's redeployment back to Santiago to conduct earthquake damage assessment. Evan, Cable, Mary Blalack, and Seth Tayman were presenting administrative and logistical matters to Mike. The discussion was now centered on the Mars Program.

"We need a great deal of independence if this is going to work, Mike," suggested Mary Blalack. "Not to mention job security that won't be called into question whenever there's a change of administrations or a tragic mishap. I don't have to tell you this ambitious Mars colonization program will create more tragedies."

"Mary, I realize the potential for the loss of life, but we've got to accomplish our mission. The Pangaean Effect is still coming," reminded Mike Valenti. "We've got over twenty years to do this mission, and we've got to do it as one entity. We won't be able to finance the entire Mars program, but foreign support is zip until we're authorized to go public."

"We should get the Brits, Germans, and Japanese secretly on board," suggested Cable Craig. "Maybe even the French. They've all got the technological knowledge and the deep pockets we'll need."

Everyone nodded.

"The list will be long," said Mike, thinking out loud. "But other nations may not be guaranteed representation on Mars. To me, the amount a country contributes should not influence colonial selection standards. But since we're dealing with the survival of the human race, the reality is that selection will be based mostly on financial participation. How are we looking on Darwin?"

"Mike, our task is challenging. Locating the newborns is easy because we conducting initial genetic testing on all of them, but identifying the population born before routine genetic testing is going to be harder. I'm focusing on the most recent Darwin Strand populations and working back from there," explained Cable Craig.

"NOAH'S ARK will be ready to implement our population centers program in a month, Mike. I figure it'll take a good five to ten years to build and stock them properly," explained Seth Tayman. "Are we going to populate the centers with Darwins, us, or both groups?"

"Plan to create survival centers for both groups. Locate the Darwins in those areas forecasted to sustain the greatest damage. The Darwin population objectives will be funded under a black budget," noted Mike. "The Mars program may have to be unclassified when it comes to actual operations."

"That sounds good, Mike, but the use of our industrial resources to support the Mars program is going to be hard to keep black," offered Evan Leeper. "How about a ruse for the Mars effort."

"What do you suggest, Evan? There aren't many reasons to expend billions of dollars to go to Mars," responded Mike. "You know of a good one?"

"Yep, the ozone layer," suggested Evan. "It involves both poles, has been in the news for years, and can be argued to be a catastrophic threat to humanity."

"Do you know how many scientists will argue that we're completely nuts?" asked Seth Tayman. "It's a weak argument, but I have to admit it just might work."

"The Space Department can present any argument and bear the criticism, you guys. It's just crazy enough to work!" exclaimed Mary. "We could sell it, if we manipulate the scientific data to conform to our ruse."

"I'll get the science and technology folks busy researching the possibilities," remarked Mike.

Mike Valenti ended the meeting and asked Evan Leeper to remain in his office after everyone else had left. He tossed his long time friend the stack of recent U.S.G.S. data concerning national seismic activity.

"Take a look at that," requested Mike.

Evan whistled as he reviewed the national seismic survey data summary.

"Okay, elevated stats, increasing irregular seismic patterns… I like this right here," noted Evan. "Volcanic irregularities - shit, all over Hawaii by the looks of this!"

"The magma flow is increasing with the pressure from the new volcanoes in the South Pacific," provided Mike. "Even though the continent's okay now, Hawaii could be blown from the map if this keeps up."

"The activity sure coincides with the Chinese and Panamanian earthquakes, doesn't it? What do you think, Mike?" asked Evan Leeper.

"I think these earthquakes have affected the planet's lithosphere and asthenosphere," opined Mike. "And that's why we have these six volcanoes to deal with and an emergency situation developing in Hawaii."

"Now that was one hell of an explanation," remarked Evan with a smile. "You know, nobody has yet determined how stresses and strains are partitioned through semi-rigid tectonic plates, but the balance of forces at the Earth's core has definitely been affected. These Hawaiian volcanoes are time bombs just waiting to happen."

"It's just another indicator that time's not on our side, Evan. This Chinese event has affected the Pangaean Effect. We have to expect sporadic degradation of tectonic plates and faults over the next twenty years, but the Pangaean Effect will not be instantaneous now. It'll occur at increasing intervals until the astronomical effects culminate in a huge rapid global disaster. We may not have enough time to prepare for the Pangaean Effect after all, brother."

"That kinda' tosses water on our fire, doesn't it?" figured Evan Leeper. "We're going to have to hustle if we're going to beat this thing. What do you think? Population centers first, then fill them with Darwin Strand carriers, and the whole time push for Mars?"

"I believe we're forced to comply with astronomy and science," agreed Mike. "We've got to plan for the worst while hoping for the best conditions. We're going to have to insure that our programs are accelerated. In the meantime, I'm going to find a solution to the six volcanoes before Hawaii stops being Hawaii."

"Sure, Mike, I'll keep the op going in the meantime," agreed Evan. His naturally curly hair was one of the things he'd inherited from his Native American grandmother.

Evan left while Mike contacted his father. As they spoke, Mike observed through his window the dark gray storm clouds gather over District of Columbia for a late summer thunderstorm. He was looking forward to enjoying Maryland crabs in North Baltimore, where he could be with family and friends without having to worry about the Pangaean Effect.

***

President Zhu Le Ho gently massaged the laminated top of his desk as he listened to the Premier, Vice Premiers, and a few of his most essential ministers. They had discussed the earthquake in Panama, which had been more damaging than their own. Lee Jiang Ping, the Minister of State, was now discussing the questions that would be asked of China now that one of the American researchers was missing.

"What about you, Dung Yeung Song? As the Minister of Science and Technology, this should bring promising returns for us," asked the Chief of State.

"I agree," spoke up Dung Yeung in a gentle voice. "We need to know about American activities in Antarctica. Some of the advisors from the World Meteorological Organization and the U.N. Framework Convention on Climate Change believe the earthquakes are related."

"We'll wait for this American to be interrogated before we engineer our summit objectives," decided Hu Quichen. "What are the results from our own research?"

"Disconcerting, Premier," remarked Sang Jiyun, the Vice Premier overseeing special projects. "Our monitoring detected increases at the time of our earthquake and the one in Panama. I believe we caused everything. I presume the Americans are fully aware that our first earthquake caused the others, but they've been concealing it from us to suit their own purposes."

"Perhaps. Perhaps," breathed Zhu Le Ho. "I think the Americans are acting in their own interest. According to our intelligence operatives, the Americans responded quickly in Panama because they had a special monitoring team there to provide advanced notification."

"That is very true," agreed Lin Hyo, the Minister of Defense. "We had the benefit of no such monitoring team and suffered for it. Our own losses were substantial, especially those suffered by the tidal waves. The President of Panama didn't notify us, even though he had time to disperse his own forces to minimize his losses. I believe that was intentional on their part."

"Very well, then," sighed the Chinese executive. "We must insure our interests in the canal are not compromised. Lin Hyo, have the Revolution deploy to the Atlantic coast of Panama where she can be detected by the Americans, and send a strong fleet to maintain a presence along the Pacific coast. Panama is weak, and we must appear strong to the Panamanian government and the United States. Instruct our general in Panama to seize as much of that country as possible for our strategic use as a bargaining chip."

The meeting ended as it had begun, with all but the President, Premier, and Vice Premiers leaving to commence their routine duties. The small group continued talking into the afternoon and evening about provincial and national issues affecting their country.

***

Hale's Seafood was a working class restaurant and tavern that remained in business in spite of the contemporary restaurant franchises that had taken over the Baltimore area. It was known for serving Chesapeake Bay blue crabs, National Bohemian beer, and the kind of local middle class conversation that was lost on most of the college students from Loyola and Towson State that often went there for the fare. Mike Valenti's father was one of those local residents and old timers who could walk into Hale's and always find friends who were eager to speak with him. Mike Valenti, Sr. was a surgeon with legendary hands and the Chief of Neurology at the Johns Hopkins Medical Center.

"Michael, these jumbo male crabs are excellent!" praised Mike Valenti, Sr., as he snapped open the chest of an Old Bay seasoned blue crab. "They didn't have seafood like this in San Francisco!"

Mike was sucking down a Corona and had his hands covered in crab debris. Both men were grinning at the bountiful feast of the three-dozen crabs that were heaped on the table in front of them. As Mike struck one crab claw and sprayed the patrons at the table next to him with it's juices, his father was reaching for another crab.

"Yeah, dad, the crabs this year are great!" exclaimed Mike. "How did your conference go? What was it for, nerve repair surgery or something?"

Mike Valenti, Sr. belched, which was something he only did at Hale's where eating messy crabs around loud, beer-drinking friends was standard behavior.

"No, Michael, it was on advancements in laser suturing," explained Mike's father as he drank some of his beer. National Boh was a staple for the Maryland working man. "I have to keep up on all these technological changes or the young physicians will be teaching me soon!"

Mike laughed. He knew his father was one of the best surgeons in the business.

"That'll be the day, dad!" exclaimed Mike as he waved at the chubby waitress for another round of beer. "So how was San Fran?"

"It was great! I did the touristy things there years ago, so now I get to dine in style. I like the seafood. Especially the abalone. It's different," remarked Mike Valenti, Sr. "So how's Steven?"

The waitress placed the new drinks on the table and removed the empties.

"C'mon, dad, between you and Vernie, I don't want to hear any more about him!" snapped Mike. He drank deeply from his new Corona.

"Speaking of Vernie, you should marry her" advised Mike Valenti, Sr. "As for Steven, whether you like it or not, he's blood, and your mother and I have set aside a nice trust fund for him."

"What?" roared Mike, who calmed down a bit when the happy patrons turned to look at him.

"You heard me, and we'll give it to him this Christmas," continued Mike Valenti, Sr.

"Dad, Steven's in the Navy, he was adopted long ago, and he's not my son anymore," stated Mike, who slid his plate away. "Why are you doing this?"

"Because your denial has nothing to do with his blood. The family will maintain contact with him, and you're going to meet with him if only for appearances."

"No!" replied Mike, who quickly stood up.

"Where are you going?"

"The bathroom, father, with your permission!" growled Mike.

When Mike returned, his father was eating crabs again and laughing with the waitress.

"What'd you do, pass a tapeworm?" laughed Mike Valenti, Sr. "Here, have another crab!"

Mike shook his head. He had lost his appetite.

"Look, son, I'm tired of talking to doctors about laser technology and sutures. I just want to have a nice dinner with my oldest boy. Is that so bad?"

"No, dad, I've been stressed out down at Langley myself," noted Mike. "No more about Steven, though."

"Okay, and I won't talk about the dangers of lasers or the honesty of the C.I.A., right?"

"Nice one, dad," laughed Mike. "Besides, how bad can laser suturing be anyway?"

Mike's father shook his head this time.

"I liked the old suturing techniques better. Using a super hot beam of light to heal an open wound isn't easy. If you don't have a good surgical style, you could end up in a malpractice suit!"

Mike sucked on a crab claw as he listened, then suddenly stopped and slowly began to smile.

"What'd I say? Something good?" asked his dad.

"Yes!" shouted Mike, who instantly drew looks from nearby customers again. "The volcanoes are like open wounds, too!"

Mike Valenti, Sr. leaned forward, attempting to understand what his son was saying.

"What volcanoes, son?"

Mike kept his voice low as he asked his father for advice about a very classified subject.

"Well?" asked Mike.

"Theoretically speaking, yes. The application of enough heat to an open wound in the proper way will meld the skin of the wound together. It would protect and conceal the interior of the body and the exterior would be healed," explained Mike's father.

Mike leaned back in his chair.

"Dad, you're the best!" he said. "And yes, I'll go see Steven!"

"Well, whatever I just did, you are welcome!" Mike replied. "Especially if it means you'll see my grandson. Now, let's eat some more ocean scavengers!"

As the evening wore on, both men completed their destruction of three-dozen Maryland blue crabs, a dozen beers, and two crab mallets. By the time the tavern stopped serving alcohol, the two Valentis were singing songs from the jukebox at Hale's Seafood.

***

Since ARK One was no longer operating the Antarctic research site, it was George Donaldson who notified the chain of authority about the disappearance of one of his team leaders. Mike Valenti personally contacted George to find out more about the case, but it was Bubba Washington who connected the missing man with the Chinese encampment.

"That's a little far fetched, don't you think?" continued Mike Valenti in response to Bubba's remark that scientists don't disappear at a research site.

"Hell no, Doc!" swore Bubba as he chewed on a toothpick. "There ain't no predators in Antarctica and no body's been found. That U.S.G.S. dude was at the site, so he didn't get lost due to no bad weather either! On that day when Vernie's team landed in that blizzard, nobody got lost then! Who's tha' dude that's missing?"

"His name escapes me, but he was a supervisory scientist in charge of the new seismic site. He is certified in earthquake seismology, geodetics, pale seismology, solid Earth geophysics, and regional tectonics."

"That means he's one smart mutha," figured Bubba. "Just the sort of gent the Chinese would like to git their hands on. Even if that dude's not hip to our classified mission, he damn sho' knows what we were doin' there. We've been fucked, Doc!"

Mike thought for a moment. It didn't make sense to him that the Chinese would risk their international reputation for one scientist from the U.S. Geological Survey. What could they want to know?

"Damn, Doc, I kin hear you thinkin' over here," laughed the big bodybuilder.

"Bubba, you are too smart!" exclaimed Mike. "I believe the Chinese are about to learn more about us than we want them to know."

"Hell, Doc, it coulda' been worse," noted Bubba as he twisted the toothpick to the other side of his mouth.

"How's that?" inquired Mike.

"They coulda' taken one a' us," he provided.

Without a second thought, Mike picked up his telephone and contacted Myrna Ramirez, who was already pursuing the investigation as a kidnapping. By the end of the day, the intelligence organizations of the United States were busy attempting to obtain data that would support the probability that a U.S.G.S. scientist was now in the hands of the People's Republic of China.

***

It was late afternoon when Myrna Ramirez was able to meet with Mike Valenti to discuss his solution for the dangerous volcanoes that threatened to alter the geography of the South Pacific. Since she was enroute to a meeting with the head of the N.S.A. at Fort Meade, Maryland, Myrna asked Mike to ride with her. It was raining, so the traffic was moving slowly.

"So tell me again, Mike," continued Myrna as she flipped through the data Mike had provided her. "You want to use nuclear missiles on these volcanoes?"

"Underground nuclear devices, ma'am," answered Mike nervously. The noise from the rain striking the vehicle was making him speak louder. "Seven of them, small yield devices, placed at precise junctions between and at the ends of the volcanoes."

"And what, they make the volcanoes go away?" asked Myrna, who didn't like using nuclear weapons.

"No, ma'am," replied Mike. "The detonation of the nuclear devices will level the volcanic funnels and form a heat seam over the volcanic channel that will be cooled by the ocean. As my dad would explain, we're going to heal this nasty wound by using laser sutures."

Myrna was impressed. She flipped through more of the papers, reviewing diagrams and drawings of the suggested solution.

"So will it just take care of the Solomons, or will it solve our problems with Hawaii and the Pangaean Effect, too?" asked the Director of the C.I.A.

"It won't delay the Pangaean Effect, ma'am, but the neutralization of the South Pacific volcanoes should save the Solomons and Hawaii from destruction."

"Well, that's one thing the President wants," admitted Myrna. She reached for a bottle of water. "I don't know if he'll go for the nukes, but saving Hawaii might convince him. What about China, and Panama?"

"The Chinese problem will remain for years to come, but Panama's earthquake was caused by the Antarctic one," advised Mike. "I just don't know."

Myrna picked up the telephone and began to dial a number, then changed her mind.

"Using nuclear weapons on these volcanoes isn't going to be easy to approve, or execute," explained Myrna, who was deep in thought. "Get with everyone you have to and prepare a rock solid plan."

"I'll make it a good one!" acknowledged Mike.

"You'd better, because everyone in the cabinet and the Intelligence Community's going to be waiting for you to make a mistake. Now, I've got to meet with N.S.A., and you've got more planning to do."

Dr. Valenti assisted the Director of the Central Intelligence Agency into her wheelchair. When the Director was on her way up the sidewalk, the limousine pulled away from the curb. Alone with his thoughts, Mike departed to work on his plan to save Hawaii.

***

After arriving in Sydney, Australia, ARK One was flown by Royal Australian Air Force transport aircraft to Brisbane. Once on the ground, Elton Rance and his team were picked up by Royal Australian Navy Hawker

Siddley HS-748 transport aircraft and transported to the island of Guadalcanal, Solomon Islands. After a brief break, Australian helicopters took ARK One to the Australian naval vessels on patrol with the American research submarine. ARK One was finally on board a Royal Australian research ship with the comforts of home.

"Kyle Lombard," greeted the portly Executive Officer with a welcome grin. His shoulder boards had the gold circle of the Royal Australian Navy and rank of a Lieutenant Commander. Elton and the team leaders introduced themselves. "You're on H.M.A.S. Melville, mates, and you've arrived just in time for a banyan!"

"A what?" asked Elton Rance as the team followed Lieutenant Commander Lombard on deck.

"A banyan, mate! It's what you yanks would call a Barbie, or cookout," explained Commander Lombard. The Australian sailors looked at the new arrivals curiously as they passed."

"Ah heard that, son! Barbie, banyan, or barbeque, it's all tha' same to me!" exclaimed Elton when he saw the heaps of grilled meat and other food arranged on deck.

"Jolly good! We've got some beef and pork, but mostly mutton if you've a mind to try it. While the crew is dining and getting to know your team, I'll escort you to the captain's quarters. You'll enjoy Captain Collingsworth. He's a first rater and easy to get on with. After that, one of our crew transports will skip you over to your research submarine. She's just arrived in the area from a surveying mission and will surface shortly."

"Kin' ah git some chow before we go see your boss, Kyle? I'm hungrier than hell!" exclaimed Elton.

Lieutenant Commander Lombard guided Elton to the food, where he heaped some chopped mutton onto a thick bun and followed the X.O. to the commander's quarters. One of the ship's Chief Petty Officers was guiding the rest of the team through the Australian mess rituals. When Elton met Captain Collingsworth, he was briefed about the comprehensive Australian and New Zealander role in assisting the Dolphin in surveying the new volcanic area.

***

After Elton Rance suffered the humiliation of needing to be assisted into the command center of the U.S.S. Dolphin, he was escorted to the skipper's small quarters. There was another officer seated next to him. The former Ranger had been seasick and vomiting since he had eaten the grilled mutton on the Australian ship.

"Fred Herman, Mr. Rance, nice to meet you," welcomed the Dolphin's commander. "I can see you've got an upset stomach. Would you like a drink?"

"Ah'd appreciate that, Cap'n," replied Elton. "Ah' was infantry, sir, so ah' never liked the Navy or any water with salt in it. I'm just a little seasick is all. So, what's the current situation?"

"I'll refer you to Doctor Robelot, our Chief Scientist," said Captain Herman.

"Milt Robelot," introduced the grizzled scientist, who spread his surveying map out on the aluminum table. "We're using state of the art radar interferometry to measure the crustal deformation of the ocean floor in the volcanic area. Basically, radar interferometry provides us with an accurate contour map of the ocean's surface by conducting a co-seismic surface displacement along the vector from the imaged points we need to analyze. This sub is calibrated to be a geodetic station where we can use global positioning systems and trilateration to obtain a precise spatial sampling of the entire volcanic zone."

"So, what have you learned, Doctor?" asked Elton, who hated scientific subjects.

"Mr. Rance, these six volcanoes were caused by an unusual intra plate disturbance, likely the expanding Chinese event, which stressed the interior of the plates here in the Solomons. Almost every plate boundary between Antarctica and China is so stressed that they're on the verge of a major reorganization. As we speak, a new island chain is developing from the new volcanoes."

"And the Hawaiian chain will die," remarked Elton as he began to search his pockets.

"That's likely, sir," apologized Milton Robelot.

Elton fished his bag of chewing tobacco out of a pocket and offered some to his hosts. The captain was delighted to have a chew since his own ship's stores had been out of chewing tobacco for two weeks.

"Mr. Rance, do you know what would happen to the Earth's atmosphere if ten volcanoes became active at one time for more than a month?" asked Dr. Robelot.

"Naw, cain't say that ah do," replied Elton nervously. "What?"

"The magma composition of this area is high in silica, or silicon dioxide. High silica magmas are very explosive. We've conducted major element chemical analysis and determined that we're dealing with fluid fast moving silicon based basalt magma. When the explosions occur, the atmosphere over Hawaii and the

South Pacific will be filled with poisonous gases that would be toxic to mammals."

"Look, are you tellin' me these volcanoes could end up killin' people?" asked Elton as he spit into a cup.

Both men nodded.

"Ah don't get it, gents," remarked Elton. "We're in the middle of the South Pacific, an' these volcanoes ain't even topped the surface yet. What's the big deal?"

"These six are just the beginning," continued Dr. Robelot. "The Australians believe more will form soon. Given the analytical data, I have to agree with them."

"Okay, ah'll get on this ASAP," advised Elton. "You got a commo room?"

Captain Herman escorted Rance to the communications room, where Elton was able to have a conversation with Bubba Washington. Before the sun had set on the Solomon Islands, the Pangaean Task Force was making contact with the Australian government.

***

After wiping messy bird guano from his compact disk player, Derrick Blasdale squatted down next to one of his tired team members to inspect the newly formed cliffs where the Panamanian peninsula had once been. It was unsettling to stand in the middle of the lush countryside and look down freshly cut rock into the rough ocean below.

"It's a bitch, huh?" noted a team member named Carlos as he looked down at the churning tide. There were bloated bodies and debris scattered over the threatening swells. "This area looks like God took a sharp knife and cut a hunk of Panama off the map."

"I've never seen anything like this," admitted another team member. "I read about it in college, but I'll be damned if I ever thought I'd see the day a quake could do something like this. The fault didn't shift, it split."

"Yeah, well, this tectonic shit's not supposed to happen for a million years, guys," said Derrick as he stood. His knees were scarred from kneeling down on the rough ground. "You see the strength of the after shocks on the monitor? If they start to increase, we're leaving!"

"Can you imagine how quickly our own west coast could drop into the ocean now? What's our next move?" asked one of them.

"Damage assessment for the Doc," advised Derrick. "SOUTHCOM is doing their own, but NOAH'S ARK needs to get as much data about this area as possible. Once we're done, we can extract from Panama and get back to the old red, white, and blue!"

***

The General Assembly Hall is the largest chamber in the United Nations. It has the capacity to seat over 1,800 people, and it is the only conference room at the facility that bears the emblem of the United Nations. The General Assembly is the central area of the United Nations where all 191 Member States can assemble to discuss international issues in a cooperative setting. Asi Fanon Mtume was on the floor of the assembly hall meeting with summit coordinators.

"Ah, Ambassador Washington! I do enjoy your attire today! Do you have time for breakfast?" asked the leader of the United Nations with a warm smile.

"I'm sorry, Secretary General, but I have so many matters to handle before we are prepared for the summit. I wanted to inquire about the protocol and schedule."

"Ah, yes, we will tentatively convene on October 12th, with a formal dinner for all attendees that will be sponsored by China. Will China's President and the Premier receive authorization to attend the summit?"

"The State Department did receive official requests for them to enter the United States, Mr. Fanon. Their requests will be granted. China also requested that President Fairchild should formally welcome the U.N. summit to the United States that evening."

"That is a splendid idea! Our summit goal will be to complete and approve an international agreement on actions to combat the climatic or geological changes. On October 13th, we'll have a morning welcome ceremony with a full state breakfast and entertainment provided by a troupe from my country. The Chinese, who have also requested that I serve as the guest speaker, will also sponsor our Kenyan troupe. I'll declare the summit officially open at that time. Representatives of the U.N. World Meteorological Organization, the International Centre for Science and High Technology, and the Framework Convention on Climate Change will present technological data for consideration by conferees. On October 14th, experts from all the affected countries will provide attendees with information briefings explaining how these environmental tragedies have affected their respective nations. The actual planning days of the summit will be from October 15th to October 19th. On the nineteenth, the summit will present preliminary recommendations for international cooperation and action to the General Assembly for a vote. If our goal is accomplished, the U.N. will meet the challenge of marshaling the world to support and investigate these geographical problems," finished the Secretary General.

"That is ambitious, sir," remarked Aramentha skeptically. "I'll submit your schedule to Secretary Tokuhisa, but I have several concerns. These summits often become forums for political discussions and haggling over spoils rather than science."

"That is still the way of most international symposiums, is it not, madam? We at the U.N. can merely do our best for the world. Nonetheless, the Chinese have insisted that Security Council members support the summit by openly sharing technology and unique scientific data. Most of the member nations have substandard abilities to accurately research how much these tragedies may impact them in the future. I know the Chinese and Russians are extremely curious to learn how much you Americans know and are willing to share about these geological concerns," provided Asi Fanon."

"What is the general opinion amongst your contacts about these problems?" asked Aramentha as she sought to obtain some intelligence. She moved closer to Mr. Mtume to keep others from listening to their conversation. The Secretary General took her arm a little too intimately and gently guided her away from his aides.

"Well, Aramentha, everyone is worried. My Office for Outer Space Affairs assures me these geographical events are due to climatic changes. Everyone else has suspicions ranging from the supernatural to the extraterrestrial," added the Secretary General. "The Chinese believe you're concealing your abilities to predict these catastrophes as a means of gaining political power or military advantage over them."

Aramentha Washington remained silent. As she handed Mr. Mtume a thick white envelope, she held onto the monthly cash payment of $10,000.00 long enough to make her point to the corrupt political leader.

"Defend our efforts, sir," reminded Aramentha, as Mr. Mtume stared into her brown eyes. "Our national policy continues to be to support you and the United Nations in any efforts that may affect any nation in the world. I'll make a note to inform the President about your concerns and the fears of the Chinese government. I'm sure he will personally contact you about this subject."

***

The jubilant Chinese combat team arrived back at the expedition site to find it being rapidly disassembled. There was a bitter wind that was disrupting work activities. Commander Jia Yonguan, the commanding officer of the tactical unit, led the line of exhausted soldiers into the icy base. Commander Jia was dragging the one-man sled that contained the drugged American scientist. Colonel Quien walked out to meet the returning unit, impressed with the Chinese naval infantrymen and their ice-covered commander.

"I trust your mission was successful?" greeted Colonel Quien.

"Yes, Colonel," replied Jia Yonguan in a tired voice. His white facemask and goggles were streaked with snow. "We weren't followed after we captured the American, but I'll feel better when he's on board our extraction aircraft. Would you like to see him?"

"If you don't mind. Is he still sedated?"

"Of course, sir," replied Commander Jia as he moved the insulated coverings from the American's upper torso. "He was actually snoring during the trip and hasn't stirred since we tied him onto the sled. Have the elements affected his health, Doctor?"

Colonel Quien knelt in the snow and briefly examined the unconscious American. He was heavily sedated, but his weak pulse was even. There was a pack of Merit brand cigarettes and butane lighter in the man's flannel shirt pocket that the Colonel removed. The two officers strolled away from the rest of the unit to chat as they smoked the rare American cigarettes.

"What did you see that would be of interest to me?" asked the expedition commander.

"The Americans have an efficient operation, complete with generated electricity, modular dwellings, and military vehicles. There were a few white painted vehicles that bore the identification of the U.S. Geological Survey, but the most suspicious ones were unmarked. The modular units and large research tent were marked with identification numbers that were different from those of normal geological units."

"Really? Intelligence indicates that this was a standard geological research site," said Dr. Quien.

"I know American military vehicles when I see them. The all terrain vehicles were camouflaged, which is unusual for non-military units operating under international treaties. This encampment is clandestine."

"What else was irregular, Commander?" asked the colonel as he tossed away his expired cigarette butt.

"The tented unit at one research site was vacant, but it had been occupied at some point. There were old excavations in the glacier at selected points at the site area that had not been covered. Most importantly, the site appeared to be only partially occupied, and the scientists we observed were wearing fresh equipment."

"Most interesting, Commander. There is apparently much we do not know. Our prisoner will be very helpful in clearing up these concerns," said Colonel Quien Lo Chen.

As the two men spoke, the sounds of approaching Chinese airplanes could be heard in the distance. In less than two hours, the entire Chinese expeditionary force had departed Antarctica. The American hostage regained consciousness somewhere over the South China Sea, where he was brutally knocked into unconsciousness again by Commander Jia Yonguan.

***

Elton Rance gathered ARK One in the small galley of H.M.A.S. Melville for an operational briefing. In spite of the cramped quarters and limited living space, morale was slowly improving. Most of the team resented being redeployed so soon, but none of them complained about the tropical location.

"Well, people, we've got some new poop," began Elton Rance as he worked a chew of tobacco around in his mouth. He was dressed in a yellow polo shirt and blue shorts that had drawn jokes from his team members. "Accordin' to the Aussies, these volcanic eruptions are part of a plate disruption that moves smack dab into the Solomon Islands and Hawaii from Antarctica. Their assessment is that the new volcanoes are causing one of the dormant volcanoes on the Solomons to become active again. The Solomon Islands are in mortal danger. I already heard from the Doc, and he says they're working on a plan to destroy these bad boys. So, we're going to leave the research staff on board here to assist the squids. The rest a' us will deploy to the Solomons to research the geological situation there until the Doc figgers this out."

"I thought we were the cavalry, Ranger!" spoke up Glenda Moses.

"Not this time, Vernie! Now, I want Brian Olson's staffers to brief us on the Solomons, then I'll explain to y'all how we're going to do this."

The Mission Staff leader provided an in-country briefing of the political details, languages, religions, and demographics of the tiny island nation.

"The Solomon Islands have a wide variety of native languages, poor transportation system, and an agrarian economy," continued Brian, whose ability to quickly orient the ARK team to host nation problems was invaluable. "This isolated country is slightly larger than the State of Maryland, so we're going to rely on satellite imagery and radio geological technology to give us a better chance of finding geological abnormalities here. Infrared mapping will also provide us with possible rips in the terrain."

Brian Olson continued his briefing, explaining that over 400,000 people lived on the Solomon Islands. In his slow talking Michigan way, he also briefed them in detail on the death of a lumberjack on Guadalcanal who died after falling into a magma pool. He also advised them that the deterioration of the precious coral reefs along much of the 5,313 kilometers of coastline was due to increased changes in ocean temperature caused by the subterranean volcanic activity.

"Thank you, Brian. People, we're going to have to conduct a split deployment to cover these islands before the Doc gets here," explained Elton as he consulted his clipboard. "Vernie's team will deploy to Guadalcanal, Bellona, and the Rennell islands in succession. Team Two will cover the New Georgia Islands and Choiseul. Team Three's got Santa Ysabel, Anuha, Malaita, and Parasi. Team Four's assigned Makira and the Santa Cruz Islands. We'll be based out of Honiara, where I'll set up headquarters."

"Hey Ranger, why isn't the U.S.G.S. down here to do all this monitoring?" complained Clyde Savage, the leader of Team Two.

"Because the C.I.A.'s got to keep this as secret as possible," emphasized Elton. "The U.S.G.S. is already knee deep in shit monitoring existing sites and they ain't responsible for foreign missions. All we gotta do is research the magma an we kin' git tha' hell outta heah!"

The ARK One members agreed with Penellas. Guadalcanal was a tropical paradise with warm constant temperatures. They all knew it was going to get warmer if the volcano there erupted as predicted.

***

The National Security Council was with President Fairchild at the Pentagon when he placed his call to the President of the People's Republic of China. He had the call on speaker for the benefit of the N.S.C. members, and Dan Tokuhisa had provided a Chinese translator in the event that one was necessary. Although President Zhu Le Ho and Premier Hu Quichen spoke English, it was usually a problem to have a complete conversation when either party became too excited or angry.

"Mr. President, it is an honor," greeted Zhu Le Ho in adequate English. The man's soft voice had to be amplified. "What is the purpose of this call?"

President Fairchild first asked questions about the state of affairs in Beijing since the earthquake. After a silent pause, Alex Fairchild got directly to the point.

"President Zhu, I'm missing a geologist from our research site in Antarctica, and I'm officially asking you if your scientists might have located him?"

Everyone in the Pentagon's secure conference room stared at the telephone set. The Chinese weren't accustomed to the President's blunt style. There was a long silence as the N.S.C. waited for an answer.

"That's quite unfortunate," said President Zhu Le Ho in his gentle voice. "The weather there is lethal."

"Yes, how can we be of assistance, President Fairchild?" asked Premier Hu.

"I want to know if China abducted our geologist from our research site in the American Highlands?"

"We are offended by your request, President Fairchild. We Chinese are not in the habit of conducting terrorist acts against the United States," noted President Zhu Le Ho. "It is not China that extends its borders by exploiting the resources of the world's poor nations."

"Who was this man?" asked the Premier.

"I question your honesty, gentlemen," challenged the President as he motioned for his Secretary of State to speak. "And I have the data to support my position."

Secretary Tokuhisa waited for the cue from President Fairchild, who motioned for him to proceed.

"Our satellites show that a group of personnel departed your site and moved to within fifty meters of our encampment about twelve hours ago," offered Dan Tokuhisa. The Chinese waited to answer.

"You're correct," responded President Zhu. "We sent out a patrol to conduct some tests, but they returned after they observed another camp. They reported no sighting of a lost foreign scientist," explained Premier Hu. There was no hint of anxiety in his voice.

"Bullshit!" swore General Vann under his breath.

"The United States will not tolerate an act of terrorism by China," warned the President, who was always willing to face the communists of the world.

"President Fairchild, the People's Republic of China is not answerable to the United States for any acts committed either real or imagined against you," countered President Zhu Le Ho skillfully. "Is the upcoming summit so insignificant that you would risk its success due to one lost scientist?"

Dan Tokuhisa and Myrna Ramirez both gestured for the President to watch what he was saying.

"It's understandable that you're concerned about your missing scientist," soothed Premier Hu. "But you cannot blame China for your lack of accountability. May we announce this to the press? They could possibly be of assistance in locating this man if you believe he was actually abducted. China does not want war."

The President of the United States reluctantly backed down. He did not want the press to be involved.

"No, thank you. We'll continue to investigate this matter, gentlemen," said Alex Fairchild firmly. "I will not create an international incident which would jeopardize the spirit of cooperation between our two countries, at least not until I have the proof I need."

"Ah, that's most reassuring, President Fairchild," replied President Zhu Le Ho jubilantly. "I will direct our team in Antarctica to conduct a search for your missing man. May we be of more assistance to you?"

"This is bullshit!" whispered General Jim Vann to those in the room. The President glared at him.

"I appreciate that, President Zhu, and I'll contact you if we need anything else," replied Alex Fairchild.

"There is more, President Fairchild," continued Premier Hu Quichen onto the next subject. "There is an increased American military presence near the Panama Canal since the earthquake. We're concerned about the presence of your troops in our strategic area."

"In light of the Panamanian tragedy, gentlemen," replied the President in a nasty tone of voice that he would soon regret. "We sent troops into Panama to assist people there. This has nothing to do with politics."

"Everything has to do with politics," warned President Zhu Le Ho. "I will not have American military troops in Panama now that my country is responsible for the canal's operation."

"And I caution you, President Zhu," countered Alex Fairchild as he nervously took a drink of water. "We've responded to a formal request for emergency assistance from President Diaz and we will not leave until that sovereign nation directs us to do so. While there, we will not interfere with your activities in the normal course of operating the canal."

"We will see," countered President Zhu.

After the President completed his call, the National Security Council had a heated discussion about the

Chinese summit and the missing American researcher. In the end, none of the attendees wanted to risk an international escalation of tensions because of one abducted scientist. General Vann had no intention of giving up on the missing U.S.G.S. scientist so easily.

***

President Zhu Le Ho knew there was little the foreigners could do in this situation. The Americans were conducting their own clandestine research in the same area. Revealing their own activities, along with involving a Chinese expedition that was present in the area without international authorization, would spark various investigations and inquiries that could place the American research in the world spotlight.

"They will not believe our presence there was to search for oil," remarked Hong Xu Ho, the Minister for National Security. "I think their satellites and spy planes may have even detected the actual abduction. I don't like it, Premier Hu."

"The Americans know we're in Antarctica," stated the Premier. "But it is difficult for the Americans to prove our activities and present them to the international community without incriminating themselves. This scientist places us in a position where we no longer have to speculate about geology, earthquakes, and how they will affect our future. This American geologist will provide us with most of the answers we need to know before the summit in the United States."

***

The White House Chief of Staff entered the crowded pressroom, which was much smaller than it appeared to be on television. It was a standing room only crowd that consisted of Secret Service agents, cameramen, reporters, and staffers. The pressroom chairs were old and worn from too many years of use, so the seated reporters usually treated the room with disrespect. The floor was already awash with discarded notes and papers. On the front of each press room seat cushion were the nameplates of the famous network correspondents and their news agencies.

"Good afternoon, ladies and gentlemen," began Kurt Farley as he adjusted his wire-rimmed eyeglasses. "The President will explain to all Americans that the upcoming Chinese summit on world environmental change has been approved. In an effort to provide complete disclosure to the United Nations community, the United States has decided to provide the world with sensitive classified information regarding the cause of these environmental disasters. And please limit your questions to the information being provided."

As the clamoring reporters raised their hands for questions to Mr. Farley, the President and Dan Tokuhisa were on their way to the pressroom from the Oval Office. The Secretary of Defense, Secretary of Space, and Director of Central Intelligence were also present.

"Remember, Mr. President, that you've got to present this just the way we rehearsed it," reminded Myrna Ramirez as she wheeled her way toward the concealed

Oval Office door. "You must sound anxious and concerned about the information we're leaking."

"I understand," acknowledged Alex Fairchild. He cleared his voice as the White House staff makeup artist applied the finishing touches to his tanned face.

"If they begin to ask specific questions you can't answer, tell the reporters to refer to the scientific data being distributed by the Space Department. That information looks very official and sensitive, so it will serve to validate your position," noted Andrea Mangone.

"My scientists will form a nice thick wall behind you, sir, complete with official lab coats and nice thick colorful folders," added Mary Ann Smith, who was pleased to be making a television appearance. "We'll also be available for televised meetings on all the appropriate networks and cable programs."

"I want you to attend every one of them, Mary Ann," directed Alex Fairchild. "This ruse is your responsibility to pull off."

Mary Ann smiled as she nodded, thankful for the opportunity to get so much press. The Red Bluff, California native had aspirations of one day serving as the chairman of a Silicone Valley Fortune 500 company.

"It's time, Mr. President," announced one of the White House aides as he opened the door to the hallway.

The entourage followed the President to the White House Press Room, where he was formally announced and entered the cramped room amidst a flood of flashbulbs and noise. The Space Department scientists were gathered behind him.

"My fellow Americans, it is my duty to inform you that the Earth's fragile ozone layer has deteriorated to the point of seriously jeopardizing our very existence as human beings," began the President with a concerned look on his clean-shaven face. "The damaged ozone layer has caused our fragile planet to begin to react to our lack of coordinated efforts to repair it. The future of Earth relies on immediate action by the nations of the world to reverse the damage.

"The press has been provided with data from the Space Department, so the presentation of the technical details will fall into the capable hands of Secretary Mary Ann Smith. My goal is to advise you, the American people, that immediate measures must be taken to prepare for environmental tragedies that might occur.

"The United States will enact national measures as follows," provided Alex Fairchild in a more upbeat tone. "First, the Surgeon General and the National Institutes of Health will conduct nationwide blood testing of the entire population of the United States to determine how ozone depletion is affecting the people of this great country. Second, I've directed that the Space Department accelerate completion of the international space station so that we can research the affected ozone areas from space. To prepare for possible American disasters, I have also directed the Department of Defense and Secretary of the Interior to establish regional areas where critical disaster items and equipment will be stored in newly constructed facilities for possible future use.

"These are only preventative measures. The United Nations summit is going to do more to prepare the world for any tragedies as they combat the effects of our unstable ozone layer. There is currently no timetable for the completion of this ambitious program, but I will present more specific goals in future press conferences with the American people. Thank you."

As soon as the President finished his speech, reporters frantically competed for the opportunity to ask questions. Based on the advice of his Press Secretary, Alex Fairchild was only to answer questions from the major networks and newspapers. The first news anchor he selected was Brock Edmund from C.B.S.

"Mr. President, is the release of this classified information in response to Chinese concerns that the United States is intentionally withholding scientific data for political reasons?" asked the fifty six year old television news veteran with the brown hair and distinguished graying temples. "And if that's the case, why are we just learning about this threat to our nation?"

"Thank you, Brock. I've always enjoyed the fine people at CBS," soothed the President as he staged his practiced response. "The recent disasters you've all witnessed confirmed our suspicions about the ozone layer, but we were not going to cause undue stress to the American people without more credible evidence. Asi Mtume, the Secretary General of the United Nations, motivated me to take action to ease the fears in the international community."

President Fairchild selected the gray haired veteran conservative reporter from N.B.C. next.

"Tom, how's the single life?" asked the President in a friendly tone. He was being cocky now.

"Just fine, Mr. President," replied the famous news anchor. He was dressed in a tailored gray Canali suit. "Does the Congress approve of these measures, or is this strictly an Executive Branch action designed to bring more publicity to your troubled administration?"

"Congress has been involved in this process from the start. We have their approval and support, Tom," stated the President. "We're attempting to save lives, not gain more press. Yes, Diane?"

The President pointed at Diane Finn, the leggy blonde anchor from A.B.C.

"Mr. President, how much time does the world actually have to solve this ozone problem? You're making this appear to be extremely urgent, not to mention life threatening," Diane asked.

"It is extremely urgent, Diane," answered the President with a smile. "Our scientists have cautiously estimated that we have until the year 2025 to make changes in the ozone layer. The effects of the ozone are poisoning our bodies in ways we're only beginning to understand. These natural disasters will escalate as long as we ignore the problem. The United States cannot afford to wait for a regional disaster like China or Panama. We have to take action now."

"Mr. President!" shouted Cecily Chang from Fox.

"How can I ignore the lovely lady from Fox?" asked the President as he deviated slightly from his scheduled list. Kurt Farley motioned in vain to get the President's attention.

"Is this ozone problem a cover up for some greater threat to our national survival, Mr. President?"

Alex Fairchild visibly paled when the smiling Chinese sweetheart slipped that question in unexpectedly. Kurt Farley's eyes sank back in his head as he groaned under his breath. There was a hush in the room as every eye and news camera settled on the President's pale face. More camera flashes could be seen and heard during the President's extended silence.

"Yes, Ms. Chang, this is a government cover up," admitted Alex Fairchild with a slight smile, attempting to be cocky again. "It's a plot to cover up a significant threat to humanity without causing panic, and the ozone layer's the unfortunate culprit."

The room was quiet for a moment longer. There was uneasy laughter as everyone took the President's response as a joke. Kurt Farley breathed a sigh of relief, while Alex Fairchild continued answering questions.

"Bernard Phillips, C.N.N.," identified the President, who was ready to end the news conference.

"Afternoon, Mr. President," greeted the distinguished black news anchor. "Can this ozone deterioration adequately justify the huge expenditures you're suggesting for an expanded space program and the creation of regional storage sites in this country?"

"Yes, Bernie, we already have an aggressive space policy involving Mars which was budgeted well into the next fifty years. We're merely accelerating the program to combat the ozone problem. There will be full disclosure to the American people," lied Alex Fairchild. "But I will take whatever action is necessary to guarantee the safety of the people of the United States."

Before Bernard Phillips could ask another question, the President selected Myrka Celeste Nespral, the voluptuous Cuban American news anchor from Univision, a popular nationwide television network.

"Thank you, Mr. President. The viewers of Univision want to know why there has been so little aide provided to the people of Panama," offered the stunning brunette from Miami, Florida. "Since the terrible earthquake, our Panamanian viewers have been claiming that American aide has been too slow. According to our sources, the people there are starving and homeless."

"Unfortunately, Mrs. Nespral, our disaster plans did not include regionally stocking Panama prior to that event. We are, however, better able to prepare for similar devastation in our own country," steered Mr. Fairchild away from the question for a minute. "I'm in daily contact with President Diaz, and he is satisfied with our quick response to assist the people of Panama. With each day, we're improving the lives of the people there."

More hands rose into the air as President Fairchild ended his news conference. Back in the Oval Office, he knew his performance had been poor.

"What do you think?" he asked his departmental advisors. "How'd I do?"

"I about shit my pants when Cecily asked you if there was a cover up," admitted Kurt Farley.

"If I may, sir," interjected Andrea Mangone as she rubbed her haggard face. The West Point graduate was strictly business. "You fielded the question well, but everyone observed your initial reaction. I think we're going to run into trouble with the public. There are too many scientists out there right now who will turn against us just to make more money as popular critics."

"This just buys us time," reminded Myrna Ramirez. "And time's what we need. When the world learns about the Pangaean Effect, we'll already be committed to facing it. Our national security depends on this."

President Fairchild closed his eyes, which was enough of a hint to the White House Chief of Staff to empty the room. The President's speech had already begun to affect the thinking of the other world powers, which were seeking reassurance from the United States that the world's geological instability was not going to be catastrophic or without a solution.

Chapter Thirteen

"Solomon's Steps"

Derrick Blasdale and ARK Four remained in Panama until the seismic data reflected that there was no longer an imminent threat of more earthquakes there. On the other side of the world, Elton Rance was enjoying the air-conditioned comfort of an Australian military building when Bubba John Washington returned his telephone call. The two men had been communicating frequently since ARK One's arrival in the Solomons.

"It's gettin' colder'n a muthafukka up heah, Ranger," greeted Bubba John with his usual earthy flare. The call was so clear that it sounded like the big weightlifter was across the street. "You're down there in gyat damn paradise an' I'm watchin' the leaves fallin' today."

"Thas' a fact, Bubba John! There's more leg here than I've seen since Bangkok back in '81!" admitted Elton with a grin. "Say, you talk to the Doc?"

"Roger that, brutha. He's got no problem with yo' split mission configuration," explained Bubba. "You've got full authorization to coordinate our activities there. You'll be seein' some foreign intelligence officers down there soon, Ranger. Hey, here's the Doc and Seth Tayman right now."

"Doc?" asked Elton over the telephone.

"How's it going, Ranger?" asked Dr. Valenti in a tired voice. "I've requested an immediate satellite surface and subsurface analysis of the volcanic zone. I want ARK One to get ground readings A.S.A.P. Find the magma and monitor the readings until remaining there becomes untenable. If the readings are correct, the Solomons will have to be completely evacuated. The glitch is that the Australians and the New Zealanders don't believe the problem's that serious. If you have to, inform them of our activities without disclosing too much about identity. After Panama, too many lives could be lost being too cautious."

"Awright, Doc, but what's the plan?" asked Elton. "Ah hear you've got a good one!"

"We're going to neutralize the volcanoes by placing tactical nuclear landmines under the ground between each of the funnels and at both extreme ends," explained Mike. "They'll create a large molten seam that will seal the volcanoes."

"You don't say!" exclaimed Elton. "Who's gonna run that mission?"

"NOAH'S ARK with the Defense Department," replied Mike. "The Navy will do the mission and I'll be deploying with them. As soon as I know more, I'll let you know. It'll be soon, though."

"Damn, ah' guess these folks are in deep shit, huh?" asked Elton. He spit tobacco juice into his cup.

"Hey, Ranger!" said Bubba. "You tha' man!"

"Well, Bubba John, you know ah'm your dawg!" laughed Elton. "ARK One's on site and humping!"

"Thas' what I'm talkin' about, my brutha!" exclaimed Washington. "Ranger's on fire, Doc!"

"Ranger, I want your team out of there before those islands go hot," directed Mike Valenti. "No hero shit!"

"Roger that, Doc," acknowledged Rance. "My people always come first!"

"I know, Ranger," noted Mike. "You're going to have one hell of a time leaving the Solomons. Just stick to the mission and we'll take care of the rest."

"Roger that, Doc. If this area goes hot, you kin best believe we'll be getting' out of heah!"

"One other thing, Ranger," cautioned Mike. "If a volcano erupts on Guadalcanal, there'll be carbon dioxide, hydrogen, carbon monoxide, and sulfur dioxide vapors in the air. As of now, I want you to discreetly increase your Mission Oriented Protective Posture (M.O.P.P.) just in case. That way you'll have your protective masks and chemical suits handy. You copy?"

"Ah copy, Doc," replied Elton.

"We'll talk to you soon, Ranger," said Mike with a smile. "Stay on cool ground."

After the telephone conversation ended, Elton Rance returned to his desk where he was meeting a liaison of the local Australian military.

***

President Alexander Fairchild was sitting at his cluttered Oval Office desk with his head in his wrinkled hands. The recent television and newspaper polls reflected poor reviews regarding his mediocre speech. The President's delayed reaction to the question posed by Cecily Chang of Fox News did little to sell his presentation to the American public. His advisors weren't attempting to raise his spirits.

"Sir, the Gallup Polls aren't completely bad," comforted Kurt Farley. "The public bought the ozone argument, but I wonder what the Chinese will say."

"The Chinese won't do shit," chipped in Dan Tokuhisa irritably. "They're sitting on our scientist and can't risk an international incident either."

"I sure as hell hope not, Dan. Look, I've already asked Speaker Kip Brewster and Grouper Johnson from the Senate Space Committee to make a televised appearance with me," provided Alex Fairchild. "That will quell the government conspiracy issue for good."

Myrna Ramirez placed some official folders in front of the President to sign.

"What the hell are these, Rosy?" asked President Fairchild with a frown.

"Executive Orders, Mr. President," replied Myrna. "These are all covert E.O.s authorizing NOAH'S ARK authority to neutralize the volcanoes."

"Did Congress review and approve this?" asked the President. He picked up a golf ball from the desk and played with it as he was thinking. "What about Senator Georgoulis and Representative Unger?"

"All of their reviews are attached, sir," replied Myrna. "We've covered the bases."

"It's good paper, Mr. President," supported Tell Summers, the Attorney General. He had his Stetson in his lap. "The Supreme Court's been briefed on the situation, too."

"I just wish we could tell the public," said the President.

"I know, sir, but that would cause a panic and put this in the U.N.'s slow political hands," advised Myrna Ramirez. "We need to act quickly and decisively."

President Fairchild read and signed each Executive Order. When he was finished, Myrna Ramirez handed them to one of her assistants for posting and copying to intelligence files, Presidential intelligence databases, applicable Congressional committees, and the Chief Justice of the Supreme Court of the United States.

***

The two foreign intelligence officers arrived on Guadalcanal to meet with Elton Rance and convince him that an evacuation wasn't necessary. The ARK One Mission Staff was prepared for the visit, which had been scheduled by Mike Valenti back at the Pangaean Task Force headquarters.

"Welcome, gentlemen," greeted Elton Rance in his cleanest English.

"I'm Vice Admiral Virgil Hanks, Mr. Rance," introduced the Royal Australian Navy Chief of Intelligence. "This is my colleague from New Zealand, Commodore Dove."

"Dylan Smith Dove, Mr. Rance, a pleasure," said the New Zealand naval intelligence officer. "We've been asked to meet with you and get an American perspective on the volcanic activity here."

"That's affirmative! Ah' don't like small talk, so let's cut to the jugular," said Elton. "Our combined research shows the six new offshore volcanoes are gonna cause a volcano in the Solomons and make Hawaii disappear.

My boss figures you need to consider evacuating the Solomons A.S.A.P."

Admiral Hanks chuckled, completely amused by the suggestion. Commodore Dove, who was less responsible for the region, looked at the admiral for comment. Both men were uneasy about an evacuation.

"That's bloody insane, Mr. Rance, which is why our governments have sent us. We have limited naval or air resources to conduct such a mission. I've looked at our own data and believe it's likely the Solomons would survive a volcanic eruption," opined Admiral Hanks.

"You're kiddin' right?" asked Elton. "We're gettin' small volcanic earthquakes everyday here. You and I ain't scientists, but my people tell me the situation is critical. My boss is never wrong."

"Perhaps that's true, sir, but you don't evacuate an entire country just because of one potential volcano threat. You don't even know where this volcano will erupt. We're used to such events here in the South Pacific," added Commodore Dove. "We've got nine volcanoes in New Zealand, and we don't evacuate our citizens unless they're in imminent danger. If we're to consider a future evacuation, we'll need English support to pull it off."

"Heavens, Dylan! Are you entertaining this bloody notion?" criticized Admiral Hanks. "The Solomon Islands are an independent nation, after all. They're mostly aboriginal people…."

"Who are loyal to the crown, Virgil," reminded Commodore Dove.

"Look, admirals, ah' don't need any negativity or shit about the Aborigines!" spoke up Elton. "The ca-ca's about to hit the fan, an' you guys don't understand that

Hawaii might be evacuated next! Look, until you hear from another proper authority, y'all are evacuating the Solomon Islands on my order!"

"I don't know who you are, or what your position is within your government," began Admiral Hanks.

"Let's settle this shit right now!" interjected Elton as he stood up and pulled a slim black wallet out of his shorts. "I have the position and the authority!"

Rance displayed the rare badge and credentials for both flag officers to examine.

"Now what's a C.I.A. Special Agent doing in charge of a geological operation?" asked Admiral Hanks, who was clearly shocked to learn that Rance held such a high level of trust and confidence in the C.IA.

"I see," noted Commodore Dove. "So, I assume you've received authority from your government?"

"You got it, Commodore," acknowledged Elton. "Our operational name isn't important, but our mission is, sir. I wouldn't even be here if this wasn't serious."

"Were you in Antarctica, then, or China or Panama?" asked Admiral Hanks.

"Now that you're goin' to be in the loop, yep, I was in Antarctica," admitted Elton as he fished his chewing tobacco out of his pocket. "Our teams deploy everywhere, but none of 'em were able to stop what happened in China or Panama."

"That explains alot," recalled Commodore Dove. "But our lads don't predict the same level of destruction for the Solomons."

"Maybe not in the way of earthquakes," agreed Elton. "The way ah' see it, the Solomons are fucked."

"In that unsavory context," noted Commodore Dove. "Are these regional volcanoes linked to any of the other geological events?"

"Roger that, Admiral! The Antarctic earthquake was tectonic, just like the Panamanian one was," continued Elton. "Ah don't know much about it, but they're all a result of the big Chinese earthquake, too. We stumbled on them six baby volcanoes by accident, but they were caused by a tear in the plate that's threatening to destroy Hawaii and the Solomon Islands."

While the two naval intelligence officers remained silent, Elton Rance connected them to Dr. Valenti, who briefed them on the situation. After the videoconference was over, Admiral Hanks sighed, and then leaned forward in his seat.

"I understand things much better now," Admiral Hanks admitted. "We weren't convinced that the plate damage was so significant as to be a threat to the Solomons, our region, or Hawaii. Now Dr. Valenti is telling us that the solution requires the use of nuclear munitions. Australia and New Zealand both have strict anti-nuclear policies, even during a war in which we could face defeat. This definitely needs to be discussed by echelons above our own intelligence levels."

"Agreed, Admiral, but the Doc says we're evacuating this place and doing the blow with or without your approval," replied Elton. "Ah'll take your policy concerns up with the Doc, but time's a wastin' in the meantime for the Solomons."

"We'll support you, old boy," said Commodore Dove. "Approval of the nukes is another thing."

Elton nodded. As they moved on to the issue of Hawaii, a volcanic tremor occurred.

"That's a bigger one than most," advised Elton. "They're getting worse."

"I see, Agent Rance. Will you be evacuating Hawaii while we're evacuating the Solomons?" asked Commodore Dove nervously.

"No, sir!" exclaimed Elton. "Hawaii is only going to suffer if these six volcanoes ain't destroyed! And my country ain't goin' to let that happen! We're goin' to level them baby volcanoes, even if y'all don't approve of the decision!"

Both intelligence officers nodded in agreement. They were both impressed with the ability of the United States to engineer worldwide public and scientific opinion to shroud its efforts to repair the planet. As they shook hands with Elton and departed, another volcanic earthquake shook the ground.

***

Doctor Connor Peabody awakened with a throbbing pain pulsing through his swollen jaw. He had been having nightmares since last losing consciousness. As his weak eyes attempted to focus in the darkness of his quiet surroundings, Dr. Peabody began to remember what had happened to him. He recalled being struck, so he attempted to raise his hands to check the condition of his throbbing face. That's when Connor Peabody learned that he was strapped down to a steel hospital gurney with tight leather straps.

"Now how the hell did you get in here, Connor?" he groaned out loud, only to cough up blood and teeth.

Peabody pulled at his restraining straps. The changing lights and strange sounds of the medical equipment near his bed came to life. With another painful groan, he laid back on the table. The bitter taste of his own blood in his dry throat made him gag.

"You ain't in Antarctica anymore," muttered Connor. "C'mon, Connor, you dumb ass, think!"

Dr. Peabody was just beginning to remember being shot when the hidden door to the cold dark room opened. The dim light from the whitewashed hallway blinded him as an unknown number of strange people in green medical scrubs entered the room. The door closed, leaving Peabody in the darkness again with the strangers. He wondered if aliens had abducted him.

"Welcome to China," said a distinctive Asian voice in perfect English. "I am in need of information only you may provide. From this moment on, you will answer our questions truthfully and completely. If you do not, I will cut off each of your fingers and toes at their joints for each answer that I deem to be insufficient. If, by the end of our interview, you have no fingers or toes left, I will liquidate you by breaking each bone in your body until you beg for death and I allow it to claim you. Do you understand?"

Connor nodded, slowly realizing that he was being held as a hostage. Connor believed American rescuers had to be coming for him. He took a deep breath and remembered that he was just a civilian.

"John D. Owen," answered Connor. That was the only name he could make up.

Analysts at an offsite entered the name into their computer system and learned that there were no board certified scientists by that name in the United States. The information was transmitted back to the interrogator, who said something in Chinese to the torturer.

Peabody's scream was amplified by the emptiness of the examination room. The torturer sliced off the small finger of Peabody's left hand with surgical scissors and let the amputated digit fall to the floor. As the geologist screamed, the torturer tied off the wound and placed the bloody scissors over the ring finger. Peabody became instantly quiet.

"Your name!" demanded the interrogator.

"Connor Brian Peabody, Jr., sir!" screamed the terrified geologist. "From New Haven, Connecticut! You cut off my fuckin' finger, you son of a bitch!"

Peabody couldn't see the interrogator smile in the darkness. The Chinese man waited for silence.

"For whom do you work?"

"With the U.S. Geological Survey!" Connor replied, crying. The scissors were poised against the ring finger on his injured hand. "Please don't hurt me anymore!"

Over the next two hours, the Chinese learned that Connor Brian Peabody, Jr., was a geologist with over ten years of experience with the US Geological Survey. He also possessed a Top Secret security clearance with access to Special Compartmented Information. After the loss of two more fingers, the interrogator learned that a C.I.A. team had been investigating special environmental problems in Antarctica and that some evidence had been found.

"Why were you selected for this deployment?" asked the interrogator in a caring voice. "Are you in the C.I.A.?"

"No, sir! I'm with the Geological Survey! We learned that the plate irregularities are indicative of an inter-regional disruption in geologic plate stability," explained Peabody.

"How does this affect China?"

"It affects everyone. The world's plates are interconnected and interlocked. A major instability in one causes tectonic events in others," continued Peabody. "Your old fault rapidly deteriorated and caused the instability of the region much sooner than conventional geological theorists could have predicted."

"Doctor, do you know what's caused the instability in China's fault?" asked the interrogator.

"No! Nobody knows what the hell's causing it!" nearly screamed Peabody as he felt more pain. "We were there to find out why!"

After three more hours, the interrogator knew enough about the Antarctic mission to realize that the Americans did not know what had caused the original earthquake in China. The lights were turned on, and the room was rapidly filled with attentive caring medical professionals. Dr. Peabody's amputated fingers were promptly removed and he was suddenly given the best medical treatment in the People's Republic of China.

***

The 20th Special Forces Group (Airborne) arrived at the U.S.G.S. Antarctic site via LC-130 transport during a routine resupply flight. The Army Reserve Green Beret team was to conduct an area reconnaissance of the vacated Chinese encampment for the purpose of locating or detecting any evidence of the presence of Dr. Connor B. Peabody, Jr.

The twelve-man team arrived with several attached elements, to include a canine team that was specially trained to locate human remains. There was also a special three-man team of Alaskan Army National Guardsmen who were Native American experts in tracking in polar environments. The Yupik Indians were unique men who lived and hunted most of their lives in severe cold weather that was similar to Antarctica's. These tough wilderness experts were assigned the task of finding clues at both research sites that might lead to new information about the missing scientist.

"The team's up, Captain Sparks," reported Master Sergeant Steven Simmons, the Team Operations N.C.O. He had the cold eyes of a seasoned veteran.

"Airborne, Top!" acknowledged the Detachment Commander, whose ebony features stood out in contrast to the snowy surroundings. "We had a lot of shut eye on that lift over here, so let's get moving! Chief?"

"Weather's a go, Cap," advised the Executive Officer, Chief Warrant Officer Tim Wood. "I just got the latest weather report. The Yupiks are fired up, mostly complaining about the mild temperatures."

The Green Berets laughed. They were hard men with high and tight haircuts that matched their attitudes.

"Those Yupiks are definitely hard core, Chief," informed MSG Simmons. "I wish we could get more of 'em to sign on and go to J.F.K., but they have such a strong family ties that its hard as hell to get 'em to join."

SGT Samuel Tlaak saluted when he approached the two officers. He was armed with an old M-16 assault rifle that was perfectly maintained.

"I figured it would be colder, sir," complained SGT Tlaak in his thick voice. "We scouted out the last area where the scientist was seen and found this for you."

SGT Tlaak handed CPT Sparks a collection bag that contained a small layer of ice.

"What do we have?" asked CPT Sparks. His youthful features hid the fact that he was a seasoned killer of his country's enemies by the age of twenty-five.

"We uncovered a boot print near the place where the vehicle's parked," explained SGT Tlaak with a smile that accentuated his brown leathery facial features. "And it ain't no American boot print from what I can tell."

"No shit? I figured the amount of time that's passed since this guy's disappearance would've screwed us up," remarked CW2 Wood.

"Unless the weather's extremely bad, a track like a boot print can last as long as a fossil in this environment. You just have to check the layers of ice for the print. We didn't have no problem picking up their trail, sir," said SGT Tlaak. "What time are we crossing the line of departure for the Chinese camp?"

"In about an hour, Sarge," responded MSG Simmons. "Get your people checked out one last time."

The Yupik's traveled light and were ready in fifteen minutes. MSG Simmons went to complete mission preparation with his section sergeants. In less than forty-five minutes, the Special Forces team would be on its way to the vacated Chinese expeditionary site.

***

When Mike Valenti arrived at the U.S. Army Special Forces Diving School at Key West, Florida, the underwater demolition team assigned to Operation NOAH'S ARK was already onsite and training for the emplacement of the nuclear devices on the six volcanoes. The Key West Army base had become the temporary home of U.S. Navy Sea Air Land (S.E.A.L.) Team II and their support structure. S.E.A.L. Team II had been selected by the U.S. Special Operations Command to install and detonate the nuclear devices that would destroy the six submarine volcanoes.

After an Army military police sergeant escorted Mike to the base headquarters, he was directed to the post commander's office. It had not been easy to convince politicians that the use of nuclear weapons was absolutely necessary. When Mike entered the commander's office, everyone was waiting for him.

"You must be Dr. Valenti," said an Army Major General as he extended his hand in greeting. "I'm General Collier, the Commander of the Special Forces Dive School. This is Dan Warner from the Atomic Regulatory Commission, and Commander Chuck O'Connell from S.E.A.L. Team Two."

"Nice to meet you," responded Mike to the group.

Mike accepted a cup of coffee and took a seat.

"Mr. Warner's filled me in on the mission, Dr. Valenti," began General Collier with a supportive smile. "And the young S.E.A.L. commander's given me his input. They both seem to think you're nuts."

Mike smiled, unsure of where the general was going with his remarks.

"That's a good thing coming from S.E.A.L. Team II, Doctor," added Commander O'Connell with a smile.

"Why is that?" asked Dan Warner, who was a Korean War veteran and an advocate of the use of nuclear weapons under appropriate conditions.

"Sir, if a mission ain't a little crazy, then it ain't for the S.E.A.L. navy!" grinned the Navy Commander.

"Doctor, why don't you brief me on what's going to take place this week," directed General Collier.

"General, you have my operations plan in front of you," began Mike with a sip of his coffee. "NOAH'S ARK elements, which are in position in the Solomon Islands and at the site of the six volcanoes, will support S.E.A.L. Team II in the emplacement and detonation of seven Medium Atomic Demolition Munitions. One M.A.D.M. will be installed at the base of each volcano. This week, S.E.A.L. Team II and their support elements will rehearse the operation. I'll be the NOAH'S ARK C.I.A. operative working with the S.E.A.L. Team. Upon completion of our training, we'll deploy to the South Pacific and destroy the six threats."

General Collier grunted, "M.A.D.M.s? Hell, I thought those were dropped off our inventory years ago!"

"They were, General," said Dan Warner. "Atomic land mines haven't been upgraded since 1986 because of the more common use of air and sea delivered nuclear munitions. When Dr. Valenti came to us with his mission requirement, we figured the use of atomic land mines is more practical because they're being placed underground in an ocean environment."

"Why is that, Mr. Warner?" asked the General.

"Well, sir, the mission calls for a simultaneous detonation of seven nuclear devices of stationary targets. That is ideal for M.A.D.M.s, which can be detonated like conventional mines. They're lightweight, weighing just over 400 lbs, and can be implanted at any ocean depth."

"What about the S.E.A.L.s, Mr. Warner, are they trained to use those munitions?"

"No, general, but they will be," explained Dan Warner. "I've spoken extensively with Dr. Valenti and his technicians, and coordinated with the commander of the Benjamin Franklin class submarine that will deliver the S.E.A.L.s and the munitions to the target area. We're all operating on the same sheet of music."

"Good," said General Collier. "What about you, Commander O'Connell? Is this type of weapon going to be a problem for you hard cases?"

"Negative, General," answered the highly motivated S.E.A.L. Commander. "I'll be in charge of the assigned team, and I've already inspected the nomenclature of the M.A.D.M. It's definitely sea transportable, waterproof, and it's contained in a W-54 hard plastic carrying case. With a yield of about 1 kiloton, each bomb will do the job as Dr. Valenti's specified, and it's simple in construction. It consists of a packing container cylinder, warhead, code-decoder unit, and a firing unit. We can do this mission, General."

"Then enjoy your stay in Key West, gentlemen, and keep me advised," directed General Collier.

After a refill of their coffee cups, the three members of the nuclear training management team departed the general's office and headed over to the training area. For Mike Valenti, who hadn't been diving in years, this was a very apprehensive time.

***

In spite of the changes in weather since the Chinese extracted from the area, the Yupik scouts easily found and followed the Chinese trail back to their original research site. They also identified the tracks of a human sled. Although the Green Berets were in peak condition, the Yupiks led the way and easily out paced their elite companions. The Army canine team failed to detect any human remains during the trek, which supported the theory that the scientist had been abducted. When the Team reached the Chinese site, the Yupiks were barely sweating. The Green Berets were winded.

"Top, establish the patrol base," ordered Captain Sparks as he checked his map. It wasn't much use without the Global Positioning System device he carried to accurately pinpoint their location. "Have the Yupiks and Section A initiate the area reconnaissance of the objective area as planned. Section B has security."

"Airborne!" acknowledged MSG Simmons.

By the end of the day, the Green Beret unit had set up camp and was conducting a detailed search of the Chinese area. It took two days of tedious searching in the terrible cold for the team to locate any evidence.

When SGT Tlaak ran over to speak with SPC Andoe in their native language, CPT Sparks and CWO Wood waited impatiently to hear the news.

"It's a cigarette butt! American made from the looks of it, sir!" identified SGT Tlaak, in very bad English. "SPC Andoe found it near two more sets of footprints. My guess is that their lead man with the sled met with a guy from the camp. I figure they got the cigarette from whoever was on that sled!"

"Very good!" praised CPT Sparks as the butt was placed into an evidence bag. "Sergeant Tawney!"

The Intelligence and Operations Sergeant for Section A responded with a shout.

"Sir?" responded Sergeant First Class Shannon Tawney. His left uniform shoulder bore both the Ranger and Special Forces tabs.

"Get in touch with the U.S.G.S. camp and get information about the brand of cigarettes the victim was smoking while he was here," directed Reggie Sparks.

"Then notify H.Q. about our find. And see if S.O.C.O.M. can find someone who can match up boot prints!"

"Airborne!" acknowledged the senior sergeant.

"Hey, Captain," said CWO Wood as he lifted an evidence bag. "That may not be necessary."

Captain Sparks laughed when he saw that there was a frozen pack of Merit brand cigarettes sealed inside the bag. They had found the evidence they needed.

***

Following a full day of training at the Key West facility, Mike Valenti had formed a great appreciation for the skills of the Navy's S.E.A.L. personnel. As a basic diver, the NOAH'S ARK leader had a hard time keeping up with the S.E.A.L. divers as they practiced and practiced the deployment of the nuclear land mines. The elite sailors were easy to get along with and had fun as they worked, but they expected Mike to adapt quickly.

Mike learned on the first day of training that his son was a member of the mission team. That confused him. When their day was over, Mike was exhausted. While the S.E.A.L. Team talked in the locker room about going to the base happy hour, Mike saw Steven and approached him.

"Excuse me," interrupted Mike as the group of sailors spoke about the day's training. They knew his status and position, and became quiet. "Steven Valenti?"

"That's Petty Officer Steven Gunther, sir," corrected Mike's son with a touch of anger.

Mike was taken aback by his son's tone of voice.

"Yeah, sorry," Mike apologized. The S.E.A.L.s looked at their companion for an indication of whether they should stay or leave Steven to speak with his father.

"Hey, guys," said Steven as he stepped out of his dive suit. "I'll meet up with you at the N.C.O. club."

"You do that, Sparky!" shouted one of Steven's buddies as the team left Steven alone with Mike.

Mike waited until the locker room was empty.

"We haven't had a chance to talk since I saw you this morning, Steven," began Mike with difficulty.

"What's to talk about, Doctor? You may be the civilian honcho on this mission, but that don't mean shit to me," explained Steven as he checked his equipment. "All you are to me is a sperm donor."

"Well, that's correct," admitted Mike, who was at a loss for words. "Between Gilman, your mother's family, and the Maryland Gunthers, you're a first class citizen now. I'm just glad you grew up so well."

"You know, Doctor, I respect the Gunthers for always making me a part of the family," remarked Steven. "Which is more than I can say for yours!"

"Now that's not true, Steven! My dad…."

"Grandfather's always been there for me, true, but what's your excuse?" shouted Steven.

Steven waited for a response, and when he received none, began to leave.

"Wait, Steven!" insisted Mike.

"For what, you fuckin' loser!" bellowed Steven. He threw his diving mask down the hall. "You didn't want me! You gave me away!"

"No, that's not true, Steve!" began Mike. "It was your mother's family! They couldn't stand me!"

"Only my friends call me Steve!"

"Fine, Steven, fine! But I couldn't stand your mother! She and her family made it impossible to be with you!" shouted Mike in return. "They wanted me to marry her and work for her father!"

"Whatever, dude," grunted Steven. "The Hessions and Gunthers are my family. They have been for my whole life! Now, we have to work together, but I don't have to like it, or you. Understand that?"

"If that's how you want it?" answered Mike.

"Yeah, that's how I want it," said Steven. "And don't mix with my team mates. You don't belong with us. Not yet. Have a good day, Doctor."

Mike said nothing as Steven left the locker room. As he completed dressing, another group of divers from the U.S. Army entered the steamy area and entered into the same type of banter and discussions that the S.E.A.L.s had done. They ignored Mike, too.

***

Glenda Moses and her team deployed to the Rennell Islands, which were the farthest islands from Guadalcanal for her patrol zone. From that location, she could obtain critical readings in support of ARK One's mission. They were conducting a detailed investigation of potential volcanic sites using geodetic, seismic, and paleomagnetic measurements.

"We've been getting zip for results, Vernie," commented Gregory Kryolok as they walked along a narrow trail. "With this thick growth, we could be standing on top of a magma source and never know it."

"We've still got a few more islands to go before we're done," said Glenda. "And we don't have much time before the nuclear phase begins. According to the satellite data, there should be a hot spot on the ridgeline."

"You've got it, Vernie," said Lewis T. Griffith as he took the lead and headed for the ridgeline.

In the distance, they could hear something that sounded like boiling water. None of the team members realized what they had found until L.T. nearly walked into a hissing puddle of thick liquid rock.

"Oh shit!" exclaimed L.T. as he leapt back and fell butt first into the thick foliage.

"Let's spread out and check the area, guys," directed Glenda. "I'll take samples of this find."

"Is the Special Staff ready to conduct immediate testing of these samples, Vernie?" asked L.T. Griffith.

"Yep. They can do X.R.F.," replied Glenda.

"Wet rock chemical analysis?" asked Loomis.

"Not really, Loom," said Glenda. "X.R.F. stands for X-ray Fluorescence Spectrometry. We cool the sample, then heat it and fuse it at 1,120 degrees centigrade with a flux. When the sample's melted, it's poured into very thin molds which produce solid disks that provide us with a precise glass surface that permits us to determine the chemical composition of the sample."

"Sounds state of the art, doesn't it, Greg? I'd like to see that in action," said Cowboy.

"It sure does," replied Greg Kryolok. "I heard back on Guadalcanal that we can have sample results in less than twenty four hours. Now we'll be able to put any magma by its unique chemistry."

"Exactly. We'll be able to compare samples from this site and other volcanic activity in the area to determine if they're all related," added Glenda.

"I have another one over here, Vernie!" notified Quentin Smith.

"Great, Cowboy, I'll be right there!"

"Hey, Vernie, why don't the magma pools cause forest fires around here? It makes no sense to me," explained Ken Loomis as he examined a magma pool.

"That's easy," replied Vernie. "The foliage is so moist that it's difficult to ignite forest fires."

As the team continued to isolate, catalog, and obtain samples of their magma finds, the rest of ARK One was also locating similar volcanic ponds and streams in their patrol areas. With each sample being sent for XRF analysis, ARK One would be able to compare the volcanic rock from the Solomon Islands with those from the six new submarine volcanoes.

Chapter Fourteen

"East Meets West"

The short husky commander of the 1st Battalion, 325th Infantry (Airborne), was standing tall in the passenger seat of a High Mobility Multi-purpose Wheeled Vehicle (H.M.M.W.V.) that was mounted with a .50 caliber machine gun. The M1025 vehicle was the battalion commander's primary means of transportation when he was maneuvering on the ground. As the Scout Platoon screened the colonel's forward zone of advance, the lead airborne infantry company was moving in the same direction behind the security force.

"Romeo Charlie One, this is Sierra One, over," transmitted the voice of the Scout Platoon Leader, whose unit of armed H.U.M.M.W.V. vehicles was well ahead of the traveling rifle companies.

The Scout Platoon was task organized with a mixture of H.U.M.M.W.V. vehicles mounted with M-60 machine guns, TOW anti-armor missiles, and STINGER anti-aircraft weapons.

"Go for One, over!" barked back the battalion commander irritably.

"One, we've got visual contact on an unknown estimated company sized infantry element in well-entrenched defensive positions within our area of responsibility!" reported the Scout Platoon Leader.

As the Scout Platoon Leader read off the grid coordinates to LTC Reid, the Operations Officer located the contact on his map. LTC Reid began to swear.

"Fuck! Sierra One, can you confirm the nationality of the visual contact?" asked the commander.

"Negative. Estimate Papa Romeo Charlie. Unit is not Panamanian, over!" replied the platoon leader.

"What're the god dammed Chinese doing taking up real estate in my assigned area of Panama?" bellowed LTC Reid. A pair of Chinese fighter jets passed by overhead. In seconds, there were huge explosions around him. "Raise Colonel Stanliss, S-3. I need career guidance and close air support now!"

"Airborne, sir!" replied the Operations Officer.

"One, shit! We've got small arms contact!" shouted the Scout Platoon Leader over the radio. Rapid loud popping noises could be heard in the background. "Request authority to return fire!"

LTC Reid was about to reply when he heard machine gun fire instinctively being returned by the Scout Platoon. In his keen analytical mind, World War III was beginning with the Chinese right in his assigned operational area.

"One, Sierra's returning fire and conducting a withdrawal under pressure!" reported the platoon leader, using his own initiative to protect his small unit.

"Roger, Sierra One, make your passage of lines per S.O.P.," directed LTC Reid. He heard a rapid increase in gunfire, then the connection terminated.

"Sierra One, over?" queried LTC Reid.

"One, this is Sierra Two in command!" reported the Scout Platoon Sergeant, who was clearly in the middle of a withdrawal under heavy gunfire. "Sierra One's K.I.A! We'll have to police up his body later!"

"Carry on!" ordered LTC Reid.

"Colonel Stanliss is on the horn, sir."

"Get Sierra some smoke to cover their withdrawal!" ordered LTC Reid. "Have air cav patrol likely enemy avenues of approach. Now!"

The S-3 dismounted and made his radio contacts.

"Romeo Charlie One," reported LTC Reid.

"This is Delta One Zero," said the Brigade Commander. "Are you in contact with the Chinese?"

LTC Reid explained the situation and asked for authority to counterattack.

"Negative, conduct a hasty defense," ordered COL Stanliss. "Do not return fire unless your units are pursued or fired upon. Air Force has identified enemy aircraft in your area and will respond. Copy, over?"

"Roger, out," acknowledged LTC Reid.

"We've already returned fire, sir," noted the S-3. The colonel's driver scanned the woods for an enemy.

"I know that, Major!" snapped LTC Reid as he grabbed his own handset. He'd made his decisions. "Alpha One, this is Romeo Charlie One, over."

"Alpha One, over," responded the commander of "A" Company.

"Movement status, over," requested LTC Reid.

"Alpha One's the lead element," reported the Company Commander. "We have contact! Switching movement to bounding over watch and attacking, over!"

"Negative! Conduct a hasty defense in depth oriented on heading one eight zero, and coordinate Sierra's passage through your lines," ordered LTC Reid. "Bravo will be on your left. Charlie will be on your right. Sierra will become the battalion reserve. Fire only if fired on, over."

"Roger, out," replied the Company Commander.

The S-3 relayed the battalion commander's orders to the rest of the battalion's company commanders. The sounds of artillery smoke could be seen in the distance.

"Romeo Charlie One, this is Oscar Echo Zulu, over," said a new voice over the radio. The S-3 reached for the handset, but LTC Reid waved him off.

"Oscar Echo Zulu, this is Romeo Charlie One, over," responded LTC Reid.

The sounds of a jet in flight could be heard during the radio transmission.

"Charlie One, just call me the Haymaker! You've got Chinese bogies in you're A.O. and some trouble on the ground, so I'm here with four Foxtrot four by fours to take 'em out, over," declared the Haymaker.

"Roger that, Haymaker," acknowledged LTC Reid, who was happy to have the F-16 aircraft supporting him. "What do you need from me, over?"

"Charlie One, weapons hold on anti-aircraft, pop purple smoke along your friendly lines, and get as small as Hussein's pecker, over!" advised the Haymaker. "We've got two Chinese bogies on our radar now. Stand by for open chutes and red shit, over."

"Roger, out!" growled LTC Reid to his driver. "Get me up to Alpha's positions! I want to see the Chinese positions!"

As the machine gun equipped all terrain vehicle took off creating a break in the jungle foliage, other tactical vehicles followed it. In the distance, the small platoon of reconnaissance vehicles passed through Alpha Company and headed to reserve positions in the rear area. As the American F-16 fighters entered into a brief and violent dogfight with the Chinese aircraft, Apache gun ships approached to cover the battalion's defensive actions.

***

Following a meeting with Colonel Stanliss, Lieutenant Colonel Butch Reid hopped into his command vehicle and directed his driver to return to his battalion area. Since the initial combat, diplomatic meetings were taking place between Panamanian, American, and Chinese officials to resolve the standoff.

"Give me a SITREP, S-3!" directed LTC Reid as he adjusted his sweaty camouflaged cap. His face and arms were covered with green and black camouflaged grease paint. "What's the latest intelligence update?"

"Sir, we're defending against a motorized P.L.A. rifle regiment with tanks, artillery, air defense, and air support," detailed the Operations Officer. "Type 85 II Main Battle Tanks were observed in positions in their rear, and they have fighters flying sorties over our lines. Fortunately, our Air Force has gained air superiority."

A Chinese fighter screamed overhead and dropped bombs in the battalion's area.

"It's more like air parity from my point of view! Those commies bombed the shit out of the brigade command post! What about our lines? Any more probes?" asked LTC Reid. "Those bastards have been violating the cease fire since the paper was signed!"

"None reported, sir. Since brigade's tied our hands by limiting our defensive activity to security patrols in our immediate area, we're at the mercy of the Chinese units. If they decide to attack us, we're going to be caught with our pants down!" said the S-3. "This whole idea of doing nothing ain't right, sir!"

"I concur, Major! I was trained to seize the initiative - to be bold and audacious! Major, isn't Bravo our best company when it comes to infiltrations and exfiltrations?" asked LTC Reid.

"Yes, sir!" acknowledged the S-3. "They've got the master blaster, Sergeant First Class Randall."

"Is he that tan beret we got a few months ago?"

"Yes, sir! Randall's about as hard as they come," said the S-3. "He's Airborne, Ranger, Pathfinder, a Jump Master, and he's got close combat experience. Shit, he earned his first Combat Infantryman Badge in a Ranger unit in Somalia. He used to teach jungle school, too."

"Good. We're not going to sit on our asses while I'm in command, Major," advised LTC Reid. "Defending is proactive, so we're going to conduct a nice little patrol of our own to find out what the Chinese are planning. Here's my concept of the operation."

As LTC Reid explained his plan to his staff officers, the ground commander of the Chinese unit was reviewing the positions and status of the soldiers under his command who were entrenched on the other side of the American lines.

***

At 19:45 hours on the third evening following the firefight with the Chinese forces, a reconnaissance patrol from Bravo Company was preparing to depart the friendly front lines of the 1st Battalion, 325th Infantry (Airborne). The patrol's mission was to infiltrate the Chinese defenses and capture one of their senior officers.

SFC Jake Randall was lean and mean like the Rangers bred warriors to be in the 75th Ranger Regiment. At five foot five and one hundred and fifty pounds, SFC Randall was a dark skinned black man with a taste for killing for his country. More than any other qualification, SFC Randall was a leader of men.

SFC Randall issued verbal corrections for his team leaders to make. They were all dressed in camouflage uniforms with boonie hats. Each man wore olive drab tactical vests that contained water bladders. Each vest also contained radios, flashlights, hand grenades, personal ammunition, combat knives, and other essential equipment.

"Staff Sergeant Ball," said SFC Randall to his Recon Team A leader. "Have each of your four men go over their camo paint. It's got to be on thick so their skin won't shine when they sweat."

"Yes, Sergeant," acknowledged SSG Ball.

"SSG Garcia, same goes for you," continued Randall with his Recon Team B leader. "Plus, Get SGT Brooks another bipod for his Squad Automatic Weapon. The one he's got is so loose it rattles when he carries it. And switch his ammo for that SAW from belt to drum."

"You got it, Sarge," said SSG Garcia.

As SFC Randall issued corrections, the Bravo Company First Sergeant dropped by to inform him the patrol would depart friendly front lines at 20:00 hours. The seventeen man reconnaissance patrol was finally ready to depart the battalion area.

***

The skies over Panama had become very dangerous since the initial combat between the forces of the People's Republic of China and the United States. The Panamanian Air Force had committed their fighter aircraft against the Chinese air units. During the course of the dogfights, most of the Panamanian aircraft had been destroyed. As the remainder of the Panamanian air units returned to their bases, the commander of the 12th Air Force was coordinating the air battle from his Forward Operating Location at the Eloy Alfaro International Airport in Manta, Ecuador.

"General Foster, we've got limited air superiority," advised Lieutenant General Miles to the SOUTHCOM Commander over an audio-visual real time satellite link. As the Commander, 12th Air Force, LTG Miles was responsible for American fighter and air support assets that were dispersed over the Caribbean, Central, and South America.

"Casualties and losses?" asked General Foster.

A staff officer handed LTG Miles a staff update.

"We've lost 6 F-15's, 8 F-16's, 2 F-18's, a KC-135 tanker, and the Panamanian Air Force lost 14 F-15's and 22 F-16's," detailed LTG Miles in a stern but heavy voice. "The worst is that we lost 13 pilots and crew."

"General, you must destroy the remaining Chinese aircraft and achieve air superiority," ordered the SOUTHCOM Commander.

"Yes, General. I haven't committed my reserve F-16 wing that's based here in Ecuador," answered LTG Miles. "We're on continuous ops, and none of our F.O.L.'s in Aruba, Curacao, Costa Rica, the Netherlands Antilles, or here in Ecuador have been attacked. The Chinese are attempting to maintain local air superiority over the battle area."

"The main battle area is what concerns me!" reminded General Foster. "Get control of those skies within 24 hours. The 82d's got control of the ground battle, but they won't keep it if the Reds keep pounding the shit out of them with their helicopters and aircraft. I have the remainder of the 18th Airborne Corps ready to deploy to Panama, and that includes the 3d Infantry Division and 1st Cavalry Division. I'm not putting those men and hardware in flight to have them shot to hell and gone enroute to their drop zones and landing sites, so I need air supremacy fast!"

"Yes, sir!" acknowledged LTG Miles.

With his mission and timetable specified, LTG Miles sat down with his weary staff and mapped out the details of the air war. As his senior officers planned for air superiority, the pilots and aircraft of the U.S. Air Force took their toll on the air assets and well protected air bases of the People's Republic of China in Panama.

***

As Recon Team A crawled in single file under a muddy rat filled thicket, SFC Jake Randall checked the illuminated dial of his olive drab watch and waited for the three remaining patrol elements to signal that they were moving. He had rigged all-purpose nylon cord between the departure points. Each element leader would pull the cord at the time of their departure, which would signal SFC Randall that they were moving.

The three remaining elements pulled on their signal cords at 20:00 hours. As an experienced night fighter, SFC Randall would use the entire period of darkness in which to operate. Using aerial intelligence photographs, SFC Randall decided to cross through enemy lines along four heavily foliated narrow gaps between the Chinese positions. He would then penetrate the vulnerable Chinese support area and locate their command post. The patrol would then find a senior Chinese officer and capture him.

The mission was more dangerous than it sounded. Light infantry operations involving an infiltration of enemy lines required stealth, proven skill, and superior leadership. Anything could happen during a mission into hostile territory. As an expert in field craft, SFC Randall knew that if anything could go wrong, it would. He was experienced enough as a combat leader to consider Murphy's Law when he prepared patrol order.

Using his radio, SFC Randall contacted the Battalion S-3 to give his SITREP, "Romeo Charlie Three, Foxtrot Four Oscar, over."

"Romeo Charlie Three, over," replied the Battalion S-3. He sounded nervous over the radio.

"Contact points one to four, over," reported SFC Randall, indicating his patrols had crossed friendly lines.

"Roger, out," acknowledged the S-3.

SFC Randall checked his watch as he low crawled through the briars after Recon Team A. Recon Team A would move 700 meters along a muddy streambed to a half downed tree. Recon Team B would cross at contact point three and pass along the western edge of a shallow swamp to a deeper stream area. Security Team A would proceed 800 meters to a hill and rally at an old rusted out Panamanian propeller plane that was covered with jungle growth. Security Team B, which had the longest route to travel, would pass through the eastern edge of the same swamp and cross the stream.

Confident in his team leaders, SFC Randall took a position near the rear of Recon Team A while Staff Sergeant Richard Ball led his men to the downed tree. After ten minutes had passed, automatic gunfire erupted from the left flank where Security Team A was moving. The Chinese gunfire was not returned, and subsided after five minutes had passed. In response to the unknown threat, the distant Chinese artillery units launched white phosphorus parachute flares that slowed the patrol's movement.

When Recon Team A was at the most dangerous part of their infiltration lane where the road and stream were closest to an enemy occupied hill, SGT Thomas Earl, the point man, halted. Everyone froze. Someone was approaching the patrol! SFC Randall gave SGT Earl the signal to kill the enemy intruder!

SGT Earl crouched like a hungry panther. A tall streetwise man from Brooklyn, he slowly withdrew his sharp M16A3 rifle bayonet from his vest. The airborne trooper didn't look back at anyone for help. Like all elite soldiers, he was skilled in hand-to-hand combat.

The approaching Chinese soldier was walking through the jungle with his weapon carelessly slung over his right shoulder. He was more concerned with the heat and mosquitoes than any Americans that were in the area. SSG Earl rose up, gripped the surprised Chinese soldier, and expertly sliced his throat. He held the dying man as he quietly lowered him to the ground.

Recon Team A reached the rally point at 23:00 hours. A place for the patrol to assemble, the rally point was a small bridge located west of the suspected Chinese command post. SFC Randall took SSG Earl with him to conduct a leader's reconnaissance of the objective area.

Security Team A arrived at 23:20 hours and reported that the Chinese had detected them. One man was grazed in the shoulder, but was able to continue with the patrol. Once they had been observed, the team moved west, then turned north to continue their infiltration. Recon Team B arrived at 23:30 without any difficulties. Security Team B arrived at the rally point at 23:45 hours. SFC Randall and SGT Suarez returned to the rally point at midnight. Both men were tired and sweating. A steady rain was beginning to fall.

"Listen up! We've got good Ranger weather now, and that enemy C.P.'s located just east of that abandoned farm tractor," pointed SFC Randall. "Shit, if we could call in a fire mission, we could wipe these dudes out in a heartbeat. They're so bunched up it's not funny."

"Any movement around the command post, Jake?" asked SSG Ralph Daniels, the Security Team A leader. "Any tanks or armored personnel carriers?"

"Too much movement," replied SFC Randall. "I didn't see any tanks or A.P.C.s in the area, but I saw fuel for them. Their security's good, though, mostly because there's so damned many of them walking around. We've got to take advantage of the rain to pull this one off."

The movement to the abandoned tractor was slow and dangerous. There were several Chinese trucks moving along the nearby road, and wary Chinese guards were posted between the road and the headquarters. They positioned themselves near a latrine and waited for an hour before targets of opportunity appeared.

At 02:30 hours, two officers left one of the Chinese tents. They were smoking cigars and walking slowly with their hands behind their backs. SFC Randall recognized senior officers because they carried pistols.

SFC Randall motioned for SSG Garcia to assist him. While one officer was inside the latrine, the other Chinese officer waited outside for his turn. With practiced precision, SFC Randall and SSG Garcia silenced and dragged the stunned officer aside without incident. SGT Brooks and SGT Ficke eagerly waited in the dense undergrowth for the other officer to exit the latrine. The air around the outhouses smelled terrible.

The Chinese officer inside the outhouse called out for his companion. Not hearing an answer, the officer cautiously stepped out of the tent with a Type 54 pistol in his hand.

SGT Brooks and SGT Ficke quickly disarmed the officer, wrestled him to the ground, and secured him. The Chinese command post had not yet been alerted.

"Let's move out! Being at this executive shitter is sure to get us in trouble. Follow me!" he ordered, as he said the famous motto of the infantry.

After a quick dissemination of intelligence, the patrol departed. In the distance, sounds of alarm could be heard back in the Chinese area. There was sporadic gunfire and frantic shouting amongst the enemy soldiers. It was obvious that the Chinese had finally figured out that some of their precious officers were missing.

By 05:30 hrs, the patrol crossed friendly front lines to the safety of the 82d Airborne Division. Their prisoners were immediately processed through the chain of command to the division intelligence officer, where the Chinese captives were identified and questioned. Initial inquiries revealed that SFC Randall and his patrol had captured the Regimental Commander and his assigned Communist Party political officer!

The first reaction by Colonel Stanliss when he learned about the mission was terrible. When LTC Reid reported to his brigade commander, COL Stanliss was full of rage and criticism.

"You disobeyed my orders, Colonel Reid! I won't tolerate insubordination from my battalion commanders! Successful or not, you've created a god damned international incident by kidnapping two of their officers!" reprimanded COL Stanliss. "How the hell am I supposed to explain this to the commanding general? Dammit, Butch, you know how sensitive the situation is! I haven't heard shit from the division commander since we handed over those officers to the G-2!"

"Colonel?" asked the Brigade S-3 as he cautiously interrupted the loud counseling session.

"What is it?"

"General Foster's on the field telephone, sir."

The brigade commander swore in his most foul language as he yanked the telephone up to his ear.

"Yes, General, it was my first battalion," explained COL Stanliss. "Yes, sir. LTC Reid acted on my orders.

Airborne, sir! SFC Jake Randall from Bravo Company was the patrol leader. Sir? Airborne, sir!"

The brigade commander turned and LTC Reid was surprised to see him smiling.

"General Foster commends your initiative," reported COL Stanliss, somewhat confused by the conversation. "Both of the Chinese officers are being transported back to Washington for further processing. The Pentagon's very interested in our catch, but I'm still not pleased that you disobeyed my orders. You won't get an award for this, but write commendations for every trooper on that patrol and I'll sign them."

"Airborne, sir!" barked LTC Reid with pride.

As the Battalion Commander departed the command post, he paid no heed to the compliments from his fellow officers. With a small leap into the seat of his command vehicle, LTC Reid was off to continue the war.

***

On October 12, 2006, the President entertained the Prime Minister of Great Britain, who was in Washington for an inspection of the new and improved British embassy. It was his last stop before going to New York for the summit. Taking advantage of the Prime Minister's visit, President Fairchild agreed to hold a secret meeting on geological issues with Prime Minister Trevor Manly in the Oval Office.

"You've read and heard the briefings, Trevor?" asked Alex over a glass of rare cognac.

"Yes, Monty. I'm very concerned about the immense financial forecasts, but I'm convinced about the outcome," stated Trevor Manly as he took an appreciative sip from a crystal snifter. "It's bloody outrageous to imagine the world shifting like that with us on it, but your three pronged approach to surviving this precessional event is positively ingenious!"

"Well, the tectonic research is still a mystery in many ways, Trevor, but our Mars program is moving ahead. We've also got a lot of work to do to build and stock the population centers," explained Alex Fairchild.

"When do you want us on board, old chap?"

"Technically, you already are, Trevor. Due to the volcanic situation in the Solomon Islands, the Australians and New Zealand have already been informed about Pangaean Effect, too."

"Yes, I've had considerable problems obtaining their silence and support for the use of nuclear weapons to combat the problem," explained the Prime Minister. "But even they recognize that a rift in a tectonic plate that close to home could spell their own doom."

"We're all doomed, Trevor," reminded Alex.

"That may well be, old son. But time has a way of providing solutions, even to astronomical problems like your Pangaean Effect," stated Trevor. "Let's get these volcanoes destroyed, then work on saving the world again from the bigger threat."

"I agree with that."

"Well, you have Britain's support, Monty."

"Thank you, Trevor," responded the President.

"Since this is a long term budgetary plan, we'll commit to funding one fifth of your projected budget with our intelligence funds," decided Trevor Manly. "We'll offset expenses even more and provide jobs in Britain by building as many of the materials or equipment you need throughout the commonwealth during the course of this project."

"Perfect! So what are your concerns about the Chinese summit, Trevor?" asked the President.

"None, actually, old son. I expect the Chinese to ask for our intelligence about their earthquake. What about you? Are there any other issues you want to discuss?"

"No," lied President Fairchild. He couldn't tell Manly about the missing scientist yet. "I just worry this summit will result in disclosure of the Pangaean Effect."

"I don't think so. They'll all be using the ozone layer as the cause of the problem," said Trevor with a knowing wink. "I hope you can pull that one off, Monty. Its a brilliant delaying tactic, even though it was damaged on delivery."

"Don't remind me," groaned Alex Fairchild. "You're the only ones we're sharing this information or mission with, Trevor. It needs to stay that way."

"Done," agreed the Prime Minister.

The two men continued their discussion and enjoyed their drinks, both pleased with the spirit of cooperation between their two nations. The Prime Minister also had some interesting things to say.

"Monty, we know about the Darwin Strand," offered Trevor Manly cautiously. "That's what your task force has been researching with your Dr. Cable Craig."

"I don't know what you're talking about, Trevor," lied Alex Fairchild, who was surprised by the admission. "Anything the C.I.A. does is classified."

"I was hoping for more honesty, Monty. In the interest of fair play, I will tell you the information came our way by a defunct agent who independently infiltrated your research project," admitted the Prime Minister as he handed the President a thin manila folder that contained a brief outline of the Darwin Strand program. "We didn't disseminate the information, but we did verify it."

"And the agent?" asked President Fairchild.

"He was liquidated last year after he solicited the Russians to purchase unrelated classified information," said Mr. Manly. "Fortunately, the Russians never learned about your Darwin program."

"I'm disturbed by your admission, Trevor. "Spying against an ally is wrong," noted Alex Fairchild.

"Every country in the world will know about your entire program in a very short while," advised Trevor Manly. "It's inevitable. As for the espionage, the spy was an independent, not someone contracted by us. We've had our own strange genetic events since 1975, too. You'll see it in that file. Our Chief of the Secret Intelligence Service has been collecting historical data since our informant made us aware of your Darwin Strand. Even our national health centers failed to make a genetic connection to the small number of mutations that have been occurring in our general population. We tallied it all to the ozone layer, pollution, or nuclear energy problems, not some astronomical force of nature preparing humanity for it's greatest tragedy. It's amazing, actually."

"Trevor," remarked Alex Fairchild. "Have you considered our proposal about the Solomons?"

"Considerably," breathed Trevor Manly. "Lord willing, nature will wait until the Crown can mobilize an evacuation program. In the interim, I've tasked the Australian and New Zealand governments with being prepared to conduct immediate evacuations of the island before the neutralization of the volcanoes."

"I appreciate that, Trevor," said the President as both men took a longer drink from their glasses than either of them would have liked. "Let's hope none of this will be necessary."

***

The massive state dinner for the opening ceremony of the United Nations summit was held in the grand ballroom of the Waldorf Astoria hotel. It was a stressful time for Daniel Tokuhisa and Aramentha Washington, who were working under confusing U.N. directives while arranging for security and protocol.

In order to make the meeting between the summit host and the host nation as smooth as possible, Secretary Tokuhisa had personally made arrangements in advance that were suitable for both parties. An accomplished linguist, Daniel Tokuhisa spoke several languages, including Mandarin Chinese and Cantonese. Secretary Tokuhisa's linguistic abilities made his dealings with the Chinese officials much easier.

When it was time for the President to meet with President Zhu Le Ho in the U.N. Security Council conference room, entourages from both countries converged on the location. The initial meeting would occur between the two presidents, who would be allowed to have one interpreter and one assistant present.

"It's unfortunate that we meet under these circumstances," said President Fairchild as he shook hands with the Chinese president. "On behalf of the people of the United States, I want to extend our thanks for your decision to host this important summit."

"On behalf of the People's Republic of China, I am proud to be here to sponsor the summit. In spite of your aggression in Panama, I'm looking forward to your welcome speech and the assistance you'll be able to provide the United Nations concerning the ozone layer and these many world disasters," offered President Zhu Le Ho with a forced smile.

President Fairchild nodded, unsure of what to make of President Zhu's casual reference to the ozone layer. While there was a cultural barrier that was hard for him to understand, the President had the feeling that President Zhu was concealing something from him.

"Of course, President Zhu Le Ho," said Alex Fairchild cautiously. "We have a wide range of information that we'll be sharing with China and the concerned nations."

"Very good. There is much to discuss," stated the Chinese Chief of State. "I will express my own views following the summit."

***

The formal dinner took place without any difficulties. Most of the member nations were present for the summit, which drew more attendees due to the publicized interest of the Chinese in the world disasters and the conflict in Panama. It was highly unusual for both the President and the Premier of the People's Republic of China to attend any United Nations function together. That made the summit even more intriguing.

President Fairchild's speech to the assemblage drew a standing ovation from the crowd. The President's remarks were very convincing. He stated that the depletion of the ozone layer was the primary cause of the world's natural geological disasters. Everything appeared to be going very well.

After the Kenyan national dance troupe performed some colorful native dances during breakfast the following morning, Secretary General Asi Fanon Mtume caused a stir when he chose not to be the guest speaker. The Secretary General humbly deferred his place to President Zhu Le Ho, which the crowd enthusiastically accepted. As President Zhu Le Ho slowly made his way to the podium, the American officials seated at President Fairchild's table were suspicious of this unannounced change in schedule by the Secretary General.

"Welcome, everyone, to the United Nations Summit on the investigation of world geographical issues," said the Chinese President into the microphone. "The People's Republic of China is prepared to present a different view for consideration by the member nations."

President Fairchild suddenly became nervous.

"While the President of the United States has so graciously offered the argument that the ozone layer is the cause of the world's natural disasters, our scientists have been working with the Secretary General to determine the true cause of these disasters. We have learned that the culprit is not the ozone layer, but the growing instability of the tectonic plates on which the world's continents and oceans are supported. That instability is caused by astronomy, and the Americans have known this all along. Rather than share their knowledge, the United States concealed it and let thousands die as a result. In order to facilitate international cooperation, the People's Republic of China, with the intellectual support of our Nanjing

University of Science and Technology, and the United Nations Framework Convention on Climate Change, is now sponsoring the new United Nations Symposium on Tectonic Research."

Everyone in the room applauded.

"The Pangaean Effect just went public, Mr. President," muttered Dan Tokuhisa.

"What the hell's going on?" asked the President under his breath as President Zhu Le Ho received a standing ovation. Several attendees looked at the American table with new suspicion and anger.

"I was afraid of this, Mr. President," uttered Aramentha Washington in an attempt to cover her ass.

"If you were, you sure as hell didn't tell me, Ambassador!" snarled Alex Fairchild as the applause subsided. "I just got boffed, and I didn't enjoy it!"

Kurt Farley sank back into his chair as the President of China continued his speech. Daniel Tokuhisa, along with Aramentha Washington, both occupied their time by taking copious notes about the speech. The President was visibly angry as a score of camera flashbulbs exploded around him.

"While I compliment the United States on their research findings, it is not their place, nor should we expect it to be their function, to be the solitary voice of the nations of the world on international issues of this kind. That task falls on the United Nations alone. At the request of Secretary General Mtume, China has found the true cause of the tragic geological disasters. The People's Republic of China asks you now to appoint China as the host nation for this new international program so that we may find the solutions now."

The crowd shouted and applauded, which made President Zhu Le Ho bow and smile at the audience.

"I recognize the supreme efforts of the United States, and I now ask President Alexander Fairchild to join me on this stage in a gesture of cooperation and peace in support of this new symposium."

As the crowd gave the Chinese leader another standing ovation, there was a lot of quick discussion at President Fairchild's table. The dining room was filled with applauding people waiting for the President of the United States to join the Chinese president on stage.

"Protocol, sir," warned Dan Tokuhisa. "You have to join him on stage or we'll be insulting China and the United Nations. We can resolve the other issues behind closed doors."

The other advisors agreed.

"I know an ambush when I see one," he said with a media smile on his face and a wave to the crowd. He placed his napkin on the table and rose to join the Chinese leader on the stage.

***

Following his embarrassing appearance on stage with President Zhu Le Ho, President Fairchild spent the rest of the afternoon chewing out his advisors. The United States was now in the impossible position of working under the Chinese on the new U.N. geological project. President Fairchild was so upset that he was considering the removal of some of his top advisors and cabinet members, especially Aramentha Washington.

"Mr. President, there's a new development," advised Dan Tokuhisa as he put his hand over the telephone receiver. "I've got Andrea Mangone on the line. She's reporting that the combat between the Chinese and the 82d Airborne has increased. But she's also reporting that the 82nd captured the regimental commander and political officer of a Chinese units."

"Christ, just what I need! What do you think, Dan?" asked the President with increasing cynicism and renewed disapproval of his Secretary of Defense. "Do I need to fire some generals and colonels, too?"

"The prisoners are a good bargaining chip, sir. They'll want their political officer back first, but I'm sure the Chinese don't want us to have much time to debrief their elite officers," advised the Secretary of State.

The President nodded as he took a long moment to think about this new development.

"Aramentha, arrange a conference with the Chinese president."

"Consider it done, Mr. President," said Ms. Washington as she gladly departed the hotel room.

"Dan, are we going to get an opportunity to interrogate the prisoners before we attempt an exchange for Doctor Peabody?" asked President Fairchild.

"Yes, Mr. President. These soldiers are technically prisoners of war, so we can question them and obtain intelligence," explained Dan Tokuhisa.

The telephone was ringing again. It was the C.I.A. Director.

"What now?" asked Alex Fairchild, as Mr. Tokuhisa handed him the telephone. After a lengthy conversation, President Fairchild hung up the telephone.

"Checkmate!"

"Sir?" asked Dan Tokuhisa.

"At least someone's taking the ball and driving it down the fairway! NOAH'S ARK sent their Special Forces team to Antarctica and they found a pack of cigarettes and a cigarette butt at the Chinese camp. The pack of cigarettes matches the lot number supplied to the research site and a priority D.N.A. analysis of the saliva on the butt matches that of Dr. Peabody!"

Secretary Tokuhisa dropped back into his chair with a deep sigh of relief.

"Now I can clean up this whole mess!" exclaimed the President, who slammed an open palm on the desk. "Yes! We finally have the proof we need! Now, let's go see the Chinese and put them in their damned place!"

Chapter Fifteen

"The Summit"

A small flotilla of U.S., Royal Australian, and Royal New Zealand vessels of war were assembled approximately 15 nautical miles southwest of the six volcanoes. Mike Valenti was onboard the American flagship, the aircraft carrier U.S.S. Ronald Reagan (CVN-76). Mike had befriended the carrier commander, Admiral Zack Pruitt. The two men were on the bridge of the huge carrier waiting for the Sea Stallion helicopter pilots to complete their pre-flight inspection.

"I just spoke with Commander O'Connell, Mike," advised the Admiral. He turned in his big chair and watched the helicopter pilots at their tasks. "Those pilots will be done in about five minutes. You ready"

Mike was sweating and felt like vomiting. The Admiral noticed, but waited for his new friend to answer.

"Yeah, Admiral, I'm ready," mumbled Mike nervously. "I'm as ready as I'll ever be."

"You need to check your attitude, Major! I'm the commander of this vessel and you'll respect me!"

"Yes, Admiral!" barked back Mike with newfound fear for his friend.

"Right now, you're a C.I.A. boss getting ready to save the world. I expect you to set an example! You're scared, and that's normal. You're about to put seven nuclear mines in the ground underwater and detonate them," explained Admiral, who lit a cheap cigar and began puffing on it. "That takes guts! Guts to envision it, and guts to do it. So get it done, Major!"

"Thanks, Admiral," responded Mike with a much improved attitude. "I will."

"Don't thank me, Major. Impress me, and them," demanded Admiral Pruitt as he pointed at the group of Navy S.E.A.L.s walking toward the helicopter. "Those young sailors are the Navy's best. They're so full of piss and vinegar that they'll do this mission just because it's crazy! But they won't tolerate the honcho, even a C.I.A. agent like you, choking and puking when it's time to bet his own badge and put his life on the line!"

"You're right about that, sir," admitted Mike.

"Damn right I'm right!" growled Admiral Pruitt. "Besides, the scuttlebutt's that one of those fine men is your son. That correct?"

"In a way, Admiral," replied Mike. "I fathered him, but I gave him up for adoption when he was born."

"You know him now, though, right?"

"Yes, sir. We're acquainted, but he doesn't care for me much, and I'm okay with that," explained Mike.

"Bullshit!" said the Admiral. "He may not call you daddy, but he wants to know what kind of stock he comes from. He wants to know if his old man can cut it."

"You've got a point," agreed Mike.

"I didn't get these stars looking through a telescope, Major. I earned them! Now, you get out there and do the do, then come on back here and deal with the consequences. You got that?" asked the Admiral.

"Yes, sir!" answered Mike in a motivated voice.

"Much better, Major Valenti!"

"Anything else, Admiral?" asked Mike as he picked up his gear bag and saluted the admiral.

"You've got the U.S.S. Kamehameha attack sub as the S.E.A.L. Delivery Vehicle. The N.R.-1 Deep Submergence Craft sub will follow it. Once your team departs the Kamehameha in the mini-sub, the Kamehameha will move into a patrol pattern fifteen nautical miles from ground zero. The N.R.-1 will deposit each 400-pound mine on site, and then depart. When you're all wired and hot, make sure your timer's accurate. Then you get into that mini-sub and hustle your butts back to the safe zone and secure that rig to the Kamehameha," directed the Admiral.

"Aye, aye, sir!" responded Mike, who was surprised to blurt out such a Navy response.

"Good, now get off my bridge!" ordered the carrier commander with a nasty look on his face.

Mike made his way down to the flight deck. As he went, some of the sailors wished him luck. When Mike arrived on the hot flight deck, one of the officers escorted him to the helicopter where the twelve members of S.E.A.L. Team II were waiting for him.

"The team's ready, Doc," shouted Commander Chuck O'Connell as they shook hands. "This helo's going to ferry us over to the sub."

"I'm ready!" Mike said as he handed his dive gear over to one of the S.E.A.L.s. "Let's go!"

When everyone was on board, the Sea Stallion took off. The Kamehameha was surfaced with its conning tower hatch open and crew waiting on its narrow deck. Covered in sweat, Mike remembered that millions of people were depending on him.

***

One hundred and fifty feet above the ocean floor, the U.S.S. Kamehameha special operations nuclear submarine approached the danger zone of the six marine volcanoes. The nuclear powered N.R.-1 Deep Submergence Craft submarine followed behind her. The N.R.-1 was equipped with extendable bottoming wheels, viewing ports, exterior lighting, television and recording equipment, an object recovery apparatus, and various gripping and cutting tools that permitted the submarine to conduct object installation and recovery on the sea floor. On the top deck of the Kamehameha, the mini-sub that contained Mike Valenti and the members of S.E.A.L. Team II was secured. As both submarines reached their operational area, the S.E.A.L.s were notified.

"That's us, Doc!" announced Commander O'Connell with a genuine smile. Everyone was equipped and ready. "Chief, prepare to get underway."

"Aye, aye, sir!" responded the team chief.

"Recheck your equipment, Mike," directed O'Connell. "We've got seven hot nukes to emplace, wire for sound, synchronize for firing, fuse on time, clear the area, and blow!"

When the mini-sub was well under way, Commander O'Connell made contact with the N.R.-1 and proceeded to the first nuclear site.

"I've never understood why we can't just use the Kamehameha to do the mission," commented Mike.

"The big sub's carrying our nukes on deck and they're all set for installation, but she's not designed to emplace something as fragile and explosive as a nuclear device. So that's where we underwater demolition guys earn our pay in the Deep Submergence Craft. The Navy's not gonna let a nuclear sub be close to those nukes while we wire them up!"

"That's not very comforting," remarked Mike, as he looked forward through the viewing window at the murky ocean. "I thought it would be clearer down here."

"You're kidding, right?" said Commander O'Connell. He motioned for one of his men to come forward. "The water down here's hotter than a Filipino whore house on a Friday! This ain't like working in that clear water at Key West, but we'll get the job done."

"Get everyone ready to dive, Chief. We're near the first bomb site," ordered the Team Commander.

As the mini-sub came within sight of the first nuclear land mine, Mike looked through the window and observed that the water and sea floor was unstable. A volcanic earthquake made the mini-sub tremble and shift in the current. Dirt and debris was visible in the water.

"Would you want that big sub to wire nuclear bombs in this environment, sir?" asked Commander O'Connell.

"I get your point now," agreed Mike, who watched Steven move up next to O'Connell.

"Sparky, it's mostly your show once we have that nuclear excuse for a depth charge released to us. Let's do it by the numbers, just like we trained to do."

"You got it, skipper," acknowledged Steven.

"Let's dive!" ordered Commander O'Connell.

With two men remaining in the mini-sub to operate it, the rest of the team entered the tumultuous sea. Mike

Valenti swam close to Commander O'Connell. He didn't want to get lost as the S.E.A.L. Team swam toward the first nuclear weapon.

***

The installation of the first six nuclear devices went smoothly in spite of the volcanic earthquakes. As the S.E.A.L.s completed their swim from the mini-sub to the last mine location, Mike noticed slight changes in his seismic readings. As Commander O'Connell and his crew worked on the last bomb, Mike analyzed the data.

"Shit, Sparky!" swore Commander O'Connell as they shifted the 400 lb. nuclear land mine into the hole the NR-1 had created. "Be careful with that detonation wire! We're on the last leg of this mission!"

"Sorry, skipper," responded Steven Gunther as he moved his det wire out of the way of the mine as it slowly dropped into the hole.

"Roger that, Sparky, but we've got to do this by the numbers," advised Chuck O'Connell. "You double check the wiring?"

"Aye, aye, skipper," answered Steven. "They all tested hot. We're ready."

"Commander," said Mike with concern in his voice. "The tremors are becoming return quakes toward the Solomons, too."

"What's that mean, Doc?" asked Chuck O'Connell as they released the wire from the spool and began to swim away from the last mine.

"That means there's new volcanic activity beginning in the direction of the Solomon Islands," said Mike. "We've got to notify the surface commander."

"Well, we're finishing up here, Doc," said Commander O'Connell. "Go back to the mini-sub and tell Tommy what you need done."

Mike left the S.E.A.L.s. While he was completing his call, a large volcanic earthquake shook the underwater terrain and tossed the divers around in the current like lost debris. When the last of the team members made it back to the mini-sub, Commander O'Connell was relieved.

"That bit the bag big time!"

"You got that right, skipper!" agreed Steven Gunther with a deep breath.

"Tommy, get us the hell back to our detonation grid!" ordered Commander O'Connell. "But take it easy. We've got seven wires to extend to our det point."

When the mini-sub reached it's detonation point on the edge of the safety zone, Commander O'Connell, Steven Gunther, and Mike Valenti entered the ocean again. It took fifteen minutes to attach the wires from the nuclear bombs to the mini-sub's firing assembly.

"Looking good!" praised Chuck O'Connell as he gave them the thumbs up. "All the wires test okay. Chief, test the firing assembly!"

"Aye, aye, skipper," responded the Chief Petty Officer over the radio.

The three men waited as the tests were done.

"Skipper, the sub's firing assembly test was negative," advised the Chief.

"I'll be god damned!" swore Steven as the three men looked at each other in the murky water. "That's what we get for hooking up Cold War bombs to computer age electronics during an earthquake! Shit!"

"Calm down, Sparky," advised Chuck O'Connell. "We've got another firing assembly on the mini-sub."

As Steven Gunter worked with the Chief to install the spare firing assembly, Mike checked his seismic readings. Another volcanic earthquake occurred, this one stronger than the last.

"We've got to blow these nukes before these volcanoes create another one in the Solomons!" warned Mike as they held onto each other in the violent current. "They're like contractions during a mother's labor and the baby's about to arrive!"

"I know, Doc!" responded Chuck O'Connell with equal worry. "We'll do this somehow!"

After the firing system was replaced, Chuck O'Connell helped Steven inspect the connections. The test of the new device was negative, too.

"No way this is happening!" exclaimed Steven with more anger in his voice. "Piece of shit!"

"What now?" asked Mike, who was confused about the situation. "We're running out of options."

"Copy that, Doc," acknowledged Commander O'Connell, who was thinking all of the time. "Sparky, all the wires are still testing hot, affirmative?"

"Roger," responded Steven as he double-checked his wires again. "Each line to the nukes is positive."

"Then we have to do this manually," decided Chuck O'Connell without any emotion in his voice. "We have manual firing devices for multiple demolitions."

Mike didn't know what that meant, but he knew by the looks on the faces of Chuck O'Connell and Steven Gunther that it wasn't the preferred way of conducting nuclear demolitions. As Commander O'Connell attached the wires to his own firing device, he looked around at the debris filled water.

"Doc, you and Sparky go on back to the mini-sub. Instruct Tommy to move to the safety zone and link up with the Kamehameha," directed Chuck O'Connell. "Notify the chain of command what the situation is. I'll detonate the nukes in exactly fifteen mikes."

Steven stowed his tools and pulled on Mike's arm, but it didn't work.

"No way, Commander!" exclaimed Mike when he realized what was happening. "You can't detonate these bombs and stay in the water here! That's suicide!"

"That's the only way it's going to get done, Doc. These firing devices are manual for a reason," said Chuck O'Connell, who received a positive test result. "I'll be okay. Just look for me on the surface."

"Sir, I'm responsible for this equipment failure," admitted Steven. "I'll stay here and do the job."

"Negative, sailor! Get going!"

"Sir, we could detonate from inside the mini-sub and probably survive the ride," offered Steven.

"Sparky. I'm not risking everyone when one man can do this!" explained O'Connell. "Now get going!"

Steven began to leave, but Mike wouldn't depart.

"Unless you use that diving knife on me, I'm not going, Commander," advised Mike. "This is my mission, and I'm ordering you back to the mini-sub."

Commander Charles O'Connell hesitated to answer, unsure of what to do now that the civilian mission commander was countering his decision.

"I'm the Commander down here, Doc, so back off!" warned O'Connell as he recovered from Mike's directive, but he had forgotten that their underwater communications system allowed for the entire team to listen to the transmissions.

"Commander O'Connell, there hasn't been a mutiny since I can remember," spoke up Master Chief Petty Officer Tommy Sands from the mini-sub. "But we came on this mission together and we ain't leaving no man behind, not even a C.I.A. Special Agent that just became a brother S.E.A.L. Now with all due respect, sir, can we fire these nukes?"

With that said, Commander O'Connell and Mike Valenti followed Steven Gunther back to the mini-sub. When they were all on board, all hands could tell their commander was upset with them.

"Well?" asked Chief Sands without waiting for his boss to reprimand them. "What're we waiting for?"

Commander O'Connell looked at his men.

"Fire in the hole!"

Commander Charles O'Connell detonated the seven nuclear land mines that were emplaced at the ends of the six marine volcanoes. With an eerie silence, followed by a jolting simultaneous explosion, the last thing Michael Valenti remembered experiencing was being flung into the side of the craft's interior steel wall. As the mini-submarine was swept away by the nuclear current, the occupants of the small vessel were knocked unconscious and left to the mercy of the sea.

***

"Gawd bless it! This ain't supposed to happen so soon!" swore Elton at the top of his lungs as a strong volcanic earthquake shook the ground. "When's the Doc gonna blow those nukes? If it don't happen soon, we're gonna be roasted like luau hogs!"

"What's the word?" asked Willian Penellas. "Any news from Doc or the Navy?"

"Ah don't need the ground to open up to know that paradise is gettin' hot and shot!" said Elton as he paced the ground. "Hey, Frasier! Get with the Aussies an' coordinate our emergency extraction now!"

"You got it, Ranger!" replied Frasier Owens, the Mission Staff Movement and Deployment Officer. He was responsible for ARK One logistics. "We leaving the non-essential equipment?"

"Roger that!" acknowledged Elton, still pacing. "Lem, get on the radio an' call in the teams A.S.A.P. We kin use the local Australian choppers for that. Hey, an' git on the secure phone. Ah need to notify Bubba John of the situation heah!"

"On it!" replied Lemuel Stokes, the ARK One Operations and Plans Officer.

As Elton Rance and the Mission Staff conducted their activities, the ground beneath their feet rumbled and groaned like it was in pain. In the distance to their west, seven nuclear mushroom clouds filled the beautiful South Pacific skyline.

"Damn!" swore Glenda Moses as the group realized what was happening.

"That should save us and the Hawaiian Islands, too," hoped Elton Rance with a bit of awe in his voice over what was happening in the distance.

As ARK One watched the detonation along with everyone else, the volcanic earthquakes under their feet immediately stopped. Elton looked at Glenda for reassurance.

"Maybe," hoped Glenda with extreme caution and doubt in her voice.

Elton looked at the ground beneath his feet, along with everyone else who realized that the volcanic tremors had stopped.

"I think the Doc did it, Vernie!" remarked Elton with a slight bit of relief in his voice.

As the members of ARK One and the villagers around them began cheering at the mushroom clouds in the distance, the ground belched and a huge volcanic earthquake that was more powerful than any of its predecessors jolted the ground.

"I was afraid of this, Ranger!" Glenda shouted. "Those nukes probably saved Hawaii, but we're going to have our volcano whether we like it or not!"

"Suit up, people! Let's grab our gear and head for some cover!" ordered Elton Rance above the noise.

As the mountain over Guadalcanal split open and exploded, ARK One and the people of the Solomon Islands frantically ran for cover. The dirt filled eruption of a new land volcano replaced the view of the seven mushroom clouds that continued rising in the distant sky.

***

The meeting between President Alexander Montgomery Fairchild and President Zhu Le Ho was hastily arranged. Daniel Tokuhisa had not been able to properly arrange for the multitude of protocols associated with meetings between two heads of state. After the two executives met, they squared off without exchanging pleasantries. Premier Hu was also there.

"We have two of your officers, President Zhu," said Alex Fairchild directly.

"Yes, President Fairchild?" asked President Zhu Le Ho, who could not conceal the concerned look on his elderly face. "Both men were captured in uniform during hostilities. I would like them returned at once."

"I don't think so," remarked President Fairchild.

He handed a package to the Chinese leader, who examined it without opening it. It was a thick bubble wrapped plastic package.

"What is this?" asked Premier Hu Quichen, who was seated next to his president.

President Fairchild merely smiled and waited as President Zhu Le Ho slowly opened the small package. The premier was very nervous.

"Is this some capitalist trick to influence the outcome of this summit?" Hu Quichen asked as he watched Zhu Le Ho pull the contents out of the bag.

"What does this mean? Is the United States interested in more tobacco exports to China?" asked President Zhu Le Ho as he examined a crumpled pack of Merit cigarettes and the cigarette butts accompanying it.

"That," began President Fairchild. "Is a pack of cigarettes found at your expedition site that bears the fingerprints of one Dr. Connor Brian Peabody, Jr., the scientist who is missing from our Antarctic site. The two cigarette butts were smoked at your site by two of your own men. Mr. Peabody's favorite brand, and the lot from which he purchased them, were provided to the scientists in Antarctica by the U.S. Air Force."

President Zhu Le Ho was shaken by the news. He had heard about American technological advances in forensic science. Premier Hu Quichen looked at the pack of cigarettes and the marks where the fingerprints had been detected on the plastic wrapper.

"Our comrades located your Dr. Peabody just before they departed Antarctica," explained President Zhu in an expert lie. "Due to our slow communications network, we just received the information that he was found. I will personally insure he is returned to you. Is it acceptable to deliver him to the embassy in Beijing?"

The President smiled, appreciating the Chinese leader's ability to lie so well.

"That would be fine, sir," accepted President Fairchild. He didn't offer to reciprocate with the return of the Chinese captives. "And he had better be well."

"What about our countrymen?" asked Hu Quichen, who was getting angry with President Fairchild for not offering to return his soldiers.

Alexander Fairchild glanced first at his Secretary of State, then at the two Chinese leaders seated in front of him. The President was beginning to enjoy international politics and intrigue.

"The United States will return your officers," replied Alex Fairchild. "They were captured during a routine patrol by one of our airborne units. Rather than kill the men, we chose to capture them. May I return them to your embassy in Washington after our scientist has safely arrived in the United States?"

President Zhu Le Ho nodded his head, realizing all too clearly that the Americans had achieved a political advantage. This was more than a prisoner exchange between two adversaries.

"I like you, President Zhu," lied Alex Fairchild. "You know the rules of politics, and you know how quickly one piece of bad information can turn the international community against you."

"What are you saying?" asked Hu Quichen.

"I'm not saying anything. I'm telling you that the United Nations Symposium on Tectonic Research will not take place in the People's Republic of China under your sponsorship."

"You cannot dictate our national policy or relationship with the United Nations," hissed Hu Quichen. "We will do as we please."

"That's where you're wrong, Premier," countered President Fairchild. "If the People's Republic of China doesn't remove itself from sponsorship and defer that sponsorship to the United States, I will personally get in front of the United Nations and give the complete information about your nuclear test that made the world's tectonic plates unstable. I will disclose information about your unauthorized Antarctic mission, your abduction of a civilian American scientist, and your unsolicited military incursion into Panama during a humanitarian mission by the United States."

"Don't threaten me, President Fairchild," remarked President Zhu Le Ho. "Even as we speak, a naval task force is on its way to the Pacific coast of Panama to protect our interests there. One of our nuclear submarines will be arriving on the Atlantic coast as well. If you want to escalate this into a world war between nuclear nations, China will face you with honor. We will not cede sponsorship of the symposium."

President Fairchild was an expert at political maneuvering. General Vann and Daniel Tokuhisa had insured that he wouldn't go to a political gunfight without a hell of a gun and a lot of ammunition. With a sly smile, President Fairchild handed Zhu Le Ho a folder.

"In that folder, sir, you'll find your defeat well in hand," noted President Fairchild. "I've got two carrier task forces converging on Panama from both sides of that country, with orders to engage any belligerent nation that interferes with the Panamanian government or the U.N. humanitarian effort there. And that submarine you're talking about has been tracked by the navy since it left Antarctica! You'll find the latest positions of your vessels listed on the first page. Go on, look at it!"

President Zhu Le Ho read the page. He was so angry that his hands were shaking.

"The Roosevelt Corollary authorizes the United States to intervene and enforce the expulsion of any foreign incursion into the Americas. I will enforce that rule unless you recall your fleet and withdraw your forces within twenty four hours."

"The People's Republic of China will use nuclear force to defend herself," remarked the Premier.

"You should know something right now," snarled President Fairchild. "The United States isn't afraid of a country whose nuclear arsenal and relies on a triggering system that doesn't work. If you can't properly detonate a stationary nuclear weapon, I know you have no ability to launch your strategic missiles. Back off, gentlemen, or I'll make this an international summit the United Nations and your enemies will never forget!"

President Zhu Le Ho was speechless.

"That is outrageous!" exclaimed President Zhu.

"Is it?" countered President Fairchild. "The nuclear test that failed and caused the deaths of so many failed because your standard triggering device is bad. How would you like the world to learn you're no longer a nuclear superpower?"

President Zhu and Premier Hu examined the data in the file President Fairchild had provided them.

"What about China's role in the symposium?" asked President Zhu Le Ho. "Can we participate?"

"Of course, President Zhu," replied the President. "You'll have an honorable place as peaceful partners working with the world toward resolving tectonic problems. Do you accept?"

"The People's Republic of China accepts your offers, President Fairchild," agreed President Zhu Le Ho with a grimace. "We will withdraw our forces to our original locations and recall our naval forces. Your scientist will be returned in exchange for our two soldiers, and we will defer the symposium over to the United States as a matter of scientific necessity."

President Fairchild wasn't satisfied.

"Negative, President Zhu. You'll withdraw completely from Panama and yield all control of the canal to that country. The United States will pay for your contractual loss, but I don't want any Chinese forces or presence in the New World again."

President Zhu Le Ho nodded and confirmed his agreement by shaking hands with the President. A military advisor appeared at the door. President Fairchild excused himself to meet with the attaché.

"How did it go?" asked the President of his military advisor. "Was the detonation successful?"

"Yes, Mr. President," responded the Colonel. "According to naval intelligence and the Commander of the U.S.S. Ronald Reagan, the six volcanoes were neutralized, and readings in Hawaii have been steadily decreasing. Unfortunately, a volcano did erupt on Guadalcanal as a result of the nuclear detonations."

"Oh, my God," remarked the President. "What are we doing to help the people there?"

"Sir, the evacuation of the Solomon Islands is underway, but the situation there is critical."

"Thank you, Colonel," responded the President with a stressful sigh. "Well, Danny, we saved Hawaii at the expense of Guadalcanal. How do I to live with that?"

Daniel Tokuhisa shrugged. He was used to international trade offs in the name of American survival.

"You did the right thing, Mr. President. Now we help the people of the Solomons as best as we can."

The President looked hard at his Secretary of State, realizing that he really didn't like him very much.

"You're an asshole, Tokuhisa," remarked the President. "A heartless asshole."

"Yes, Mr. President, and that's why you pay me to do what I do," responded Dan Tokuhisa. "Now, are you going to let the Chinese know you saved them, too?"

President Fairchild entered the room and sat down. President Zhu Le Ho was curious about what to expect next.

"A few moments ago, President Zhu, the United States detonated nuclear weapons in the South Pacific to neutralize damage caused by your failed nuclear test. The detonation was successful, but the Solomon Islands will have to be evacuated. I expect your full support for this action as we've already discussed."

"Of course, President Fairchild," agreed President Zhu Le Ho.

By the time the President had showered and had a strong nightcap in his hotel bedroom, the rest of the world had heard the news that nuclear weapons had been used to extinguish the volcanoes in the South Pacific.

***

When Admiral Pruitt was able to reestablish contact with vessels in the fleet, he requested a status update of the S.E.A.L. Team. The news wasn't good. Following the explosion, sonar contact with the mini-sub had been lost during the tidal waves. Contact not been regained, and the waters around ground zero were filled with floating debris.

"Get Agent Washington on the horn," directed the Admiral to one of his staff officers. "He's next in the chain of command down here. He can notify C.I.A. that we've lost contact with Valenti and the S.E.A.L.s."

"Aye, aye, Admiral," responded the staff officer.

Another officer handed the Admiral a message.

"X.O., direct two destroyers and our support ships to proceed immediately to Guadalcanal to assist in the evacuation of the islands," ordered the Admiral. "Instruct the rest of the task force to conduct rescue operations and bomb damage assessment."

As the officers on the carrier's bridge executed the Admiral's commands, search aircraft were dispatched to look for the mini-sub or any survivors of S.E.A.L. Team II. For radiation safety issues, the search was limited to the safe area around ground zero.

***

Elton Rance evacuated as many ARK One members as he could on the available helicopters until the falling debris made it impossible for continuing flight operations. Most of Glenda's team had chosen to remain with Elton so the other ARK members could extract. As rescue vessels from the U.S. and her allies conducted beach rescues, thousands of Solomon Islanders were stranded in the surf. Thick clouds of pyroclastic flow and rivers of lava were flowing down the volcano into the urban areas of Guadalcanal. Debris from the spreading eruption cloud was falling to the ground with deadly results.

"Oh, shit!" exclaimed Glenda as she looked over her shoulder to see a boulder bouncing off of the ground and coming their way. It careened into local civilians as it bounced into the sea. All around the ARK One team, the sounds of the erupting volcano were being matched by the screams of the wounded and dying.

As Cowboy Smith attempted to raise their designated rescue vessel on the portable radio, Team One quickly realized that they were about to be covered with ash and pumice from the eruption column. Rance was screaming into his radio as Glenda grabbed a couple of children that had fallen and were choking on the thick ash that had filled the air.

"Ranger!" shouted Glenda above the sound of the eruption as they reached the beach. "These protective suits are going to be lead weights in the water!"

"Shit, Vernie! The whole mountain's disappeared from what ah kin tell!" shouted Elton. "We ain't got no time left! We've got to keep suited up and masked or we'll choke on the ash and pumice just like everyone else! The ground's shakin' too much for us to help anyone that's stuck on land!"

"What are your orders, Ranger?" asked Glenda.

"We'll just git about waist deep in this heah water and wait for rescue, Vernie! Ah'll git us outta here!"

As the islanders began choking and dying from the gases and fumes in the air, ARK One members tossed as many people as they could into the boats. Cowboy was retrieving women and children that were lying on the beach and unable to move on their own. As the team continued assisting in the rescue efforts, several of the rescue vessels were also destroyed or damaged.

"This ain't good!" shouted Elton to the rest of his companions as he grabbed an injured team member and raised him up to a withdrawing vessel that was already overcrowded with desperate screaming passengers. "There just ain't enough boats to get all these folks out!"

"I'm not taking a place on any boat while there's women and kids still waiting to go!" shouted Cowboy Smith to them all. "It ain't right, and you know it!"

Elton nodded as he cleared some of the thick ash off of his protective mask lenses.

"Vernie, you're going on the next boat!"

"No way, Ranger!" responded Glenda. "Not while my team's still here!"

Before he could argue his point any further, a familiar voice blared over their hand held radios.

"Y'all need a ride today, Ranger?" sounded Bubba John Washington's deep voice over the radio.

"Bubba John? We sure do, son! Where you at?" shouted Elton as he tried to make out any boats that might be within sight of him. "Ah cain't see you at all!"

"Hang on, Ranger!" calmed Bubba to his friend. "I've got your locator chips on the G.P.S., so findin' you's the easy part. I'm coming in right now!"

As the sounds of a slowing boat indicated Bubba's proximity to their location, Elton's chemical detection equipment began to light up again.

"Bubba, you've got to clear the area now!" shouted Elton as he looked over his shoulder and realized what was happening. "Gas! Gas! Gas!"

"Awright, Ranger, we're going, but we'll be back to get you!" roared Bubba's voice over the radio.

When the huge explosive cloud of poisonous gas consumed ARK One, they huddled together and disappeared in a huge cloud of poisonous smoke and ash. The sounds of the rescue boats as they rapidly departed the area made people shout for help as the deadly gases killed most of them.

***

Three hours had passed and the captain and crew of the U.S.S. Ronald Reagan had not been able to locate any survivors of the stricken mini-sub. All of the assigned vessels in the area that were not involved in the Solomon Islands rescue were busy using their aircraft and technical sensors to locate the missing bomb team. After five more hours had passed, the search was meeting with negative results.

"What's going on at Guadalcanal?" asked Admiral Pruitt with a frown.

"The C.I.A. group's extracted, with the exception of Team One and the ARK One leader," replied the Executive Officer from his post. "They're presumed missing, and toxic gases and hot pumice are preventing any rescue efforts until further notice."

"Goddammit! What about civilian casualties?" asked the Admiral as he checked the field reports.

"Estimates for the dead are 7,000, Admiral. The last estimate on wounded was approximately 16,500. There are still thousands of survivors on land or waiting on the beaches for extraction."

"Thank you," responded the Admiral. "And the situation at ground zero?"

"The seas are stabilizing, Admiral. We've got clearance to re-enter ground zero," responded an officer on the Admiral's staff.

"Instruct all warships to search there by sector and find that mini-sub!" ordered the Admiral. "Now!"

The staff officers and sailors scurried to comply with their commander's instructions. A communications officer interrupted the Admiral, who was looking at the many helicopters and aircraft searching the sea.

"Sir, the President is on the secure line."

The Admiral picked up the telephone and attempted to sound as commanding as possible.

"This is Admiral Pruitt, Mr. President."

"Admiral, I understand the nuclear detonations were a success?" asked the President in the usual way that commanded an affirmative response.

"Yes, Mr. President. The six volcanoes were neutralized," explained the Admiral. "There's a cooling seam of rock where they used to be, and there's no seismic data that would indicate any further eruptions."

"Excellent, Admiral! You've all done an excellent job! Where are the heroes? Doctor Valenti, and the S.E.A.L.s?" inquired the President.

"They're missing, Mr. President," advised the Admiral. "There was an error with the mini-sub's firing system, so they did it manually. When the nuclear devices were detonated, the mini-submarine with its crew was struck by the nuclear wave and may have been lost."

"That's unfortunate, Admiral," remarked the President, with sorrow in his voice. "Search until we have the remains or locate the mini-sub. Please keep me informed, especially if and when you cease your rescue efforts and list them as lost at sea."

"Yes, Mr. President," acknowledged the Admiral.

As the search for survivors continued, Admiral Pruitt leaned back in his chair and angrily puffed on his cigar. The rest of his officers avoided him. It was apparent that he was in a foul mood.

***

Stuck at the bottom of the sea some fifty miles west of ground zero, the stranded mini-sub was lifeless and dark. There were broken seals and leaks that had been caused by the shock wave from the nuclear detonation, and there were several men inside the vessel that were beginning to come to life again after being unconscious for hours. The first man to awaken was Master Chief Petty Officer Tommy Sands, who was the hardest and most experienced man on board.

"Commander O'Connell? Wake up, sir!" urged the Chief as he checked the vital signs of his men.

As the S.E.A.L. Team leader began to awaken, Chief Sands sat down at the sub's helm and attempted to bring the vessel back into service.

"Hell, we're at least twenty five miles from ground zero!" exclaimed Chief Sands as he worked with the control panel. "You okay, sir?"

"I'm at fifty percent, Chief," replied Chuck O'Connell as he checked Mike Valenti and the rest of his men. "Slick's got a broken arm, but everyone else looks okay. Doc, wake up! What about you, Chief?"

"Well, sir," remarked the Chief as he smacked the control panel. "I'm in the fight, Skipper. I've got some lacerations that the sharks might like, but otherwise I'm good to go. That's a nasty gash on your hand, though."

"We'll need lunch soon, so we'll eat any sharks you attract," boasted Chuck O'Connell, who ignored his bleeding hand.

When Mike Valenti opened his eyes, he could feel the throbbing pain over his eyebrows and on his cheeks. He gingerly touched his face and realized that he was bleeding from cuts that occurred when he hit the wall of the submarine following the nuclear detonation.

"We're alive?" asked Mike, who was still dizzy.

"Just barely, Doc," spoke up Chief Sands. He was the only man functioning well at that point. "We're on the bottom of the ocean under a mound of sand."

"C'mon, Doc, help me with the others," directed Chuck O'Connell, as he began waking and tending the wounds of the others. Mike immediately went over to Steve Gunther, who appeared to be fine. Unlike the others, Steven's body was very warm.

"What's wrong, Doc?" asked Chuck O'Connell.

"I was checking Steve's vitals," replied Mike. "His body temp is really good considering it's so cold in here. Everyone's suffering from exposure, but he's not."

"That's right, Doc!" spoke up Chief Sands. "You don't know about Sparky, do you? He's got the unique ability to change his body temperature. When we're underwater and everyone else is freezing their balls off, old Sparky's warm and cozy like a sea lion!"

"That's right," spoke up one of the other team members. "During our S.E.A.L. training, Sparky was the only guy who didn't freeze in the cold waters of the Pacific Ocean. You watch, Doc, when we get into the open water again, Sparky will swim around warm as a walrus. That's why he's so good at demo work. He's got warm hands no matter how deep we work."

Mike was shocked by the news, but he kept to himself the knowledge that Steven Gunther was a Darwin human. As the nuclear team recovered from the detonation, Chief Sands worked on the mini-sub.

"Sir, I've got the sub's life support up, but she won't be getting out from under this sand. And stuck here, the surface ships won't find us on sonar. We'll have to abandon ship," advised Chief Sands.

"Roger that, Chief," acknowledged Chuck O'Connell. He was wrapping his hand with a sterile dressing. "Can we launch the emergency signal buoy?"

"Negative, skipper," replied Chief Sands.

"Let's prepare to dive, Chief," directed Commander O'Connell, as he pulled on his equipment. "Doc, I need your help getting the wounded ready to dive, too. We've got to move fast if we want to get out of this sub in one piece!"

***

The Director of the Central Intelligence Agency wheeled herself from the television set where she had been watching the press coverage of the nuclear detonations in the South Pacific. The President and

Assistant NOAH'S ARK Director Evan Leeper had notified her that Mike Valenti, the S.E.A.L. Team, and members of ARK One were missing. As she nervously checked her make up, Evan Leeper peeked into her office and asked for permission to meet with her.

"Come on in, Dr. Leeper. I heard the news," she stated. "I hope we find everyone alive."

"Yeah, Rosy, that would be great," agreed Evan, who was worried about his best friend.

"But I know you're not up here to comfort me, right?" noted Myrna with a smile. "What's up?"

"I just wanted to brief you, Rosy. Our analysts in Hawaii report that seismic activity throughout the region has decreased," explained Evan, as he referred to his notes and reports. "Unfortunately, the magma is centered now under Guadalcanal in the Solomon Islands. The volcano that's erupted formed at Mount Makarakomburu, which is 2,447 meters above sea level. It's located about ten kilometers from Nouindui, which is the coastal town where Ranger and the ARK One headquarters were located. There have been secondary volcanic earthquakes that indicate that nearby Mount Popomanaseu may become a volcano, too."

"What about the evacuations and rescue efforts?" asked Myrna.

"The evacuation of people to the safer western and eastern ends of the island is in progress," explained Evan. Those populations along the southern coast, which are in the direct path of the eruption, are cut off from land and air evacuation. Ships in the area evacuated an estimated four thousand personnel. Thousands more are currently stranded due to pyroclastic flow and toxic fumes that have caused vessels to cease operations until the situation improves. The sea rescue should be able to resume within twelve hours."

"That's a long time to sit in the surf or roast on the beach. Can the people survive until then?"

"I don't know, Rosy. I hope so," sighed Evan, who was exhausted.

"So what about the future of Earth, the United States, and NOAH'S ARK?"

"The destruction of the six volcanoes has put us back on the normal Pangaean Effect time schedule. That means we've still got until 2025 to prepare for it," detailed Evan. He ran his hands through his naturally curly black hair. "The Mars and Darwin projects are moving along. We'll be ready, Rosy."

She nodded and stretched in her wheelchair.

"That's good news, Evan. The whole point of this was to save Hawaii and anyone else we could, and we did it for the most part," she said. "Let's just hope we don't have anymore problems like this until 2025."

"I agree, Rosy, but we probably will."

"I know we'll have increasing challenges, Evan, but please let me be optimistic right now," stated Myrna with a soft smile. "We'll do more planning and talking after Mike and the members of ARK One are recovered."

As the two intelligence managers continued talking, the telephone lines began to light up as more information concerning the volcanoes and rescue efforts arrived for the Director. It was a very stressful time for the C.I.A. and the members of Operation NOAH'S ARK at Langley, Virginia.

***

When the S.E.A.L. Team opened the mini-sub, wet sand and water poured into the hatch. Helping each other, the divers exited the small vessel and slowly began their ascent to the surface. Chief Sands monitored their progress and their health. All of them were bleeding someplace. The water was extremely cold, in spite of the tropical surface climate. As they continued to swim toward the surface, it became clear to all of them that the blood from their wounds was leaving a trail.

"Sparky, we're going to have company," warned Chuck O'Connell as they swam. "This is shark country."

"Gotcha, Skipper, I've got your back," responded Steven as they swam. Armed with a shark stick that contained a shotgun round on the end of it, Steven Gunther slowed his ascent and waited for the arrival of any sharks that would be drawn to the blood trail.

When they reached the surface, five large sharks were circling the group of divers. The S.E.A.L.s released their floatation devices and Commander O'Connell activated their rescue homing beacon. As Mike and the other divers waited, Steven remained underwater.

"Are you going to help him?" asked Mike as he swallowed a bit of seawater when he chanced to speak.

"Sparky? Nah," replied Commander O'Connell. "He'll do just fine, or he'll ask for help if he needs it."

After ten minutes of waiting, a large white and gray object coated with blood floated to the surface. It was a hammerhead shark that was approximately 10 feet long. Mike nearly urinated in his wetsuit when he saw the dead predator so close to the group.

"This is sushi for us and food for all those other sharks, Commander," said Chief Sands. He reached out, pulled the shark closer, removed his knife, and cut a hunk of meat out of the dead fish before pushing it away from them. Other sharks immediately fed on the dead one.

Coming from the east, the sounds of approaching helicopters filled the air. The S.E.A.L.s began to cheer. Within minutes, they were being hoisted into a rescue helicopter and returning to the U.S.S. Ronald Reagan.

When the helicopter landed on the deck of the aircraft carrier, Admiral Pruitt was there to greet them. It was a huge celebration with most of the carrier's sailors there to cheer the heroes of the nuclear detonation. Admiral Pruitt quickly pulled Mike Valenti aside to inform him of the situation at Guadalcanal.

"You're kidding!" exclaimed Mike to the Admiral. "I thought this mission was a success!"

"It was, son, but Mother Nature threw a wrench in part of it," reassured Admiral Pruitt. "The worst part's that some members of your ARK One team are missing on the shore near the volcano and can't be rescued until the toxic fumes are reduced."

Mike was devastated. He asked for the list of names of the missing and nearly cried when he saw that Glenda Moses was one of them.

"Admiral, I've got to get there, now! Those are my people trapped on that island!" shouted Mike.

Admiral Pruitt looked at Mike's bleeding cuts and weary face. He shook his head.

"Negative, Doctor. As soon as I can get them rescued, or their bodies recovered, I'll see to it, but you're in no condition to fly right now. Besides, you can't get in there until the toxicity in the air stabililizes."

As the S.E.A.L.s listened to Mike's protests, they spoke amongst themselves. The Admiral waited, too.

"Look, Admiral, I just spoke with Bubba Washington. He spoke with my team just before he withdrew from the island," explained Mike. "That means they're alive and need to be helped! Now, I need an aircraft to take me to the boat Bubba's on. He'll attempt another rescue with me right now!"

"And how are you going to get to the beach and survive all those fumes?" asked the Admiral.

"The mask filters they're wearing and suits will last another three hours," explained Mike as he gathered up his equipment again. "And we can use our dive suits and enter the beach underwater. When we get to the shore, we'll rescue my people and swim out to the boat!"

The Admiral frowned.

"We'll go with him, Admiral," said Commander O'Connell proudly. "He's one of us now."

Admiral Pruitt shook his head and smiled.

"Okay, Major Valenti, you've got my approval," agreed Admiral Pruitt. "Go get your people!"

Mike Valenti and the S.E.A.L.s saluted the Admiral and threw their gear back on the helicopter, which cranked up it's engines and prepared for another flight. Mike shook hands with the Admiral and followed his new comrades onto the aircraft. As they took off, Mike caught Steven looking at him. It was not a look of anger or hatred as he had seen on previous occasions. Petty Officer Steven Gunther silently shook Michael Valenti's hand. The silent gesture left tears in the eyes of both men. Mike had finally earned his son's respect.

***

Bubba Washington was on the deck of a Royal Australian patrol boat when he heard a helicopter approach from the northwest. He had been assisting the Australians with the transfer of their passengers to one the larger support vessels in the area.

"Bubba!" came Mike's voice over the radio in Bubba's hand. "You there?"

Bubba knew the Doc was excited when he failed to use proper radio and telephone procedures.

"I'm here, Doc, over," responded Bubba.

The helicopter approached the boat and hovered over its forward deck. Bubba stood under the chopper's skids waiting for his boss to join him. He noticed the S.E.A.L.s were with him, too.

"Damn, Doc, you look like shit! Did you have to bring the Navy wit' you?" asked Bubba with a smile.

The S.E.A.L.s hopped off the helicopter after Mike Valenti and put their equipment on deck. With a wave to the helicopter pilot, the aircraft left the new arrivals to prepare for their next mission. Bubba helped his boss and the S.E.A.L.s as the vessel got underway.

"We came straight from the carrier, Bubba. Any changes?" asked Mike as he prepared to dive.

"Naw, Doc, not at all," answered Bubba, as the boat moved toward the beach. "We was about to pick them up when a toxic cloud arrived and forced us to leave. We tried again, but Vernie shouted for us to go."

"And you went?" asked Mike.

"Gyat damn right, Doc! We'd have died, too!"

"Fine. Bubba, everyone on board has to suit up and mask right now. When we get to the toxic area, the S.E.A.L.s and I will enter the water and swim to shore. We'll locate our team and then I'll call you in. We need to pick up our people first, rescue any others, transport them to safety, and continue the rescue. You got it?"

"Yeah, Doc, I copy," responded Bubba, who knew Mike had to be worried about Glenda.

When the Australian vessel arrived at the edge of the toxic cloud area, Mike Valenti and the S.E.A.L.s slipped into the water and disappeared. When they were underwater and away from the vessel, Bubba ordered it to withdraw a safe distance from the toxic fog. There were no sounds coming from the island other than those of the dead and dying under the erupting volcano.

***

Using underwater lights to make their way through the murky water, Mike Valenti and the S.E.A.L. Team swam past hundreds of bodies floating in the surf. When they reached the shore, the team surfaced in the darkness and found the thick air filled with volcanic particles. After leaving the water, the S.E.A.L. Team quickly found the few bodies lying among the dead that were wearing protective suits.

"Church!" shouted Mike as he turned over the one form he could recognize any place in the world. "Dammit, Church, talk to me!"

"They're all here, Doc!" shouted Chuck O'Connell as he quickly checked each downed man.

When Mike looked at Glenda's face through the mask, it appeared as though she had succumbed to the effects of the intense heat that was associated with volcanic clouds.

"Check their vitals as best as you can, then let's get them to the water," directed Chuck O'Connell, who had begun working on Elton Rance.

None of the ARK One members was conscious, which made the task of getting each of them into the water for rescue more difficult.

"Bubba, we're ready," said Mike into his radio.

"We're on the way in now," responded Bubba.

As the sounds of the boat became louder, Mike and the S.E.A.L.s moved their charges into the sea. As they walked up to their shoulders in the choppy sea, they had to push aside the floating bodies that bobbed up and down around them. When the naval vessel cautiously approached and stopped next to the rescuers, Bubba assisted them by lifting each survivor into the boat.

"They alive, Doc?" asked the big bodybuilder through a mask that looked much too small to fit his face.

"Barely, Bubba. We need to get them out of these suits. They've got heat exhaustion!" advised Mike.

When everyone was on board, the boat backed away from the shore. When they were clear of the toxic cloud of carbon dioxide and sulfuric acid, everyone removed their chemical suits. Chuck O'Connell and Bubba began dousing the rescued team members with fresh water to cool them down and hydrate them.

"Church?" asked Mike as he caressed Glenda's face. "Wake up, honey!"

After a painful moan and a coughing fit, Glenda finally opened her eyes. Tears ran down her face when she saw Mike. After they kissed and held each other tight, the woman that had begun this mission in

Antarctica was finally ending it in the arms of the man she loved.

"Dim, how are my people?" asked Glenda.

"Greg Kryolok and Ken Loomis didn't make it, Church," explained Mike. "I thought they'd been rescued before our arrival, but that wasn't the case. Everyone else made it, though."

As the boat approached the hospital ship that was located with the rescue fleet, Mike looked into Glenda's blue eyes and cupped her face in his two hands. The group on board became quieter when they observed Mike Valenti get on his knees next to Glenda Moses.

"Church, I want to spend the rest of eternity with you," said Mike. "Will you marry me?"

"Yes, Dim, I'll marry you," answered Glenda with a stream of tears falling down her cheeks. "But only if your son will be your best man."

Mike nodded, and Steven Gunther walked over to kneel down beside his father. Steven put an arm around Mike and took Glenda by the hand.

"I'd be proud to be your best man, dad, and I'm proud of both of you," said Steven, whose eyes were also filled with tears.

As the S.E.A.L. and Australian crew members cheered and applauded the tender moment that occurred in the midst of the erupting volcano and the devastation it had created, Mike kissed Glenda and held her tight under the eyes of a hospital ship filled with smiling Solomon Islanders, medical personnel, and the rescued members of Operation NOAH'S ARK.

About The Author

James L. Copa resides in Miami, Florida with his wonderful son. He has been employed with the U.S. government for over twenty years, which includes honorable military service in the U.S. Army, Army Reserve, and Army National Guard as an enlisted soldier and commissioned light Infantry officer. James L. Copa holds the rank of Major in the U.S. Army Reserve. He has a Bachelor of Arts degree from Loyola College, and a Masters Degree in Public Administration from the University of Baltimore.

James likes being a father, and he cherishes true love, life, and the enlightenment of the soul. He is deeply spiritual, a genuine gentleman, and he believes that brotherhood is a moral obligation for all of us.

Printed in the United States
17301LVS00001B/10